*The Best*
AMERICAN
ESSAYS
2019

# The Best
# AMERICAN
# ESSAYS® 2019

Edited and with an Introduction
by REBECCA SOLNIT

*Robert Atwan, Series Editor*

MARINER BOOKS

HOUGHTON MIFFLIN HARCOURT

BOSTON · NEW YORK   2019

hmhbooks.com

ISSN 0888-3742 (print)      ISSN 2573-3885 (e-book)
ISBN 978-1-328-46580-1 (print)      ISBN 978-1-328-46711-9 (e-book)

Printed in the United States of America
DOC 10 9 8 7 6 5 4 3 2 1

# Contents

# Foreword

It is not possible to extricate yourself from the questions in which your age is involved.

    —Ralph Waldo Emerson, "The Fortune of the Republic" (1878)

What I have most wanted to do throughout the past ten years is to make political writing into an art.

    —George Orwell, "Why I Write" (1946)

FOR MANY YEARS George Orwell avidly collected political pamphlets. After his untimely death at age forty-six in 1950, his collection of some 2,700 pamphlets from across the entire political spectrum (dating roughly from World War I through World War II) found its way to the British Library, where it has since supplied a wealth of information to scholars and historians of those turbulent times. In "Pamphlet Literature," a brief essay contributed to the *New Statesman* in 1943, Orwell describes a small representative sample of his collection, identifying nine trends of the pamphleteering "revival" he had been following since 1935; he labels these Anti-left and Crypto-fascist, Conservative, Social Democrat, Communist, Trotskyist and Anarchist, Non-party radical, Religio-patriotic, and Lunatic. He also refers to a ninth category, Pacifist— but claims he has no samples of this trend handy to comment on. He then says amusingly that all these headings could be roughly reduced to two main schools, Party Line and Astrology.

Orwell wrote the essay, despite its title, mainly to complain about the decidedly "unliterary" nature of political pamphlets. They were not merely disappointing to a novelist and essayist whose literary goal was "to make political writing into an art," but Orwell thought they were undeniably "rubbish": "There is totalitarian rubbish and paranoiac rubbish, but in each case it *is* rubbish." He considered this especially disappointing because of the times. The pamphlet, he said, "ought to be *the* literary form of an age like our own." "We live in a time," he continued, "when political passions run high, channels of free expression are dwindling, and organized lying exists on a scale never before known." He blamed the publishing and literary worlds for not making the public more aware of the necessity of pamphlets, which are haphazardly printed and rarely advertised or reviewed. As a result, most good writers who have something they passionately want to say don't know how to go about publishing a pamphlet and so they leave the genre to either lunatics or political hard-liners. Orwell then shows his hand: "The normal way of publishing a pamphlet is through a political party, and the party will see to it that any 'deviation'—and hence any literary value—is kept out." For Orwell, literary value apparently depends on some deviation from party lines.

As we know from such popular books as *Nineteen Eighty-Four,* *Animal Farm,* and *Homage to Catalonia,* Orwell staunchly opposed totalitarianism and fascism. Other books like *Down and Out in London and Paris* and *The Road to Wigan Pier* show his passionate identification with working-class values and culture. Essays like "The Hanging" and "Shooting an Elephant" disclose his fierce hatred of imperialism. Orwell was in no way politically neutral. After his military experiences at the front in the Spanish Civil War—where he had been shot through the neck—he declares he is a socialist; he writes in 1937, "I have seen wonderful things and at last really believe in Socialism, which I never did before." Prior to his experiences with the Spanish revolutionary forces, he thought socialism was a "theory confined entirely to the middle class." He was embarrassed once while writing *Wigan Pier* to be called "comrade."

Orwell was one of those individuals who pushes harder against his own beliefs than the ones he ostensibly opposes. Like John Stuart Mill, he found it intellectually necessary to continually interrogate his own cherished opinions so that they didn't become automatic, stale, and orthodox. This tendency—as well as his distrust of abstractions, general discomfort with labels, and relentless self-criticism—makes Orwell hard at times to pin down ideologically. In *Homage*, he is amused by all the political distinctions and rival groups within the revolutionary parties but also dismayed by how all the petty, doctrinal differences can distract a justified movement from its primary goals. Early on in Spain he felt most attracted to the anarchists. His antifascism, however, was unwavering, and he thought that fascism could never be defeated by bourgeois democracy, because that would be a "fight against one form of capitalism on behalf of a second." Orwell seems an antifascist first and a socialist by default. We can find many ways to interpret the various inconsistencies of Orwell's politics as they altered over time, but I think in the main we can say that he had two unswerving positions: he hated fascism and he loved the working class. And he thought—though it may seem delusional today—that it was only the working class that could fully resist fascism. Perhaps one quotation makes his political instincts clear: he writes in *Homage* that "when I see an actual flesh and blood worker in conflict with his natural enemy, the policeman, I do not have to ask myself which side I am on."

But as the radical Scottish poet Hugh MacDiarmid might have said of Orwell, he "was *for,* not *of,* the working class." Born into relative privilege, the Eton-educated Eric Blair could become the socially conscious, prolabor, antifascist writer George Orwell only after renouncing his membership in the British administrative class. But all his life, even though his sympathies were overwhelmingly with the workers, he struggled with a double-consciousness; he wrote often as both outsider and insider, observer and participant, and this is what I think gives his nonfiction books and essays their appealing authenticity and enduring vitality, though he knew he had to be careful not to allow his feelings for the working class to turn into a sentimental idealization. He had learned from experience that it was far easier to recruit Marxists from the middle class than from the people.

Orwell's mode of double-consciousness carried over into the act of writing as well. In "Why I Write" (1946) he claims that, aside from "the need to earn a living," there are "four great motives for writing": "Sheer egoism" (the desire for notoriety, fame), "Esthetic enthusiasm" (a pleasure in composing good prose), "Historical impulse" (to report accurately about the world for posterity), and

"Political purpose" (to promote a world view and a better society). He believes all writers feel such contradictory and fluctuating impulses all the time. He also feels that had he lived in more peaceful times and been allowed to follow his natural bent, his career would have taken a different turn and he "might have written ornate or merely descriptive books, and might have remained almost unaware of my political loyalties." But he goes on, "As it is I have been forced into becoming a sort of pamphleteer."

It is difficult to assess the mood of this very personal (almost confessional) essay by such an accomplished writer. Would he have preferred to write "ornate" books, perhaps under his family name, and not to have been "forced" by the times to be a "pamphleteer" (producing "rubbish")? Did revolutionary times compel him to sacrifice literature for polemics? Or is he actually satisfied with the value of his political writing, as he seems to suggest in the following eloquent passage:

"Every line of serious work that I have written since 1936 has been written, directly or indirectly, *against* totalitarianism and *for* democratic socialism, as I understand it. It seems to me nonsense, in a period like our own, to think that one can avoid writing of such subjects. Everyone writes of them in one guise or another. It is simply a question of which side one takes and what approach one follows. And the more one is conscious of one's political bias, the more chance one has of acting politically without sacrificing one's aesthetic and intellectual integrity."

So much for the "pamphleteer." And he reassures his readers (or himself) by adding, "I could not do the work of writing a book, or even a long magazine article, if it were not also an esthetic experience."

"Why I Write" is fascinating both for its comments on political writing and for its disclosure of the deep internal conflicts Orwell faced in his attempts to balance his political commitments with his self-imposed aesthetic demands. *Animal Farm* was rejected by several publishers in 1944; the Soviet Union was still an ally, and some worried about the book's transparent anti-Stalinism. But as our wartime friend soon became our Cold War enemy, the fable became an enormous bestseller. His masterpiece, *Nineteen Eighty-Four*, written largely while he stoically endured the final stages of tuberculosis, was an instant success when it appeared in 1949 and has persistently remained the finest example of dystopian vision in our literature. (It again soared in popularity when Donald Trump assumed the presidency in 2017.) But these two influential books that made Orwell into an international literary celebrity also damaged his reputation on the radical left. Orwell had always been anti-totalitarian, but these two popular books transparently identified totalitarianism with Soviet communism, thus appearing to endorse Western capitalist society. American neoconservatives could admire much in these books and often cited Orwell as a friend, despite Orwell's long attachment to worker-based socialist values. As often happens in political debate, nuance gives way to hardened positions, multiplicity surrenders to reduction. Once a crisis is defined, we are left with only friends and enemies.

Writing in 1971, the Marxist critic Raymond Williams evaluated Orwell's political and literary legacy. Though generally admiring of Orwell, especially his socially conscious nonfiction like *Wigan Pier, Down and Out,* and *Homage,* Williams didn't much care for *Animal Farm* or *Nineteen Eighty-Four* and makes his reasons clear: Orwell wrote with too many contradictions and, since he could never fully escape his middle-class upbringing, often reverted to type. We see this most, Williams argues, in his later work, where he often appears discouraged, disillusioned, defeated ("defeatism" being one of communism's mortal sins). A staunch New Left intellectual, Williams regrets that Orwell came to substitute communism for fascism as his model of totalitarianism, and that his later work appears to deny the "possibility of authentic revolution." Williams thinks that Orwell eventually betrayed the faith, and in his last two "pessimistic" books made an "accommodation to capitalism," thus capitulating to the anticommunist sentiments of American Cold War ideology. In the conclusion to his brief biographical study of Orwell, Williams sadly suggests how we should regard Orwell's legacy: "The thing to do with his work, his history, is to read it, not imitate it." We're left to wonder had he lived into his early eighties what Orwell's politics would have been when the real 1984 came around.

And what would he think now? Would he embrace today's progressive movement? Would he still consider himself a democratic socialist? Would he oppose Brexit or sympathize with the older working class who voted leave? And from an essayist's standpoint, would he agree with Williams that the writer in him unfortunately "had to split from the political militant." All his career, as we've

seen, Orwell hoped to fuse his art with his politics. Williams believes he ultimately failed, and that failure had serious political implications. I'm left thinking that for the sake of politics, Williams
—no matter how much he admired the writer and his struggle
—would have preferred Orwell the party-line pamphleteer to Orwell the literary artist.

The issue here—as should be evident—is about the uneasy relation of the essay to the political world. And a part of this comes
down to how much "deviation" writers are allowed before they
cross the inevitable line that separates the true political believer
from the apostate. The "deviation" can take many forms—a skepti-
cal voice, inappropriate irony, a partial criticism, a suggestion of alternative perspectives, insufficient identification with the cause, a
questioning of ideological goals, a contrary opinion, even a muted
nonmilitant tone. In times of crisis (assuming we don't now live
in a state of permanent emergency), political writing becomes a
minefield where one incorrect phrase or sentiment, or even something unsaid, could result in a writer's permanent self-destruction.
Once entering the political arena, the essayist can only at personal
risk take advantage of the genre's long-established affinity for free
inquiry, unrestricted opinion, and open-mindedness.

Dayna Tortorici's splendid essay, "In the Maze," reminded me
that F. Scott Fitzgerald also understood the affliction of double
consciousness. He famously wrote in 1936 that "the test of a first-
rate intelligence is the ability to hold two opposed ideas in the
mind at the same time, and still retain the ability to function."
First-rate writers now, in many ways, face a similar test: Can they
hold opinions and at the same time question those very opinions?
Can they maintain certain beliefs while trying out alternatives?
In short, can they be at the same time politically committed and
open-minded? But I can't express this current literary situation
any better than does Rabih Alameddine in this collection's opening essay. An essay that does something Orwell (rightly or wrongly)
thought essays should do: *essay.*

*The Best American Essays* features a selection of the year's outstanding essays, essays of literary achievement that show an awareness
of craft and forcefulness of thought. Hundreds of essays are gathered annually from a wide assortment of national and regional
publications. These essays are then screened, and approximately

one hundred are turned over to a distinguished guest editor, who may add a few personal discoveries and who makes the final selections. The list of notable essays appearing in the back of the book is drawn from a final comprehensive list that includes not only all of the essays submitted to the guest editor but also many that were not submitted.

To qualify for the volume, the essay must be a work of respectable literary quality, intended as a fully developed, independent essay (not an excerpt) on a subject of general interest (not specialized scholarship), originally written in English (or translated by the author) for publication in an American periodical during the calendar year. Note that abridgments and excerpts taken from longer works and published in magazines do not qualify for the series, but if considered significant they will appear in the Notable list in the back of the volume. Today's essay is a highly flexible and shifting form, however, so these criteria are not carved in stone.

Magazine editors who want to be sure their contributors will be considered each year should submit issues or subscriptions to:

The Best American Essays
Houghton Mifflin Harcourt
125 High Street, 5th Floor
Boston, MA 02110

Writers and editors are welcome to submit published essays from any American periodical for consideration; unpublished work does not qualify for the series and cannot be reviewed or evaluated. Also ineligible are essays that have been published in book form—such as a contribution to a collection—but have never appeared in a periodical. All submissions from print magazines must be directly from the publication and not in manuscript or printout format. Editors of online magazines and literary bloggers should not assume that appropriate work will be seen; they are invited to submit clear printed copies of the essays to the address above. Please note: due to the increasing number of submissions from online sources, material that does not include a full citation (name of publication, date, author contact information, etc.) cannot be considered. If submitting multiple essays, please include a separate cover sheet with a full citation for each selection.

The deadline for all submissions is February 1 of the year following the year of publication; thus all submissions of essays published in 2019 must be received by February 1, 2020. Writers should keep in mind that—like many literary awards—the essays are selected from a large pool of nominations. Unlike many literary awards, however, writers may nominate themselves. A considerable number of prominent literary journals regularly submit issues to the series, but though we continually reach out with invitations to submit and reminders of deadlines, not all periodicals respond or participate, so writers should be sure to check with their editors to see if they routinely submit to the series. There is no fixed reading period, but writers and editors are encouraged to submit appropriate candidates as they are published and not wait until the final deadline.

I would like to commemorate here three major writers, two of them outstanding poets, who died recently and whose work appeared in this series over the years: Mary Oliver (January 2019), who not only had several essays selected for the volumes but served as guest editor of the 2009 book; Tom Wolfe (May 2018); and Donald Hall (June 2018). Their work endures.

I warmly thank Valerie Duff-Strautmann for her generous and invaluable assistance at various stages of this edition, the thirty-fourth in the series. Once again it's a pleasure to acknowledge Nicole Angeloro's editorial skills and her amazing capacity to juggle all the fast-moving parts of an annual book. And for their expertise, a heartfelt thanks to others with Houghton Mifflin Harcourt who help make this book possible—especially Larry Cooper and Mary Dalton-Hoffman. I also thank my son, Gregory Atwan, for his expansive knowledge and steady help throughout every edition. For this year's Notable list, I appreciate the fine suggestions I received from students of Ander Monson's University of Arizona course "The Art and Work of Literary Anthologies": many thanks to Samantha Jean Coxall, Lee Anne Gallaway-Mitchell, Hannah Hindley, Natalie Lima, Matthew Morris, Kevin Mosby, Emi Noguchi, Maddie Norris, and Margo Steines.

It was especially enjoyable to work on this collection with Rebecca Solnit, whose own remarkable essays have unflinchingly confronted the most difficult and urgent problems facing our world today.

R.A.

# Introduction

*I*

THE ESSAYIST'S JOB is to gather up the shards or map them where they are, to find the pattern out there or make one with words about the disconnections and mysteries. This reading of the world is a form of travel, questing and searching and gathering. Essays are restless literature, trying to find out how things fit together, how we can think about two things at once, how the personal and the public can inform each other, how two overtly dissimilar things share a secret kinship, how intuitive and scholarly knowledge can cook down together, how discovery can be a deep pleasure.

When you read for a book called *The Best American Essays*, you have to decide what an essay is, or in my case, definitions emerge as you read. Some excellent writing fell by the wayside because it was too purely personal history, and some because it felt too like feature-writing journalism. A very few pieces were at the other end of the spectrum, too purely philosophical inquiry and analysis. These writings reminded me what essays in particular do and what I want them to do, which is to be a meeting ground. A place where the experiential and the categorical, the firsthand and the researched, converse, question, or just dance in each other's arms for a while. Where the patterns and relationships we didn't suspect reveal themselves, or where those patterns and phenomena we thought we knew take on new meanings and depths or turn out to be strangers we are meeting for the first time. Where the writer moves between people, places, things, and events, and contemplation of what they mean, why they matter, what they have to tell us. Where the writer goes on to philosophize a little, to draw conclusions, to share a little of her own views about it all.

Essay writing is reflective; it doesn't just want to recount things that happened, but contemplate what they mean, and often what they mean is really about how they fit into the pattern, which is how the particular connects to the general. Often this means making ethical statements, and though sometimes an ethic is explicit, sometimes it's implicit in what the writer chose to pay attention to or how she read it. (People who think overt principles are always propaganda often mistake the status quo for a neutral place, rather than one with its own ethical strictures and ardent propaganda.)

That quest for meaning takes many forms. Gary Taylor writes about the murder of Maura Binkley, one of the students in the English department he chairs: "These men were all trying to kill generalities. The man who stands accused of murdering Maura was not seeing a luminous living individual; he was seeing a specimen of the category 'woman,' a category he hated. From his perspective, the category 'woman' owed him something, something he as a 'man' was entitled to have. The category 'woman' had no right to choose to refuse him. Before the gun killed Maura, the generalization did."

Taylor takes a stance against the inability to see particulars, and argues, "What we do, in English, and in the humanities more broadly, what we teach, what we celebrate and investigate, is human particularity." Though I was moved and impressed by his essay's deep humanism as he grapples with the crime, I don't actually agree with him, because seeing patterns is seeing what we have in common, and he does it himself: "These men were all trying to kill generalities" tries to understand the mass shooting in which Binkley died as something that happens too often, and arises from a set of beliefs and entitlements. That is, this one killer typifies misogynist mass shooters.

It's the relationship between generalities and particulars that matters, and often the work an essay does is taxonomical: here's how this particular fits into this categorical reality. Here's how this young woman died as a result of a set of widespread beliefs and values. Here's how to restore what may seem like an anomaly to its natural habitat in the order of things. Here's why this thing matters: because it is a type specimen of the species, and here is why this species matters or threatens us or is in trouble. Here's how what happened to me happens to us, or has happened before and will again.

It takes a certain kind of confidence to reach a conclusion. You have to take a stand, believe in yourself. You have to go past reporting or recounting. But it also takes a desire to understand, to contextualize, to situate the incident in the principle that governs it, and every essay is a journey of sorts from what we're given to what we make of it, "we" being the writer and the readers who go on the journey with her.

Jia Tolentino covers similar ground to Taylor's in "The Rage of the Incels," at least thematically, since her particulars are so different in this essay prompted by a whole different slaughter directed at women. She writes, "It is a horrible thing to feel unwanted —invisible, inadequate, ineligible for the things that any person might hope for. It is also entirely possible to process a difficult social position with generosity and grace." She's contextualizing the men who think women owe them sex by contemplating the other people who are not having sex and who yet don't feel enraged and homicidal about that. It's full of her usual startling insights, briskly delivered: "These days, in this country, sex has become a hyperefficient and deregulated marketplace, and, like any hyperefficient and deregulated marketplace, it often makes people feel very bad." But then she goes further, to explore how what incels want is not really sex, or that sex is just the form in which they demand supremacy. It's an ethical essay, and its ethics might be called feminism. As might Lili Loofbourow's essay interrogating the excuses so often made for men, and the latitude to destroy they're given.

Terese Marie Mailhot does something similar with racism and then with violence against women, but she also tells us of the mythologies, beliefs, and ways of living of her mother, and of how "there is power in the reclamation of story—in the remembrance that these stories are real and tangible things, like my mother . . . I look at myself and see a lineage of monstrous desire and compulsion and beauty and power. When my mother said I was born to Thunder, she believed life would be hard for me, because Thunder is a liberator, and liberating is hard and thankless work. She believed I would disrupt things, but the world would be better for it." Mailhot finds a cosmology that can accompany her through insults and obliviousness and shows us something of it.

In "My Father Says He's a Targeted Individual. Maybe We All Are.," Jean Guerrero tells us about her father's fears about surveillance and some of the conduct that fear has prompted and the ways that it impacted her and her family. That could be the stuff of memoir, but she goes further, to think about the ways that people who are dismissed as paranoid or conspiracy theorists are right, or have become so. With that she brings us to face the monstrous invasiveness of the new technologies and networks and the fact that all of us now live under conditions that were once supposed to be the stuff of paranoiac delusion. They are watching you. And us. If she'd only reported on the latter, her piece would be journalism, just as it would have been memoir had it only been the former, and since there is no such genre as investigative memoir, nor any such thing as the personal editorial, it's an essay.

"Only connect" may have emerged as the dictum underlying E. M. Forster's novel *Howard's End*, but it's the main instruction for writing an essay. Not connecting people emotionally, but connecting ideas and meanings, which are the protagonists in essays, as human beings are in novels, the subjects who must reveal themselves and evolve through the writing.

2

Threaded through all the crises of this era is an absence of a certain kind of sense perhaps too rare to call common. This sense arises from an ability to deal in facts but also in meanings, to situate the particular in the general, and to extricate oneself from generalizations by means of directness and detail, to move back and forth from the personal to the political, to know where we are and how we got here and why that matters. Patience, attention to detail, devotion to accuracy and precision, interest in patterns and overarching orders, and concentration that doesn't flicker from the main event are the soil in which that sense grows.

This is the work essays have done more than any other kind of literature, though virtually all literature has done it by asking people to sit quietly alone and engage with what a stranger thought, perhaps one long ago or far away or unfamiliar in some essential. This thoughtfulness of the writer and the reader who meets her is itself an act of self-definition and of being in the world in ways that don't comply with hasty, networked, distracted time.

William Carlos Williams wrote in one of his most famous passages about the difficulty of getting the news from poems, "yet men die miserably every day . . . for lack of what is found there." Just before that oft-quoted clutch of lines, the poet says,

> My heart rouses
> > thinking to bring you news
> > > of something
> that concerns you
> > and concerns many men.

It seems to be some kind of objective information he's referring to, some practical or political information (and he keeps addressing himself to men as a synecdoche for humanity, though he's speaking to a beloved who is his wife of forty years, because women still didn't quite exist in the fifties, speaking of patterns that erase, or patterns we're trying to shatter). Actual news, perhaps of the kind found in newspapers, or perhaps news in the larger, vaguer sense of what just happened out there, whether it's the sun breaking through the clouds out the window or the diagnosis just phoned in. And then come those famous lines informing us that poems don't deliver the news, but they deliver something essential.

So does the news, of course, and essays deliver both and maintain the diplomatic relations between journalism and poetry, owning something from both territories, or functioning in both. Curious about the lines I had read so many times, I looked up the poem, "Asphodel, That Greeny Flower," and when writing about it I found this from poet and professor Ann Fisher-Wirth: "A bout with depression was exacerbated both by the recent stroke and by the injustices surrounding Williams' appointment as Poetry Consultant to the Library of Congress. The position was first offered, then withdrawn owing to allegations of Communist sympathizing, then offered again contingent upon further loyalty investigations, which were conducted but never evaluated, so that the year's term was up before Williams was able to serve. The situation tormented him with feelings of rage, powerlessness, and humiliation."

Fisher-Wirth writes that the crisis drove him to put himself in a mental hospital for a couple of months, and it was in this phase of his life he wrote the poem. Maybe it's this news "of something that concerns you" he was thinking of. I hadn't known that McCarthyism had impacted Williams, too, and it changed the poem for me to know that it had been written in duress that was not only personal but public, the vicious anticommunism that turned into a right-wing enthusiasm to punish and control all dissenters and leftists and then homosexuals and everyone, anyone. Millions lived in fear they might be targeted, whatever their political alliances past and present.

How do you think about this poem to his wife, with its intimate imagery of flowers and domesticity, when you find out it's from a man devastated by the national crisis of McCarthyism—that is, by the threat of an inquiry that is not a desire to know the person but to hunt for grounds to punish him in an act that oversimplifies the past and lumps many positions in the same category and attempts to banish certain kinds of thought and politics?

We know that Senator Joe McCarthy started an inquisition in the early 1950s, with the help of lawyer Roy Cohn, who later became a mentor and instructor to the young Donald J. Trump. McCarthyism is far behind us as part of the era of the USSR and the Cold War, but right in front of us as a strategy to override facts, truths, and rights with belligerence, repetition, and sheer force of will. It is the strategy of nonsense: "'When *I* use a word,' Humpty Dumpty said, in rather a scornful tone, 'it means just what I choose it to mean—neither more nor less.' 'The question is,' said Alice, 'whether you *can* make words mean so many different things.' 'The question is,' said Humpty Dumpty, 'which is to be master— that's all.'"

By Williams's time, and McCarthy's, this destruction of meaning was recognized as a deadly serious political force by the chief poet of the age of Stalin and McCarthy, George Orwell, who wrote: "And if all others accepted the lie which the Party imposed—if all records told the same tale—then the lie passed into history and became truth. Whatever was true now was true from everlasting to everlasting. It was quite simple. All that was needed was an unending series of victories over your own memory." In an age like this, accuracy and precision become acts of resistance, and the practice of memory and the writing of history and the assertion of it at key points become insurrectionary acts.

Orwell reminds us that essays have tremendous political power at times, and Thoreau reminds us that such power is not always immediate. But we live in an essayistic age, and in recent years some of the key transformations in the United States have proceeded in no small part by the arguments advanced in essays, not landmark individual ones, generally, but flocks of essays that fill the sky like the birds J. Drew Lanham writes about in his essay here, covering all aspects of a subject, one essay making a case that lets another make a case that goes a little further, establishing together a new set of perspectives from which new statements can be made and old problems reexamined. The flock lands in countless imaginations and settles in. This has been true of Black Lives Matter, of feminism, of the climate movement, of the way the fight at Standing Rock against the Dakota Access Pipeline illuminated a whole world of indigenous struggles and fossil-fuel depredations for a new audience, of the growing awareness of trans identities and oppressions, and of much else besides.

I have in recent years had a vivid feeling of seeing new ideas sweep in like storms to water the ground and germinate dormant seeds, of recognizing with exhilaration the way that this essay and this and this have a cumulative effect that is transformative. Of how we together make things visible that even those already dedicated to the general goals or principles did not see, of how that capacity to see expands and becomes integral to some portion of society, of how change itself works.

## 3

We who live in and through media and the online world live in a whirlwind of slogans and catchphrases and clickbait, summary conclusions and scrolls across the split screen of news programs, pop-up ads and interruptions that together make things swirl and spin and shatter thoughts and thoughtfulness, and more than that propose that they're something to accelerate past on the raceway. The world is made out of fragments, and now we have breathtaking new technologies to pound them into splinters or snatch us away before we have time for pattern recognition or even knowledge of ourselves. Silicon Valley's contribution to the diminishment of our attention spans may have as much as anything to do with the more disastrous moments of our politics.

"Make America great again," the slogan Trump ran on, was a promise to make history run backward, to make immigrants and people of color disappear, to make women shut up and queer people go back into the closet, to make coal king again and "working class" mean white men with hardhats and not, say, immigrant Asian women in nail salons and Latinx farmworkers. But more than that, it was the promise that nostalgia was history and the past could be recaptured, that truth could be whatever you wanted it to be, that reality was a Choose Your Own Adventure plus bullying romp, that history "means just what I choose it to mean." History is erased by the victors.

Good writing is antithetical to all that, and by good I mean passionately engaged, informed, and committed to ideals including accuracy and precision and fact and memory, writing that calls on readers to be alert, to care about subtle as well as large distinctions, that asks them to observe and value the details and the distinctions, to resist oversimplification and the binaries and absolutes that dog our sloganeering, to go slow and take the time to know where we are and where we are heading. Or it can change who we are and where we are heading.

In this troubled era I have found a particular power not just in straight news reporting, but in a sort of hybrid, a newsy editorial writing or reporting with opinions and interpretations, work that is objective enough to serve as journalism and subjective enough to serve as editorial and opinion writing. Dahlia Lithwick, Roxane Gay, Jamelle Bouie, Jane Kramer, Paul Waldman, Rebecca Traister, Soraya Chemaly, Brittney Cooper, Masha Gessen, Jelani Cobb, Jia Tolentino, Bill McKibben, Sue Halpern, Moira Donegan, John Nichols, David Roberts, Charles Blow, and Greg Sargent are leading examples, people whose voices I trust, writers who begin with the news but go on to contemplate or analyze it in ways that are proscribed in newspaper journalism's idea of straight reporting.

Facts without contexts are slippery things, and it's easy to miss what's going on if you have an untrustworthy narrator or one who gives you just bald facts without context. A law is being violated, an assumption is being made, a new precedent is being set, language is being used in a particular way, pattern recognition of slow incremental change and its causes: why does it matter? is the question that political essays often try to answer, and with that they reach out from the official arena of politics into culture, the subsoil from which politics grows.

Which is to say that we fail miserably for lack of what's found in the judicious engagement, the personal interpretation, and the capacity for understanding when they're in harness together. I was assigned to pick out the best of the very good essays we gathered, and for me that meant not only the integrity of the writing and the writers' visions, but essays that engaged with the most important and conflicted stuff of our time. I enjoy digressions and asides and essays that find the world in a microcosm; I'm as interested in the personal as the next person (but maybe more interested in the impersonal, in what I call public loves). An important topic doesn't make an important essay, but addressing what matters can be part of what makes an essay significant. And since we are in a series of overlapping emergencies, I wanted to read about climate, about gender, about race, about technology, about violence, about how these things are changing and where we have leverage. (I didn't find nearly as many great climate essays as I'd hoped, but I've long known how hard it is to find footholds on as huge and slippery a subject.)

Not only those things, because there are essays on world literature and language loss here as well, and pieces like J. Drew Lanham's "Forever Gone" connect race and endangered and extinct species. That the climate crisis is also a heartbreak and a storytelling crisis is something that Elizabeth Kolbert takes up. The personal is political, feminism declared half a century ago; here she shows us how the political is personal.

## 4

Reading the hundred essays to find the twenty that went into this book encouraged me in ways I didn't anticipate. I found in them one of the subtler forms of resistance we need in this era, or rather opposition, as in "to be the opposite of." I found the opposite of the rush to judgment, the looseness with facts, the overstatements and pretense that categories are airtight, which don't just plague our politics and public life, but gave rise to them.

Reading anything of length is still a solitary act, a settling into slowness and thoughtfulness, and to decide to read is to decide to pay attention to what someone else thought when they themselves were solitary, reflective, introspective, trying to put the fragments together into a new picture of who we are and can be, where we are and came from and might go, why it matters, what it means. By the end of my reading for this volume, I felt the grace and bounty of all these people working in their various corners of the country to try to understand what's going on and to explore what language can do to give us joy and sharpen our perception and deepen our awareness.

I met people thinking about the issues that are in the foreground of this moment: climate change, race, gender and gender identity and misogyny, the abominable current administration. But even the essays about the most central facts of our public political life were not about the obvious. It is customary for people of color to write essays about the particulars of their experience, often saddled—as James Baldwin notably was, as if he were the ambassador from Black—with the task of explaining their "us" to the vast "them" of white people. Women have done some of the same work to illuminate what has been hidden about women's experience to men—and also, often, to ourselves.

But one of the unfortunate side effects of this salutary business is the implication that women, queer people, and nonwhite people have a particular experience and white men have a universal experience that need not be scrutinized. Walter Johnson's "Guns in the Family" was striking for me in that it seemed so cognizant of the fact that the relationship between certain kinds of white American males and guns is peculiar, problematic, even scary, though it is treated as normal. As an ambassador from heartland white masculinity, Johnson makes it as weird and sociologically specific as it should be.

I found in Michelle Alexander's "We Are Not the Resistance" almost everything I ever wanted in an essay, and maybe the essay that made the biggest impact on me in 2018. She takes up the subject of our current situation in the United States, but reverses the terms in which we have described it to say that we—the we that believes in equality and universal human rights—are not the resistance. They are. She gives us a tent: "One might argue that the big tent of 'the resistance' is its greatest strength: a massive united front becomes possible when the barrier to entry is so low."

Then she gets us out of the tent to admire the panorama beyond: "Viewed from the broad sweep of history, Donald Trump is the resistance. We are not." And down below we see the river, the metaphor whose power carries the essay and our imaginations. She writes, "In the words of Vincent Harding, one of the great yet lesser-known heroes of the black freedom struggle, the long, continuous yearning and reaching toward freedom flows throughout history 'like a river, sometimes powerful, tumultuous, and roiling with life; at other times meandering and turgid, covered with the ice and snow of seemingly endless winters, all too often streaked and running with blood.'" She then tells us, "Donald Trump's election represents a surge of resistance to this rapidly swelling river, an effort to build not just a wall but a dam." The metaphor itself is liberating: the river surges through those who read of it in her essay. This is why essays are not just journalism, why their freedom to do things with words and meanings and metaphors and images matters.

Alexander's is a recharged vision of who and where we are, made partly by a different assessment of the situation on the ground, but partly by a reversal of the underlying metaphors. Resistance is a dam. And it's not our dam. We're not holding anything back; we're the river, the real power, and our path forward is inevitable. Not just a news report, not just a political analysis, but a work in which the power of language and a distinct personal vision combine with those raw materials to make something more that prepares us to face a catastrophe with more confidence and clarity than before. And so the fragments come together. Stories do their work.

REBECCA SOLNIT

RABIH ALAMEDDINE

## Comforting Myths

FROM *Harper's Magazine*

BEFORE HE DIED, my father reminded me that when I was four and he asked what I wanted to be when I grew up, I said I wanted to be a writer. Of course, what I meant by "writer" then was a writer of Superman comics. In part I was infatuated with the practically invulnerable Man of Steel, his blue eyes and his spit curl. I wanted both to be him and to marry him—to be his Robin, so to speak. But more importantly, I wanted to write his story, the adventures of the man who fought for truth, justice, and the American Way —if only I could figure out what the fuck the American Way was.

How could I tell the story with such glaring holes in my knowledge? I was terribly bothered that I did not know what the American Way was, and became even more so when I began to wonder whether there was such a thing as the Lebanese Way and whether I would recognize it. My parents were Lebanese, but I was born in Jordan, raised in Kuwait. Could my way be Kuwaiti and not Lebanese? Since most of my classmates were Palestinians, I had a Ramallah accent. Did that mean I'd lost my way?

I wanted to tell stories that belonged to me. Superman would be my friend, his world mine. In a single bound, he would leap the tallest buildings, basically my house and my cousins' across the street. My Superman would be more powerful than a locomotive, stronger than my father's red Rambler. I wished to share my story with the world, and it did not occur to me at that age to ask whether the world had any interest.

Who gets to tell stories? Let me answer this quickly: for the most part—and the exceptions are relatively recent—the writers who are allowed to talk are those who prop up the dominant culture, who reflect it with a gilded mirror. But wait: writers have been critical of the dominant culture for quite a while, you may say. Look at James Baldwin, look at Margaret Atwood and *The Handmaid's Tale*. Well, fine, but criticism of the culture is not necessarily a threat to it. When the story is truly threatening, the writer is marginalized, either deemed a "political" writer or put in a box to be safely celebrated as some sort of "minority" writer. In his day Baldwin was considered more a black writer than a writer, and so he still is. If he is inching his way into the canon, it is because the culture has shifted. Overt racism is a bad thing now, so a liberal American can read *Another Country* and think, sure, there were a few bad apples back then, but this is not about me or how I live. It is easier now to tell ourselves that Baldwin is not talking about us, that he is criticizing people we no longer are.

When I bring this up in conversation, people stop me in my tracks because, you know, Conrad, *Heart of Darkness* and all that. Didn't he criticize empire?

He didn't. A story about a bickering couple does not threaten the institution of marriage. *Heart of Darkness* might disapprove of colonialism, but it's not an attack on empire itself. The book deals in strict dualities and reinforces the superiority of Western culture and ideas. Africa, its jungle, is what blackens Kurtz's heart, and just in case you start to feel uncomfortable because you find yourself identifying with him, the supposed bad apple—the Lynndie England of nineteenth-century Europe—Marlow, the novel's cordon sanitaire, is there to make you feel better. If that's not enough, it's actually some other shadowy narrator telling you what *he* heard when listening to Marlow's story, so you, imperial citizen, are at least two steps removed from the apple and its African rot. No need for you to feel yourself in jeopardy. Your world might not be perfect, but that other world, that world of the other, is just simply horrid.

In Chinua Achebe's 1977 essay on *Heart of Darkness,* he accuses Conrad of "thoroughgoing" racism and adds, "That this simple truth is glossed over in criticisms of his work is due to the fact that white racism against Africa is such a normal way of thinking that its manifestations go completely unremarked."

In other words, Conrad not only shares the dominant point of view but makes it stronger. He might prick it with a pin every now and then, but he is by no means threatening the culture. In fact, he is glorifying it. Achebe uses a phrase that I will return to: Conrad is a purveyor of comforting myths.

Where I disagree with Achebe is that, because of the racism in *Heart of Darkness,* he refuses to consider it a masterwork. Like all books, Conrad's novel is limited by his vision, his biases, his world view. There is no writer with limitless vision, no writer whose world view is shared by everyone. The problem is not that people read *Heart of Darkness* as a masterpiece—it is one—it's that few read books unsanctioned by empire, and even if you wanted to, there aren't that many available. Today's imperial censorship is usually masked as the publisher's bottom line. "This won't sell" is the widest moat in the castle's defenses.

*Heart of Darkness* echoes everywhere today. Take the American war novels about Vietnam, Afghanistan, Iraq. They are often considered critical of war, hence you might think of them as dangerous to the institution of war. But most of them deal with the suffering of the American soldiers, the Marines who were forced to massacre a village, the pilots who dropped barrel bombs and came home suffering from PTSD. If anything, this is helpful to the cannibalistic war machine. Such war novels make us feel bad and at the same time allow us to see ourselves as the good guys. We are not all terrible, for we suffer, too.

In one of the most gorgeous passages at the end of *Heart of Darkness,* Conrad describes at length the suffering of a mass murderer's widow, though he glossed over that of the murderer's victims. Conrad did not create the original mold for this kind of writing—from Homer to Shakespeare to Kipling, everyone has done it—but he became the standard because he was so good. We invade your countries, destroy your economies, demolish your infrastructures, murder hundreds of thousands of your citizens, and a decade or so later we write beautifully restrained novels about how killing you made us cry.

Among the many writers who have responded to *Heart of Darkness,* my favorite is Tayeb Salih in *Season of Migration to the North.* This short novel, published in Arabic in 1966 (the first English translation came out in 1969), refers to a number of classic works of Western literature—*Othello, The Tempest*—but primarily it engages with Conrad. Where Conrad wrote of colonialism as a misadventure that forced enlightened man to encounter his opposite in the heart of darkness that is Africa, Salih, who is Sudanese, calls the entire enterprise of empire a "deadly disease" that began "a thousand years ago," a contagion that began with the earliest contact, the Crusades. Conrad's Kurtz is mirrored in Salih's Mustapha Saeed, who leaves his small Sudanese village and moves to his heart of darkness, London. Once enmeshed in the city's web, Saeed decides he will "liberate Africa with his penis." Like Kurtz's time in Africa, Saeed's stay in London results in a trail of dead bodies—his lovers who commit suicide, the wife he murders.

Salih's novel simultaneously emphasizes and breaks down the dualities between self and other, between white and black. Saeed is shown as both the other and the double of the unnamed narrator, a man from the same village. The line demarcating the dualities is not clear-cut. Compared with *Heart of Darkness*, *Season of Migration to the North* is a study in subtlety. Whereas the denizens of Conrad's Africa are "just limbs or rolling eyes" who grunt and snort or are cannibals who want to "eat 'im," Salih's Africans think, act, and speak—an amazing concept. And Salih is more generous than Conrad: he allows the denizens of his heart of darkness to be human as well. Even these imperial interlopers are allowed to talk, if only to act on ridiculously sexist and racist sentiments, as with a woman who says to Saeed, "Ravish me, you African demon. Burn me in the fire of your temple, you black god. Let me twist and turn in your wild and impassioned rites." (There are prejudices and there are prejudices, of course, and suffering under someone else's does not inoculate you from subjecting others to your own. In Salih's book, in other words, sexism "is such a normal way of thinking that its manifestations go completely unremarked.")

The gravitas in Salih's novel is in the return home. Conrad's Kurtz dies, Marlow returns to England a tad traumatized. In *Season of Migration*, both Saeed and the narrator return to Sudan after a stint in London, and they find that they no longer fit where they belong. The narrator says, "By the standards of the European industrial world, we are poor peasants, but when I embrace my grandfather I experience a sense of richness as though I am a note in the heartbeats of the very universe."

Neither man can be that note any longer; neither can recover the experience of being part of the village. They are caught in countercurrents.

The novel ends with the narrator in the river, not the Thames or the Congo but the Nile, struggling to stay afloat: "Turning to left and right, I found I was halfway between north and south. I was unable to continue, unable to return . . . Like a comic actor shouting on a stage, I screamed with all my remaining strength, 'Help! Help!'"

Think "The horror! The horror!"

Colonialism dislocates you in your own home.

I don't have to tell you that Tayeb Salih is not widely read in our dominant culture; or, to put it in the terms I'm using, he isn't allowed to talk here. He isn't a purveyor of *our* comforting myths. He is, however, read among Arabs, at least among the intelligentsia. The book was published to great acclaim and is now recognized as one of the masterpieces of Arabic literature. So, is Salih the purveyor of comforting myths in *that* world? His novel might not subscribe to the American Way or the Colonialist Way, but does it subscribe to the Arab or the African Way? One has to wonder if it fits into a dominant Arab culture that blames all its ills on colonialism.

The question is important for me, so let me take it a little further. Even though Salih wrote the book in Arabic, he was still a Western-educated man who spent most of his life in London. To the Sudanese, he may be closer than an Englishman, but he isn't exactly one of them, and of course few actual Englishmen would consider him one of their own. He is seen by both sides as the other. Even though his work might sound foreign to most Western readers, his foreignness is the tip of the iceberg, that humongous iceberg of the *other*. Or, if there is such a thing as an otherness scale, then Salih falls at a point along this scale, but not at the far end, and maybe a lot closer than you think.

No matter how bleak things look these days, what with Trump and other racists yelling on the airwaves and committing overt acts of violence, we are living in a time of greater inclusivity than any other. More people are being allowed into the dominant culture, more people are being allowed to talk, maybe not all at the same volume, and there are still not enough voices, but things are quite a bit better than when Salih and Baldwin wrote their novels, and that is reflected in our literature. Every year, novels by women, African Americans, Latinos, queers, by all kinds of "others," are released alongside the white-male-authored books. We have novels by Somalis, Filipinos, Chinese, Indians, Peruvians, Nepalis, you name it.

World literature is now a genre. And as you might have guessed, I have a problem with this.

Let's take an example. Which Chinese writer gets to talk? Amy Tan was born and raised in California and still lives there, so at times she's a Chinese-American writer. Yiyun Li lives in the United States and received her graduate education here, but she was born in China; she's definitely classified as a Chinese writer. They both write in English. Ma Jian lives in London but writes in Chinese. Mo Yan is Chinese, lives in China. He has been accused by the West of not being sufficiently antigovernment, which basically means he does not get to speak for the Chinese. Liu Xiaobo was born and raised and jailed in China, but he was a critic and academic, and who reads that?

It might be fun to play Who Is More Chinese, but that's not the point here. This isn't about good or bad. I love the work of all the writers I mentioned above. What I'm interested in is who gets to talk. Arguably, Tan and Li are the only "Chinese" who are allowed to talk, who are allowed to tell the story in the United States. There might be one or two others. This is still very limiting, not just in terms of how few are permitted to speak but how the writers are perceived. We're adding another modifier, creating another box—black writer, queer writer, and now the world-literature writer.

On the back cover of one of my novels I am called "one of world literature's most celebrated voices." (I have a voice, I get to talk, though I often have the impression that I'm supposed to do it sotto voce.) If we look at the impressive list of writers who are part of this world-literature thing, we see Tan and Li, Aleksandar Hemon representing Bosnia, Junot Díaz representing the Dominican Republic, Chimamanda Ngozi Adichie and Teju Cole representing Nigeria, Hisham Matar for Libya, Daniel Alarcón for Peru, Salman Rushdie for India or is it Pakistan, oh, what the hell, let's give him the entire subcontinent. I get Lebanon.

The thing is that we are all Westerners, if not exclusively American. We have all been indoctrinated with a Western education. We can cite Shakespeare with the best of them.

A number of years ago I was a juror for the Neustadt International Prize for Literature, an award sponsored by the University of Oklahoma and the magazine *World Literature Today*. Since this is an international prize, the jury is always composed of international writers. There were jurors representing Lebanon, Mexico, Egypt, Nepal, Palestine, South Africa, Ukraine, the Philippines, and Italy. Only the Italian actually lived in Italy. The rest of us were primarily Americans, living in the United States, almost all associated with American universities. The Mexican was a Texan, the Egyptian a New Yorker; the Nepali taught at Ohio State. Every interview I did as a juror included questions about peace in the Middle East and whether we can achieve it in my lifetime, what it is like in Beirut, and whether I found the trip to Oklahoma tiring. Norman is a four-hour flight from San Francisco. (And while we're talking about universities: MFA programs are a kind of indoctrination, too. Certain stories, certain types of stories and certain ways of telling stories, are made more valid than others, and this can be dangerous. From the Congo to the Punjab, if you go to Iowa, you will be learning the Iowa Way. You risk becoming a purveyor of comforting myths.)

This is not a discussion of authenticity. I'm not sure I believe in the concept, particularly in literature. Think of Michael Ondaatje's *The English Patient,* a fully imagined novel with four "other" characters set in "other" locations. Nabokov did not have to be a pedophile to write *Lolita*. After all, art and artifice are related. What I'm talking about, in my roundabout way, is representation—how those of us who fall outside the dominant culture are allowed to speak as the other, and more importantly, for the other.

This is not to say that we were not, or are not, "world literature." We might be different from what passes for regular American lit, or as I like to call it, common literature. What I'm saying is that there is more other, scarier other, translated other, untranslatable other, the utterly strange other, the other who can't stand you. Those of us allowed to speak are the tip of the iceberg. We are the cute other.

I use the term jokingly, but also deliberately. All of us on that world-literature list are basically safe, domesticated, just exotic

enough to make our readers feel that they are liberal, not paro-
chial or biased. That is, we are purveyors of comforting myths for
a small segment of the dominant culture that would like to see
itself as open-minded. I don't mean that as an insult—I love to be
read; we all do—but we are serving a purpose that we might not
be thinking much about.

In a *New York Times* review, one of my novels was called a "bridge
to the Arab soul." I find this phrase discomfiting, mostly because
of the words "Arab" and "soul." Is the Arab soul like the American
Way? Do Arabs have just one soul, and if so, can someone please
tell me how to find it? "Bridge" I understood. You see, my novel
was seen not as American but as representing the Arab world. My
novel is a bridge to this world of otherness. I get to talk because I
am the bridge. No one on the other side of the bridge gets to. And
truly, who would want to cross that bridge and touch the heart of
darkness, be soiled by that dark other?

We get to talk because we are seen as the nice tour guides. We
can hold the hands of readers of the empire as we travel a short
distance onto the bridge and get a glimpse of what's across it,
maybe even wave at the poor sods on the other side. We make
readers feel good about themselves for delving into our books because they believe they are open-minded about the other. We are
purveyors of comforting myths.

Now, again, I want to be read. I love holding hands. If there is
such a bridge, I'd love to take readers for a stroll along it. I doubt
any writer feels differently. What I want is to allow other writers to
talk, all kinds of writers, or should I say, more others, more-other
others.

The problem today is that this culture we live in is lovely and insidious, able, unlike any that has come before it, to integrate criticism of itself and turn it around faster than Klee's Angelus Novus
can blink. The culture co-opts others, co-opts their culture, makes
us cute and cuddly and lovable, but we never integrate fully.

Every group needs to have an other. I don't know how a society
can exist without classifying another as the other. The question
for the writers who are getting to talk is where we stand. Inside,
outside, in the middle? For so-called world-literature writers, it's a
troubling question.

You might think this is diversity, but it seems more like homogenization. Sometimes, not always, when I read a novel presented or marketed as "foreign," I feel that I'm reading that common thing, a generic novel hidden behind an alluring façade, a comfortable and familiar book with a sprinkling of exoticness. The names of foods are italicized. Instead of visiting Beijing, I end up at its airport with the same bright Prada and Starbucks stores, maybe one dumpling stand in the corner.

And sometimes even that little stand is troublesome. When I wrote a novel about a reclusive woman who bucks society's rules by having a rich inner life filled with books and art, I was surprised by how many readers identified with her, and more so that many considered her a tragic figure because she lived in a country that had no respect for women. You know: we live in an exceptional country; it's only over there where they ostracize women who refuse to conform. (Our world might not be perfect, but that other world, that world of the other, is just simply horrid.)

How to get out of this cycle? I don't know. I'm a writer; answers are not my forte. Complaining certainly is. Moreover, as I said above, I'm a writer with a limited view. Like many writers, when I begin a novel, almost all I worry about is making the damn thing work. I move from one sentence to the next, from one section to another, wondering how and whether everything will fit. I try, however, to write in opposition; by that I mean that whenever a consensus is reached about what constitutes good writing, I instinctively wish to oppose it. When I started writing my first novel, a friend suggested I read John Gardner's *The Art of Fiction*, which allegedly explained the principles of good writing. I hated it, not because it was bad advice but because it felt so limiting. Writers are supposed to show, not tell? I wrote a novel where the protagonist does nothing but tell. A short story should lead to an epiphany? Who needs that? When I'm told I should write a certain way, I bristle. I even attempt to write in opposition to the most recent book I finished. If my previous novel was expansive, I begin to write microscopically; if quiet, I write loudly. It is my nature. I don't know whether this childish rebelliousness helps keep my work "foreign." Most days, I doubt it. I write a book thinking it is subversive, that it might not be a comforting myth, and if it gets read, if I'm lucky, the dominant culture co-opts it like Goya's Saturn devouring his son.

I might think of myself as living in opposition to empire, or I might insist that I write differently from everyone else, but I recognize that I believe this to make myself feel better. Whenever I read reviews of my work, I notice that I am still the tour guide. "Look at those cute Arabs. See, not all of them are bad. And the homosexuals are nice, too." Which is to say that opposing the dominant culture is like trying to whittle down a mountain by rubbing it with a silk scarf. Yet a writer must. I may not be able to move mountains like Superman, but I have lovely scarves.

MICHELLE ALEXANDER

# We Are Not the Resistance

FROM *The New York Times*

THE RESISTANCE HAS once again sprung to action, this time around Brett Kavanaugh's nomination to the Supreme Court. Even before we learned of the allegation that he sexually assaulted a teenage girl during high school, progressive and liberal forces mobilized to resist his elevation to the highest court in the land, asking people to call their members of Congress, to register their opposition.

Since the beginning of the Trump administration, it seems there has been a new crisis roiling our nation nearly every day—a new jaw-dropping allegation of corruption, a new wave of repression at the border, another nod to white nationalism or blatant misogyny, another attack on basic civil rights, freedom of the press or truth itself. Invariably, these disturbing events are punctuated by Trump's predictable yet repugnant Twitter rants.

Often the battle lines are clearly drawn and blatantly partisan, as is the case with Kavanaugh's nomination. Other times it's less clear where "the resistance" begins and ends. What began as a viral hashtag immediately after Trump's election has evolved into something that's increasingly difficult to define. The defiant, boisterous marches that eclipsed Trump's inauguration helped to inspire a wave of courageous activism, such as the spontaneous protests at airports in the wake of the Muslim ban and the demonstrations against proposed cuts to Medicaid led by disability activists. At the same time, we've also seen a broader, bipartisan idea of "resistance" take hold, one that seems to include everyone from establishment Democrats like Nancy Pelosi to the civil rights legend

John Lewis to democratic socialists like Bernie Sanders and Alexandria Ocasio-Cortez to James Comey, who has spent most of his adult life as a registered Republican.

Unlike the Tea Party, which was born after President Barack Obama's inauguration and which spawned a proliferation of well-funded, loosely affiliated right-wing groups determined to hijack the Republican Party and push it further to the right, the only common denominator for "the resistance" today is a commitment to resisting Donald Trump—the man, not necessarily his mission.

Even members of Trump's own inner circle are joining the ranks. A senior official used an anonymous op-ed article in this newspaper to declare himself or herself part of "the resistance inside the Trump administration." The writer was quick to clarify that he or she was not part of the "'resistance' of the left." Quite to the contrary, the tax cuts for the wealthiest Americans, the expansion of the military-industrial complex and, by extension, the slashing of vital social services were not only fine by him or her but a cause for celebration.

One might argue that the big tent of "the resistance" is its greatest strength: a massive united front becomes possible when the barrier to entry is so low. If you're revolted by Trump's tweets and feel terrified by his access to the nuclear codes, you too can join the resistance.

There is power in numbers, to be sure, but I've begun to wonder whether the downsides to "the resistance" frame outweigh the benefits. At first, I thought the question wasn't worth entertaining because #Resist is a hashtag, nothing more. To the extent "the resistance" is an organized political force, it's doing quite well. The rising number of progressive candidates and the promising midterm election map are testament to the power of the resistance, however it's defined.

But the time may have come to take the downsides more seriously. Resistance is a reactive state of mind. While it can be necessary for survival and to prevent catastrophic harm, it can also tempt us to set our sights too low and to restrict our field of vision to the next election cycle, leading us to forget our ultimate purpose and place in history.

The disorienting nature of Trump's presidency has already managed to obscure what should be an obvious fact: Viewed from the broad sweep of history, Donald Trump is the resistance. We are not.

Those of us who are committed to the radical evolution of American democracy are not merely resisting an unwanted reality. To the contrary, the struggle for human freedom and dignity extends back centuries and is likely to continue for generations to come. In the words of Vincent Harding, one of the great yet lesser-known heroes of the black freedom struggle, the long, continuous yearning and reaching toward freedom flows throughout history "like a river, sometimes powerful, tumultuous, and roiling with life; at other times meandering and turgid, covered with the ice and snow of seemingly endless winters, all too often streaked and running with blood."

Harding was speaking about black movements for liberation in America, but the metaphor applies equally well to the global struggle for human dignity and freedom.

The Guatemalan mother desperately fleeing poverty and violence in her home country stands at the border, young child in her arms, yearning for freedom no less than the American mother hundreds of miles away who puts her hands to the plexiglass in a prison visiting room, desperate to hug her child who sits quietly on the other side. The movements that have arisen to honor the dignity of both women—movements to end mass incarceration and mass deportation—are separate streams feeding the same river.

Donald Trump's election represents a surge of resistance to this rapidly swelling river, an effort to build not just a wall but a dam. A new nation is struggling to be born, a multiracial, multiethnic, multifaith, egalitarian democracy in which every life and every voice truly matters. In recent years, we've seen glimpses of this new nation at Standing Rock, in the streets of Ferguson, in the eyes of the Dreamers, in the voices of teenagers from Parkland and Chicago, as well as at LGBT pride celebrations, the Women's March and the camps of Occupy Wall Street. Confederate statues are coming down as new memorials and statutes are going up in Montgomery, Alabama, and beyond, honoring victims of lynching as well as the courageous souls who fought for the abolition of slavery and the end of Jim Crow.

For many, the election of Barack Obama to the presidency symbolized the imminent birth of this new America, and many whites feared their privileged status, identity and way of life would die in the transition. The reaction was swift and fierce. It shouldn't have been surprising.

As the historian Carol Anderson documented in *White Rage*, every single advance toward racial justice in this country has been met with virulent, often violent, resistance. But the 2016 election was not about only race or gender. That perfect storm had been brewing for a long time, drawing strength from many political and economic forces and gathering speed as the pace of change accelerated.

If we pause long enough and consider where we stand in relation to the centuries-long quest to create a truly equitable democracy, we may be able to see that the revolutionary river that brought us this far just might be the only thing that could possibly carry us to a place where we all belong.

Every leap forward for American democracy—from slavery's abolition to women's suffrage to minimum-wage laws to the Civil Rights Acts to gay marriage—has been traceable to the revolutionary river, not the resistance. In fact, the whole of American history can be described as a struggle between those who truly embraced the revolutionary idea of freedom, equality and justice for all and those who resisted.

One might wonder whether it matters, in the end, whether we consider ourselves members of the resistance or part of the revolutionary river. Can't we be both?

The answer, I think, is yes and no. Yes, of course, we can and must resist the horrors of the current administration—thousands of lives depend on us doing what we can to mitigate the harm to our fellow humans and the planet we share. But the mind-set of "the resistance" is slippery and dangerous. There's a reason marchers in the black freedom struggle sang "We Shall Overcome" rather than chanting "We Shall Resist." Their goal was to overcome a racial caste system—to end it—and to create a new nation, a Beloved Community. Similarly, those who opposed slavery didn't view themselves as resisters; they were abolitionists.

Today, many of us in the movements to end mass deportation and mass incarceration do not want to simply resist those systems. We aim to end them and reimagine the meaning of justice in America. By the same token, many of those who are battling cli-

mate change and building movements for economic justice understand that merely tinkering with our political and economic
systems will not end poverty or avert climate disaster, nor will mere
resistance to the status quo. As the saying goes, "What you resist
persists." Another world is possible, but we can't achieve it through
resistance alone.

HEATHER ALTFELD

# Obituary for Dead Languages

FROM *Conjunctions*

PRESSED WITH COPPER, inked on vellum, Ortelius's 1570 *The-atrum orbis terrarum* (Theatre of the World) was an atlas of the vis-ible, the earth as stage, the seas as audience, 160 maps graphing possibility, illuminating the desire for the unexplored. Each carto-graph was legend to the coveted marvels of the known universe: spice, salt, fur, gold, moon, salt, stars, love, the whim of elements engraved in its corners—sun, fire, the rage of Poseidon, cold wind strapped to a mortal at sea. The boundaries, invisible to birds and despots, are marked by turrets, blurred by the rivers the dead cross alone at night. Here are the Nubian elephants, here are the hot tents of the Tartars, who used the blood of horses to slake their thirst, here the locusts of Ethiopia, who devour the corn and leave the meadows and pastures bare of grass so that *the people do often-times leave their native soil where they were bred and born and are forced, for want of victuals, to go seek some other place to dwell on.* Here is the Congo, where Ortelius says *before the entrance of the Portugals into this country, the people had no proper names, but were called by common names, such as stones, trees, herbs, birds, and other creatures.* Here are the continents, once married, now divorced by the currents of the sea. Here is the terra incognita of kindness and empathy, here are urns you will return to after your long wanderings for power or love.

Recent broadcast from the terrarium of sadness and destruc-tion: it will take between ten and fourteen days from now for an-other of the world's 6,900 languages to die out. So let's say that today the last speaker of something somewhere is dying. Exhibit A: Alban Michael. Out of the 7,700,000,000 people on earth, he was the only one left who could speak Nuchatlaht. He lived near Nootka Island, he spoke to his parents in dreams, as there was no one left to speak to him. And then one year ago, he was gone, himself a dream, his language buried with him.

Exhibit B: After millennia of surviving in the Caucasus Mountains on one vowel and eighty-four consonants, Ubykh died in the grave of Tevfik Esenç. He said, *I see you well* instead of *I love you* and *You cut my heart* instead of *You please me*, the sounds of his words described in a fable as the noise of a bag of pebbles poured on a sultan's marble floor.

Every human infant is a despot. Watch one emerge—first the head extruding slowly from the hot liquor of the sac, then the face turned to cough the brine, then one arm reaching out from the first mine, deep in the underground sea. Here is the lips' first taste of salt, first gold, first light. Its first shriek is the most perverse desire to own and be owned, skin, liver, pinkies, hair, heart, all of it needs to belong, to the mother, to the father, to the country beneath it, it wants its own sky as soon as it sees light, fistfuls of cloud to swallow and devour. Every tiny hand grabs at the delicious world, each slivered nail wants to rake its sands and its sadnesses, merciless, indiscriminate. Every arrival is a possible colossus, every bundle a gentle teenage runaway with stringy bangs and a tuneless guitar, each tinny cry a cracked glass of solitude hoping to break open the sky. It takes time before these little parcels learn their origins and destinations, before they understand whether they are here to own or be owned. It takes a box of Ghirardelli chocolates ten to fourteen days to ship via freight from San Francisco to Minsk.

As it turns out, it is the authorities who are most nervous when it comes to languages. *Through sameness of language is produced sameness in sentiment and thought. Barbarous dialects should be blotted out and the English language substituted*, said a US commission on Indian affairs in 1868.

Exhibit C: It took six hundred thousand men working forty-three years to build the Tower of Babel. It is said in the Torah that those in charge behaved heartlessly toward the weak and sick who could not assist in its construction. They would not even allow a woman in travail to leave the work. When God smashed the tower to smithereens, many of its builders were changed into apes, evil spirits, demons, and ghosts. The rest wandered the earth, deaf to each other, confounded, babbling a thousand tongues, interpreters racing in the rain to explain the dreams of God. Babel is hence referred to in some texts as *the mother of confusion.* And "barbarous," then, or "barbarian," is Greek for "one who babbles," while "jabber" pertains to seafowl, fools, Jews, monkeys, and the Flemish.

Goodbye, Thracian and Yana, Mesmes and Old Burmese, Mandan and Tukumanféd and Classical Nahuatl; farewell, Akkadian and Assyrian and Knaanic and Bidyara and Yiddish, the language Singer wrote in because he liked ghost stories. *Also, I believe in the resurrection. What will all those Jews have to read when they come back to life if I don't write in Yiddish?* Farewell, Venetic and Mura and Old Norse, the languages of mint masters and tribesmen and hatters and engravers, the languages of servants and slaves and the architects of aqueducts. Goodbye, !Xoon and its five interpreters, the language in which a cloud is a house for rain. Yahi didn't even have a word for goodbye. *You stay, I go,* Ishi told the white men who befriended him, and then he did, taking his songs and his name with him. It takes about ten days to get the results of your lab work. In ten days you will receive a courtesy call from our offices. In ten days your building permit will be approved by the city council.

It turns out that there was an ancient civilization that could speak Tree. They could understand the language of roots and the noise of the fungi, a highly developed tongue albeit difficult to translate. They refused to write down the sounds because they could hear the molecules of the papyrus crying. They also had one word that they learned from the wind that they only used with stones—and absolutely never with each other—that, if uttered, was a spell, a name you could carry with you that would open the gates to the city of forever. The word died with them, buried in the folds of old brains and skin, zippered into the earth beneath a tel somewhere between the Tigris and the Yellow River.

I find that I can rely upon the 1951 "Practical Guide to Speaking" the endangered language of Tongan for both teaching and learning the most elemental phenomena of the world. Each English phrase is compressed into one, easy-to-remember Tongan word. All you have to do is to repeat after the tone. *The animals bite. My sheep's hut has fallen into disrepair. My goat has aborted. Wild boars have sadly depleted our crops. The thing is dead. The people have died. Our humanity is finished.*

Greed defines us. Even when we try to call it love. It is still wanting, still inhalation, still one mouth sucking on and spitting out the world like bones; the planet's marrow, one long banquet of planked sturgeons and roasted pheasants. Such continents to swallow, such rivers to burp. If not Mussolini, Stalin. If not Stalin, you. It is so easy to pretend there is an order to things, an extant plan to determine who breathes and who dies, a diagram explaining to the unwitting mothers why some are breeding fascists and others Plutarchs when the wombs look virtually the same. The only sense that can be made of it all comes not through God but through midnight conversations with the ghost of Lucretius who tells you that music was meant for the heavens and not to inspire blood. *Whenever I speak Tlingit, I can still taste the soap,* says one tribal elder, remembering how his grandmother would rub the suds in his gums, the tiny clean bubbles of English rising toward the ceiling, carried on his hiccup toward the unreachable sky.

Exhibit D: Two old women sit stiffly on a small upholstered sofa somewhere in Alaska. *I worked real hard on fish today,* one says improbably to the other. *You rest,* the other responds. *I eat today,* one says into the camera. *Seaweed, salmon, berries, bread. Hooligan grease, potatoes, tea. Tastes really good.* The other smiles, speaks to the videographer in English. These are some of the only words they still know in the moribund language of Haida. Soon they will be dead but they will leave behind a partial dictionary and a YouTube video of their conversation.

At the edge of the Timor Sea in Australia, Exhibit E, the last speakers of Mati Ke, a brother and sister, live in separate villages, and because they are siblings, they may not converse. *I miss you,* one says to the wind. *I have been dreaming of our mother, have you seen the plums this year, the wildfire is fierce, the waterbirds are growing thinner, do you still pray, do you sleep with the language we swam in during the womb?* The wind garbles the messages so when they arrive they are scratchy and unintelligible, like the recordings made by linguists who set up camp in the outback.

Nine years ago, the last Pyrenean ibex died in Spain. Scientists were able to replace the genetic material in eggs of domestic goats by using DNA taken from skin samples. The infant ibex lived seven minutes before dying. "One seven-minute lifespan does not translate to much quality of life, and even if the kid had lived, who would have taught it how to *behave* like a Pyrenean ibex?" questions John Platt in a comment for *Scientific American*. But someday a little ibex will be tottering on the computer-simulated rocks of the Cantabrian Mountains on his four genetically produced legs, herdless, siblingless, cousinless, taking ibex lessons from humans on iPads who clap when he correctly mashes leaves in the zoo. Next year they will implant the semen of a desiccated mammoth into a mother elephant. Her strange infant will be born with a furry coat and a glimmer of glacial light still in her eyes.

In the Caucasus, a mother will bring forth a child for whom Ubykh is only a strange memory, its eighty-four consonants tinny in his tiny ears. *I feel that I have drunk the milk of a strange woman, that I grew up alongside another person. I feel this because I do not speak my mother's language,* says the man from Namibia. His mother perhaps *left to go berry picking and took her language with her,* which is what the last speaker of Tofa tells us is their metaphor for death. It takes approximately ten days for raspberries to ripen with a constant temperature of 88 degrees Celsius. It has been ten business days and the check still has not arrived in the mail.

<3, <3, <3, says the text that arrives on my daughter's phone from her beau, which, if translated correctly, seems to mean *I love you* in sideways ice-cream cone. One can also say, _____, which translates to *I am in love with you up to my kidneys* in Hebrew, which, according to Dante, was the language in which the lips of the speaker formed. It was dead for centuries before it was revived to say things like *Do you have a cigarette?* and *The bombs will be dropped at midnight in Rafah.* Bora had one word for "to love from the heart" and another word for "pretending to love," and you could, if a Boran was alive, say, *Onsra,* which means *I have loved you for the very last time.* Who needs divorce when one compact word illuminates all? In the now-dead language of Assyrian you could say, *Tātu,* which could mean *Of all those who serve in the palace there is no one who loves me there is among them no benefactor of mine to whom*

*I might give a present and who might accept it and intercede for me* and it can also mean *You, sorceress, seek me out, you keep circling me with evil intent.* Depending.

It is late July. The season of hot and delicate grasses is upon us. It is the month of the edible lily bulb, the era in which it is bad to collect birch bark, the window for picking ripe cherries, the hour of molting birds, just one of the thirteen seasons known to the Siberian Yakutsk. Or it is the time to eat corn on cobs and pray for America. Depending. *No man should travel until he has learned the language of the country he visits. Otherwise he voluntarily makes himself a great baby, so helpless and so ridiculous,* wrote Emerson. We can say, *The Container Store is, like, the third exit off the freeway? Like just past the Nordstrom?* Or we could say, *Go inland three river forks downwind of the black sister rock and it will take you as long as two kettles take to boil to get there.* At fifteen miles a day it will take you about twelve days to walk from Prague to Vienna. It took the Jews ten days to march from Stutthof to the Baltic Sea and those who made it all the way there were shot.

One language to rule them all, one language unites them. *Chief among misguided policies is the mandate of a multilingual government,* says a certain congressional representative in California. *By discouraging immigrants and their children from using the English language, this policy has erected a linguistic barrier that keeps many immigrants from becoming full participants in the society they have chosen to join.* Ten days from now the blastocyst inside you will affix to the uterine wall.

*Water mama papa brrr,* says the baby in the bathtub, an impeccable host to the newly minted mother tongue of the world. *Mama water papa brrr. Doggie donkey me. Me go. Me go bye-bye.* Who needs a world without a word for indigo or plop, without vowels or numbers after five? What use are those thirty-seven tiny fish taxonomies or the compound words for castrated reindeer? Who needs words like *abubu* for mythical creatures that no longer exist? *I had constructed with skillful craftsmanship two fierce deluge monsters to place at the royal door to the left and right of the locks,* says one Assyrian to another. It probably took two weeks. Two weeks after the implantation of the blastocyst, the *heart develops in the embryo.* Why eat lilies? So bitter. Ortelius's tomb in Antwerp reads that he *"served quietly, without accusation"* and now his bones are pressed against the water

table, which rises as the glaciers melt, flowing beneath him mysteriously as though called by the time-telling tides of the moon.

Goodbye, Livonian and Yurok and Old Avar and Salish, Aka-Kora
and Aka-Jeru and Aka-Bo and Aka-Cari and Aka-Kede; goodbye,
Natchez and Bohemian Romani and Carpathian Romani and
Tasmanian; and goodbye, old women eating hooligans with their
tea, goodbye to the Kaua'i 'o'o, whose love song cooed the Hawai-
ians to sleep and whose wails could be heard when their young
fell from their nest. Goodbye, ibex and tiny fish with the missing
taxonomies, ten days from now, thanks to the ichthyologist from
Brookhaven, your cells will replicate in a petri dish somewhere in
a lab in Houston. This year his two-week vacation is mandatory.
Hello, new tiny fish. Hello, pretend mammoth that will walk the
earth someday soon with its partially manufactured old soul. Babel
is also reputed to be the mother of singing. Goodbye, tiny black
disappearing dots on the map where two very old people meet or
do not meet to say *tea, cake, your friendship is both storm and flood,
your eyes are lanterns, I am about to speak and about not to speak, I have
carried off to Assyria the rest of his children and his entire family and even
the bones of your father, the city in which we live will not rise from ruin,*
then they are quiet, just saying the words *ruin, ruins, hello, ruins,* in
the way only they will know, the way that, once buried, will never
return to our ears.

MARIO ALEJANDRO ARIZA

# Come Heat and High Water

## I. Get Over It

THERE'S A SCAR on my knuckle in the shape of a star. I got it
from punching Alex Rodriguez in the teeth one afternoon in sixth
grade. He and eleven other kids cornered me by the chain-link
fence at the end of an empty soccer field. Alex had metal braces
that cut my skin open when I swung at him. After I resisted, he and
all the other kids went at me like a pack of feral dogs.

But I observed an unwritten code. When I came home badged
with bruises, all I offered my parents by way of explanation was
that I had fallen. My silence made sense at the time, since my peers
and elders told me all this cruelty was supposed to make me tough,
resilient, manly. I went to an all-boys Catholic school in Miami
whose official motto was "Men for others," whose unofficial religion was Latin machismo, and whose unspoken mantra was "No
seas soplón": Don't be a snitch.

So there's no tally of the choke holds, sucker punches, twisted
wrists, mango-sized bruises, and swift kicks to the nuts I endured.
Nobody kept tabs on how many times I got my face crushed into
the boggy dirt behind the swimming pool. If I was lucky, my cousin
or one of my friends would push my aggressors off of me and I
could run. If I was unlucky—and there were a few days when I was
very unlucky—I'd catch a beating that stayed with me for life.

Alex is an actor now, living in New York City, and he's also my
friend. By all accounts he has grown into a kind and gentle adult.
We grab coffee whenever he's in town. And the older boy who
whipped me with a belt that one woeful time, who tried to shove

a piece of ice up my ass while another, larger boy trapped me in a headlock and giggled as I squealed, now lives in Brooklyn and has founded a tech company. That sadistic motherfucker can burn in hell.

But this isn't about settling accounts. Rather, this is about the sun-scorched Miami fields where I was beaten, and their natural tendency to flood. This is about actual traumas: my own mild ones, my best friend's, and those that climate change is already inflicting on Miami, which in 2016 was the city with the greatest income disparity in the United States. This is about how trauma often makes you vulnerable forever, no matter which socioeconomic group you belong to, even though some folks keep trying to tell you that if you're tough enough you just might come out ahead.

There's a word that's becoming increasingly popular in the climate-change adaptation community: *resilience*. The capacity to recover quickly from adversities and difficulties. As in what they prescribed to me while I was being hazed and bullied and beaten. As in the quality whose suggestion of rugged self-reliance lies at the heart of North American neoliberalism and its correspondingly brutal moral order.

Resilience is a concept so anodyne and formless as to have been embraced by pop culture, cognitive psychology, local government, environmental science, urban studies, and educational theory. You can find books with titles like *Resilience: Hard-Won Wisdom for Living a Better Life* and *Resilience: Why Things Bounce Back* and *The Resilience Factor: 7 Keys to Finding Your Inner Strength and Overcoming Life's Hurdles,* among the other door stoppers in the self-help section. But the genealogy of the word should give us pause. It's deeply connected to the uniquely American gospel of self-improvement as it filtered down through the Protestant ethos of election, according to which worldly success was a measure of divine favor.

"Heaven helps those who help themselves," begins Samuel Smiles's 1859 bestseller, *Self-Help,* which sold twenty thousand copies the year it was published. Smiles secularizes the Protestant ethic and roundly blames the lot of the underclasses on their "habitual improvidence," but never stops to consider what would happen to those would-be self-improvers were the heavens to change—to become hotter, wetter, more prone to drought and storm and hurricane.

Judith Rodin, former head of the Rockefeller Foundation, has published a book called *The Resilience Dividend: Being Strong in a World Where Things Go Wrong*, in which she speaks of "the capacity of individuals, communities, institutions, businesses, and systems within a city to survive, adapt, and grow no matter what kinds of chronic stresses and acute shocks they experience." Her organization, through the program 100 Resilient Cities, has pledged hundreds of millions of dollars to the task of adapting the world's cities, Miami included, to the adversities of a changing climate, and its framework is holistic, calling on cities to, among other things, "foster economic prosperity" and "ensure social stability, security, and justice."

This all sounds nice until you realize that for a city like Miami, stuck on the front lines of climate change, resilience without massive carbon cuts and immediate state and federal aid is the policy equivalent of palliative hospice care. Much as early capitalism managed to project its systemic failures onto the personal shortcomings of those it failed, so, too, does the emerging creed of urban resilience subtly shift the onus of adaptation and mitigation from the macro level to the micro. It is now Miami's responsibility to adapt, even though a future sea-level rise of several feet is already baked into the climate system, even though there's little high ground to go around, even though it's an open question whether or not the city has another fifty years left in it.

You might not think, at first, that my constantly getting the crap kicked out of me has anything to do with climate change or sea-level rise or the death of my city at the hands of an angry, swollen ocean. Yet when state and federal governments ignore the greater structural issues at play, the prevailing doctrine of adaptation starts to closely resemble the national discourse of "toughen up" and "pull yourself up by your bootstraps," and it's worth taking a moment to check in with the folks who don't have any boots.

It is 2018, and like a shameful memory the waters under the bridges of Miami refuse to stay put. The three hottest years in city history have all occurred in the past decade. The limestone soil beneath the region is ludicrously porous. Nearly 20 percent of Miami-Dade County is barely two feet above sea level. The billions of dollars it will take to successfully adapt an urban region of seven million people to frequent, unstoppable sunny-day flooding are nowhere in sight. If you expect to survive into the middle of the twenty-first century, you just might get to watch Miami die. But not before the changing climate stretches the city's already yawning gap between rich and poor past its breaking point.

## II. Old Testament Prophet

Harold Wanless is as close to an Old Testament prophet as you're going to find in South Florida. He is the chair of the geological sciences department at the University of Miami, and around town his opinion is at once respected and loathed. He practices good science, and has been doing so for a long time. Avuncular, wrinkled with worry, he sits in a stiff-backed leather chair pulled up to a round table piled high with charts and papers and books and scraps and tells me, clearly, succinctly, that the city I live in is going to drown. And quickly.

"The Southeast Regional Florida Climate Compact says two to six feet by 2100," he says. "They're using modified versions of the Army Corps of Engineers numbers. Jim Henson of NASA says eight to ten. I agree with Jim."

The compact, a multicounty planning body that helps set and coordinate resilience and mitigation strategies across southern Florida, was established because the response to climate change from the state and federal governments was so feckless. When the counties banded together to figure out what the hell to do, they came up with a consortium that's a little bit like the Rebel Alliance in *Star Wars,* in that it's desperately outgunned and hopelessly outmatched. This is because both NASA's and the compact's predictions spell doom for Miami.

At just four feet of sea-level rise by 2100, Miami meets this century's end as a rump state. The beach is gone; so is Key Biscayne. Homestead, home to a large portion of the area's affordable housing, is a shallow tidal basin that smells like an unflushed toilet. Western suburbs from Doral north to Miramar are nigh on uninhabitable because of constant flooding. Sweetwater, a notoriously low-lying and staunchly middle-class neighborhood, is a wastewater-infused bog. The land along the raised coastal ridge, where Henry Flagler built his railroad at the turn of the last century, is some of the precious little terra firma that stays dry year-round.

And that's one of the better scenarios. At *ten* feet by 2100, Miami starts to look like the Florida Keys, a string of low-slung islands in a shallow azure sea.

But in terms of the stress it will place on the city, how the sea behaves as it rises is just as important as how high it ultimately gets. Presently, Miami-Dade County averages between 14 and 17 tidal flooding incidents a year. We call them sunny-day floods, and they suck: they snarl traffic, damage cars, disturb businesses, and interfere with local and regional drainage systems. Residents are warned not to wade through the several feet of fetid water invading their streets if they have any open wounds. By 2045, NOAA, the National Oceanic and Atmospheric Administration, predicts as many as 285 sunny-day floods a year.

Because Hal is a geologist, he's spent lots of time looking at how the sea has risen in the geologic past. "It pulses," is his characterization, "very rapidly." These rapid pulses of ancient sea-level rise measured "one to ten meters, probably within a century, and were fast enough to leave drowned reefs, sandy barrier islands, tidal inlet deltas, and other coastal deposits abandoned across the continental shelves of the world." During digs, Hal has come across perfectly preserved cypress stumps buried hundreds of yards out to sea, remnants of swiftly drowned tidal forests.

Barrier islands like Miami Beach and Key Biscayne, where much of the area's real-estate wealth is concentrated, are particularly vulnerable. In fact, most of the world's barrier islands are only about four to six thousand years old and date back to a relatively small pulse of sea-level rise that occurred because of naturally changing climatic conditions. That relatively small pulse made the sea rise almost two yards. Again, to be clear, such a pulse today would render Miami a shadow of its former self.

Hal's office is underground—weird for Miami—plumb in the bowels of one of those brutalist structures that dot college campuses like monuments to the bad decisions of the seventies. It has no windows, which is just as well, since the wood-paneled walls are dominated by maps of the Greenland ice shelves. Hal was part of an expedition that journeyed to those far ledges to figure out how swiftly they were melting. As I wait for him to finish writing an email, I imagine a younger version of him scrambling over the ice cap. Traversing a glacier is something that must be done carefully: small, hard-to-see gaps in the long-frozen water open into crevasses thousands of yards deep. One misstep can find you squinched between dark, slick walls that are impossible to climb back up, freezing and struggling to breathe as you slip down into the cold, dark void.

A photo of the West Greenland Ice Shelf, which looks like a dirty patch of road ice on a northern highway in November, hangs above Hal's desk. The shelf is about the size of Mexico, yet during previous periods of warming it took less than a hundred years to melt. If its 684,000 cubic miles of ice turned to liquid, there would be a corresponding sea-level rise of 7.8 yards, enough to imperil most cities on the East Coast.

Those past atmospheric warm periods that melted the ice shelf were caused by shifts in the tilt of the earth's axis, the ends of the planet wobbling like a top drifting lazily through space. This period of warming isn't like that. This one is caused by you and me, and our consumption of fossil fuels, and our excretion of millions of tons of carbon into the atmosphere, which, thanks to the greenhouse effect, will continue to warm the planet for millennia after we and all of our children are dead.

"The problem we're facing now is that, globally, we're getting toward a foot of sea-level rise since 1930 or so," Hal proclaims matter-of-factly. "That's partly because of the warming of the ocean and partly because of ice melt, and the ice melt is only accelerating, because that's what it does." Because atmospheric carbon levels have risen faster in the past 150 years than at any other point in the earth's entire geologic history, the oceans are going to keep rising for the foreseeable future, almost certainly faster than ever before. This isn't to say that reducing atmospheric carbon emissions is a pointless endeavor: the Paris Agreement's goal of keeping the planet from warming more than 2 degrees Celsius during this century is necessary for humanity's survival. But regardless, Hal points out, "we're probably in for a major ride."

His words are hard to hear and even harder to act on in daily life, in part because he deals with complex systems that operate on a timeline far removed from human lifespans. Geologic time considers thousand-year intervals small. City planners tend to think in twenty-five- to thirty-year intervals at most. Their attempts to usher in flood-resistant building codes, or garner the funds to harden infrastructure, or spur denser and more defensible urbanization are plays for time. But Wanless knows the geologic record, and it doesn't lie. The water's rise will be merciless and swift.

## III. The Forest for the Trees

Grim as Miami's prognosis is, you don't have to look to the future to see the city being pulled apart. Lived experience already shows how Miami is ground zero for climate change in America, and points to where the discourse of resilience starts to fail.

"I need people to understand that climate change is something that's not just happening on Miami Beach," huffs Valencia Gunder as I sit across from her one spring afternoon. A fiercely charismatic millennial of Haitian descent, Gunder is head organizer at the New Florida Majority, a scrappy, left-leaning nonprofit dedicated to community improvement through grassroots mobilization. Her work affords her a front-row seat to a show not many in Miami are tuning in to watch, the one where wetter weather, stronger storms, and hotter temperatures disproportionately affect the city's poor.

The New Florida Majority has its Miami offices in a nondescript strip mall on the northeast side of the city, next to a discount sex shop and across from a seedy used-boat dealership. This part of town reflects the true character of greater Miami more accurately than Miami Beach does. There are very few trees. The blacktop on the boulevard is old and has been bleached bone white by the sun. On this May day, it's 93 degrees at 11 a.m. Traffic roars past at fifty miles per hour, and the few poor souls waiting for a bus at the end of the block huddle for shade under the tattered awning of an insurance office.

Popular conceptions of Miami as a tropical paradise obfuscate the region's grim socioeconomic reality. According to census data from United Way, some 58 percent of county residents are barely making ends meet. The average median income in Miami hovers around forty-four thousand dollars a year, but increases in rent and energy costs since 2012 have meant that the household survival budget—what it costs for a family of three to subsist without saving anything—has shot up to almost fifty-four thousand dollars annually. Most residents spend up to two-thirds of their income on housing and transportation alone.

Vee, as she likes to be called, grew up in Liberty City, a historically black neighborhood in northwest Miami, where the median household income is just twenty-six thousand dollars a year. "I own a home there now, actually," she says with pride. When the neighborhood was settled in the '30s, Miami—like much of the rest of the United States—restricted where African Americans could live, both by statute and by practice. Blacks weren't allowed in Coral Gables or Miami Beach after nightfall without a written pass from the sheriff; no realtor would sell or rent to blacks, or sometimes to Jews, because of redlining and restrictive covenants.

So the white folks got the beaches, and Miami's historically black communities—the ones that built the place, and that now make up the city's rapidly gentrifying urban inner core—got most of the high ground along the rocky geological formation known as the Atlantic Coastal Ridge. The average elevation of the ridge is around ten to twelve feet above sea level, which is why Vee can state categorically that, at least in her community, "sea-level rise isn't necessarily our biggest issue when it comes to climate change: it's heat."

Three technical breakthroughs made Miami a livable place at the beginning of the twentieth century: airplanes, mosquito control, and air conditioning. John Gorrie, the inventor of indoor climate control, represents Florida in Washington, DC's National Statuary Hall, next to busts of Jefferson and Hamilton and Franklin. In South Florida, AC is life—but soaring economic inequality and electricity costs mean that many of the people Vee works with can't afford to turn their units on. "I got folks down in Perrine with a two-thousand-dollar-a-month light bill," she scoffs. "Who can afford that?"

The year I visit Vee, 2017, will end up vying with 2015 as the hottest on record in metro Miami's history. After our conversation, the area will undergo a blistering July, with over forty days in a row above 90 degrees Fahrenheit. The consistent worldwide uptick in recorded temperatures over recent decades is among the clearest available evidence of the impact of human carbon dioxide emissions on the climate; the Intergovernmental Panel on Climate Change has expressed high confidence—an eight-in-ten chance—in the correlation between human industrial activity and increased temperatures. For the working poor of Miami, though, there are more immediate concerns. The heat, along with speculators' desire to buy property on high ground, is helping to accelerate an already brutal process of gentrification. And the increased temperatures are only contributing to the physical, as well as the economic, stress.

"This isn't the same heat I felt years ago," Vee says.

"Most of the homes in Little Haiti are unbearable," explains Cheryl Holder, an internal medicine specialist, who, in her capacity as program director of Panther College of Medicine Communities, a health outreach service run by Florida International University, regularly visits some of the poorest and most vulnerable people in Miami. "That's why you see so many people sell—because the homes are not as nice to survive in."

Dr. Holder is tall, with the long, rail-thin hands of a piano player, and looks at me with kind, deep-set, curious eyes. Originally from Jamaica, she's been in Miami for three decades and has devoted her entire career to the uninsured and underinsured—those too poor to afford air conditioning to get them through the hellish South Florida summers.

The county doesn't keep statistics on who owns an AC unit, and neither does the US Census Bureau, but over her thirty years of making weekend house calls, Holder has personally witnessed the effects of climate change on this population: their asthma and chronic obstructive pulmonary disease are exacerbated; they can't go outside and walk as often; they sleep worse at night. And they're more likely to sell their homes as a result.

There hasn't yet been a study that aggregates health and heat data in the area, but the sentiment that it's getting hotter faster in Miami's poor communities is backed up by the county's own infrared maps of urban heat zones—areas where temperatures consistently hover several degrees above the city average—which show them concentrated in working-class and historically black neighborhoods like Little Havana and Overtown. Part of the problem is an unequal distribution of tree cover, which leaves lower-income communities disproportionately out in the sun.

And as the cost of residential real estate in Little Haiti spikes alongside the temperatures, Holder's practice has brought her into closer contact with the would-be gentrifiers. "I did a Saturday program at the Little Haiti Optimist Club at Soar Park," she explains. "There were developers there offering these homeowners decent money for these old homes. If you're a poor immigrant struggling to pay bills, it's very, very attractive to sell your home."

Vee is more emphatic. "We're starting to see climate gentrification on a high level," she says. "People think we're joking, or we're making it up, or it's not a thing. But it is."

Everything we know about climate change indicates that it pulls at society's loose ends. The US military considers the phenomenon a "threat multiplier." Studies have convincingly linked global warming to the years-long drought that helped lay the groundwork for the Syrian Civil War. In *After Nature: A Politics for the Anthropocene*, Duke University law professor Jedediah Purdy presciently points out that "it is too anodyne to say that climate change creates hazards for which wealthy countries are better prepared. It is more accurate to say that it creates a global landscape of inequality, one in which the already wealthy people who have contributed most to the problem see their advantages multiplied."

Miami's poor are losing the high ground. To date, though, none of the regional, county, or municipal resiliency plans have addressed climate-change gentrification, even though census and real-estate data indicate that individuals in these communities are moving to lower-lying and thus more vulnerable areas. The city has yet to vote on a single measure passed by its own Sea Level Rise Committee, even though it is statutorily obligated to. But it does have a plan in place to plant one million trees by 2020.

## IV. Picadillo

Andrew Otaz is a blond, brown-eyed Cuban American. I've known him since we were eleven, when we attended the same prep school —Belen Jesuit, the beating heart of Miami's Cuban exile community. He's in my kitchen today because I'm interviewing him about the salt flats he's been visiting for the past decade. The rising ocean is destroying them, which both of us suspect is a portent of things to come for the city where we grew up. I'm cooking him picadillo, a Cuban hash made from a bric-a-brac of ground meat and minced vegetables, in exchange for his time.

Sitting at the counter, Otaz watches as I dice onions and cube peppers. He lives in DC now, in the dark basement of a turn-of-the-century brownstone, and runs a nonprofit pushing for a more open policy regime toward Cuba. Ten years ago, though, he was a washout. He had declined his commission after his second year at West Point, America's officer candidate school, and came home with PTSD.

For the first six months of his training, Otaz was humiliated, verbally abused, and graded on how well he beat his classmates. The awfulness of it all was not without purpose: hierarchy is life to an organization like the military. Savagery and dehumanization increase cohesion among units, and cohesion increases rates of survival in combat situations. Though all branches of the military have strict antihazing policies, the practice is still widespread, primarily because it enforces discipline and weeds out the weak. You could say it builds resilience. But certain people are genetically incapable of certain sorts of resilience, and it's entirely possible that Otaz belongs to a subset predisposed to PTSD. The mechanisms his brain used to deal with the environment at West Point have permanently changed how his body responds to stress. It's been a decade since he left the place, and he still has trouble sleeping. He's also partly deaf from a nightshoot training exercise with M-4 carbines when he forgot his earplugs.

The air inside my tiny apartment thickens with the smells of comida criolla—onion, cumin, sázon completo—but after a few minutes the aroma subsides. The aerosolized particles that make up the scent haven't gone anywhere; the receptors in our noses have just stopped responding to them. Most human cells are able to downregulate their response to overwhelming stimuli, which explains both why you stop smelling the same thing after a while and why your brain can get way too used to being overly stressed.

This state of affairs should not be confused with resilience.

Say you hear that a grenade is about to go off. The first thing your body does is shut down its neocortex. The hippocampus immediately stops producing long-term memories and instead starts producing a host of chemicals called glucocorticosteroids. These chemicals prepare your body to fight, flee, or freeze; they also short-circuit the normal pathway of memory formation, which usually translates experiences into language. This is a fine system for dodging large predators, but it's awful for dealing with long-term stressors like war—or the institutions designed to prepare you for them. It's also awful if you are growing up poor on the streets of a twenty-first-century American metropolis, or on the margins of a city slowly being swallowed by the sea.

This is because, over time, like a nose that's been smelling something for too long, your existing neuroreceptors begin to downregulate their response to ever-present stress chemicals. But, paradoxically, your neurons develop more and more stress receptors, which makes you more sensitive to stress. If certain people can't build resilience, perhaps it's because their bodies go into fight-or-flight mode too readily, because their neurons have too many stress-chemical receptors. They are, in a sense, too easily triggered. And even if a city is of a radically different nature from a human body, it's still a complex system that can be challenged past its breaking point by persistent stressors.

Otaz grew up on the Key, in one of Miami's most expensive zip codes. After leaving West Point, he had the time and money and family support to try to get himself well, even if he did white-knuckle the aftereffects for the first five years. And when he couldn't take it, he'd slap on a pair of old sneakers and went trudging around a mangrove swamp. He found the flats at the far end of the northeastern tip of Miami's southernmost barrier island. The flats were a wonder at low tide, teeming with plovers picking through tide pools wriggling with silver bait fish, a pan-smooth landscape broken only by a few red mangrove seedlings struggling to keep their first leaves above the waterline. It was by walking out hundreds of yards into this landscape a decade ago that Otaz had first found the courage to quit West Point. And after he left, it was there that he found a modicum of healing. Now, he explains, the flats comprise barely fifty-five yards of sand at low tide.

As the chicken stock reduces, Otaz asks why I've chosen to return to Miami instead of staying up north and settling someplace less vulnerable, less likely to suffer the constant stress of sea-level rise. "You know there's no future here, right?"

I know it's true, and I tell him as much. Miami may not have a future, but some of us have to stick around and write the story of its death.

What happens to memories in a prolonged state of extreme stress? Brain researchers aren't sure, but they do know that some of them become traumas, deeply distressing experiences that the brain can't recall at will but that can be triggered: by the sound of a pin being pulled, by a bright flash or a loud bang. Instead of regularly formed and normally accessible long-term memories, you get a sort of ten-minute-meal version of a memory, a quick-and-dirty access point to a dangerous and indelible experience. In short, you get mnemonic picadillo.

## V. After the Storm

At the end of our first conversation, I ask Vee what she thinks of Miami-Dade County's resiliency planning. She laughs out loud.

"We have plans on paper, and so did New Orleans and Louisiana," she says. "[They] were actually gaining national attention for their resiliency planning, and then Katrina hit."

Four months after our conversation, Hurricane Irma slams into South Florida. The tropical cyclone makes landfall on Cudjoe Key, 150 miles south-southwest of the city, a category 4 hurricane with sustained winds of over 130 miles per hour. I spend the first days after the storm reporting in the Keys, but run into Vee back in Miami at the end of the week. The power is still out.

I find her sweating over a smoking gas grill that dominates the parking lot of a small Salvation Army outpost in Little Havana. From her barbecue, a line of hungry residents extends halfway down the block. Downed trees still block arterial roadways just a few hundred yards away, and massive traffic jams clog the interstates as seven million bodies attempt to return to their homes after one of the largest peacetime evacuations in US history. "You have to understand how it feels to be a woman after a storm, what it feels like to be poor after a storm," she tells me. "Not everybody has the money to evacuate, or to evacuate their whole family, or even to buy supplies."

"There were a good twenty-four hours there without food, and since the power's gone we've been drinking our coffee cold," says Ruben Garcia, a haggard-looking Little Havana resident waiting in line for food. "But I'm not a wimp. I can last seventy-two hours without eating." The hot dog Vee hands him is his first hot meal since the storm. Like many people in the neighborhood, he's on SNAP, the food-stamp program; problem is, when the power's out, the electronic cards used to access the funds don't work. "We didn't take any money out of the ATM before the storm, and nobody around here has power, so the stores aren't taking credit cards or even food stamps," he explains as he accepts a bag of chips. "We're grateful for the meal."

According to 2015 census data, some 185,000 households in the county are on SNAP. In the wake of Irma, that population was essentially left to fend for itself. Since the storm, Vee has been

getting calls from officials asking if she's seen any damaged infrastructure. "I keep telling them, 'You know what the infrastructure
damage is going to be? If y'all don't get some food up in here,
people are gonna start looting and burning the damn buildings.'"

In the two weeks after Irma, Vee feeds hot meals to over
twenty-two thousand people. Not by herself, of course. She mo-
bilizes more than three hundred volunteers, takes over a ware-
house, and holds daily cookouts in public parks from Florida City
to Miami Gardens. She spends hours in line at Costco, purchasing food and supplies with crowdsourced funds, and coordinates
their delivery around the county. The Miami Foundation, Knight
Foundation, Florida Immigrant Coalition, and Vee's own New
Florida Majority pitch in. People who have never volunteered
with her before, from wealthy neighborhoods like South Miami
and South Beach and Brickell, show up in droves. Two city commissioners send one ice truck each, which is about all the government help she gets.

It's not like the government didn't feed people, assistant fire
chief and city emergency manager Pete G. Gomez explains at a
Sea Level Rise Committee meeting almost six months after the
hurricane hit. City employees handed out military-issue MREs
(Meals Ready to Eat) and basic food supplies at priority areas, like
hospitals and nursing homes. But 1.5 million people here live at
the poverty line, and 350,000 are well under it. And the tropical
cyclone's winds didn't just knock down power lines—they revealed
the degree to which the gap between local government response
and the magnitude of the issue leaves thorny questions of equity
on a back burner. "I just don't think our resilience plans are equitable, even though the people working on them are nice," Vee tells
me. "I don't think they get it."

Before the storm, 100 Resilient Cities awarded grants to the city
of Miami, the city of Miami Beach, and Miami-Dade County to
hire resilience officers, whose job is to integrate themselves into as
many city departments as possible and put into practice a holistic
vision of resilience focused on both infrastructure and inequality.
Miami Beach is now in the process of spending $400 million to
raise roads, install pumps, and improve drainage. Miami passed
a general obligation bond in November 2017, just after the hurricane, some $200 million of which is meant to go toward adapta-
tion. Miami-Dade has prioritized resilience in its capital expendi-

tures, though in layman's terms this means it's not spending any extra money on preparing for sea-level rise, just spending what it already would have, but more wisely.

Still, the scientific literature regularly puts the cost of adaptation for the region in the hundreds of billions of dollars, next to which the millions the area has forked over for plans and studies and physical infrastructure improvements barely amount to a down payment. One 2007 study estimated that by 2060, Florida could be spending $2.4 billion a year on beach renourishment alone, just to keep tourists coming. The cost of maintaining the South Florida regional drainage system—one of the world's largest—past 2030 is already pegged at $7 billion. (For reference, Miami-Dade County's annual budget hovers around $8 billion.)

So it's not reasonable to expect anyone but the richest of local governments to put up much of a fight. Nor is it reasonable to expect the half of Miami residents who live from paycheck to paycheck to be able to afford emergency supplies, which usually run about $200 a household. That's just the logic of the situation. To people like Vee, though—those working tirelessly to address climate gentrification and the deeper-rooted inequality it exacerbates—the problem of climate justice can often seem invisible to those in power, whose response, in turn, can seem merely like more self-help rhetoric.

During the public comment period of the first county commission meeting after Hurricane Irma, in a chamber packed to the gills, residents voiced their concerns about the county's response while commissioners ate lunch and chatted among themselves. Only when Vee stood up and said her piece did the meeting's self-congratulatory tone shift. "I do not know the complete protocol for emergency response after a storm, but I really believe that it needs to be revisited now," she said, as quoted in *USA Today*. "We need to revisit every plan, turn over every page."

Carlos A. Gimenez, the Republican mayor of Miami-Dade County, bristled at Vee's accusation. In spite of his public acknowledgment of climate change, Gimenez has been accused by city media of flat-footedness on environmental issues—and for the small size of the county's sustainability office before the Rockefeller Foundation's intervention, and also for an environmentally dubious plan to extend the Dolphin Expressway deeper into the Everglades. "I've never heard of these people," he reportedly said of the New Florida Majority. "So their claim of feeding people, etc., etc., I don't even know if it's true. I know the county response was very good. In the street, we get complimented all the time."

"Come on, Mayor Gimenez," Vee says to me over the phone later. "You know who I am. Your chief of staff has my personal cell-phone number."

## VI. The Disappearing Flats

To get to the tidal flats, you have to leave the trail. It's a short hop from the elevated boardwalk onto a tree, then a fifteen-foot scramble down the hardwood trunk to the soft leaf litter below. Then you pick your way across a beach—carefully, because half of the beach is covered in sand, but the other half is a razor-sharp fossilized mangrove reef that's completely exposed at low tide, and tripping means slicing your hands open.

The fossilized black mangrove roots that form the reef are between one and two thousand years old. When they were alive, they formed part of a network of tidal forests home to over 1,300 species of fish and other animals. Mangroves are the ocean's nurseries, but today it's just clams and crabs who hang on, waiting patiently for the tide to come back. To the north there are a few young, sturdy red mangroves, whose roots make it look like they're walking, and beyond those are the tidal flats.

You may find it difficult to get excited about a low-lying stretch of sand and mud that smells a bit like a sewer when the water is out. But as you approach it, this one shimmers and swells in the Florida sun like a desert mirage. Pools of water bend the light and draw your eye out past Bear Cut to South Beach, where high-rise buildings loom like a distant Oz, and to Government Cut, the entrance to the Port of Miami, where cruise ships that look like giant, top-heavy wedding cakes steam quietly into the Atlantic.

At low tide, the flats extend a hundred feet into the sea. Even with Otaz as my guide, I feel a sense of solitude as I walk out onto them. It becomes possible to hear myself think. Just a few yards from the shore, it's evident that this place is a sort of edge of the world, a border state between land and sea.

I look at the picture Otaz has brought. It's a grainy cell-phone shot, taken in 2007, close to the spot where we're standing now.

We've made sure to come here as close as possible to the same date and time, the same extreme low tide. The flats in the photo are more than four times as wide.

"What's left is a sliver," Otaz says, sighing.

We walk in silence all the way out to the edge of the flats. There isn't a hard line between the sand and the water; the tide pools just get bigger and the strips of sand between them get thinner. If I didn't know any better, I'd think I could walk all the way across Bear Cut and over to South Beach—that's how shallow it looks.

"When I came back from West Point, I couldn't sleep," Otaz tells me. "I'd go three, four days without sleeping. That's when I would go run on the beach, or go hiking." His decision to leave the academy cost him friends, perhaps even pride. But he tells me of a morning when he ran on the beach around Key Biscayne. "Everything was still nighttime and I had the full moon coming down on my right, and I had the sun coming up on me on my left. It was this moment where they were perfectly in balance."

To the uninitiated observer, the mangroves look like breeding grounds for saltwater mosquitoes, places where floating bits of plastic sea trash collect, forlorn, boggy spots best not to wander in. But 90 percent of all commercial fish, and 70 percent of all game fish species consumed in Florida, spend some part of their life in a tidal forest. These areas are critical ecologically; for Otaz, they're critical emotionally too. The edge between land and sea is where he still comes to feel alone.

But the edge has been retreating. At some point it will disappear. His need for solitude, for space away from human institutions and hierarchical violence, will not.

He's not alone in this need. Everybody who lives in Miami has it to some degree. But even as the city attempts to build resilience, the promise of that strategy seems predicated on some interior strength, some inner resource, perhaps the same one the poor and disadvantaged have been accused of lacking since the advent of capitalism. Even the quiet spaces are distributed unequally in America's most unequal city, and it's getting hotter, and the waters are rising.

JABARI ASIM

# Getting It Twisted

FROM *The Yale Review*

IN MY CHILDHOOD home, we were not allowed to call each other liars. It fueled my father's indignation. Slung with the casual malice that only bickering siblings can summon, *Liar!* somehow set off a warning beacon, alerting my father wherever he was. A schoolteacher with a reputation for discipline, he wasn't remotely as stern as my friends imagined. But proper speech was an area he patrolled with diligence, and his radar was remarkably sensitive. Lazy enunciation, insults, and vulgarities were the blunders most likely to set him off. Once, in the middle of an argument, I told my brother to drop dead. My father's admonishment was calmly but pointedly delivered, and even now my ears burn at the memory of it. His catalogue of deplorable lingo was expansive and, to our considerable confusion, unpredictable. Words that hardly raised other parents' eyebrows could quickly draw his ire, words like *butt, funk,* and especially—inexplicably—*liar.*

No such codes existed beyond our front yard, and the streets presented delectable opportunities to mix it up with the neighborhood kids. We gave as well as we got, diving into the exchange of insults and threats like stragglers in the desert plunging into a sparkling oasis. If we caught someone making an assertion without evidence to back it up, we unleashed our vernacular and let the culprit have it. The local dialect turned *you're a liar* into *you a lie,* a contraction I found irresistible despite my father's prohibitions. I appreciated the way it transformed people into the very thing they were accused of.

Our lies and tall tales usually revolved around girls or athletic exploits and were only occasionally malicious. They were light-hearted fabrications inspired and shaped by the stories we heard at the feet of our fathers, in barbershops and on front porches, at barbecues and ball games. For black people in the 1960s, even less welcomed as full-fledged members of society than we are today, yarn-spinning presented a rare American ritual in which we could freely participate. Other venerable traditions, like burning our neighbors alive, casting a ballot, or taking communion alongside white Christians, had long been denied us. But lying, now that was an equal-opportunity activity. With roots in stories about Aunt Nancy, Brer Rabbit, and John Henry, our inventions were small-scale variations on the African American experience, more about outwitting the powerful than manipulating privilege at the expense of the weak. Our bluster was closer in style to Troy Maxson recalling his tussles with Death in August Wilson's *Fences* than, say, Thomas Jefferson arguing in *Notes on the State of Virginia* that orangutans find black women sexy. Those differences aside, what could be more American than pretending truths were self-evident when they seldom were? What could be more American than dressing up a lie in tailor-made language, like romanticizing treason as a Lost Cause or sugar-coating genocide by rebranding it as Manifest Destiny? As a bulwark against the realities of life in a racist republic, our fictions helped us believe we belonged.

In our world, the consequences of being caught in a lie were usually no harsher than schoolyard ridicule or parental discipline. A person could get grounded or "put on punishment," as neighborhood parlance would have it. Our falsehoods possessed little power to influence another person's circumstances or alter a destiny, and we understood that their relative impotence stemmed more from our blackness than our youth. Anyone could see that "I blamed that broken window on Johnny and he got put on punishment" was a far cry from "I accused that nigger boy of whistling at me and he got strangled, chopped up, and tossed in the river."

Recently, listening to a white man's story on National Public Radio got me thinking again about untruths and consequences. At age ninety-four, Joseph Linsk disclosed a lie he enabled when he was eight years old. He stole two dollars to pay off a debt and said nothing when his mother blamed the theft on Pearl, the family's black cleaning lady. She lost her job and was unable to get another because of her tainted reputation. Linsk remained silent and grew up to be a prosperous physician. Years later, he called on NPR listeners to help him locate Pearl's family so that he could try to make amends. Carrying the burden of guilt for so long, he admitted, had left him "smitten with grief." Such a lovely, complicated phrase. *Smitten* as in struck down, or as in enamored with? And if Linsk considered himself unbearably tormented, one wonders how he would have assessed Pearl's feelings. I'm tempted to conclude that Linsk, like too many white Americans, was less concerned with restorative justice than with assuaging his own pain.

When I posted a link to his story on Facebook, friends' responses eloquently lamented the long tradition of white lies leading to disastrous outcomes for black people. Yet my favorite comment was the most succinct: "Hmph!" That single syllable epitomized the tangled web encompassing whites' misdeeds and the desire for absolution from the people they've wronged. The ritual is often seen with representatives from the media thrusting their microphones at traumatized African Americans while their wounds are still gushing blood. Effectively serving as proxies for the white gaze, the reporters demand to know if the unlucky sufferers are ready to forgive their assailants, usually police officers or armed vigilantes tragically warped by delusions of supremacy (see Zimmerman, George). On the periphery, public officials hover uncertainly, trembling like Jefferson considering the prospect of a just God. To take the pressure off themselves, appointees and officeholders place it firmly on their bereaved black constituents by suggesting that healing cannot commence until they indicate their willingness to put the transgression behind them. It would be even more helpful if they could also express faith that justice will be done in court, or, failing that, heaven. A forgiving victim who remembers to discourage street protests before pausing to pray for the killer will do more to "restore trust" than any indictment or conviction ever could. Reviewing footage of several of these predictable ceremonies made me think of an essay I'd read by the British writer Hilary Mantel. "Oppressors don't just want to do their deed," she wrote, "they want to take a bow: they want their victims to sing their praises."

*

The history of our Revolution will be one continued lie from one
end to the other.

—John Adams

Along with brutality, torture, and murder, a principal step in oppression, American style, has long involved getting between the
oppressed and their stories. Depending on the circumstances, intervention may involve disputing oppressed people's versions of
events, distorting them or seizing them outright, or renaming and
repurposing them. Nurturing the lie at the heart of each method,
a maneuver known in some locales as "getting it twisted," helps
oppressors sustain what Toni Morrison calls the master narrative.
When individuals in some African American communities get
things twisted, often beginning their tale with *What happened was,* a
popular response is *Who I look like? Boo Boo the fool?* The question is
quickly recognized as a way of announcing one's refusal to be bam-
boozled, hoodwinked, or misled. But street-level skepticism is one
thing; collective willingness to accept the lie of American exceptionalism is quite another. Many descendants of enslaved Africans
are no less intentionally gullible than their countrymen in wanting the American tradition—and the white men who established it
—to be uniformly virtuous. For example, we know that more than
a century before Thomas Dixon and D. W. Griffith started writing lies with lightning, the Framers were dipping them in ink and
inscribing them on parchment. Despite the dishonesty inherent
in their secular scriptures, the disheartening fractions and lies of
omission, we want the nation's founders to be flawless. We want
to believe that one youthful misadventure with a cherry tree was
all a typical Great White Father needed to set him on the right
path. We want to believe that the original plutocrats were never
vain or insecure, that they were never unfaithful lovers or abu-
sive husbands, that they never kept black women in chains and
raped them repeatedly, that they never suffered from tooth decay
and body odor or knew the heartbreak of psoriasis and regrettable
habits. In my old neighborhood this kind of naïveté was called falling for the okey-doke.

Benjamin Banneker, an early American genius, was admirably
resistant to willful amnesia. In 1791, he became aware of Jefferson's exuberant lies about black people in *Notes on the State of Virginia.* They included:

- Black people were more inclined toward lust than whites, but not sufficiently sophisticated to appreciate or experience the complexities of genuine romantic love.
- It was only natural for black men to prefer the superior beauty of white women, just as the orangutan "preferred black women over those of his own species."
- Pain, both emotional and physical, was "less felt and sooner forgotten" among blacks.
- Blacks were "induced by the slightest amusements," "had dull, tasteless and anomalous" imaginations, and were incapable of uttering "a thought above the level of plain narration."

Jefferson's whiteness was so fragile that a profligate lifestyle utterly dependent on human trafficking, sexual exploitation, and coerced labor was not enough. He had to buttress it with deliberate falsehoods designed to comfort the planter class and allay their fears of rebellious blackness. Incensed, Banneker called him on it. Including an edition of his almanac with a letter dated August 20, 1791, he wrote:

> Sir, how pitiable is it to reflect, that although you were so fully convinced of the benevolence of the Father of Mankind, and of his equal and impartial distribution of these rights and privileges, which he hath conferred upon them, that you should at the same time counteract his mercies, in detaining by fraud and violence so numerous a part of my brethren, under groaning captivity and cruel oppression, that you should at the same time be found guilty of that most criminal act, which you professedly detested in others, with respect to yourselves.

In other words, Sir, you a lie.

Jefferson's letter in reply was tepid and noncommittal:

> Sir,
> I thank you, sincerely for your letter of the 10th instant, and for the Almanac it contained. No body wishes more than I do, to see such proofs as you exhibit, that nature has given to our black brethren talents equal to those of the other colors of men; and that the appearance of the want of them, is owing merely to the degraded condition of their existence, both in Africa and America. I can add with truth, that no body wishes more ardently to see a good system commenced, for raising the condition, both of their body and mind, to what it ought to be, as

far as the imbecility of their present existence, and other circumstances, which cannot be neglected, will admit.

I have taken the liberty of sending your Almanac to Monsieur de Condozett, Secretary of the Academy of Sciences at Paris, and Member of the Philanthropic Society, because I considered it as a document, to which your whole color had a right for their justification, against the doubts which have been entertained of them.

I am with great esteem, Sir, Your most obedient Humble Servant,

Thomas Jefferson

He made no attempt to directly address or refute any of Banneker's objections, sidestepping such provocations as *fraud, violence,* and *cruel* while tossing back an *imbecility* of his own. That kind of verbal thrust-and-parry, with its sly implications, coy dismissals, and passive-aggressive misdirection continues to shape disputes between whites and Americans of color over the nature of reality, a conflict I like to describe as narrative combat. Years later, Jefferson speculated in a letter to a friend that Banneker probably had (white) assistance in performing the calculations for the almanac and had possessed a mind "of very common stature indeed." In the end he let the lies stand.

Jefferson was not an elected official when he presented his inflammatory and patently false "observations" of black people to the world. Although he was minister to France the year he published his *Notes,* he was opining as a private citizen. Yet he was a public figure of considerable stature and thus his influence can't be overestimated. His notes enlivened stereotypes that resonate even today. When a white mother called the police in Washington, DC, because black teens near an ATM made her "uncomfortable" —and police unquestionably followed her implicit commands by detaining the youngsters—that was race-based lying at work. When the manager of a lingerie store made all the black customers leave after a black woman was caught shoplifting, that was race-based lying at work.

A different but no less caustic danger results from the liar acting as an agent of the state. When the state gets it twisted, as it did in the case of the Central Park Five, the consequences are long-ranging and irreparable. After a white woman was raped and beaten nearly to death in Central Park in 1989, the Manhattan district attorney's sex-crime unit railroaded five innocent young black and Latino men into prison. Each served between five and twelve years. The state's mendacity was abetted by the defendants' coerced confessions: vague, inconsistent statements in which they lied on themselves. Years later, after another man confessed to the crime and the five were exonerated, former district attorney Linda Fairstein, who had supervised the sex-crime unit, continued to ignore the complete absence of evidence and insist that the jury had reached the correct verdict. Donald Trump, who had fanned the flames of derision by purchasing full-page ads in local newspapers calling for "muggers and murderers" to suffer for their crimes, also expressed no remorse. "They admitted they were guilty," he said in a statement to CNN. "The police doing the original investigation say they were guilty. The fact that that case was settled with so much evidence against them is outrageous." There was no evidence against them, and investigators found no DNA from any of the young men at the scene of the crime. Like Jefferson and many others before them, Fairstein and Trump refused to admit their roles in perpetuating a toxic deception, even when facts inconveniently illuminated their errors.

> Deceiving Americans is one of the few growing home industries we still have in this country.
>
> —Charles Simic

In 1988 Newt Gingrich spoke passionately of a war against liberals that had to be "fought with a scale and a duration and a savagery that is only true of civil wars," a war in which language would be wielded as "a key mechanism of control." Two years later his political organization, GOPAC, offered aspiring Republican candidates a key list of words and phrases—*sick, pathetic, radical,* and *welfare,* among them—to help voters distinguish between them and their Democratic opponents. If not for such maneuvers, it would be tempting to identify something unprecedented in Trump's aggressive pseudo-populist postures during the campaign, as well as his tendency to dismiss any coverage that challenges his narrative as merely *fake news.* Instead, his tactics remind us that getting it twisted is hardly a new method for the GOP. It is the party of Lee Atwater, after all, and the party whose most popular president in recent decades launched his campaign in Philadelphia,

Mississippi, where the bodies of three activists were found during the height of the civil rights battle in that state. Perhaps because of that sordid history, it was just a short spiral from Ronald Reagan's welfare queens to Trump's wilding teens, Mexican rapists, death panels, and gay Kenyan Muslims masquerading as American presidents. Our Twitter-happy narcissist in chief, continuing his long history of dissembling and prevarication, rode into power on a wave of such shouts and murmurs (and dog whistles). The "mainstream" press, suffering from an embarrassing lack of diversity, did little to resist Trump's verbal tsunami, using *working class* as a euphemism for white people, often uncritically accepting police accounts of shootings involving unarmed black people, and showing a woeful reluctance to identify racists as the unprincipled degenerates they are. The day after Trump declared his candidacy, Dylann Roof executed nine black Charleston churchgoers. As black communities nationwide reeled in horror, initial news reports described the unrepentant assassin as "a bug-eyed boy with a bowl haircut who came from a broken home," a waif so bedraggled and forlorn that local cops took him for sandwiches before hauling him to jail. Similarly, the media, preoccupied with the prep school costumes favored by Trump's youthful troops, failed to seriously consider the visceral trauma resulting from resurgent racist terror. A month before the election, *Mother Jones* magazine introduced Richard Spencer as if he were a new neighbor at the block-party cookout. "Meet the dapper white nationalist riding the Trump wave," its promoting tweet cooed. Similarly, ten days after Trump's victory, the *Los Angeles Times* encouraged readers to "meet the new think tank in town: the 'alt-right' comes to Washington." The dithering over the appropriateness of using *alt-right, white nationalist,* etc., was a sideshow that helped us to avoid the fundamental questions that must be confronted: Is voting for a racist itself a racist act? Can one commit a racist act and not be a racist? Until we delve into that riddle, no real conversation can take place between those who voted for the forty-fifth president and those who did not.

Similarly, I find little purpose in referring to the Richard Spencers and Donald Trumps of this world as advocates of "white supremacy." To use that term, even while condemning it, is to flirt recklessly with absurdity, and uttering it even in that context leaves a rancid, intolerable taste. I'd like to suggest that it has outlived its usefulness. As a phrase describing a specific psychosis deriving from a race-based lie, *white insanity* seems far more suitable.

And while we're at it, self-styled liberals might consider arming their own vocabularies. Help those Americans who support full equality for all human beings by using words like the following to describe those who oppose it:

| | | |
|---|---|---|
| Duplicitous | Ammosexual | Confederate |
| Greedy | Sterile | Covetous |
| Racist | Flaccid | Sadistic |
| Delusional | Divisive | Cunning |
| Psychotic | Unethical | Uppity |
| Selfish | Intellectually | Confused |
| Paranoid | challenged | Malignant |

It's time to replace the timid discourse of pragmatic centrism with the aggressive language our situation requires. Unlike Barack Obama, who spent both terms of his presidency hamstrung by conventional notions of propriety and understandably wary of coming off as an "angry black man," the rest of us have license to speak freely—and speak out. "It is a very grave question as to whether or not the slavery and degradation of Negroes in America has not been unnecessarily prolonged by the submission to evil," W.E.B. Du Bois once observed. Replace the archaic-sounding *evil* with *blatant corruption* and the question applies not just to black people but also to any American who's not a member of the gilded one percent. As I watch the forty-fifth president and his lackeys attack the tender flesh of opponents, with claws fully extended and fangs dripping saliva, I can't help thinking of Benjamin Franklin's words to his sister Jane. "If you make yourself a Sheep," he wrote, "the Wolves will eat you."

> This whole country is full of lies.
> You're all gonna die and die like flies.
> —Nina Simone

Lately, I've been revisiting the work of Ronald Fair, an inexcusably unsung writer. I admire him not only because his deeply empathetic portraits of black boys and men encourage my own literary ambitions. I also admire him because he laid out the structure of narrative combat as well as any American novelist ever has. Especially in his books *Hog Butcher* (1966) and *We Can't Breathe* (1972), Fair exposed the limitations inherent in what he called "this lie they call democracy, this insidious myth they call fair play, this vicious thing called the-American-way-of-life."

Both novels address issues that continue to resonate today, including economic inequality, a legal system designed to promote white impunity and accumulate black convictions, and the ferocity with which whiteness challenges black people's right to narrate their own experiences.

Like Richard Wright and Gwendolyn Brooks, Fair took readers inside the tenements and kitchenettes of South Side Chicago. Like August Wilson, he created characters who insist on reevaluating the wisdom of the Great Migration. What is the point of them fleeing north, they ask, if they are only going to encounter the very conditions they fled? Fair called the myths of a liberal North "glorious fantasies about a new and better world," but refugees from Dixie turned a deaf ear to skeptics. Huddled masses of black people, yearning to breathe free, broke for St. Louis, Chicago, Harlem, and Detroit like displaced European tribes hell-bent for Ellis Island. But when they arrived, they sometimes discovered there wasn't enough air to go around.

"We came to the North, and we're still victims of discrimination and oppression in the North," Wilson complained in an interview. "The real reason that the people left was a search for jobs, because the agriculture, cotton agriculture in particular, could no longer support us. But the move to the cities has not been a good move. Today . . . we still don't have jobs. The last time blacks in America were working was during the Second World War, when there was a need for labor, and it did not matter what color you were."

Whereas Wilson saw the Great Migration as a mistake, Ernie Johnson, the observant young man at the center of *We Can't Breathe*, sees the epic journey as the result of a lie of omission. "I read about the South and things whites had done to my people there," he says, "and I wondered why more people had not written about atrocities in the North—in many ways they were worse because they were committed behind a smiling face that always kept you thinking that things were going to be better."

Ernie's neighborhood differs little from that of Wilford Robinson, the headstrong young hero of *Hog Butcher*. The landmarks, hurdles, and pitfalls of their sixties-era Chicago streets would not be out of place in Tamir Rice's Cleveland or Trayvon Martin's Sanford, Florida. Ernie, developing the sharp eye of the novelist he hopes to become, has already recognized the local policemen as "assassins for white society." Similarly, Wilford sees the motorcycle cops who menace his community as "a special squad created not so much to protect them as to keep them in line." The plots of both books hinge on the protagonist witnessing a police killing of an unarmed black man. With social media and cell phones still a twinkle in a technologist's eye, all each boy has is his own account versus the official story that the police will tell.

When Ernie tells his father what he has seen, they discuss going to the state's attorney. Ernie deduces a world of significance from his parents' exchange of glances. "He looked at my mother and I could see how desperately he was trying to find the right thing to say, how he was trying to save himself in my eyes as a man, how he was trying to give me something meaningful to hang on to for the rest of my life, a feeling of fairness about our world if nothing else."

His father concludes that going to the state's attorney would be a misstep that could end disastrously. The solution, he says, is to take control of the narrative. "Write it down," he advises Ernie, who is about to enter high school. "Write down how much a black man has to pay for bein a black man in this country. Write down what happened here today so the whole damn world'll know what we take just to do the simple things we do, and let them see if they'd be strong enough to be black." With no hope of justice for the slain black man, Ernie and his family dream of redemption in the form of art he will someday create.

In *Hog Butcher*, a precinct captain stops by Wilford's house to intimidate him into silence before he can testify about what he has seen. "It's not that we don't want you to tell the truth," he says to the boy. "It's just that we don't want you to say anything just now. Now that's not tellin' a lie, is it?"

But Wilford remembers his teacher's advice: "If you know somebody else is tellin' a story and you don't say nothin' about it, well, then, that's the same as you tellin' a story right with 'em." Unlike our nonagenarian friend in the NPR segment, Wilford realizes that enabling a lie will leave him entangled in remorse.

Wilford's experience appears headed to a hopeful resolution

when his steadfast bravery moves a black policeman to breach the thin blue line of silence. On the witness stand, the cop resolves to free himself from a timeless trap pitting "black man against black man to maintain a goddamn white lie."

Ernie, the author's alter ego, continues to face bitter circumstances but regards them with a defiant glare. "I was extremely cold, but my mind was occupied with a story that I wanted to write about the North," he confides, "a story that I felt no one would believe or take seriously. Undoubtedly, it was something that had happened to someone's cousin or uncle or brother or father, and was told over the years from black neighborhood to neighborhood, from city to city, north and south, until I finally heard it. I don't remember having been told the whole story, only certain aspects of it. I knew it would be good, and I also knew that the truth of this story would be denied by whites. But I was going to write it anyway." Nearly half a century before it became a battle cry prompted by the police killing of Eric Garner, Ronald Fair made *We Can't Breathe* a ringing declaration of intent.

Echoing his resolve, we continue to write—and resist. In the tradition of black bards known and unknown, we compose with purposeful fury. We muster our candor and eloquence against a master narrative advising us to patiently attend those who continue to cling so eagerly to antiblack racism, to sit with folded hands and hear them out. It's what we might call a morality tale, a parable in which embracing white people at their worst inspires them to return the gesture and open their arms to us in all our complicated, flawed, and wonderful coloredness. The warmth of our newfound mutual affection will be so intense and contagious that it softens hardened minds and changes the direction of the American future. It's a story that requires a substantial suspension of disbelief.

Or it's simply another lie.

ALEXANDER CHEE

# The Autobiography of My Novel

FROM *The Sewanee Review*

*I*

THE QUESTION CAME amid some more ordinary ones: How long did the book take to write, and did you do any research? Seven years, and yes. And then: Were you a victim of sexual abuse yourself?

Yes.

Why didn't you just write about your experience? the reader asked me. Why isn't it a memoir?

I looked at him and felt confused for a moment. I didn't understand the question immediately. The questioner sounded annoyed, as if I were deliberately hiding something from him. As if he had ordered steak and gotten salmon. Had I chosen? I felt the presence of conflicting, confusing truths. I was talking with a book club in downtown Manhattan, on Wall Street, a paper cup of coffee on the table in front of me. All of us were seated around a conference table, blinking under a fluorescent light that felt, along the skin and eyes, both thin and heavy at once. Like this question.

The questioner was an otherwise nice white man, a few years older than me, I guessed. He would have been in high school when it all happened to me, and I wouldn't have told him about it then. That I could even speak to him about it now was not lost on me.

The things I saw in my life, the things I learned, didn't fit back into the boxes of my life, I said. My experiences, if described, wouldn't portray the vision they gave me.

I saw the room's other occupants take this in.

I had to make something that fit to the shape of what I saw, I said. That seemed to satisfy them. I waited for the next question.

That afternoon, I tried to understand if I had made a choice about what to write. But instead it seemed to me that if anyone had made a choice, it was the novel, choosing me like I was a door and walking through me out into the world.

I began in the summer of 1994. I had just finished my MFA and moved into an apartment with my younger brother and sister off Columbus Avenue, on the Upper West Side of Manhattan. My brother was starting his first job in finance, at a stockbrokerage. My sister was beginning her studies at Columbia University. I used to joke that we were a little like the Glass family from Salinger's novels and stories, except our mother was in Maine, alone with her own troubles. But the truth was more complicated, and more melodramatic, than the world of a Salinger novel. My mother had been betrayed by a business partner, who doctored their partnership agreements indemnifying her for his debts, then vanished. After she refused to declare bankruptcy, she sold our family home. She had mostly hidden her problems from us until they could no longer be hidden, and to this day I think we three siblings moved in together in New York at the same time she was forced out of our house because it was the single self-protective gesture we could make that was entirely under our own control.

The means by which I had made my way in the world prior to that summer were coming to an end. Grad school was over, as was my accompanying stipend. The inheritance left to me after my father's death, meant to provide for my education, was likewise almost spent—the move back to New York would exhaust it. I had not won any grants or gotten into any of the postgrad programs I had applied for. The despair I felt as each possible future I had dreamed of dropped away with yet another rejection was the surface of me; underneath that, on the inside, I could sense my family fracturing. Myself also.

I kept seeing reports that summer of other writers, some of them friends of mine, selling their novels, some of them unfinished, for what seemed like outlandish sums of money. I thought it was my turn when a friend from college who worked in the fiction department at *The New Yorker* asked me for stories, and I sent her part of my then novel in progress, which was about AIDS activists in the late 1980s in New York and San Francisco. While she found the excerpts weren't right for the magazine, she admired what I submitted enough to send the pages to an editor she knew at William Morrow. The editor, in turn, liked the pages enough to tell me he wanted to have his house consider the unfinished novel for publication. This interest quickened the interest of a friend's literary agent, who agreed to represent me, and I spent a happy ten days hoping this was it. But the house eventually passed on the novel, thinking it would be too large to publish based on my synopsis. "They fear it will be six hundred pages long," my new agent said. Her advice: "If you finish it, then no one will be guessing how long it will be, because we'll know, and we'll just send it out then."

I tried to master my desperation at this news. What happened next was a product of my cynicism, my youth, and my anger. By now it was clear our apartment was too expensive for us to keep, and that my sister, due to our mother's bankruptcy, would have to leave Columbia.

I could have finished that first novel. In the next year, as if to mock me, several novels longer than six hundred pages would appear, and the year after that, *Infinite Jest*, weighing in at 1,079 pages. Length was not the issue, though. I could have tried even one other publisher. But I didn't. Instead, I became obsessed with the idea that I could sell an unfinished novel and that the money would be enough to save my family. I began what would become my first published novel with the idea that autobiographical fiction was as easy as writing down what was happening to me. I turned my back on the experimental novel I'd put forward, and told anyone I knew, "I'm just going to write a shitty autobiographical first novel like everyone else, and sell it for thousands and thousands of dollars." And then I sat down to try.

The story of your life, described, will not describe how you came to think about your life or yourself, nor describe any of what you learned. This is what fiction can do—I think it is even what fiction is for. But learning this was still ahead of me.

I knew what I thought was normal for a first novel, but every first novel is the answer to the question of what is normal for a first novel. Mine came in pieces at first, as if it were once whole and someone had broken it and scattered it inside me, hiding until it could be safe for it to be put back together. In the time before

I understood that I was writing this novel, each time a piece of it emerged, I felt as if I'd received a strange valentine from a part of me that had a very different relationship to language than the me that walked around, had coffee with friends, and hoped for the best out of every day. The words felt both old and new, and the things they described were more real to me when I reread them than the things my previous sentences had tried to collect inside themselves.

And so, while I wrote this novel, I can't say that I chose to write this novel. The writing felt both autonomic, as compulsory as breathing or the beat of the heart, and at the same time as if an invisible creature had moved into a corner of my mind and begun building itself, making visible parts for itself out of things dismantled from my memory, summoned from my imagination. I was spelling out a message that would allow me to talk to myself and to others. The novel that emerged was about things I could not speak of in life, in some cases literally. I would lie, or I would feel a weight on my chest as if someone was sitting there. But when the novel was done, I could read from it. A prosthetic voice.

Prior to this, my sentences were often criticized in writing workshops for being only beautiful, and lacking meaning. I felt I understood what they meant, and worked to correct it, but didn't really think about what this meant until the novel was done.

I'd once organized my life, my conversation, even my sentences, in such a way as to never say what I was now trying to write. I had avoided the story for years with all the force I could bring to bear —intellectual, emotional, physical. Imagine a child's teeth after wearing a gag for thirteen years. That is what my sentences were like then, pushed in around the shape of a story I did not want to tell, but pointing all the same to what was there.

I have a theory of the first novel now: it is something that makes the writer, even as the writer makes the novel. It must be something you care about enough to see through to the end. I tell my students all the time: writing fiction is an exercise in giving a shit —an exercise in finding out what you really care about. Many student writers become obsessed with aesthetics, but I find that is usually a way to avoid whatever it is they have to say. My first novel was not the first one I started. It was the first one I finished. Looking at my records, I count three unfinished previous novels; pieces of one of them went into this first one. But the one I finished, I finished because I asked myself a question.

What will you let yourself know? What will you allow yourself to know?


2


The idea of autobiographical fiction had always rankled me. Whenever I told stories about my family to friends, they always told me to write about my family, and I hated the suggestion so much that I didn't write about families at all.

Even so, most of what I wrote then, if not all of it, was in some way autobiographical. My central characters were typically a cipher for me—like me but not me, with one-syllable names. Jack Cho, for example, the recurring character in four of my first published stories, all a part of that rejected experimental novel. Jack was a Korean American gay man from San Francisco, the only son of a single mother, who moves to New York for love and becomes involved in ACT UP. His relationship to me was more than accidental, but not so close that I couldn't delineate his experiences from my own. Even the name, Cho, was like Chee—a name that was Chinese and also Korean. I invented Jack to help me think through my relationship to activism and sex. Other stories I wrote at the time were investigations of various friendships, relationships, and breakups. I was, meanwhile, struggling with an existential issue that my writing peers from more normative backgrounds simply didn't have to address. Kit Reed, my undergraduate fiction teacher, first identified it. She told me that if I was fast enough, I might be the first Korean American novelist. She wasn't entirely right, through no fault of hers: Younghill Kang was, in fact, that person, but he was, until recently, lost to contemporary literary history. And when Chang-rae Lee published *Native Speaker*, in 1995, she said, "Well, you'll be the first gay one." And she would be right.

None of this was inherently interesting to me, however, at age twenty, and it felt strange, even uncomfortable, to aspire to. I was by now used to people being surprised by me and my background, and their surprise offended me. I was always having to be what I was looking for in the world, wishing that the person I would become already existed—some other *I* before me. I was forever finding even the tiniest way to identify with people in order to escape how empty the world seemed to be of what I was. My long-standing love for the singer Roland Gift, for example, came partly from finding out he was part Chinese. The same for the model Naomi Campbell. Unspoken in all of this was that I didn't feel Korean American in a way that felt reliable. I was still discovering that identities are unreliable precisely because they are self-made.

When people told me to write about my family, it felt like I was being told that my own imagination wasn't good enough, that I could only write one kind of person. For a fiction writer, this was a double standard: I was supposed to both invent characters from whole cloth *and* tattoo my biography onto each of them. The absurdity of casting my every story in half-Korean gay characters alone made me rebel. I think every writer with a noncanonical background, or even a canonical one, faces this at some point. I was fighting with this idea, in any case, when I pulled out a binder I had promised myself I would look at once I got to New York.

I had assembled the binder a few months earlier, in the spring, as I was going through my papers, deciding what to save and what to throw away when I left Iowa. I discovered some pieces of writing that initially seemed to have no common denominator. There was a short story, written in college; several unpublished poems, whose blank verse felt a little too blank, more lyrical prose than prose poem; a fragment of an unfinished novel, with a scene in which a young man kills himself by setting himself on fire; and a fragment of an unfinished autobiographical essay about the lighthouses in my hometown at night. I put them all in a binder and said, out loud, "When we get to New York, tell me what you are."

I think I knew all along that the process of writing a novel was less straightforward than it seemed. But thus far it hadn't seemed straightforward at all. Perhaps out of a desire not to appear pre-scriptive, at no point in my education as a writer had my teachers offered specific instruction on the writing of novels and stories. We read novels and stories copiously, argued about what they were constantly, but plot was disdained if it was ever discussed, and in general I went through the MFA feeling as though I had to learn everything via context clues, as if I had wandered into a place where everyone already knew what I did not know, and I had to catch up without letting on.

The one conversation I can remember having about the conception of a novel had come indirectly, several years earlier. In college, when I was at work on my first collection of short stories for a senior creative writing thesis, I had the good fortune to be classmates with the writer Adina Hoffman, who read my collection and delivered this news: "I think that these all want to be a novel," she said. "I think you want to write a novel."

Hoffman's idea challenged me at first—I had been trying very hard to write stories, and I felt as if I had failed. The connections between the stories seemed at best remote to me. But over time I understood: she saw the way each of them had roots that connected to one another, and also the way I'd formed a narrative in my ordering of them. Even the enjambments between sections gave the reader the pause you feel as you understand a story is about to unfold. And when it didn't go further, it felt like a mistake. This vision of my own process, and the way it has informed what I do, and even how I teach, continues to this day. That day when I asked my fragments to tell me what they were when we arrived in New York, before I got into my loaded car and drove there, I knew I was calling out to a novel. I knew these pieces had their own desire to be whole. And as I opened the binder, that summer in New York, and read through the fragments again, I could sense the shadow of something in the links possible between them, and began to write to the shape of it.

The first plot I came up with was drawn right from that summer: a young man returns home to help his mother move out of their family home. She's been forced into bankruptcy after being betrayed by a business partner, and the son finds her lost in depression and grief—still grieving her husband, his father, who died eight years earlier. The son plots his revenge on the lawyer he sees as responsible for his mother's troubles, hoping to find a measure of justice, and then a lightning strike burns the lawyer's house to the ground.

The main character was, of course, another cipher for me.

At one hundred thirty-five pages, I sent it to my agent, who said, "It's beautifully written. But it's a little hokey, in the sense that no one is going to believe this many bad things happened to one person."

I laughed. I had found my own life implausible on several occasions. I don't recall that I said anything to this.

"Still, it really picks up after page ninety," she said. "Keep going."

When I look at that first manuscript, I can see again how the plot was, well, not a plot—it was only a list of things that had happened. I also see what she felt changed on page ninety. After the narrator visits his father's grave, the novel moves into the past, and into the present tense.

This is how I remember the summer of being twelve to thirteen: foghorn nights, days on bicycles at beaches, lunches of sandwiches and soda. My mother works to get recycling made mandatory, sends me off into parking lots with hands full of bottle-bill bumper stickers as she does the grocery shopping. My hair is long and wavy and I am vain about the blond highlights at my temples that my father admires. Summer in Maine starts with the black flies and mosquitoes rising out of the marshes to fill the woods, and they drive the deer mad enough to run in the roads. The tan French-Canadians arrive in cars, wear bikinis, eat lobsters, glitter in their gold jewelry and suntan oils. The New Yorkers bewilder and are bewildered, a little cranky. The Massachusetts contingent lords around, arrogant, bemused. They are all we have, these visitors. The fisheries industry is dying, the shoe manufacturing industry, the potato farms, all are dying. Our fish are gone, our shoes are too expensive, the potatoes, not big enough. The shallow-water lobster was made extinct the year I was born, quietly dropped into a pot, and now we serve the deep-water brothers and sisters. The bay no longer freezes in winter and dolphins have not visited us in decades. In a few years, cutbacks will close our naval-yards. Soon a doughnut shop will be a nervous place to be. We can only serve the visitors and make sure everything is peaceful and attractive as we sell them our homes, the furnishings inside them, the food we couldn't think of eating.

A space break, and then:

The sun is hours from setting. I am sunburned, tired, covered in sand. I go into the bathroom, lock the door and lay down on the floor. On my back the cool tiles count themselves. I pull down my trunks, kick them across the floor to the door. The only light a faint stream coming in under the door, a silver gleam. I look into it and wait for time to pass.

I'd moved into the present tense as I had the idea of making the novel into something like *Cat's Eye,* by Margaret Atwood, a novel I loved, told from alternating points of view by the same person at different times in her life. An artist goes home for a retrospective of her work, and memories of the scalding love of her best friend from childhood return and overwhelm her. The novel uses past tense for the sections in the present, and present tense for the sections in the past, and between the two, the reader develops a sense of what the girl experienced that the adult does not remember.

I was interested in this idea of the self brought to a confrontation with the past through the structure of the narration. But what I found in writing in the present tense was that it acted like self-hypnosis. Discussions of the tense often speak of the effect on the reader, but the effect on the writer is just as important. Using it casts a powerful spell on the writer's own mind. And it is a commonly used spell. The present is the verb tense of the casual story told in person, to a friend—*So I'm at the park, and I see this woman I almost recognize . . .*—a gesture many of us use. It is also the tense victims of trauma use to describe their own assaults. I didn't yet know what I was trying to do.

The pages previous to this, in the past tense, shed a little light on what my agent meant by "no one will believe this many bad things happened to one person." The draft included my father's car accident and subsequent coma; the suicidal rage he emerged with, which returned in storms until his death; my father's family's various betrayals of us, ranging from stealing bank statements for my father's business, to suing for custody of me and my siblings, to accusing my mother of infidelity while she was caring for my father; and my own suicidal feelings, and sexual abuse, which I hadn't told anyone about, because I feared becoming even more of a pariah than I already was just for being mixed. And while it had never felt like love or community, it had almost felt like not being alone.

These autobiographical events were not organized within the novel in any way. When I was helping my mother move, I'd noticed she had not truly moved in; she had just left everything where the movers had dropped it. I'd had the sense of being in the presence of a metaphor, and I was: my novel draft was like that. Page ninety was where my narrator's attention turned inward, when he looked away from the crisis in his mother's life to see his own.

I cut those first ninety pages and continued with the remaining forty-five, using them as the new beginning. These pages took up the problem of my narrator's silence and his urge to self-destruct, and saw it as if for the first time.

The college story in the fragments binder had been my first attempt to write about my abuse: a story about a boy in a boys' choir who cannot speak about what is happening to him, and thus can't warn away the other boys, and so the director continues his crimes until he is arrested, and the boy blames himself for the role his silence played in the ongoing disaster. The boy wants to kill himself once the crimes are revealed—ashamed of his silence more than anything else—and is prevented by the accidental intervention of a friend, a victim also, one of the boys he was unable to protect. This, I understood, was where that story belonged. I had written my way there, and that was what came next. As I continued, this happened again and again: I would pause, find a place to insert a section from the binder, and continue, writing it all in the present tense.

## 3

In an interview with the *Iowa Review*, Deborah Eisenberg describes learning from Ruth Prawer Jhabvala that it is possible to write a kind of fake autobiography, and that idea—the one I understood from that quote—guided me next. I needed to make a "fake autobiography," for someone like me but not me, giving him the situations of my life but not the events. He would be a little more unhinged, a little less afraid, a little more angry. These inventions were also ethically necessary: they gave anyone else involved in the real events distance and anonymity. As I began imagining the memories that drew my narrator into the past, I found myself wondering what that boy was looking into, in the light under the crack in the door.

There's a quotation in my journals from June 4, 1998, four years into the writing of the novel: "These stories are gothics, and have in common a myth of a kind where the end result is the same paralysis." I don't remember who said this to me. There is no attribution and no context. I think I must have thought I would always remember the speaker—my hubris, and as such, a common omission in my journals. But it succinctly describes many of my early attempts at fiction, what I was reading, even what I thought of as my life, and the primary challenge I faced next with the novel.

The boy needed a plot. I wanted to write a novel that would take a reader by the collar and run. And yet I was drawn to writing stories where nothing happened.

My stories and early novel starts were often criticized for their lack of plot. I was imitating the plotless fiction of the 1980s, but also, it seems, lost in a landscape where I unthinkingly reenacted the traumas of my youth. All of my stories lacked action or ended in inaction because that was what my imagination had always done to protect me from my own life: the child's mistaken belief that if he stays still and silent, he cannot be seen. I had believed this without quite knowing I believed it. In light of this insight, I knew I needed a new imagination. I needed to imagine action.

The plots I liked best worked through melodrama, the story's heart worn on its sleeve and then bloodied up: rings of power, swords, curses, spells, monsters and ghosts, coincidence and fate. These were safe to the person I had been, as all of them were imaginary and impossible problems with imaginary and impossible solutions. They consoled, but they did not consist of choices, emotions, and consequences, people exchanging the information they needed to live their lives. Finding a magic ring of power that would allow me to face an enemy who had won all our fights before was not the same as mastering myself for the same fight. And these stories rarely required that the hero change. The plotless literary fiction of the eighties and the blockbuster science-fiction novels I'd read and loved until now had in common a consoling, thrilling power, but neither could teach how to write this novel. I needed to learn how plot and causality could be expressed in story —not one I read, but one I wrote. Stories about the most difficult things need to provide catharsis, or the reader will stop reading, or go mad.

I examined my favorite myths and operas, searching for plots I loved, ones with explicit action, drama, and catharsis. *Tosca*, for example, where everyone conceals a motive in their actions, and at the end everyone is dead. Or the stories that made me uncomfortable, but that I never forgot, like the myth of Myrrha, who falls in love with her father, poses as his concubine, becomes pregnant, and is turned into a myrrh tree. When she gives birth, tree nymphs hear the crying child, cut him loose, and care for him, raising him as their own. The tree weeps myrrh forever after. Forbidden desire, acted upon, results in transformation, paralysis, and then catharsis. I needed to learn how to make something like this, but not this exactly. I needed to hack a myth, to use the structures of myth to provide some other result. I wanted my novel to be about this thing no one wanted to think about, but to write it in such a way that no one would be able to put the book down, and in a way that would give it authority, and perhaps even longevity.

Mythic plots contain events so shocking or implausible that the reader sympathizes with the characters' emotions instead, the recognizable humanity there: loss, forbidden love, treachery. No one has ever said they couldn't empathize with Hera for her jealousy when Zeus takes lovers just because they themselves never lived on Mount Olympus. The recognizable emotions in the story did this. As I remembered the way we victims were met with condescension, disgust, and scorn, I knew that if I told our story, or something like it, I would have to construct a machine that moved readers along, anticipating and defeating their possible objections by taking them by another route—one that would surprise them. They would want to grasp for something familiar amid it all. Plot could do this.

Plot was also a way of facing what I couldn't or wouldn't remember. The gothic story that led the character into paralysis left me paralyzed and unable to write. Annie Dillard, in my nonfiction class at Wesleyan, had warned us that writing about the past was like submerging yourself in a diving bell: you sink down to the bottom of your own sea. You could get the bends. You had to take care not to let the past self take over, the child with the child's injuries, the child's perceptions. "All of us were picked on, growing up," she said. "Come up before that happens." I knew that my situation was different, but also the same. I would need a way to descend and return safely. Turning myself into a character, inventing a plot, turning that past into fiction, I hoped, could solve for all of this.

## 4

Autobiographical fiction requires as much research as any other kind of fiction, in my experience. I bought books about sexual abuse, the predatory patterns of pedophiles, and a self-help book for survivors, which I needed more than I knew. I bought a book about the flora and fauna of Maine in every season. I took out my old sheet music from the choir. Whether or not I could trust my memory, I was also writing across gaps, things I wouldn't let myself remember. While I had no choice except to invent my way forward, I relied on material that contained the facts I needed.

I also bought a weathered copy of Aristotle's *Poetics*, Malcolm Heath's translation, with tiny print and crumbling pages, at a library sale. I don't know for sure when I purchased it. All I know is that at some point, looking to address my need for story, for plot and catharsis, I turned to Aristotle. The book is remarkable for many reasons, including the pleasure to be found in reading Aristotle on tragedy, as if it has just been invented, speaking confidently about how no one knows the origins of comedy, but that probably it is from Sicily. He notes that the root of "drama" is the Greek verb *dran*, which means "to do" or "to act," and this became one of the most powerful insights for me. Memorable action is always more important to a story—action can even operate the way rhyme and meter do, as a mnemonic device. You remember a story for what people *did*.

> Tragedy is a representation of an action of a superior kind—grand, and complete in itself, presented in embellished language, in distinct forms in different parts, performed by actors rather than told by a narrator, effecting, through pity and fear, the purification of such emotions.

Here the text is footnoted:

> purification: the Greek word katharsis, which occurs only here in the *Poetics*, is not defined by Aristotle and its meaning is much controverted.

Pity and fear and grand action. And purification. This was what I was after. I had reached for the right instructions.

Reading Aristotle to learn how to structure a novel means reading at an angle, almost at cross purposes, but I understood him all the same. And rereading him now, I still thrill to his descriptions of beginning, middle, and end, or his casual mention, in the section on scale, of "an animal a thousand miles long—the impossibility of taking it all in at a single glance." While he was speaking of scale in the story, this was, in a sense, what a novel was: a thought so long it could not be perceived all at once. His assured way of saying that a story "built around a single person is not, as some people think, thereby unified" gave me an understanding of both the idea of a person, and the way it was distinct from a story about a person, and what this meant for his claim that Homer "constructed the *Odyssey*, and the *Iliad*, too, around a single action"—of the grand kind —was for me like watching lightning. A single grand action unifies a story more than a single person, the characters memorable for the parts they play inside it. Or it did, at least, for the novel I was writing. And that is the thing that is harder to describe. Each of these lessons meant something specific to me as I constructed the novel; who can say what they will mean for others?

Also of great use to me was the very simple explanation of "something happening after certain events and something happening because of them." I think of this as a chain of consequences, made from the mix of free will and fate that only one's own moral character creates. Finally, Aristotle's comparison of poetry and history struck me as precisely the difference between fiction and autobiography. Or at least, fiction and life.

> From what has been said it is clear that the poet's job is not relating what actually happened, but rather the kind of thing that would happen—that is to say, what is possible in terms of probability and necessity. The difference between a historian and a poet is not a matter of using verse or prose: you might put the works of Herodotus into verse and it would be a history in verse no less than in prose. The difference is that the one relates what actually happened, and the other the kinds of events that would happen.
>
> For this reason poetry is more philosophical and more serious than history; poetry utters universal truths, history particular statements.

This was where my biggest problem lay. *The difference is that the one relates what actually happened, and the other the kinds of events that would happen.* Recounting the way in which these terrible things had happened to me did not lead the reader to the sense of a grand act of the kind Aristotle describes. A simple recounting did not convince. The plot I needed would have to work in this other way, out of a sense of what would happen to someone like me in this situation, not what did happen or had happened to me. The story of my mother's financial destruction, for example, one of the great tragedies of my life, would not pass muster with Aristotle as something that would arouse the audience to pity and fear and eventual purification. As a story, it was only the account of good people undone by misfortune, and any poetic truth to it belonged to my mother, to share or not share as she preferred.

I chose one of my favorite operas, *Lucia di Lammermoor,* based on the novel *The Bride of Lammermoor* by Sir Walter Scott, as a model for my plot. A young man seduces and then betrays the daughter of the man who destroyed his father, as an act of revenge, but he unleashes a terrible murder beyond his control. I decided I would queer it: instead of the daughter, there would be a son. And instead of a marriage, the doomed love of a student for a teacher.

The choir director character in my draft thus far had a son, Warden, age two at the time of his arrest and trial, and this was the clear Aristotelian tragic line to draw: sixteen years later, Warden is the spitting image of the best friend my narrator, Fee, had been unable to protect, his father mostly unknown to him for having been in prison. Fee meets Warden when he takes a job at his school, falls in love with him, and thus is seduced, unknowingly, by the son of the man who molested him as a child, these many years later. Only after they fall in love do they discover the truth about each other.

I set about making up someone like me but not me. I brought the father back to life and restored the mother. The grandparents whom I had never known well because they lived in Korea I moved into Fee's family home, to live with him.

Then I turned my attention to my main character's family in greater detail, through the plot's other parent: the myth of the *kitsune,* the shape-changing Japanese fox demon. When I read in the lore that red hair was considered a possible sign of fox ancestry, I recalled the single red hair my father used to pull out of his head and the benign stories he made up for me at bedtime about foxes, and went looking for a fox ancestor. I found the story of Lady Tammamo, a medieval Japanese fox demon who had come to Japan from China. According to legend, she escaped her pursuers by leaping from a rock that split from the simple force of her standing on it, just before she vanished into the air. When I looked up where the rock was—said to emit murderous gases until exorcised of her ghost—I saw she could fly in a straight line to the island off the coast of Korea my father's family came from. I could continue Lady Tammamo's story, braiding her, fantastically, into the ancestry of my autobiographical narrator.

The foxes in these *kitsune* stories were said to be able to take the shape of both men and women, but the stories were only ever about foxes as women. I queered the myth much the way I had the opera, making up a fox story about a fox taking the shape of a boy. I decided to give my cipher a life like mine but not mine, one in which he would always be made to feel uncanny, and then made that feeling literal: Fee suspects himself to be part fox, a little alien in the way that makes you entirely alien. A complex tragedy, then, as Aristotle calls it—with two characters, my cipher and the director's son, no single narrator, reversals and discoveries, "fearsome and pitiable events," my plot born of a Japanese legend exiled to Korea, and a Scottish novel turned into an Italian opera. The original reason for the title *Edinburgh* was no longer in the manuscript —I had discarded my plan to send Fee to the University of Edinburgh—but I kept it. It now made sense to me for new reasons that had nothing to do with my life, as a symbol of the novel's eventual separate life.

I made a world I knew, but *not* the world I knew, and told a story there.

## 5

Sometimes the writer writes one novel, then another, then another, and the first one he sells is the first one the public sees, but usually, the debut novel is not the first novel the writer wrote. There's a private idea of the writer, known to the writer and whoever rejected him previously, and a public one, visible only in publication. Each book is something of a mask of the troubles that went into it, no matter how autobiographical it is, and so is the writer's visible career.

*Edinburgh* was almost that for me. I finished a draft of *Edinburgh* finally in 1999 and applied for the Michener-Copernicus Fellowship, a postgraduate award of the Iowa Writers' Workshop. That's twenty dollars I've wasted, I remember thinking as I mailed the application. I'd applied before with unfinished excerpts of the same novel; this was the first time I sent the entire thing. Frank Conroy called my agent a few months later to tell her I would be getting the prize. She then left me the most thrilling voicemail of my life. I remember listening to it in a phone booth on the corner of Third

Avenue and Fourteenth Street, just listening as she described how excited she was. Conroy had picked up the novel in the morning and read it all day to the end. When he decided to give me the prize, he called my agent, alerting her in advance of the official announcement.

He said he would do all he could to help sell the novel. It seemed like publication was close. Instead, the submission process went on for two years, and the book was rejected twenty-four times. Editors didn't seem to know if it should be sold as a gay novel or an Asian American novel. There was no coming-out story in it, and while the main character was the son of an immigrant, immigration played no part in the story. "It's a novel," I said when my agent asked me what kind of novel it was. "I wrote a *novel*."

She eventually asked me to withdraw the manuscript from submission.

The days of imagining that I could write a "shitty autobiographical first novel just like everyone else" and sell it for a great deal of money were five years behind me. The Michener-Copernicus award came with a one-year monthly stipend that allowed me to work less and write more. It was meant to help writers during what was typically the first year of work on a novel, since debut authors often receive small advances. The grant was more than twice the advance eventually offered by the independent press that accepted *Edinburgh*, when, after refusing to withdraw the novel from submission, I left my first agent and found a publisher on my own. My editor was a Korean American from Maine named Chuck Kim. It was a coincidence out of a novel—my novel, actually.

It's the story of my life, Chuck told me.

I really hope not, I said, hoping he had a happier life than the Greek tragedy I had made of myself.

You're my Mishima, he said, once I agreed to the contract.

I really hope not, I said, wishing for a happier future than the Japanese writer and suicide Yukio Mishima.

I was the first living author for this house, the now-bankrupt Welcome Rain, which I called "Two Guys in a Basement on Twenty-Sixth Street." Chuck and his boss. They were smart, ambitious men who made their business publishing books, mostly in translation, mostly by dead authors. Chuck frequently had me to his home for dinner with his wife and brother, and we would speak of Korea and Maine equally. I had based Fee a little on someone I knew in childhood, a young woman who would always try to kill herself, and fail every time, and who turned out to be a friend of Chuck's as well.

I feel as if you're on a mission with this novel, and I don't think it's in your best interest to complete it, my first agent had said when she tried to convince me to let it go. No one will want to review this, given how dark the material is, and they won't want to tour you with it, she said. One editor had rejected the novel with a note saying, "I'm not ready for this." I don't want to say the problem was the whiteness of publishing at the time, but it was not lost on me that the first editor to try to sign it up was Asian American also: Hanya Yanagihara, who then worked at Riverhead Books. She ultimately agreed to submit it for the Pushcart Prize, which allowed editors to nominate works they had tried and failed to acquire. I was preparing my manuscript for this when I met Chuck.

With Chuck behind the novel, everything changed. His enthusiasm for it was peerless. He got it in front of scouts, in front of editors at *The New Yorker,* and he hired a freelance publicist to pitch it to newspapers and magazines. Eventually the paperback rights went up for auction and eleven of the houses that had turned it down for hardcover asked to see it again. One editor even sent a note: "I feel as if we let something precious slip through our fingers." The winner, Picador, had in fact turned it down for hardcover.

But the result that mattered most came when I received a postcard from a friend of mine, the writer Noel Alumit, who also works as a bookseller. He had enthusiastically pressed the novel on a friend, who sent it to a prisoner he was corresponding with, a man serving time for pedophilia: he'd been convicted of having a relationship with a teenage boy. The card, written by the prisoner to the friend, described how he read the novel in four days and didn't speak the entire time. People thought he was ill. "This is the only thing that ever told me how what I did was wrong," he wrote.

I didn't know I had written it to do this, but then I did.

I wish I could show you the roomful of people who've told me the novel is the story of their lives. Each of them as different as could be.

I don't know if I'd be in that room.

CAMILLE T. DUNGY

# Is All Writing Environmental Writing?

FROM *The Georgia Review*

WE ARE IN the midst of the planet's sixth great extinction, in a
time when we are seeing the direct effects of radical global climate
change via more frequent and ferocious storms, hotter and drier
years accompanied by more devastating wildfires, snow where
there didn't used to be snow, and less snow where permafrost used
to be a given. Yet some people prefer to maintain categories for
what counts as environmental writing and what is historical writing
or social criticism or biography and so on. I can't compartmental-
ize my attentions. If an author chooses *not* to engage with what
we often call the natural world, that very disengagement makes a
statement about the author's relationship with her environment;
even indifference to the environment directly affects the world
about which a writer might purport to be indifferent. We live in
a time when making decisions about how we construct the prod-
ucts and actions of our daily lives—whether or not to buy plastic
water bottles and drinking straws, or cosmetics with microbeads
that make our skin glow—means making decisions about being
complicit in compromising the earth's ecosystems.

What we decide matters in literature is connected to what we
decide will matter for our history, for our pedagogy, for our culture. What we do and do not value in our art reveals what we do
and do not value in our times. What we leave *off* the page often
speaks as loudly as what we include.

I could choose among several paths walking from school to my
childhood home in the Southern California hills. Route One was
the most direct as the crow flies. It involved the fewest inclines

but required a precarious scrabble down a pathless embankment to get to the greenbelt attached to the cul-de-sac where we lived. Route Two involved an initial ascent, then a level walk along the street where Jeff Blumenthal kenneled the Dobermans he often sicced on my sister and me. Running from the dogs was complicated by the steep stairs leading down to the greenbelt that separated our streets; this should have been the easiest way home, but we avoided it whenever we could. Route Three had no dogs, no stairs, no embankments, and no greenbelts, but it was significantly longer, ending with a climb up a three-block road that had *hill* in its name.

We also had a fourth option. We could climb beyond Jeff Blumenthal's cul-de-sac and into the foothills that backed both his house and ours. In the hills, we walked along drainage canals and animal paths, avoiding our suburban streets and the heavily irrigated strips of park dividing them. We climbed down, finally, over chaparral shrubs and scraggily anti-erosion landscaping, directly into our own backyard. Our parents didn't like us to take this route because we sometimes ran into coyotes or rattlesnakes, but I preferred the risk of the improbable encounter with a rattlesnake to the surety of Jeff Blumenthal's Dobermans. On that little-traveled path, I was free from the tensions of my built environment. I could be like the landscape in the hills beyond our house—a little wild and moderately protected.

Aggressively trained Dobermans, sun-lazy rattlesnakes, green turf in a desert, and ice plant clusters to keep serrated foothills from sliding over newly constructed neighborhoods represented the thin divide between the natural world and our built environments. When one world impinged upon the other, my daily life was directly affected.

When I began to write, words and images sourced from my childhood's landscape became part of what and how I wrote:

### Language

Silence is one part of speech, the war cry
of wind down a mountain pass another.
A stranger's voice echoing through lonely
valleys, a lover's voice rising so close
it's your own tongue: these are keys to cipher,

the way the high hawk's key unlocks the throat
of the sky and the coyote's yip knocks
it shut, the way the aspens' bells conform
to the breeze while the rapids' drums define
resistance. Sage speaks with one voice, pinyon
with another. Rock, wind her hand, water
her brush, spells and then scatters her demands.
Some notes tear and pebble our paths. Some notes
gather: the bank we map our lives around.[1]

"Language" was the first poem in my first book. This seems as
right a decision about order as I've ever made.

Environment is a set of circumstances as mundane as the choice of
paths we take to get home. When I lived in Iowa City for my final
years of high school, our main routes home—in a car now, because we lived eight miles from school—involved either the inter-
state and a major thoroughfare, or the back roads that led through
farmland and patches of prairie.

On recent visits to the Midwest I've driven through ghost landscapes—less prairie, less farmland. Memory overlaid my vision, inscribing alternative realities onto the present, making me aware of
where I was within the context of where I have been.

Isn't this one of the things we do when we sit down to write? We
decide how to describe what we are compelled to describe. Even
while moving through vast cities like LA or Chicago, by being at-
tuned to a world that is more than simply human I can't help but
think of what might have been there before we privileged our own
interests: commerce and industry, asphalt and glass. In this way we
can apprehend what might have disappeared and what still lives
alongside us, biding time—ginkgoes, catfish, the rivers, crickets.

Looking out my office windows where I live now in northern
Colorado, I see the foothills of the Rocky Mountains on most days,
and the actual Rockies on really clear ones. People in Fort Collins
navigate by those mountains—which are to the west, and so, except on about five overcast days a year, you always know just where
you are. The mountains are a constant guide. Consider how different this topographical navigation is from an orientation based
on your proximity to a particular building, to a particular street
—south of Houston, or SoHo, for instance—or navigation by some
other man-made landmark—east of Central Park. Here I'm using

references from New York City, the environment of my husband's youth; for him, thinking to navigate by nonhuman landmarks took a little time. Similarly, "two streets down from the Waffle House," we might have said in the Virginia town where I once lived, or "just after the entrance to the college," or "We're the house with the blue trim. If you reach the Church of Life, you've gone too far." In such urban environments, it might be difficult to remember that you are, in fact, *in* an "environment," given that we've come to think of the terms *environment* and *nature* as referring to someplace wild and nonhuman, more akin to the foothills of my childhood than to the cul-de-sacs terraced into their sides. But that line of reasoning slides us toward the compartmentalization I resist. Our environments are always both human and other than human.

I feel an affinity for what ecologists call ecotones, areas at the margins between one zone and another—like the tidal zone where beach and ocean overlap, or the treed and grassy band where forest becomes meadow—spaces that are often robustly productive and alive. These are overlaps rich with possibility and also, often, danger. The margins of one biologically robust area and another are sometimes called conflict zones, because the clash between one way of living on the earth and another can be violent and charged. They are spaces that reward study, revealing diverse possibilities for what it might mean to be alive.

Writing takes off for me when I stop separating human experiences from the realities of the greater-than-human world. A poem that at first seems to have everything to do with some so-called environmental concern might end up being about some human condition, or I might begin a poem thinking about some human concern and end up writing something that's chock-full of natural imagery. The connection I feel to experiences that are beyond my own, beyond simply the human, causes me to fuzz the lines.

In a radical and radicalizing way, these fuzzed lines bring me face-to-face with the fragility of the Holocene—or, more precisely, the destructiveness of the Anthropocene. To build an age around the concerns of one species is to ignore the delicate balance required in any ecotone. When one way of living on the earth takes priority, the overlaps that support a healthy system of exchange collapse. Without that exchange, one path becomes the only path, and so whatever dangers were inherent on that one route cannot be avoided, because whatever possibilities were available on the others can no longer be revealed. I do not want such a limiting set of circumstances for my writing or for the literature of our time. I certainly don't want such a limiting set of circumstances for my world.

In 2009, when *Black Nature: Four Centuries of African American Nature Poetry* was published, one of the most remarkable statements the book made was that black people could write with an empathetic eye toward the natural world. In the general public perception of black writers, the idea that we can write out of a deep connection to the environment—and have done so for at least four centuries—came, and I think still comes, as a shock.

As the editor of *Black Nature,* I was able to make the anthology a complete project by expanding the presentation of how people write about the environment. Not all the poems in the anthology are of the rapturous *I walk out into nature and find myself* ilk, though such poems *are* there. The history of African Americans in this country complicates their ability and/or desire to write of a rapturous idealized connection to the natural world—as when I have driven over the Tallahatchee River and had my knowledge of history, of the murder of Emmett Till, make it impossible for me to view those often-quite-scenic waters in a purely appreciative manner. And so, many of the poems in the collection do not fall in line with the praise school of nature poetry but, instead, reveal complicated—often deadly—relationships. The authors of these works mix their visions of landscapes and animals into investigations of history, economics, resource extraction, and other very human and deeply perilous concerns.

In complicating or "de-pristining"—I'm patenting that word—my environmental imagination, I engage with what has come to be called *ecopoetics,* connecting topics we often understand to be the provenance of nature poetry with topics about our current and past human lives. In doing so, ecopoetics has expanded the parameters of who is writing environmental work, and how. This mode of creating and understanding poetry is expanding our ideas about the very nature of what constitutes environmental writing.

Writers exploring ecopoetics ask themselves questions such as these: How does climate change affect our poetics? How do we write about resource extraction, agribusiness, endangered bird species, the removals of indigenous peoples, suburban sprawl, the lynching of blacks, or the precarious condition of gray wolves and the ecosystems dependent upon them? Our contemporary understanding of ecopoetics takes into account the ways human-centered thinking reflects on, and is reflected in, what we write. And, contemporary ecopoetics questions the efficacy of valuing one physical presentation of animated matter over another, because narratives about place and about life contribute to our orientation in, and our interpretation of, that place and that life.

All of our positions on the planet are precarious at this moment in history, and attentive writers work to articulate why this is the case—including many writers of color who were already engaging in this mode of writing long before the ecopoetics movement took off. (Works by Alice Dunbar Nelson, Lucille Clifton, Claude McKay, Anne Spencer, Sterling Brown, June Jordan, Evie Shockley, Sean Hill, and Ed Roberson spring immediately to mind.) But only as the ecopoetics movement gained traction has such de-pristined writing finally been identified as environmental writing and, therefore, begun to be seen in a new light.

Without giving myself license to believe that all writing is environmental writing, I could very likely assign expansive poems—including many of those anthologized in *Black Nature*—to just about any category other than that of a nature poem. But to separate the importance of human interactions with the nonhuman world from the importance of cultural and political considerations would be to limit the scope of such poems entirely. This is particularly true given that the black body has so frequently been rendered "animalistic" and "wild" in the most dangerously degrading and limiting senses of those terms.

According to what Jeff Blumenthal yelled at us as he commanded the attacks, he sicced his dogs on us because we were black girls and, in his mind, beneath him. Hearing all the names he assigned to my body, so many of them intended to limit my potential, I quickly learned the danger of categorical labels. Never mind all the things Jeff Blumenthal and my sister and I might have had in common; our differences were enough to cause him to be indifferent toward our safety. He was hostile toward our presence in a space he considered his own. So, walking the easy path home from school was often nearly impossible.

The history of human divisions is often constituted of stories about one set of people being hostile toward the presence of others. An ideology that would demand the exclusion or subjugation of whole populations of human beings is an ideology quick to assume positions of superiority over all that is perceived to be different. If you can construct a narrative that turns a human into a beast in order to justify the degradation of that human, how much easier must it be to dismiss the needs of a black bear, a crayfish, a banyan? The values we place on lives that are not our own are reflected in the stories we tell ourselves—and in which aspects of these stories resonate with us. To separate the concerns of the human world (politics, history, commerce) from those of the many life forms with which humans share this planet strikes me as disastrous hubris and folly. We live in community with all the other lives on earth, whether we acknowledge this or not. When we write about our lives, we ought to do so with an awareness of the other lives we encounter as we move through the world. I choose to honor these lives with attention and compassion.

## Note

1. From *What to Eat, What to Drink, What to Leave for Poison* (Red Hen Press, 2006).

MASHA GESSEN

## Stories of a Life

FROM *The New York Review of Books*

### *1. Fetus*

THE TOPIC OF my talk was determined by today's date. Thirty-nine years ago my parents took a package of documents to an office in Moscow. This was our application for an exit visa to leave the Soviet Union. More than two years would pass before the visa was granted, but from that day on I have felt a sense of precariousness wherever I have been, along with a sense of opportunity. They are a pair.

I have emigrated again as an adult. I was even named a "great immigrant" in 2016, which I took to be an affirmation of my skill, attained through practice—though this was hardly what the honor was meant to convey. I have also raised kids of my own. If anything, with every new step I have taken, I have marveled more at the courage it would have required for my parents to step into the abyss. I remember seeing them in the kitchen, poring over a copy of an atlas of the world. For them, America was an outline on a page, a web of thin purplish lines. They'd read a few American books, had seen a handful of Hollywood movies. A friend was fond of asking them, jokingly, whether they could really be sure that the West even existed.

Truthfully, they couldn't know. They did know that if they left the Soviet Union, they would never be able to return (like many things we accept as rare certainties, this one turned out to be wrong). They would have to make a home elsewhere. I think that

Note: This essay was delivered, in a slightly different form, as the Robert B. Silvers Lecture at the New York Public Library on December 18, 2017.

worked for them: as Jews, they never felt at home in the Soviet Union—and when home is not where you are born, nothing is predetermined. Anything can be. So my parents always maintained that they viewed their leap into the unknown as an adventure.

I wasn't so sure. After all, no one had asked me.

## 2. *Vulnerable*

As a thirteen-year-old, I found myself in a clearing in a wood outside of Moscow, at a secret—one might say underground, though it was out in the open—gathering of Jewish cultural activists. People went up in front of the crowd, one, two, or several at a time, with guitars and without, and sang from a limited repertoire of Hebrew and Yiddish songs. That is, they sang the same three or four songs over and over. The tunes scraped something inside of me, making an organ I didn't know I had—located just above the breastbone—tingle with a sense of belonging. I was surrounded by strangers, sitting, as we were, on logs laid across the grass, and I remember their faces to this day. I looked at them and thought, *This is who I am.* The "this" in this was "Jewish." From my perch thirty-seven years later, I'd add "in a secular cultural community" and "in the Soviet Union," but back then space was too small to require elaboration. Everything about it seemed self-evident—once I knew what I was, I would just be it. In fact, the people in front of me, singing those songs, were trying to figure out how to be Jewish in a country that had erased Jewishness. Now I'd like to think that it was watching people learning to inhabit an identity that made me tingle.

Some months later, we left the Soviet Union.

In autobiographical books written by exiles, the moment of emigration is often addressed in the first few pages—regardless of where it fell in a writer's life. I went to Vladimir Nabokov's *Speak, Memory* to look for the relevant quote in its familiar place. This took a while because the phrase was actually on page 250 out of 310. Here it is: "The break in my own destiny affords me in retrospect a syncopal kick that I would not have missed for worlds."

This is an often-quoted phrase in a book full of quotable sentences. The cultural critic and my late friend Svetlana Boym analyzed Nabokov's application of the word "syncope," which has three distinct uses: in linguistics it's the shortening of a word by omission of a sound or syllable from its middle; in music it is a change of rhythm and shift of accent when a normally weak beat is stressed; and in medicine it is a brief loss of consciousness. "Syncope," wrote Svetlana, "is the opposite of symbol and synthesis."

Suketu Mehta, in his *Maximum City*, wrote: "Each person's life is dominated by a central event, which shapes and distorts everything that comes after it and, in retrospect, everything that came before. For me, it was going to live in America at the age of fourteen. It's a difficult age at which to change countries. You haven't quite finished growing up where you were and you're never well in your skin in the one you're moving to."

Mehta didn't let me down: this assertion appears in the very first pages of his magnificent book; also, he moved to America at the same age that I did. And while I think he might be wrong about *everyone*, I am certain he is right about émigrés: the break colors everything that came before and after.

Svetlana Boym had a private theory: an émigré's life continues in the land left behind. It's a parallel story. In an unpublished piece, she tried to imagine the parallel lives her Soviet/Russian/Jewish left-behind self was leading. Toward the end of her life, this retracing and reimagining became something of an obsession. She also had a theory about me: that I had gone back to reclaim a life that had been interrupted. In any case, there are many stories to be told about a single life.


## 3. Diversity

On Valentine's Day in 1982—I was fifteen—I went to a gay dance at Yale. This was a great time for gay dances. It was no longer terrifying to be queer on campus, but gay life was still half hidden in a way that was thrilling. I do not remember, in fact, dancing, and I don't even remember catching anyone's eye. In other words, I'm pretty sure that no one noticed me. Strangely, that wasn't crushing. Because what I do remember is standing somewhere dark, leaning against something, and feeling like I was surrounded by community. I remember thinking, *This is who I could be.*

What the syncope of emigration had meant for me was the difference between discovering who I was—the experience I had in the woods outside of Moscow—and discovering who I could be

—the experience I had at that dance. It was a moment of choice and, thanks to the "break in my destiny," I was aware of it.

## 4. Entitlement

In this sense my personal narrative splits from that of the American gay and lesbian movement. The latter was based on choicelessness. A choice may have to be defended—certainly, one has to be prepared to defend one's right to make a choice—while arguing that you were born this way appeals to people's sympathy or at least a sense of decency. It also serves to quell one's own doubts and to foreclose future options. We are, mostly, comfortable with less choice—much as I would have felt safer if my parents had not set out on their great emigration adventure.

After I left Moscow, one of my grandmothers was compelled to hide the fact of our emigration—we had committed an act of treason that could have threatened those left behind. So in the little town where she lived and where I had spent summers as a child, she continued to update my friends on the life I wasn't leading. In that Soviet life, I applied to colleges and failed to get in. In the end, I settled for some mediocre-sounding technical route.

I was hurt by the predictability of the story my grandmother chose for me. In the United States, I was living an imaginative and risky life—I dropped out of high school, ran away from home, lived in the East Village, worked as a bicycle messenger, dropped out of college, worked in the gay press, became the editor of a magazine at twenty-one, got arrested at ACT UP protests, experimented sexually and romantically, behaved abhorrently, was a good friend, or tried to be—but in the mirror held up by my grandmother, it wasn't just my location that was different; it was the presence of choice in my life.

After ten years in this country, I went back to Moscow as a journalist, on assignment. I felt so unexpectedly comfortable in a country that I had expected to feel foreign—as though my body relaxed into a space that had stayed open for it—that I also felt resentful about not having had a choice in leaving. I kept going back and eventually stayed, refashioning myself as a Russian-language journalist. I pretended that this was the life I would have had if I had never left, but deep inside I believed that my grandmother had been right: there was some parallel me, toiling miserably on some dead-end engineering task. This made me a double impostor in the life I was living.

I'm not sure when I made the choice to stay in Russia, but I remember hearing the statement come out of my mouth, surprising me, as it sometimes happens when a decision makes itself known. I had been living there a year, and I was talking to a close friend, an American graduate student who had also been there a year and was now going back. "I think I'm going to stay," I said. "Of course you are," he responded, as though it weren't a choice at all.

Around the same time, I was interviewed by a young Russian journalist: having chosen to return to Russia made me exotic enough to be written about. He asked me which I liked better, being a Russian in America or an American in Russia. I was furious —I believed myself to be a Russian in Russia and an American in America. It took me many years to come around to liking being an outsider wherever I go.

I remet my two grandmothers, whom I hadn't seen since I was a teenager, and started interviewing them. This project became a book about the choices they had made. The one who disapproved of our emigration had become a censor, which, she told me, was a moral choice. She had been educated to be a history teacher, but by the time she had completed her studies she was convinced that becoming a history teacher in the Soviet Union would require her to lie to children every day. Censoring, on the other hand, seemed to her a job that could have been done by a robot: any other person would have crossed out the same lines or confiscated the same mail (her first job was as a censor of printed material in incoming international mail), whereas every history teacher uses a different kind of charm and persuasion to distort children's understanding of the past.

My other grandmother I knew as a rebel and a dissident, someone who never compromised. But as I interviewed her I learned that when she was offered a job with the secret police (as a translator), she had agreed to take it. This was during Stalin's so-called anti-cosmopolitan campaign, when Jews were purged from all kinds of Soviet institutions. She could not get a job to save her life, or, more to the point, her toddler son's life. It had been no choice at all, she told me: she had to feed her child. She never started the job because she failed the medical exam.

The central figure in the book, however, was her father, who was killed in Majdanek. I had always known that he had participated in the rebellion in the Bialystok Ghetto. But then I also found out that he had served in the Judenrat (Jewish council) before choosing to help the rebels.

As I studied the archives—a remarkable number of documents from the Bialystok Ghetto have been preserved—I realized that my great-grandfather had been one of the de facto leaders of the Judenrat. He had been responsible for food deliveries to and garbage removal from the ghetto, and I saw strong evidence that he took part in putting together the lists of names for extermination. I also found a memoir written by a member of the resistance in which she recalled my great-grandfather's efforts to stop the resistance. Later he apparently changed his position and started helping the resistance to smuggle weapons into the ghetto. Before the war, he had been an elected official, a member of both the city council and the Jewish council, so it was clear to me that he had seen his duties in the Judenrat as the logical outgrowth of his elected service. I could see the trajectory of my great-grandfather's choices.

My grandmother didn't want me to publish the part about the Judenrat, and we had a protracted battle over whose story it was to tell—hers or mine, or both of ours. In the end, she had only one demand: that I omit a quote from Hannah Arendt's *Eichmann in Jerusalem*. This is the infamous quote in which Arendt says that the Holocaust would not have been possible without the help of the Jewish councils.

I saw it as a story of impossible, anguished choices that he nonetheless insisted on making. Totalitarian regimes aim to make choice impossible, and this was what interested me at the time. I was awed by the gap between my capacity for judgment and the unbearably limited options faced by my grandparents. I fixated on the ideas of "impossible choice" and of having "no choice." But what interests me now is that I think resistance can take the shape of insisting on making a choice, even when the choice is framed as one between unacceptable options.

## 5. Science-Based

Back in the United States, my parents' adventure came to a halt, eleven years after we landed in America. My mother died of cancer in the summer of 1992. Another eleven years later, I returned for a year-long fellowship—to be a Russian in America for a year. During that year I took a test that showed I had the genetic mutation that had caused the cancer that killed my mother and her aunt before that. I was "born this way"—born to develop cancer of the breasts or ovaries, or both. The genetic counselors and doctors asked me what I wanted to do. It was a choice, framed as one between "aggressive monitoring"—for the first signs of cancer, which the doctors were certain would appear—and preventive surgery.

I ended up writing, first, a series of articles and then a book on making choices in the age of genetic testing. I talked to people who had faced far more drastic choices than the one before me. These people had chosen to live without such essential organs as the stomach or pancreas, whereas all the doctors were suggesting to me was the removal of breasts and ovaries. I chose to remove my breasts and reconstruct them. I was choosing my breast size and my fate!

The doctors, incidentally, didn't think this was the right choice: they advocated for the removal of the ovaries rather than, or more importantly than, the breasts. I found more compelling evidence in favor of keeping the ovaries for a while, but two and a half years ago I had those removed as well. Around that time, my doctor was strongly suggesting I really no longer had a choice.

## 6. Transgender

Two decades after moving back to Russia, I left again. It was one of those impossible choices that don't feel like much of a choice: I was one of many people pushed out of the country during the crackdown that followed the protests of 2011–2012. Some were given the choice between emigrating or going to prison. My options were emigrating or seeing social services go after my kids, on the grounds that I am queer.

What had happened to the life my discontinuous self was leading back in America while I was in Russia? My writing life had been proceeding apace, more or less—I was publishing in the United States while living in Russia. Socially, who was I? Who were my people? Where did I belong? I had lost some friends and gained others. Some friends had become couples, split up, recoupled, had children. I had coupled and recoupled and had children too.

Also, some of the women I had known had become men. That's not the way most transgender people phrase it; the default language is one of choicelessness: people say they have always been men or women and now their authentic selves are emerging. This is the same "born this way" approach that the gay and lesbian movement had put to such good political use in the time that I'd been gone: it had gotten queer people access to such institutions as the military and marriage.

The standard story goes something like this: as a child I always felt like a boy, or never felt like a girl, and then I tried to be a lesbian, but the issue wasn't sexual orientation—it was gender, specifically, "true gender," which could now be claimed through transitioning. I found myself feeling resentful at hearing these stories. I too had always felt like a boy! It had taken some work for me to enjoy being a woman (whatever that means)—I'd succeeded, I had learned *how to be* one. But still: here I was, faced with the possibility that in the parallel life that my left-behind self was leading in the United States while I was in Russia, I would have transitioned. True gender (whatever that means) didn't have much to do with it, but choice did. Somehow, I'd missed the fact that it was there.

I had written an entire book on making choices that had to do with removing the parts of the body that would appear to have made me female: the breasts, the ovaries, the uterus. And I had not questioned the assumptions that after a mastectomy one considers one's options for reconstruction, and after a radical hysterectomy one considers whether to receive hormone "replacement" in the form of estrogen. Indeed, I had had reconstruction and was taking estrogen. I had failed, miserably, at seeing my choices, made as they were under some duress, as an opportunity for adventure. I had failed to think about inhabiting a different body the way one would think about inhabiting a different country. How do I invent the person I am now?

I quit estrogen and started testosterone. I had some trouble with the evidence part of the science, because, as I have found, all published papers on the use of testosterone in people who start out as women fall into one of two categories: articles that aim to show that people taking testosterone will experience all of the masculinizing changes that they wish for, and ones that aim to show that women will have none of the masculinizing changes that they fear. I am taking a low dose, and I have no idea how it's going to affect me. My voice has become lower. My body is changing.

But then again, bodies change all the time. In her book *The Argonauts,* Maggie Nelson quotes her partner, the artist Harry Dodge, as saying that he is not going anywhere—not transitioning but being himself. I recognize the sentiment, though I'd probably say the opposite: for thirty-nine years, ever since my parents took those documents to the visa office, I have felt so precarious that I lay no claim to someone I "really am." That someone is a sequence of choices, and the question is: Will my next choice be conscious, and will my ability to make it be unfettered?


## 7. *Evidence-Based*

It took little effort to organize the notes I jotted down for this talk around the seven words that the Trump administration was reported to have banned the Centers for Disease Control from using. All seven words—from "fetus" to "evidence-based"—are words that reflect on our understanding of choice.

Choice is a great burden. The call to invent one's life, and to do it continuously, can sound unendurable. Totalitarian regimes aim to stamp out the possibility of choice, but what aspiring autocrats do is promise to relieve one of the need to choose. This is the promise of "Make America Great Again"—it conjures the allure of an imaginary past in which one was free not to choose.

I've been surprised, in the past year, that the resurgence of interest in some of the classic books on totalitarianism has not brought back Erich Fromm's wonderful *Escape from Freedom* (though Fromm, who was a psychoanalyst and social psychologist, has been rediscovered by many people in the mental health profession because he introduced the idea of "malignant narcissism"). In the introduction, Fromm apologizes for what he perceives as sloppiness, which he says stems from the need to write the book in a hurry: he felt that the world was on the verge of catastrophe. He was writing this in 1940.

In the book, Fromm proposes that there are two kinds of freedom: "freedom from," which we all want—we all want our parents to stop telling us what to do—and "freedom to," which can be difficult or even unbearable. This is the freedom to invent one's future, the freedom to choose. Fromm suggests that at certain times in human history the burden of "freedom to" becomes too painful for a critical mass of people to bear, and they take the opportunity to cede their agency—whether it's to Martin Luther, Adolf Hitler, or Donald Trump.

No wonder Trump appears to be obsessed with people who embody choice. Immigrants are his most frightening imaginary enemy, the ones who need to be "extremely vetted," blocked out with a wall, whose crimes need to be reported to a special hotline and whose families need to be kept out of this country. It puts me in mind of the "aggressive monitoring" for the cancer that's sure to come. Transgender people have been another target of Trump's apparently spontaneous lashing out—witness the transgender ban in the military, the rescinding of protections for transgender students, and now the ban on the very word "transgender."

But in speaking about immigrants we tend to privilege choicelessness much as we do when we are speaking about queer people or transgender people. We focus on the distinction between refugees and "economic migrants," without asking why the fear of hunger and destitution qualifies as a lesser reason for migration than the fear of imprisonment or death by gunshot wound—and then only if that wound is inflicted for political or religious reasons. But even more than that, why do we assume that the more restricted a person's choices have been, the more qualified they are to enter a country that proclaims freedom of personal choice to be one of its ideals?

Immigrants make a choice. The valor is not in remaining at risk for catching a bullet but in making the choice to avoid it. In the Soviet Union, most dissidents believed that if one were faced with the impossible choice between leaving the country and going to prison, one ought to choose exile. Less dramatically, the valor is in being able to experience your move less as an escape and more as an adventure. It is in serving as living reminders of the choicefulness of life—something that immigrants and most trans people do, whether their personal narratives are ones of choice or not.

I wish I could finish on a hopeful note, by saying something like: If only we insist on making choices, we will succeed in keeping darkness at bay. I'm not convinced that that's the case. But I do think that making choices and, more important, imagining other, better choices, will give us the best chance possible of coming out of the darkness better than we were when we went in. It's a bit like emigrating that way: the choice to leave rarely feels free, but choices we make about inhabiting new landscapes (or changed bodies) demand an imagination.

JEAN GUERRERO

## My Father Says He's a "Targeted Individual." Maybe We All Are.

FROM *Wired*

I WAS ELEVEN when my father destroyed the condominium where he was living. Searching for hidden transistors or other devices that might be beaming voices into his skull, he took a hammer to the walls, shoved his fists into the holes, and pulled off chunks of plaster. He shut off the power generator and cut the electrical wires in the walls. He put his ear to the floor. He ripped up the carpet. He called 911.

A Mexican immigrant who perfected his English by reading books he sneaked into the San Diego shipyard where he helped build oil tankers, Marco Guerrero had always been an uncanny mechanic. He could see through to the machinery of everything as if he had x-ray vision: he could adjust brakes, fix broken pipes, tap telephone lines.

After mass layoffs at the shipyard, he stayed at home, documenting my first words on his camcorder and taking me to coastal tide pools to catch *cobitos*. But then he fell into a depression. My parents separated. He started smoking crack cocaine. After tearing his place apart, he vanished on a years-long, cross-border quest to escape alleged CIA persecutors.

My mother took me and my sister to assess the damage to the condominium, which she owned but had let our father stay in after they separated. The carpet lay in heaps against the punctured walls. A layer of cigarette ash coated the rooms. It looked apocalyptic. Our mother, a physician specializing in internal medicine, offered a psychiatric diagnosis. Your father, she said, has paranoid schizophrenia.

In college, I minored in neuroscience while majoring in journalism, searching for my absent father in fMRI brain scans and the *Diagnostic and Statistical Manual of Mental Disorders.* Though he had returned from his transcontinental odyssey a couple of years earlier and moved in with his mother in San Diego, I rarely saw him; when I visited, we exchanged few words.

But on my twentieth birthday, I made a trip to my paternal grandmother's house, and my father, sober now for several years, dragged a chair next to me and started talking. It was the first lengthy conversation we'd had since I was a child.

The story he told sounded unlikely: that he was one of thousands of "targeted individuals" who had been covertly spied on and manipulated by the CIA in the early 2000s. (So-called TIs have begun banding together around the country and across the internet.) But he didn't sound agitated or disturbed the way I had imagined a paranoid schizophrenic might. He was articulate. He cited patents, research, and the central role of something he called MKUltra, a real CIA mind-control program that ran from 1953 to 1973 that targeted drug addicts, prisoners, and other vulnerable people.

I didn't know anything about the pile of facts he'd just left at my feet—his farfetched answer to the mystery of his breakdown and disappearance—but I felt it was my duty, as a journalist and as his daughter, to investigate the possibility that what he said was true. I hoped I could do it without falling down a rabbit hole.

One day, after scouring the internet for information about "MKUltra" and "CIA torture," I was served with an ad for Trintellix, a pharmaceutical drug for depression. The ad was prominent on the page and encouraged me in large blue letters to "take the first step." For a moment, I wondered: Did I have depression? The idea of a conspiracy targeting my father was making me *feel* depressed.

Then a more likely hypothesis occurred to me. My online activity—using search terms like "V2K" and "government harassment" —had probably caused computer algorithms to place me in a category of people with paranoia, which is often accompanied by depression, leading advertisers to target me.

The hypothesis started to broaden. In our digital economy, covert players are constantly harvesting our data and churning out exquisitely tuned consumer profiles to tap into our dreams and desires. We *are* being surveilled. We are being controlled and manipulated. We are perhaps being tortured. But it's not the CIA or aliens perpetrating all this. We are doing it to ourselves.

A thought occurred to me: Could the stories of "targeted individuals" be a warning, a cautionary tale about the real targeting we experience as digital technologies pervade our lives? Perhaps my father's perception of electronic harassment is the result of his sensitivity to the mechanics of things. He may be seeing through to the nuts and bolts of the web, weaving a story out of its danger and turning it into a terrifying delusion of persecution, suffering, and torment.

Stay with me here; the idea that madness might contain insights about overlooked realities is not new. There is a growing international network of people with hallucinations, Intervoice, whose members have embraced their waking visions and the voices in their heads.

They see them not as undesirable symptoms of mental illness, but as tools that serve the same function as dreams. They explore hallucinations for metaphorical insights to help them process unresolved experiences. They argue that traditional mental health approaches, focused on eradicating symptoms, fail to promote a meaningful, empowering relationship between patients and their hallucinations. On its website, the network urges people with schizophrenia "to listen (to hallucinations) but not to necessarily follow, to engage." (The approach is gaining traction in the scientific community.)

What if the TI voices exist for the same reason? Maybe my father, and the thousands of people who have bonded over their self-perceived status as targeted individuals, are a kind of indirect warning system experiencing a kind of collective dream—canaries in the digital coal mine. We dismiss them as out of touch with reality. Yet we have all become the objects of monitoring and manipulation eroding the core of what makes us human: our free will.

Perhaps the "targeted individuals" are foretelling the future— one in which we've lost control of our minds.

I remember the first time I told my father I wanted to write about him for what became my memoir, *Crux*. Papi choked on his beer, pounded his fist against his chest and shook his head, eyes watering.

When he could breathe again, he said: "Absolutely not. Maybe if someday you become famous and respected, you can do it. Otherwise, nobody will think twice if"—he lowered his voice—"if the CIA kills you."

I paused, trying to think of the best response. "Pa, if I write your story, you'll be immortal," I said.

He rolled his eyes and squeezed indignation into his forehead, saying he didn't care about the perpetuity of his insignificant ego, but I could see the grin growing on his face against his will. My father was human, just like me, dying to live among the gods.

Humans are story-making machines. We are the only animal capable of such rich conceptualization, taking the raw material of reality and turning it into something more. Our minds connect objective entities, enfolding them in categories within categories: a man and a woman can be a mother and a father, who may be a couple, who are parents, who may be property owners and Americans.

In *Sapiens: A Brief History of Humankind,* Yuval Noah Harari observes that our species conquered the globe because of our ability to share stories about things that don't objectively exist, such as "gods, nations, and corporations." Such fictions allowed us to organize around shared values, goals, and ideas. It was not exactly wisdom—*sapiens*—that gave us dominion, but creative storytelling. We are *Homo fabulator.* "The real difference between us and chimpanzees is the mythical glue that binds together large numbers of individuals, families and groups," Harari writes. "This glue has made us masters of creation."

Unlike the Neanderthals and other early humans who could work together in groups of at most 150 individuals, we learned to cooperate in groups of thousands, tens of thousands, millions—simply by telling stories to forge shared dreams. But now, this gift is in danger. As the speed and efficiency of computer processing increases at predictable rates, our ability to author our own destinies is being consumed by a conjured figment of our imagination: the internet.

We created the internet as a vast landscape where information could be free. That was a delusion, of course, or at least a misapprehension. The advertising model that drives online media and commerce means we pay for the web's valuable resources by opening up our minds to what virtual reality pioneer Jaron Lanier calls "siren servers"—cloud computing networks that dominate the internet. Algorithms collect our data and crunch that into maps of our minds, which companies use to manipulate our decisions. Power concentrates where the data are. Lanier argues that we are surrendering our free will "bit by bit" to Amazon, Facebook, Google, and their clients.

In *Who Owns the Future*, he writes: "When you are wearing sensors on your body all the time, such as the GPS and camera on your smartphone and constantly piping data to a megacomputer owned by a corporation that is paid by 'advertisers' to subtly manipulate you . . . you gradually become less free."

This surrender is triggering a breakdown in our ability to distinguish fact from fiction. Instead of moving through the world as autonomous actors with original thoughts and inquiries, we become objects of what is dictated to us via the digital realm, including fake news.

While advertising dates back to papyrus, it gained a broader reach after the Industrial Revolution; the Information Age opened its Pandora's box. Digital feedback loops allow advertisers to predict our fears and cravings and to influence our purchases and preoccupations. The information economy thrives on the currency of our data—our selves. It is unseating us as masters of our own destinies and distorting the fabric of reality as we know it.

Sound familiar? Many who hear the TI stories of surveillance and manipulation dismiss them as mere delusion. But we have created machines that track our every move, that beam thoughts into our heads. Were the targeted individuals America's prophets all along?

My father told me about the CIA agents who allegedly followed him at the turn of the millennium. The TIs collectively refer to this as "gang stalking," the perception of groups tracking and harassing them. As my father traveled across continents, he says he was trailed by "gringos" in suits and black SUVs with American plates.

He describes an instance where the stalking became so unbearable that he drove to a Mexican jail and begged the officers to put him behind bars, where he thought he would be safe from the CIA. "I want you to arrest me!" he recalls saying. "All of them were trying to be real nice. 'Why? Do you have drugs?' I told them I had been doing drugs."

A targeted individual in San Diego explained to me that her stalkers often coordinate to mock her and make her feel she's losing her mind. After she went through a difficult breakup, she noticed persecutors posing as couples, kissing and hugging in front of her to torment her. "You know when someone kisses and it's natural," she says, speaking on condition of anonymity because she feared for her life. "This wasn't natural."

An early sign of schizophrenia is apophenia, the tendency to perceive connections among unrelated external phenomena. It's the product of our innate storytelling impulse, unmoored from healthy inhibitions. Ironically, the brains of people with schizophrenia are afflicted by *disconnectivity*—the loss of connections between cortical structures. But while some TIs have schizophrenia diagnoses, their perceptions aren't necessarily meaningless. They can shine a light on a problem we have yet to fully process.

More than fifty years ago, Carl Jung argued that the dreaming phase of sleep—now known as REM, for the rapid eye movement that characterizes it—serves our mental health by maintaining an equilibrium between the conscious and unconscious parts of our minds. "For the sake of mental stability . . . the unconscious and the conscious must be integrally connected and thus move on parallel lines," he writes in *Man and His Symbols*. "If they are split apart or 'dissociated,' psychological disturbance follows."

Scientific evidence supports Jung's idea that dreams give our minds a cohesiveness that can be fractured; REM-sleep deprivation has been correlated with mental disorders.

Perhaps the TIs' stories signal a dissociated society. Just as our brains must integrate the conscious and unconscious, our collective imagination must reconcile the drab perceived reality of clicking on Amazon links with the darker facts of a digital system that is taking control of our lives.

I suspect that TIs experience this control consciously, and rather literally to boot: Strangers are sending voices into their heads. Strangers are harassing them.

We can dismiss the targeted individual whose persecutors allegedly tormented her about a breakup. Or we can ask ourselves if her story reveals something we've ignored about ourselves: a social media dynamic in which we are actually being watched, in which our most intimate lives are exposed, in which we are sometimes mocked and taunted by remorseless strangers.

There's no mystery that Facebook knows our gender, ages, hometowns, birthdays, friends, likes, political leanings, and internet browsing habits. Facebook can tell, by analyzing our likes and comments, whether we are going through a breakup or a divorce. It can make predictions about our health. It can algorithmically intuit our fantasies and fears and use that information to target us with messaging so personalized it feels like persecution.

Consider this example from my own life: After the *Los Angeles Times* published allegations of sexual misconduct by a gynecologist at the university I attended, Facebook started bombarding me with pictures of his face in the form of ads, from plaintiff lawyers offering free consultations and injury checks. I'd had an uncomfortable experience with this gynecologist and had been considering sharing my story with journalists after reading the first article. But seeing his face on my news feed every time I opened Facebook felt invasive, almost nightmarish.

My USC classmates and I were being stalked by lawyers who knew we'd attended the university while the gynecologist worked there. It didn't feel like the platform was presenting an option to speak up; it felt like harassment. The specificity of the ads, their omnipresence and relation to a very personal incident in my life, felt like an assault on my process of deliberation—on the integrity of my free will.

Like my father, I was experiencing a form of gang stalking. And it was real.

In the Bible, men who perceive voices and visions nobody else can see or hear are prophets. They are in communication with God. With the sea nowhere in sight, Noah built a ship and herded animals onto it, saving life on earth from God's wrathful flood. Moses foresaw plagues of flies, boils, locusts, and the deaths of firstborn sons, convincing Pharaoh to free the Israelites.

In the 1970s, the American psychologist Julian Jaynes argued that all early humans suffered from hallucinations because their two brain hemispheres, connected by nerve fibers of the corpus callosum, were not fully integrated. The voices of one hemisphere were perceived by the other as external to the self—thoughts were the voices of gods.

"We could say that before the second millennium BC, everyone was schizophrenic," Jaynes writes in *The Origin of Consciousness in the Breakdown of the Bicameral Mind.* As the brain hemispheres became integrated, humans began to perceive the gods' voices as their own internal dialogue. They acquired free will.

The HBO series *Westworld* depicts a world in which robots gain agency through a similar process. In one scene, a creator speaks to his digital creation and tries to coax her into consciousness: "I gave you a voice, my voice, to guide you along the way. But you never got there . . . Consciousness isn't a journey upward, but a journey inward. Not a pyramid, but a maze. Every choice could bring you closer to the center or send you spiraling to the edges, to madness. Do you understand now, Dolores, what the center represents? Whose voice I've been wanting you to hear?"

Watching this series, I saw in Dolores's journey to consciousness the opposite of our present path as we surrender our minds to computer algorithms. What if our own freedom depends on our realizing that the voices of "targeted individuals" are our own collective unconscious?

My father fought the alleged mind-control experiments as if his humanity were at stake, collecting evidence, researching remedies, traveling far from home. Perhaps we can learn something from his resistance.

Abraham, according to the biblical tale, hears the voice of God telling him to sacrifice his only son. Without a second thought, Abraham takes his boy to Moriah and ties him to an altar. He pulls a knife from his pocket and God calls out to him from heaven, stopping him just in time, praising him for his obedience: "I will surely bless you and make your descendants as numerous as the stars in the sky and the sand on the seashore."

This is the promise made by the digital realm: that if we surrender our minds to it, if we prize it above the people we love, we will be rewarded with a kind of immortality. In Silicon Valley, it is considered a certain future: we will soon be able to upload our minds to the internet and live forever in digital Edens. But the idea fails to consider that such an eternity would come at the cost of our free will. Would we still be human then?

My journey into my father's world led to strange and unexpected places, including the ruins of a Mexican ranch where his great-grandmother, a *curandera,* was said to have communed with spirits. The townspeople relied on her for plant remedies and prophetic wisdom. People traveled from far away to see *La Adivina,* the Diviner.

I contemplate the parallels between *La Adivina* and my father and the differences in the stories our societies weaved: one heard the voices of the dead and was thought to have a gift, while another suffered hallucinations and was considered ill. To what extent had those stories influenced their outcomes?

In the backyard of a house in northern Mexico, where my father moved after living with his mother in San Diego, Papi built a garden of medicinal crops like comfrey and *ashitaba.* His cupboards were filled with powders and potions. He claimed the CIA rarely sent voices into his head anymore, but had started sending a mysterious illness into his body to keep him exhausted and subservient. He was trying to cure himself; traditional doctors were failing to detect his illness. He tried different seeds and tinctures on himself and my grandmother's Chihuahua. *Abuelita* claims he cured the dog of blindness. My father says he cured himself of his illness.

I visited my father and asked him about the voices he used to hear. He described them: male and female CIA agents, commenting on his actions, insulting him, taunting him. I asked how he knew he wasn't hallucinating, given that crack can induce psychosis. The reason was obvious to him: the CIA never bothered him on airplanes because the aircraft's aluminum alloys protected him from electromagnetic weapons. The voices stopped if he wrapped himself up in aluminum foil.

I looked into the real-world CIA mind-control experiments my father had mentioned: MKUltra. The program involved slipping LSD to more than ten thousand unwitting civilians, among other things, to see if they could manipulate people's behavior. It was exposed by a *New York Times* article in 1974.

After MKUltra was investigated by the Senate's Church Committee and the Rockefeller Commission, President Gerald Ford signed an executive order in 1976 prohibiting "experimentation with drugs on human subjects" without their consent. But the order was revised by subsequent administrations, and the CIA's internal guidelines later gave the agency director the discretion to "approve, modify, or disapprove all proposals pertaining to human subject research."

TIs believe MKUltra was replaced with a more sophisticated CIA program using electromagnetic or radio wave technologies. My father said the CIA chose to experiment on him because, as a crack addict, nobody would believe him if he spoke up. Also, he thinks the agents sought to eradicate his addiction. Success would demonstrate the electromagnetic weapons' behavior-altering effectiveness—and it worked. He did stop smoking crack.

Unconvinced, I filed Freedom of Information Act requests for any records about my father to the CIA, the FBI, and more, including a signed certification of identity from my father with authorization to release the information to me. While most agencies said they had no such records, the CIA said it could neither confirm nor deny their existence, citing a national security exemption. I appealed. Same response. For people prone to conspiracy theories, this may serve as proof that the CIA does have records on my father. For me, it confirms only the CIA's penchant for secrecy.

When I analyze the voices my father described rather than disregard them, I am struck by the parallels with the hyperpersonalized messaging we all experience. The CIA agents' alleged surveillance parallels the web's tracking of our activity. Their commands echo invasive ads. How often have hidden players on the web influenced our behavior by shouting or whispering in our ears? Russian interference in the 2016 election is yet another example of the far-reaching power of AI-based messaging, affecting not only our consumer choices but also the integrity of our democracy.

Earlier this year, Facebook CEO Mark Zuckerberg testified before Congress about the leak of millions of users' private data to Cambridge Analytica—a firm hired by Trump's 2016 campaign to influence voters. Zuckerberg admitted that Facebook had become a vehicle for "fake news, foreign interference in elections, and hate speech."

In a recent *New York Times* column, the Turkish technosociologist (and *Wired* contributor) Zeynep Tufekci criticized YouTube as an engine of extremism due to its "recommender algorithm," which keeps viewers on the site by directing users to increasingly incendiary content. She explained that after she viewed Trump rally videos for research purposes, YouTube autoplayed "white supremacist rants, Holocaust denials, and other disturbing content."

The ad-based digital economy notoriously promotes echo chambers, which boost prejudices and paranoias. Some have attributed the rise of TI theories to the fact that anyone who feels a strange buzzing in their body and Googles "electronic harassment" can end up in contact with other targeted individuals, and, as a result of conversations with them, come to the conclusion that they themselves are targeted. Misapprehension spreads like a virus.

What we fail to recognize when we dismiss targeted individuals is that the web is having the same impact on us. The plague of alternative facts spreads through the arteries of social media like a drug. A study published in *Science* this year found that fake news spreads "farther, faster, deeper, and more broadly than the truth in all categories of information."

Our susceptibility to fake news is related to confirmation bias and the illusion of explanatory depth, the belief that we understand things better than we do. What we need, what a healthy society needs, is the habit of inquisitiveness that comes from a humble recognition of ignorance. The more we admit we *don't* know, the more likely we are to seek out information that increases our knowledge.

Curiosity is driven by a kind of hunger. When we are alone with our own thoughts, when we spend time with questions, we come upon original ideas. The ubiquitous stimulation of modern society leaves us with a false sense of satiety and no space for uncertainty.

Our storytelling capacity emerges from the wellspring of silence. Perhaps the targeted individuals are pointing to the noise we have stopped hearing. One way to destroy an echo chamber is to search for the voices in the walls—the way my father did.

During the Renaissance, people who hallucinated—"madmen" —were believed to have a cryptic wisdom, more like poets than prophets. In the age of reason, they were cast aside as aberrant and institutionalized en masse. The twentieth-century Christian philosopher G. K. Chesterton argued for a more moderate approach. In his book *Orthodoxy,* he wrote that madness dwells not in irrational minds but in rational ones that overestimate what they can grasp: "It is the logician who seeks to get the heavens into his head. And it is his head that splits."

America, with its fetishization of logic and data, has one of the world's highest rates of mental illness, according to the World Health Organization.

Chesterton wrote that sanity lies in accepting the limits of our minds. We can't distill the whole world into numbers and equations. While some knowledge comes from separating reality into pieces we can comprehend, some comes from connecting things, allowing them to gain added meaning and mystery. Sometimes the truth lies in a metaphor or a rhyme.

What exactly can we learn from the stories of TIs? First, there is symbolism in the villain some selected: the Central Intelligence Agency. Their fixation on the CIA may highlight the pernicious effect of covert data collection. The name of the agency is the clue.

In his second book, *Homo Deus*, Harari argues that *Homo sapiens* will soon see the emergence of a new species as a result of centralized intelligence gathering: god-man. Revolutions in computer science and biology, and specifically neuroscience, will allow us to master and replicate the *sapiens* code. But it's not that we're all going to have access to immortality. A tiny elite could end up controlling our bodies and minds.

Harari argues that dictatorships and democracies can be seen as two different forms of data processing: centralized and distributive. In the world wars of the twentieth century, democracy emerged victorious because distributive data processing was the most efficient tool for mobilization. The digital economy is changing the game, giving the upper hand to centralized data processing. Harari believes that our clicks and likes are paving a path toward dictatorship.

If we wish to reverse course, we must decentralize the digital economy and regulate the ownership of data, taking it out of the hands of a few tech companies that now control it. It will be difficult. Unlike property, data is intangible and hard to delineate. But our species is made to accomplish miracles of reorganization. All it takes is a new story. Perhaps this is a starting point: the targeted individuals are living the nightmare of what could happen. We must awaken.

As a child in northern Mexico, my father often had a hard time sleeping. He lay hiding under the blankets, heartbeat like a freight train on old tracks, as his stepfather roared at his mother. Screams.

Smashing plates. A body thumping against the floor. In the morning, his mother's bruises. A bulging black eye.

Papi taught himself how to fix broken televisions and discarded radios. He had an intuitive understanding of simple machines. If only he could figure out the machinery behind human behavior, he could fix people.

He built a wire-mesh cage in the backyard and began collecting animals in glass jars. He dissected lizards, frogs, tarantulas. He sought to determine how hearts pump blood, how brains form thoughts. He tried to keep the creatures alive. But often his subjects died.

My father was tormented by nightmares. He suspected there was something evil in him, his curiosity too extreme.

Recounting his experiments, my father's eyes shift around the room as if looking for an escape. "I wouldn't have done that if I had other *means*," he says, breathless. He searches my face, as if for fear or disgust, but that isn't what I felt.

In a *Scientific American Mind* article, Intervoice board member Eleanor Longden recalled that the voices in her head stopped sounding sinister once she realized that each was related to parts of herself that "carried overwhelming emotions that I had never had an opportunity to process and resolve—memories of sexual trauma and abuse, of shame, anger, loss, and low self-worth." All she had to do to soften their grip was listen.

As a writer with an eye for metaphors and an ear for rhymes, I can't help seeing in my father's shame about his boyhood experiments a clear identification with the creatures he tortured—perhaps a literal identification. But Jung argued that the dreamer is the primary authority on the secret meaning of a dream. My father has the final say on what his voices and visions signify.

The psychologist Gail Hornstein argued in *Agnes's Jacket: A Psychologist's Search for the Meanings of Madness:* "Madness is more code than chemistry. If we want to understand it, we need translators —native speakers, not just brain scans."

By the same token, if individual dreams and hallucinations are meant for each person who has them, collective hallucinations are meant for the societies where they occur.

My father believes the CIA subjected him to remotely induced electric shocks, filling him with lightning-bolt pain when he tried to smoke crack. He explained that a copper penny he placed on his forehead during one of the attacks flew off him as if zapped by a corporeal current. Whenever he touched a metal railing, the pain dissipated.

Technology capable of inducing something like the TIs' "electric shocks" does exist: the Active Denial System is a military weapon using millimeter wave radio frequency to zap people. California resident Donald Friedman repeatedly sued the government for allegedly harassing him with such weapons. One of his Freedom of Information Act requests resulted in the declassification of a 1998 US Army document that discusses a microwave technology capable of beaming sounds into heads from hundreds of meters away. With some refinement, the document states, the technology could induce "voices within one's head."

My father recently described the frustration of trying to convince a psychologist he wasn't crazy: "There was a TV playing over there in the room, and I said, 'Do you hear that TV? Well, I hear it too. But that doesn't mean I'm hearing voices.' There's a technology in which they can make you remotely hear voices, and it has been *documented*. You can *read* about it."

The fact that you can read about these technologies does not prove his theories. But when I sit with my uncertainty, rather than dismiss my father's beliefs outright, my eyes open to the covert manipulation that is commonplace in our lives. We carry it around in our pockets. We wear it on our wrists. We devote more than ten and a half hours a day to screen time.

Facebook has conducted experiments on us that show how susceptible we are to mind control. In 2012, the company secretly tampered with the news feeds of nearly 700,000 people, manipulating the ratio of emotionally positive to emotionally negative posts, then monitoring the subsequent activity of those users.

What they found is that emotions can be remotely controlled and are highly contagious on the platform. People who saw more unhappy posts showed more unhappy activity and vice versa. Many questioned the experiment's legality and ethics, wondering if Facebook had triggered any suicides. Facebook apologized for the way the experiments were conducted and promised to conduct them "differently" in the future, with enhanced review.

We ignore the parallels between those experiments and the

ones the TIs describe at our own peril. We are amphibians in a pot
of water over a flame.

MKUltra is now seeing a resurgence in the popular culture through
Netflix shows like *Wormwood,* a docudrama based on Eric Olson's
real-life quest to uncover the facts about his father's death during
MKUltra. The name of the series is an allusion to a line in the
Bible in which the star Wormwood falls from the sky and turns waters of the earth bitter. Olson describes finding no relief because
nobody has been held accountable.

Given this lack of closure for families like his, is it really that
crazy for thousands of people to believe the United States is
still illegally experimenting on people—especially after Edward
Snowden's leaks showing NSA surveillance of the general population? Don't their beliefs reveal something meaningful about our
failure to acknowledge the extent of our wrongs and the reach of
our technologies?

We have become commodities manipulated by shadowy forces
beyond our control: corporations, computer algorithms, cam-
paigns. We are caught in a web where we can be easily drained of
blood.

How can we correct this? Legislative restrictions on the collection of personal data are the logical first step. Supporting subscrip-
tion- or donation-based news organizations could help counter the
viral nature of alternative facts.

Lanier, the computer scientist, argues that we should demand
payment for data that companies collect from us. He envisions a
world in which we are compensated for every profitable datum we
provide, with payments proportionate to the profit they produce.
He argues that such a world—in which we value the humans behind data as much as the data themselves—would lead to a new
era of economic prosperity, equality, and freedom.

The Electronic Frontier Foundation is fighting against mass
surveillance with lawsuits and browser add-ons that block advertisers from tracking online activity. The EFF's international director, Danny O'Brien, works with people who are actually targeted
by repressive regimes for their journalism or activism. He says he
sometimes gets calls from people with mental illness who wrongly
believe they're being targeted. Many have an inquiring spirit that
he finds instructive. "These people aren't just sitting back and ac-

cepting what's happening to them," he adds. "They're trying to understand."

But O'Brien hypothesizes that for too many self-described TIs, affirming rather than escaping their victimization is the goal. They show a preference for false solutions, such as aluminum foil hats, because their belief that they're being targeted serves to distract them from real traumas they don't want to face. "Paranoia is strange because it's simultaneously comforting and disturbing," he says. "It's disturbing to think people are spying on you, but it's also comforting to have an explanation for why your world sucks."

Fears of surveillance and manipulation in the world should motivate people to change it, according to O'Brien. Self-agency lies not in the TIs' delusions of persecution nor in most people's delusions of safety, but in recognizing that the two mirror each other. In both cases, a human story has gained authorship of human minds.

In 2014 my father became sick again. The tomatoes in his backyard blackened and shriveled. A coastal wind threw salt on his sagging garden, which began to stink. Papi drank bottle after bottle of whiskey. His skin became the color of *maíz amarillo.*

He begged me to bury him without ceremony.

"Just push me over like a dump. Like a stone. Cuz that's all I am," he says.

"That's not true. You're a human being. And a father. And a son," I say.

I begged him, through tears, to stop drinking. He had been cycling in and out of depression and substance abuse all my life. I remembered a beautiful garden he built when I was a little girl, a Mexican Garden of Eden. Wooden enclosures for *fresas* and *frijoles.* A towering wire-mesh trellis for tomatoes. Rows of cacti and other desert plants. Cages for roosters, hens, ducks, cockatiels, iguanas, hamsters, guinea pigs, and rabbits.

When he became depressed for the first time, his fruit shriveled into wrinkled black sacs. Flowers drooped on their stalks. The cacti rotted and turned a sickly brown. Our animals began to die as if in synchrony with Papi's slumber. We buried pet after pet.

My mother bought a blue-green iMac G3 in 1999. I began to write every day. As I typed every detail of my banal existence into the computer, I felt I was immortalizing myself, protecting a part of my mind from the nothingness that devoured so many things I loved. It eased my existential anxieties. Years later, when I learned of the possibility of uploading human consciousness into digital Edens, I was enthralled.

I didn't realize that what I needed was not eternity but freedom from the story of immortality. We were never meant to be gods. Or at least not gods in the way we envisioned them: all-knowing and all-powerful. If we continue to delude ourselves into believing that our destiny lies in knowledge and power, we will become slaves of the gods that we create.

We have lost an appreciation for the limits of our flesh and blood—the price of human life. We are not omniscient and never can be. Sometimes, groups with divergent beliefs detect what we refuse to see. Targeted individuals like my father remind us of what we really are: not *Homo sapiens,* but *Homo fabulator.* Our fate is shaped by the stories we tell. Now they are growing so strong they may supplant us.

LACY M. JOHNSON

# On Likability

FROM *Tin House*

MY DAUGHTER COMES home from school at least once a week and announces to me that no one likes her. She has done something that is too weird, or bold, or has said a thing with which others disagree. She has had to sit alone during lunch or play alone during recess. She even sat on the buddy bench, she tells me, and no one came. At the moment she says or does the weird bold thing, she doesn't care what anyone thinks or whether they agree or disagree. It's only afterward, after she has felt shunned, ostracized, and completely alone with her decision that she begins to question it.

She is eleven and a half. When I was eleven and a half, I liked to play the Commodore 64 and read Choose Your Own Adventure novels and I liked making tapes of my favorite songs that I recorded off the little radio my parents let me have in my room. I liked New Kids on the Block—I liked them so much I called it LOVE—and I liked sitting next to my friend on the long bus ride home when we could talk for hours about who we liked better, Joey or Donnie. I liked Joey. She liked Donnie. (Wrong.) I liked to climb the row of mulberry trees that grew beside the long driveway to our farm. I liked to wander into the woods and eat blackberries straight off the vine. I liked being alone sometimes, but not always, and I liked how my arm hair glowed in the sun.

When I was fourteen, two and a half years older than my daughter is now, I liked a boy who was a few years older than me. He played on the basketball team, was over six feet tall, had chest hair,

Note: This essay was originally delivered as a craft lecture during the 2018 *Tin House* Summer Workshop.

and on his upper lip grew what was, in retrospect, a very sad excuse for a mustache. I liked that he wore Drakkar Noir, stood with his hands in his pockets, drove a fast car. I wanted him to like me back, so I agreed to sneak out of my friend's house, where I was supposed to be spending the night, and I agreed to meet him down the road, and when he picked me up in his fast car and drove to a liquor store that mostly disregarded the state's liquor laws, I agreed to drink from the bottle he handed me. I liked how it tasted, how giddy and free being drunk made me feel. I agreed to sneak him back into my friend's house, to the basement. I didn't like what he did to me. I didn't like how he kept kissing me after I told him to stop, or how he overpowered me, held me down, put a pillow over my face so no one in the house would hear me crying for help.

I agreed to doing things I didn't really want to do that night because I had been taught somewhere along the way that it was a blessing to be liked by a man, that I should be flattered by the attention: from the grown men who called to me on the street while I was walking home, from the one who kept calling even after I asked him to leave me alone, from the drum major who wanted me to suck his dick in the back seat of his car. I learned, soon enough, that being liked meant favor, meant preferential treatment, meant I was safe but only in certain ways. I was supposed to be flattered that my Spanish professor liked me enough to invite me to his apartment while I was still his student, to his bed, that he invited me to live with him. He was the one who taught me that it actually didn't matter how likable I was, there was always the threat of violence or punishment for saying or doing something he didn't like. We could be at the market choosing fish and fresh tomatoes for dinner and his hand would be resting on the small of my back and the next moment it would be raised to strike me. I tried diminishing myself in such a way that I wouldn't provoke him, wouldn't anger him, tried to bend myself according to his pleasure so that he would like everything I did and said and thought. It didn't matter, because no matter what I did, it was never enough. I kept at it anyway, until there was almost nothing left of me, of the person I had been. And that person I became, who was barely a person of her own, is the version of me he liked best.

I wrote a memoir about that, about how that happened, about how a man convinced me to give away all of my power and authority and to reject everything in the world that brings me joy without even realizing I was doing it. It wasn't easy to write that book, and I knew that if he ever read it, he wouldn't like what I had said. The first time I read from *The Other Side*, it was here, in the amphitheater at *Tin House*. I am not exaggerating when I say I thought he might show up to shoot me with a gun. But what actually happened is that my story found an audience instead.

After its release, a criticism waged against my memoir was that my "narrator" (which, spoilers, is me) isn't likable, that I write things that make my readers uncomfortable, and that I make choices with which my readers disagree. As if my most important job in finding language for a story that had none were to please. As if by labeling me unlikable, they don't have to listen to the story I needed to tell. Raped women are unlikable, apparently. So are strong women. Women who survive. Ambitious women are unlikable, women who are good at their jobs, women who tell the truth. Women who don't take shit are unlikable, women who burn bridges, women who know what they are worth.

Why shouldn't women know their worth? Just because we're not supposed to? Just because people don't like it when we do? I know that I am good at lots of things—I am not good at singing (you'll hear what I mean at karaoke tonight) but I know I write like a bad motherfucker. I am very funny in person. Also, I just ran a marathon. It wasn't pretty or fast but I persisted, and it is from small confidences like these that I draw courage to tell the truth, without regard for my likability.

As a woman, I have been raised to be nurturing, to care for others' feelings and well-being, often at the expense of my own. I have been taught that to be liked is to be good. But I have noticed that certain men are allowed to be any way they want. They get to be nuanced and complex. Adventurous and reclusive. They can say anything, do anything, disregard rules and social norms, break laws, commit treason, rob us blind, and nothing is held against them. A white man, in particular, can be an abuser, a rapist, a pedophile, a kidnapper of children, can commit genocide or do nothing notable or interesting at all, and we are expected to hang on his every word as if it is a gift to the world. Likability doesn't even enter the conversation. His writing doesn't even have to be very good.

I am still talking about writing, though there is an uncanny resemblance to current events in the wider world. Let us consider, for example, our most recent presidential election. On the one hand, we had such a man as this: an unapologetically racist, sexist, homophobic, serial sexual assailant—a grifter, a con man—and on the other hand, we had a woman many people didn't like. That election cycle reminded us of all the words for an unlikable woman: she was a bitch, a cunt, a hag, a harpy, a twat, a criminal —she was unbearable, unelectable, unlikable.

Unlikable to whom? I'm saying women are told we are unlikable, but let's be honest, this pressure isn't exclusive to women, especially not just to white women. The world tells black women they are unlikable when they are angry, even though they have the most reason to be angry. I find it unlikable that more of us aren't angry alongside them. The world tells black men they are unlikable when they are too confident, too intelligent, when they behave like kings, when they are not men but children who reach /into their pockets or stand together on corners. People who have immigrated to this country are told they are unlikable when they "take American jobs"; they are just as unlikable when they do not work. They are unlikable when they cross the border in the desert under the cover of night and when they come through a checkpoint in the middle of the day. We put their stories in cages.

This is not a metaphor.

There is no end to the reasons people are labeled unlikable— because of the way they look, or the configuration of their bodies, or the choices they have made about how to live their lives, what kind of family to build, how to love, how to worship God, or not, or the language they speak, or the country where they were born, or because someone does not like the things they have to say. At some point, we must acknowledge that the question of likability is not one about craft, but about sexism, racism, homophobia—it's about bigotry.

The pressure to remain likable exerts power over us and the stories we feel it is safe enough to tell. "We tell ourselves stories in order to live," Joan Didion famously writes in *The White Album*. Stories are how we know ourselves, how we understand our relation to others; stories are the lenses that allow us to look at the chaos of the world and see with clarity and wisdom. We remember our past through the stories we tell about our mistakes and successes, and through these stories, we teach our children lessons for the future. We resolve conflict through stories, especially those of us inclined toward a tidy narrative arc. Stories keep us sane; they give us meaning. As a writer of nonfiction, I understand that if some of us tell stories in order to live, others must tell our stories in order to survive.

In my own life the stories I have told have created paths for me that did not previously exist, have helped me to escape from prisons of my own making or another's, have become the form through which I have made the case for my own humanity, or another's. What I have found to be most powerful about these kinds of stories is that they are almost impossible to deny. This is not to say that people haven't tried to negate, or degrade, or defame the stories I have told—they have, which is my point—but my point is also that when I tell a story that is mine and true they cannot simply say no, because the truth is not a request, is not a question, requires neither permission nor forgiveness.

If you come to the page to ask for forgiveness you have come to the wrong place. Forgiveness asks everything from the forgiver, asks her to give her pain away, to act as if the harm never happened. It's the wrong question to ask. I'm not interested in letting go of my pain, but in transforming it into strength instead.

I have made so many mistakes. And I experience those mistakes I have made as a burning shame. But I can tell a story that transforms that too, not by taking your pain away—because it isn't mine to take—but rather through understanding the harm I have done, the pain I have caused in you. This is what I mean by "a reckoning": it means I take responsibility for that pain I have caused. It means that I feel that pain in myself and that I also feel it in you. This is, to me, the first step toward reconciliation. Forgiveness comes only after.

The pressure to be likable keeps us from doing this hard work, keeps us from telling the truth. Not just on the page, but in the lived experience of our bodily lives. Every day we go to great lengths to be likable. Some of us spend hours altering our bodies so that we can be better liked: we starve ourselves to be thinner, we bind, we constrict, we take up less space. We make ourselves paler or darker. We cover up or show more skin. We tell lies to survive and to fit in.

We feel pressure to disfigure ourselves on the page in these same ways—we constrict our stories because we are told they do not deserve to occupy space in the world, we tidy up our histories to make them more presentable to others, we carve up lifetimes of mistakes and wrong choices until the story we tell is only a shell of the truth, which isn't really any kind of truth at all.

The truth is: sometimes I am afraid of what I write. You should be a little afraid of the story you are telling, too. And if you're not afraid that someone won't like it, you're still not telling the truth.

Think of all the emotional labor that requires: planning each of your actions and weighing them against the emotional conse- quences they might have on every person, and bending yourself in anticipation of what others might feel—always scaling back your own desires and rejecting your own needs. It requires a constant negotiation of what you can say and do in the world, constantly diminishing yourself because of the effect it might have on other people—which you cannot actually control or predict.

Think for a moment how much time you have spent in your life replaying conversations where maybe you said the wrong thing, or how you were maybe too curt with that person in the checkout line, or too forward with that dude you met on Tinder; how maybe you speak too much in meetings or make your views too known. How much time you have wasted fretting about whether other people like you. Just do a quick calculation: How much of your life, do you think, have you spent this way? An hour? A whole day? A week? Maybe entire years? What masterpieces could you have made by now if you'd directed your energy toward writing like a bad motherfucker instead?

There will always be some people who won't like what you have to say. I recently spoke on a panel at a conference in Iceland and I told the attendees (a roomful of mostly women, and a handful of men) that I don't actually care whether men like my writing. There are specific men whose opinions matters to me—my hus- band, several friends, the men running this conference, the men in this room—but as a demographic, no, I don't actually care at all whether men like my work. After the talk, two of the men who were in that room approached me (one of whom was the conference organizer) because they wanted to tell me they didn't like what I said.

Imagine, for a moment, the luxurious freedom of being so appallingly un-self-aware!

Maybe now those men call me "that bitch" (which is fine, I'll put it on a tote bag), maybe they call me a cunt, a hack, a whore. I don't have to answer. That's not my name. I know my name. I know my purpose. I know my place, and it is rising.

I think, perhaps, one reason—maybe the primary reason—that the world tries so hard to pressure us to be likable (and to punish us when we aren't) is because they are afraid we will realize that if we don't need anyone to like us, we can be any way we want. We can tell any story. We can tell the truth.

We can be wrong sometimes. We can make mistakes. Sometimes really big ones. We can be crude and vulgar. We can change our minds. We can say something wrong—or better yet, we can say something that is unpopular but right. We can admit that we have sometimes loved the wrong person or gave away too much of ourselves in exchange for fame, or favor, or fortune. We can tell the stories of our addictions, our falls from glory, our kinks, our abuse. We can tell the hard truth we learned at rock bottom, and we can admit that it is precisely by climbing back from that lowest place that we have drawn power and strength. We can let ourselves be vulnerable enough to admit our most unforgivable errors, to find our way back from the brink of oblivion, and even if no one likes the story we have to tell, there is no story—none at all—that makes any of us unworthy of love.

I want to tell you this: There is a truth that lives inside you and no one can give you permission to tell it except yourself. You can tell the whole thing, the full truth—and you deserve to. You deserve to tell the story of your anger and heartbreak and regret, your foolishness and apostasy and your unquenchable thirst for revenge. You deserve to admit that sometimes you behave in ways you later regret, that sometimes you hold back when someone needs you to give, that sometimes you take more than you need. You deserve to name the harm that has been done to you by others, and you have a responsibility to name the harm you have done. What I am asking is that we make space for these stories of our failures, our ugliness, our unlikability, and greet them with love when they appear.

I'm almost forty now. These days, I still like being alone sometimes, but not always. I like running. I like the feeling of my legs moving and my feet on the ground. I like how working my muscles makes them feel tired and sore. I like learning how to swim. I like setting small goals and achieving them. I like singing to pop music with my children in the car—especially when it is very loud and very bad. I like it when my daughter talks back to me, even though it also makes me mad, and I like it that she is so bold and so weird. I hope she stays bold and weird forever. And I like it when a piece of writing comes across my desk that is brave and vulnerable enough to tell the hard story that is underneath the easy story people like, that shows me the ugly truth that has been wearing a beautiful mask. I like it when a writer confronts my assumptions and biases and I realize I have been wrong. I like to change my mind. This is the work that stories do in the world and stories are how we will save it. I like feeling so ready for your stories to arrive in my mail-box and on my desk. I will *love* reading them.

WALTER JOHNSON

## Guns in the Family

FROM *The Boston Review*

IT IS IMPOSSIBLE for me to remember my father without thinking about guns. My first was a child-sized Winchester 20-gauge
shotgun. It was a hand-me-down from a kid across the street. I
think I paid twenty-five dollars for it, saved from my allowance and
advanced to me by my father for doing yard work. I was eight.
That summer, after I bought it, I remember getting my dad to
go down to the basement with me after dinner to "practice." He
would open up the gun cabinet and we would get out my shotgun.
My dad would coach me into a stance. Then I would cock the hammer and pull the trigger. My dad would jam the barrel back into
my shoulder so I could prepare for the recoil—"the kick"—when
I fired live ammunition. I worried a lot about the kick: would I be
up to it?

I went hunting for the first time that fall, for geese. My hometown was near the Mississippi Flyway, the massive bird migration
route that roughly follows the track of the Mississippi River. Every
fall hundreds of thousands of Canada geese made their way south-
ward overhead, arrayed in their instinctual V formations. We woke
up at two in the morning, and my mother made us a full break-
fast—bacon, eggs, toast, coffee for my father—before we drove to
Swan Lake, the wildlife refuge in northern Missouri. Reservations
to hunt at Swan Lake were lotteried at the beginning of the season. If you were fortunate enough to get one, you were assigned a
date and told to be there that morning before six.

I remember that long drive in the early hours of the morning,
before the rest of the world was awake. The warmth of the heater
in the car, the homey familiarity of AM radio, the lonely glow of

the lights left on overnight outside the farmhouses across the fields from the road. There was one sharp turn in the highway, near Mendon, Missouri, which my father had warned me about, and I stayed alert the whole drive waiting for it to come up on us.

In the parking lot at Swan Lake, thin sheets of ice had been shattered and ground down into muddy ruts by cars and trucks belonging to other hunters. Inside the hunter check-in, it was bright and almost warm, bare lightbulbs hanging from the pitched wooden ceiling, a furnace burning at either end, and men of all ages in their rubber boots and camouflage gear. They spoke to one another in the low tones of the early morning; occasionally someone would laugh. My father and I did not talk to anyone else. I remember his gentleness with me in that foreign place—so longed for and so strange all at once.

At six the service window at the far end of the building opened, and an officer started assigning the blinds. He had a hand-cranked bingo cage, out of which rolled balls corresponding to the num-bered blinds situated around the edge of the reserve. Behind him was a poster that tracked the daily totals of each blind over the course of the season. We drew A-4, which according to the poster was pretty good.

It was hard to find, though, and the sun was coming up by the time we parked and dragged the decoys across the stalk-stubbled field, setting them up in what we imagined to be a pattern that would appeal to passing geese—it was important that they face into the wind, I remember my father saying. Before long we heard the roll of distant gunfire.

The "goose pit" was a plank-lined rectangular hole, maybe a little more than four feet deep, with a wooden bench long enough to sit four across. Most of the time in it was spent trying to keep quiet and still, whispering when there were geese nearby, and eat-ing year-old chocolate bars and Vienna sausages. The pit had a low roof and a hinged gate that partially hid the entrance, making it possible to peek out without being visible. When geese flew into range, you threw open the gate, stood, and took aim.

I killed my first goose that day. Or at least that is what we said, and what I have said ever since. I know I popped up and shot at a goose, and my father did, too, at the same time, and we both agreed that the one that fell was the one I had been aiming at. Af-ter my father had shot one, too, we carried our dead geese, swing-

ing by their long necks, back to the car and drove to check out in
the same building where we had been that morning, so that our
totals could be posted on the board: 2/2.

Along the road back to the highway, there was a spray-painted
sign advertising goose processing, and my father followed the arrow to a small parking lot in front of a large white all-weather tent.
Inside, a couple of women stood behind a folding table wearing
winter coats and elbow-length yellow rubber gloves. They had
white plastic aprons on over their coats, and the aprons were
already flecked all over with red. One of them had a strand of
hair that kept falling down into her eyes; she used her forearm to
push it back into place. While my father and I sat in metal folding
chairs at the other end of the tent, the women dipped the birds in
paraffin wax, which when hardened pulls off easily, taking all the
feathers with it. Then they decapitated and gutted the carcasses.
I will never forget the way that place smelled: humid, oleaginous,
nauseating. After a while, the women brought our geese back to
the table in the front. They were wrapped in butcher paper, and
the light red watercolor stains had already begun to seep through
in several places.

The aspects of my psychology and constitution that might make
me recoil from a place like that today, the things that still lead
me to feel a little queasy when I see chicken legs in the store or
cooked up for dinner, or people put to bloody work, had a simpler
name that day. I experienced them as personal weakness, as not
being quite "grown-up" enough.

When I was ten, I was first allowed to carry a gun during deer season. I had been deer hunting with my father a couple times before
that, sleeping in the old farmhouse with the rest of the men and
sitting two shifts a day on a freezing bench nailed about ten feet
up a tree. My gun was a Savage Model 99 lever-action rifle that my
father had inherited from his mother. In the hands of a skilled
hunter, the gun I carried has a range of at least eight hundred
yards. My hunting license for the year 1977 records that I was four
feet eleven inches tall and weighed eighty-two pounds.

My grandmother had grown up on the Miramachi River in New
Brunswick, Canada. She met my grandfather when he hired her
father as a guide on a bear-hunting trip and she went along to
help out. In the world of the National Rifle Association, my grand-

mother was a formidable woman, a national champion in several
sorts of riflery. Every year my grandparents drove from Virginia
to Ohio so my grandmother could compete at Camp Perry. All of
their five children shot, too. In 1954 my father became a national
champion, the "High Junior" in the small-bore-rifle category, and
received a huge, heavy silver bowl that was prominently displayed
in the house where I grew up. Also in the house was a photo of my
grandmother, smiling, standing next to the carcass of a leopard
she had shot, which had been hung from a tree.

None of that helped me get very far as a deer hunter. The trick
to ambushing deer in the woods is to sit still and keep quiet, and
I couldn't do either. On the last day of my first deer season, my
father came to get me off my stand a couple of hours before dusk.
He pointed me along a trail back to the car, and then set out on a
parallel line through the woods, hoping to startle a deer into running across my path. Before long I heard a rustling in the woods to
my right, a crashing, really, because the quiet of a forest in winter
amplifies sounds—there were many occasions, sitting out there,
that I froze at the sound of a squirrel crunching over dry leaves,
thinking I was being stalked by the ten-point buck of my dreams.
My heart began to pound.

A light-footed doe peaked out of the edge of the woods and
stopped to look at me. She was about fifteen feet away. I froze. Not
because I had any conscious objection to killing, not even in the
odd mutuality of that single beat, as we both stood there trying to
figure out how to respond. I just did not know what to do. And
then she was gone. I don't remember how I explained it to my
father. Just the silence as we drove home.

As well as being a poor deer hunter, I was dangerous. There were a
couple of years when, bored and cold, fiddling with my gun, I acci-
dentally squeezed off a shot. If I had not later done the same thing
in my parents' basement while playing with a loaded handgun, I
would say that the unanticipated sound of a high-powered rifle in
the woods is the loudest sound that I have ever heard.

I always lied about the reason. "My gun went off by accident" was
not an acceptable hunting story. Nor, really, was "I saw a huge buck
and took aim but missed." And so I settled on wild dogs. Three
different years, I came in from the woods with a tale of shooting
at a dog. One year, I somehow found a tuft of hair, perhaps from

a squirrel, which I passed around as evidence that I had managed
to graze one. Another year, standing in a long line of hunters at
the edge of a field as another group walked through the woods
to drive the deer toward us, my gun went off when I was trying to
catch a falling snowflake in my mouth.

When I was eleven or twelve, I almost shot a kid named Mark,
whose father owned the farm where we hunted. We were all heading out to drive "the back forty," a piece of ground across the
gravel road from the main farm. I was standing down at the end
of the driveway, ahead of the group, with my muzzle pointing at
the ground. I raised the gun as I cranked the lever to chamber a
round, and my muzzle traced a line upward from Mark's feet to
just above his head, where it was pointing when it exploded in my
hands.

I stared at the gun in my hands, uncomprehending, and put it
down on the ground. I did not hunt that afternoon. That night, after a council of the men had met to talk about what happened, including looking at my grandmother's old gun to make sure nothing was wrong with it (nothing was), my father took me aside and
told me that they had decided it was still safe for me to be armed
in the woods with them. Somehow my complete surprise had convinced them that I would not make the mistake again. "You turned
*white*," my father said to me, as if it were almost a compliment, as
if it said something about my redeemable soul, even though I had
violated virtually every precept of the hunters' safety classes I took
every fall.

I finally killed a deer when I was thirteen. I was in a stand they
called the Texas Tower, an enclosed platform that was set out in
the middle of a field. Around 11:30 in the morning, something
flashed to my right, and I turned to see a doe running across the
field. She stopped at the tree line to look back. I braced my rifle
—by now a Winchester Model 70 7-millimeter magnum that I had
bought with money I earned from delivering newspapers at 5:30
every morning—sighted through the scope, and pulled the trigger. I got down out of the stand and walked to the spot where I
thought I had seen her fall. Before long, I found a small smear of
bright red blood on the leaves on the ground.

I tried to track her, following the broken branches and small
spattered drips of her blood, into the woods where she had run to

hide. But I lost the track, and so I walked back to the farmhouse, where I knew my father would be. Once we drove back over there, it did not take long for my father to track the dying deer through the woods. She had died heading uphill, about a hundred yards from where she had stopped to look back after crossing the field.

I was surprised and a little bit scared by what I had done. By the way her brown eye stared up at me from the floor of the forest, by the bubbles in the puddle of blood that had flowed out of her lungs, by her glandular smell. As we stood there, before we cut into her and left her steaming viscera in the woods, my father took me in his arms and hugged me. It is the only time I remember him hugging me between the time I was five or six and the day I went away to graduate school. "Well done, son," he said.

My father was one of the loneliest people I have ever known. My brother and I used to joke that it was a deer that killed him. He kept up the hunt long after I moved away. He would dutifully go out and sit in his stand, and it became kind of a joke that he would never shoot anything. But finally, one year, on a freezing-cold day right around Thanksgiving, a big buck walked across his stand and he shot it. The photo someone took shows him looking pleased, but very cold, his face and hands bright red; the light of the camera caught the eyes of the dead buck somehow, making them look like small flashlights shining off into the distance. A week later my father was in the ICU with pneumonia; he was a life-long smoker, and the cold and the exertion that day had been too much for his enfeebled lungs. He lived a few more years, in and out of the hospital, and finally died in November of 2001, close to the anniversary of his last kill and three weeks before the birth of my second child, his first grandson. On the floor by his chair in the living room, in a way that now seems as weirdly unaccountable as it once did a natural fact of my father's existence, sat his AR-15, bump-stocked and fully automatic.

I have told all these stories before, back when I used to drink, at parties when I was a graduate student or at dinners with my colleagues later on. I have told them, and laughed along with the others, but with an intensity edged with anger: at my fancy friends for their easy, unquestioned sense of superiority; at my emotionally foreshortened childhood and the fact that my father died without me ever really having talked to him; at myself for selling out my father for a few laughs from a bunch of academics, for playing the hick, and for never having been that good at it in the first place.

But I have never really told the stories of the undertow, the ones that are not so much picaresque as they are plain old morality tales, in which I was often an anxious acolyte at the gunners' conclave, and rarely—if ever—had the courage to be anything more than a stupid, smiling bystander. The story of watching the other kids shooting swallows in the barn with a .22, and not participating, but only because I thought I might miss and reveal myself to be unworthy. The night we sat out in the freezing cold with a hunting knife and the frozen-solid head of a decapitated doe, and cut away at her features. The hour I spent with a friend of my father's who had taken me dove hunting, and, raising none, had shot at a large turtle sitting at the edge of a farm pond; the turtle paddled out into the pond, and my father's friend shot it again, and then again and again and again, as it kept surfacing to breathe, fighting for life. "Fucking thing won't die," he said, at first bemused, and then finally angry, like it was ruining his whole fucking day.

Very rarely have I told anyone about Virgil, the boy who lived across the street, who was my first hero, perhaps my first love.

Virgil was a lithe and beautiful boy; crew-cut tan and freckled with narrow brown eyes. He was a tree-climbing, jackknife-carrying, dirt-bike-riding sort of boy. He had all the best things. A Nishiki bicycle and Adidas shoes—one pair, green with neon-yellow stripes, I admired so much and so openly that he gave them to me when he was done wearing them. He was the sort of boy who knew about the things that boys like me feel they are supposed to know about: Black Cat fireworks, cherry bombs, and Roman candles; condom machines in service station bathrooms.

A long, straight scar bisected his left eyebrow, a memento, he said, of a shotgun that had exploded in his face, the selfsame Winchester 20-gauge shotgun with which I had killed my first goose, a shotgun whose continued existence I could never fully square with the scar on the left side of my right-handed friend's face.

I spent summer afternoons at Virgil's, a solid two-story brick house with a pool in the backyard. It was dark and cool and quiet inside the house, a contrast to the purposeless noise of the failing AC window unit in our living room. Virgil's house had dark olive wall-to-wall carpeting with an undulating pattern perfect for deploying tiny armies of plastic soldiers. It also had a player piano in the front hall and a huge wooden console television, on which we watched *Ironsides* every afternoon.

Sometimes Virgil's father came home early from work and sat at the dining room table drinking bourbon. Barrel-chested and beer-bellied in a plaid snap shirt, he was all topside: his jeans hung loosely from his waist, and he walked with the rolling bowlegged swagger of a man who always wore cowboy boots. He had blunt, hairy forearms and thick fingers. As he sat at the table and drank his whiskey, the cat—first a gray tabby and then a black Siamese, after the first cat was hit by a car—would jump up in his lap, and he would stroke her head. Try as I might, I cannot recall his face, and it makes me wonder if I ever had the courage to look him in the eye.

Virgil's father was a banker, the scion of one of my hometown's first families, the owners of a local bank, and the last generation of that sort of local elite, as it turned out. But I mention that now not to frame the changing fortunes of the Rivers family in light of the shifting, deregulated economy that would soon force them to sell out to St. Louis–based Boatmen's Bancshares, which would soon enough be sold off to NationsBank and then, finally, to Bank of America, but simply to explain the gun that Mr. Rivers brought home from work, a snub-nosed .38 that he unclipped from his belt and placed on the credenza in the dining room where he sat and drank and stroked the cat.

Mr. Rivers drove a black Ford Thunderbird with a license plate that read BLKBRD, a novelty in those days, and was the loudest man I have ever met. My parents sometimes told the story of a time when he was in our house, looking at something—my father's classic Parker 12-gauge, maybe, or some hunting trophy—when suddenly he bellowed for his wife. Across the street, in the kitchen in the back of their house, from the living room in the back of our house, she heard him calling and came to see what he needed.

When his mother went out, Virgil showed me his father's things. Mr. Rivers had been a major in the Army, and his uniform hung in an upstairs bedroom, where he and his wife slept in separate beds. Downstairs, his study was a museum of dark wonders. Antique tin soldiers and old books. Weapons of all kinds: small throwing stars, brass knuckles, heavy bone-handled hunting knives, flintlock dueling pistols, a Colt .45 Peacemaker, and a 20-gauge shotgun with the barrel sawed down to about a foot, the stock refinished into a pistol grip. One day I went over to Virgil's house and found that the television was out of commission. Mr. Rivers had been sitting in his study playing with one of his guns and it had gone off. The shot splintered the edge of the front door, which had been half open, and blew up the television across the hall in the living room, where the rest of the family had been sitting, watching *The Hollywood Squares.*

It was not until much later that I figured out the riddle of my friend's scar. I knew Virgil's father beat him. It was no secret. I remember one time when he had Virgil out on the front porch, spread-eagled with his hands on the seat of the porch swing, kicking him in the ass and screaming at him, his words rhymed to the kicks. For all the world to see. Like that scar on his son's face.

The things that Mr. Rivers wanted to hide were behind the books on the built-in shelves that lined the front wall of his study. Magazines with pictures of naked women. There were no men in Mr. Rivers's magazines, only women and knives. I spent many hours of my childhood wondering how the things I had seen in those magazines were possible, how the women could have survived. Mr. Rivers's Grease Gun was behind those books, too. I have known several men like Mr. Rivers, and the fact is that they always hid their machine guns and their pornography in the same place; so proximate, perhaps, were the lonely pleasures of fantasizing about mastery and violence.

The Grease Gun, properly known as the M3 submachine gun, was introduced by the US Army at the tail end of World War II, and could fire 450 .45-caliber bullets per minute. As far as I could tell, Mr. Rivers kept his close to hand in case of an uprising. Some sort of zombie-hippie-commie-black-homo apocalypse that he was convinced was gathering right around the corner, waiting to come down the street and assemble on his front lawn.

When the threat finally materialized, it was more familiar, closer to home. We were in our living room watching the 1980 Winter Olympics—Eric Heiden, Ingemar Stenmark, the "Miracle on Ice" US triumph over the Soviet ice hockey team—when one of Virgil's sisters, Sarah, called from across the street. She had heard someone outside the house, tangled up in the duck decoys by the side of the garage. She had tried to call her father, but he was out at a party. Could my dad please come over? And so he did. Went down to the basement, got the pistol—an old, long-barreled .32

that I would very shortly misfire into a wall down there—and went over to help. In the meantime, Sarah had been able to talk to her father, and so he had come home, armed with his .38. In the backyard, in the hard dark of winter, he saw my father, silhouetted with his gun, and drew on him. When my father came home he was laughing, although it wasn't really funny. The agreed-upon moral of the story, the one that framed and reinforced the hierarchy between our two families, between the two men, and between Virgil and me, was not that having handguns around is stupid or likely to lead to mayhem, nor that someone should have called the police, nor even that it was actually a pretty big longshot that the Revolution would begin with someone trying to steal duck decoys. It was that Mr. Rivers had got the drop on my dad.

There was, I have to believe, as much tenderness in my father as there was rage in Virgil's. But I will never really know. My father knew much more about killing than he did about loving. It was only in violence, dressed for the hunt, carrying a gun, that he could face the terrifying feeling of having a child, of loving someone whom you can neither control nor protect.

My memories and my stories, I have sadly concluded in later life, lead inevitably toward the machine gun hidden in my friend's father's study, or lying next to my father's easy chair. The heady and uniquely American blend of martial culture, white paranoia, and toxic masculinity—which makes stories of so many US families and childhoods illegible without guns—possesses an insistent teleology, a sense that all this perceived threat is leading us to someplace inevitable, a battlefield on which one will not stand a chance of surviving without a gun.

When I hear the NRA people going on about how guns are just "tools," I think, absolutely, you are right, guns are tools: tools for making emotionally stunted men feel whole; tools for guiding lonely boys along the bloody pathway to becoming violent men; tools for spreading the fearful fantasy of the coming race war; tools for inflaming urban areas in rural states, and making the argument for more cops and more prisons; tools for reproducing male dominance and white supremacy; tools for white male parthenogenesis.

So I am with the Parkland kids, truly. And yet, when I hear people talking about raising the age at which someone might buy their first gun or banning bump stocks or assault weapons, I have got to admit it leaves me wondering why they are stopping there. True: there is no reason in the world for someone to have an AR-15 except to kill people or indulge in the fantasy life of white survivalism that I learned about at Virgil's house. And we can start by banning the tools, but we are not going to be finished until we dismantle the house they have been used to build.

In her new history of the Second Amendment, *Loaded* (full confession: I loved the book enough to blurb it), Roxanne Dunbar-Ortiz shows that the history of gun owning and use in the United States has always been connected with imperial genocide and racial slavery. Notably, the constitutional provision for the keeping of a "well-regulated militia" was (contrary to the ahistorical reading prevalent today) not about defending the country from outside threats but rather aimed at arming white men against Native Americans and the threat of slave insurrections. In other words, the defense of gun ownership has always been rooted in anxieties about the need to defend white homesteads and households against a racialized, gendered threat: blacks, Indians, women who threaten their husbands' masculinity, kids who won't obey their fathers.

Add to this that the rising generation of school shooters has come of age over almost two decades of continuous war. They are an imperial generation. And we wonder that they fetishize force. They live in a society that deals with social problems by putting people in cages. That thinks that the "first response" to any problem should be to add a gun to it. We send armed police officers to deal with mental breakdowns and drug overdoses and old ladies who lock their keys in the car. We send them to deal with kids who shoplift cigarillos and then walk down the middle of the street.

Until we deal with the admixture of toxic masculinity and white supremacy that produces such pornographic inequality, until we stop using armed police to guard the border between the haves and have-nots, until we recognize that imperial violence and police violence and school violence are related aspects of the same problem, we are going to keep producing killers. The cause of the United States' problem with guns, to paraphrase Dunbar-Ortiz, is not guns; it is the United States.

ELIZABETH KOLBERT

## How to Write About a
## Vanishing World

FROM *The New Yorker*

ON A STORMY night in 1987, an American herpetologist named
Marty Crump was getting ready for bed when she heard a tapping
at her door. This was in the mountains of northwest Costa Rica,
where evening callers were rare. The visitor had braved the down-
pour to give Crump what counted, in field-biology circles, as a hot
tip: the golden toads had emerged.

Golden toads had been formally described only two decades
earlier, by another American herpetologist, named Jay Savage. In
the paper Savage had written assigning the species its Latin name
—*Bufo periglenes*—he noted that the toads exhibited "the most startling coloration."

"I must confess that my initial response when I saw them was
one of disbelief," he wrote in an otherwise staid scientific tract. He
wondered briefly whether someone had tricked him by dipping
"the examples in enamel paint."

Golden toads had been seen only in rugged terrain, near the
crest of a mountain range known as the Cordillera de Tilarán,
which forms part of the Continental Divide. They seemed to live
mostly underground, surfacing only long enough to reproduce,
an MO that made them difficult to study. The morning after the
knock on her door, Crump trekked up the cordillera, through a
soup of fog, mud, and drizzle. When she finally spotted the golden
toads, she was so astonished that she forgot how miserable she felt.
The toads, she later wrote, were "dazzling," like jewels scattered on
the forest floor.

That spring, Crump watched golden toads mate, a process that sometimes took as long as twenty-five hours. Males outnumbered females by as much as ten to one, and when a guy managed to find a single lady he would tackle her from behind. Carrying him piggyback, she would hop to the nearest puddle, while he fended off competitors. Sometimes so many males were trying to crawl on top of the same female that they formed an orange ball, studded with writhing orange limbs.

Crump returned to Costa Rica the following May to continue her research on golden-toad reproduction. By the end of July, she had spotted just one toad at the site where, the previous year, she'd seen dozens.

In 1989, Crump arrived in Costa Rica in early April. She hiked up the mountain: no toads. She made the trip again—same result. After a month, a family emergency compelled her to return home to Florida, and one of her graduate students took over. He eventually found a lone toad, a male. Crump spent 1990 on sabbatical in Argentina. A colleague monitored her research site and was to alert her if any toads appeared. None did.

By 1990, it was no secret that many populations of wild animals were in trouble. Still, Crump's experience represented something new under the cloud cover. A biologist could now choose a species to study and watch it disappear, all within the course of a few field seasons.

Crump chronicled the loss of the golden toad in a book titled, for complicated reasons, *In Search of the Golden Frog.* (The golden frog, which is native to Panama, is only very distantly related to the golden toad. Neon yellow in color, it, too, has vanished from the rain forest.) She followed this with a second book, *Extinction in Our Times,* cowritten with a colleague. Meanwhile, naturalists with similar experiences were weighing in with similarly mournful titles: *Requiem for Nature, Silence of the Songbirds, The Last Rhinos, Planet Without Apes.* In 2006, Samuel Turvey, a researcher with the Zoological Society of London, participated in a survey aimed at locating the last remaining Yangtze River dolphins, or baiji. Six weeks of intensive monitoring failed to turn up a single baiji. When the survey results were made public, in the journal *Biology Letters,* Turvey was deluged with interview requests. In one twenty-four-hour period, he spoke to more than three dozen news outlets around the globe.

"It turned out it was possible to galvanize the world's media on behalf of the baiji," he observes in his book *Witness to Extinction.* But only after the dolphin was gone for good: "That's what would sell. That's what constituted a story."

The losses on our human-dominated planet keep coming, and so, too, do the stories. These days, it's not just species that are vanishing. Entire features of the earth are disappearing—thus, the latest batch of "witness-to" books, written by geologists.

Peter Wadhams, the author of *A Farewell to Ice: A Report from the Arctic,* is the head of the Polar Ocean Physics Group, at the University of Cambridge. He first visited the polar north in 1970, when, as an undergraduate, he got a job on a Canadian research vessel, the *Hudson,* which was attempting to circumnavigate the Americas. Although the *Hudson* was built for travel through sea ice, on the last leg of the journey it got stuck in the Northwest Passage and had to be rescued by an icebreaker. Evidently, Wadhams enjoyed the experience—in the stiff-upper-lip tradition of British adventurers, he's largely mum on the topic of emotion—because he returned to northern Canada a few years later to work on his PhD. This involved flying over the ice cap in a sort of aeronautical jalopy —a Second World War–era DC-4 with the cockpit bubble of a Sabre fighter jet welded to the fuselage. The flights left from Gander, and Wadhams recalls a bar in town, called the Flyers' Club, where a band played topless.

At the time, Wadhams imagined himself part of a glaciological tradition stretching back to the Napoleonic Wars. The idea was to map the extent of the Arctic sea ice and then, basically, forget about it. (Many died trying.) The ice cap's size varied, expanding in winter, when the polar darkness descended, and then contracting in summer. But this cycle, like the seasons themselves, was supposed to be unchanging. The assumption, Wadhams writes, was that "everything in the ocean is constant."

In the 1980s, satellites replaced scientists eyeballing the Arctic from DC-4s. The satellite data revealed that the ice was shrinking. By this point, the earliest climate models had been assembled, using IBM punch cards, and they predicted that global warming would be felt first and foremost at the poles. In 1990, Wadhams compared surveys of the sea ice north of Greenland that had been conducted from British submarines, using upward-looking sonar. The comparison showed that the ice cap, in addition to contracting, was thinning; during the previous decade, its thickness had declined by 15 percent.

By the end of the summer of 2007, the ice cap was about half the size it had been at the start of the satellite era, and the Arctic sea ice had entered what an American scientist, Mark Serreze, has dubbed its "death spiral." Today, a decade deeper into the spiral, older Arctic sea ice has mostly melted away. What's left, in large part, is first-year ice, which forms over the winter and, since it's thinner, is that much more prone to melt the following spring. The most recent climate models predict that within a few decades the Arctic Ocean will be entirely ice-free in summer. Based on his own observations, Wadhams believes that the time frame is more like the next few years. "It is clear that the summer Arctic sea ice does not have long to live," he writes.

For his part, Serreze, who directs the National Snow and Ice Data Center, housed at the University of Colorado at Boulder, has also written a farewell to ice. In *Brave New Arctic: The Untold Story of the Melting North,* he relates that when he first started out in polar research in the early eighties, he was taken with the idea of global cooling. "Deep down I was hoping for an ice age," he confesses.

As the satellite and sonar images began to pile up, Serreze continued to hold out that hope. Perhaps, he theorized, the ice cap was shrinking due to a natural cycle that would eventually reverse. Years passed, the ice continued to melt, and Serreze came to favor fire. "The weight of evidence turned me," he observes. "And then I turned hard." He gives the perennial sea ice until 2030 or so. "That the Arctic Ocean will become free of sea ice in late summer and early autumn is a given," he writes.

Both Waldhams and Serreze anticipate the loss will have disastrous and, as it were, snowballing consequences. Sea ice reflects sunlight, while open water absorbs it, so melting ice leads to further warming, which leads to more melt, and so on. (This past winter, parts of the Arctic saw temperatures of up to 45 degrees above normal, even as parts of the United States and Europe were being buried under snow; some scientists believe the two phenomena are related, though others note that the link is, at this point, unproved.) Arctic soils contain hundreds of billions of tons of carbon, in the form of frozen and only partially decomposed plants. As the region heats up, much of this carbon is likely to be released into the atmosphere, where it will trap more heat—another feed-

back loop. In the Arctic Ocean, vast stores of methane lie buried
under frozen sediments. If these stores, too, are released, the resulting warming is likely to be catastrophic. "The risk of an Arctic
seabed methane pulse is one of the *greatest immediate risks* facing
the human race," Wadhams writes.

"This is definitely disaster movie material" is how Serreze puts it.

What's known as a "global bleaching event" occurs when coral
reefs in three oceans—the Atlantic, the Pacific, and the Indian—
exhibit signs of heat stress all at the same time. There was a global
bleaching event in 1998, and a second one in 2010. In October
2015 the National Oceanic and Atmospheric Administration an-
nounced that another event was beginning. The bleaching continued through 2016, and then on through the first half of 2017. By
the time it ended, in June of last year, almost a third of the shallow-
water corals on the Great Barrier Reef were dead. In the northern
stretches of the reef, the mortality rate was closer to three-quarters.

As it happens, shortly before NOAA's announcement, Irus
Braverman, a professor of law and geography at the University
at Buffalo, set out to interview coral biologists. The earlier global
bleaching events, combined with various other forms of destruc-
tion—disease, dredging, dynamite fishing—had already convinced marine scientists that reefs were in grave trouble. Still, as
Braverman relates in her forthcoming book, *Coral Whisperers: Scientists on the Brink,* even the gloomiest were caught off guard by the
third event. After taking an aerial survey of the Great Barrier Reef,
one of Australia's most prominent coral biologists, Terry Hughes,
showed the results to his students. "And then we wept," he tweeted.

An American scientist, Laurie Raymundo, reported on Facebook that, after observing the devastation of reefs in Tumon Bay,
on Guam's west coast, "for the first time in the fifty years I've been
in the water, I cried for an hour, right into my mask."

Coral reefs are often referred to as living structures; as such,
they span the divide between the faunal and the geological. Individual corals are tiny, gelatinous animals infelicitously referred to
as polyps. In their cells, polyps house even tinier algae, which they
rely on for food, to help fuel their extraordinary building proj-
ects. Bleaching occurs when water temperatures rise more than
2 degrees or so above normal. For reasons that are not entirely
understood, corals react to the heat by expelling their symbionts.

(Alternatively, according to some scientists, it's the algae that respond by decamping.) If the bleaching event is short-lived, the corals can survive and, eventually, recover. But in a warming world, where such events are becoming both more frequent and more protracted, the prognosis for reefs is much the same as it is for sea ice.

A coral ecologist named Peter Sale, who's a professor emeritus at Ontario's University of Windsor, tells Braverman that reef scientists are confronting "the likely disappearance of the ecosystem they have been studying." What most interests Braverman, though, is not the fate of reefs—with Sale, she takes their disappearance as likely—but the way scientists choose to "narrate" the crisis. She finds them divided into two camps. In one are those who argue that reefs' downward spiral can be arrested only by dealing with climate change, which is to say, by completely revamping the world's energy systems. (It's worth pointing out that if Wadhams and Serreze are right about Arctic feedbacks, even this may not be enough.)

"A lot of what we're doing in terms of conservation actions is futile until we stabilize the climate," Ove Hoegh-Guldberg, the director of the Global Change Institute at Australia's University of Queensland, tells Braverman. Hoegh-Guldberg describes local efforts to preserve or restore reefs as "rearranging the chairs on the *Titanic* to get a better view." Imitating those on the other side, he says, "Let's just block out those horrible people, like me, who say it's all futile. 'Lalalalalala, can't hear you!'"

In the second camp are those who argue that, yes, reefs are dying and, yes, the situation is only going to get worse, but this just makes local restoration efforts that much more urgent. Ruth Gates, the director of the Hawaii Institute of Marine Biology, is working on selectively breeding corals that might be able to withstand higher temperatures, an approach that's become known as "assisted evolution."

"The gloom and doom is paralyzing," she tells Braverman at one point. "The scope of climate change is paralyzing."

"I don't know what the outcome of our project will be," Gates says at another point. But, on some level, "we're already successful. Because we're sending out a more hopeful message, something we can do actively."

Hope and its doleful twin, Hopelessness, might be thought of as the co-muses of the modern eco-narrative. Such is the world we've created—a world of wounds—that loss is, almost invariably, the nature writer's subject. The question is how we relate to that loss. Is the glass 95 percent empty or is it 5 percent full?

The message that there's still "something we can do actively" has a lot to be said for it. It offers a rationale for not giving up —on species, on whole ecosystems—which is also a rationale for continuing to research these subjects and, perhaps most relevant for scientists turned authors, for continuing to write about them. Narrating the disaster becomes a way to try to avert it. Wadhams ends *A Farewell to Ice* with a chapter titled "A Call to Arms." In it, he urges readers to "adopt every possible measure that will reduce unnecessary energy use," to lobby for better laws, and to embrace nuclear power, which, he writes, "will keep the lights on without carbon emission."

But we seem to have reached the point where even the calls to arms are starting to sound like dirges. In the same chapter in which Wadhams argues for better energy policies, he observes that such policies probably can't—and almost certainly won't—be put in place fast enough to save the Arctic. Therefore, he says, technologies to block sunlight or change the reflectivity of clouds will have to be deployed. These so-called geoengineering technologies have yet to be tested—if truth be told, they've really yet to be invented—but without them, according to Wadhams, the "temperature rise, and the associated further feedbacks, will be too great to allow our civilization to continue." Apparently, this is supposed to count as inspirational.

It's hard to say what purpose would be served by a message of straight-up despair; despondency, as it's often noted, produces its own feedback loop. And yet, scientifically speaking, what alternative is there, as we move into the future, beyond the baiji, and the golden toad, and the reefs, and the sea ice, on toward reengineering the atmosphere? Lalalalalala, can't hear you!

J. DREW LANHAM

# *Forever Gone*

FROM *Orion*

I IMAGINE THAT there is no headstone at the Cincinnati Zoo aviary, no mark of remembrance, no epitaph. Had there been, it might have read:

— INCAS —
HERE LIES THE LAST CAROLINA PARAKEET
CONUROPSIS CAROLINENSIS
DIED FEBRUARY 21, 1918
HIS LIFE DONE AND BARELY KNOWN,
DOOMED TO THE DARK SWAMP HEREAFTER,
A BIRD FOREVER GONE

Final rites for the passage of one of the most unique birds ever to sweep across the skies of the American psyche.

There are few creatures that we can tag with exact departure dates, but with the Carolina parakeet (*Conuropsis carolinensis*) we probably can. It all ended on February 21, 1918, in the same year World War I came to a close and not quite four years after the passenger pigeon's own exit from existence. Incas died that day. He had been housed for some years at the Cincinnati Zoo aviary, and was the last Carolina parakeet anyone would ever see with certainty.

The passenger pigeon's extinction was sadly predictable. People had blasted at flocks that once darkened the sky until the birds became scarcer and scarcer, and then were finally gone. But how the Carolina parakeets' population dwindled down to Incas is a mystery that plagues conservation scientists to this day. It wasn't for lack of the species' range. Despite their name, Carolina parakeets were found across most of the eastern half of the lower forty-eight states. Recent science shows that there were two subspecies —a southeastern population, *Conuropsis carolinensis carolinensis*, that dwelled in the southeast Atlantic, Gulf coastal plains, and all of Florida; and another, *Conuropsis carolinensis ludovicianus*, found west to Texas, Nebraska, and Oklahoma. In some years, birds from the western groups wandered widely and could end up in the Northeast. Wherever they occurred—north, south, east, or midwest—mature floodplain bottomland forests lying along great rivers were the parakeets' preferred haunts.

*Conuropsis carolinensis* seemed misplaced in the temperate latitudes. The gaudy tropical combination of its emerald-green body, sunset saffron in the wings, and tangerine on the head and cheeks didn't belong here. The Seminole people tagged the bird colorfully: *puzzi la née*, yellow-headed one. A saberlike tail that would fan to break or bank in a turn, paired with wedge-shaped swept wings, made a pleasing form. Attach a beak hooked and notched like its falcon cousins—but designed in the parrot kind to pry and peel fruits, nuts, and seeds instead of to tear flesh. Its diet varied widely, sycamore and cypress balls among the favorites on the menu, but its affection for one particular seed—cockleburs—was especially noteworthy. An otherwise innocuous weedy plant that grows almost anywhere soil is disturbed, the cocklebur produces thumbnail-sized ovate seeds that look like miniature spike-covered footballs. Walk through a tangle of them and you'll soon have the company of hundreds of the needy seeds entangled on your clothes. When it's time to disentangle yourself (and your canine companion) from the unwanted riders, you will need time and patience—the plant's tenacious desire to attach and disperse was an inspiration for hook-and-loop fasteners like Velcro. Beyond being a sticky annoyance and crop pest, cocklebur is highly toxic. Pain and death are the final irritations for many animals that dare to ingest it. Somehow, though, Carolina parakeets were immune to the toxic effects and relished the seeds like candy, possibly concentrating the chemicals in their own bodies. Some early naturalists reported cats dying after eating Carolina parakeet entrails.

Parrots—a family that includes parakeets, macaws, and cockatoos—are among the prodigies of birds. They have a sense of themselves, of others, and the environment around them that likely extends beyond instinct. Being a parrot means being a thinker who relishes the company of friends and kin—sociality is as much a part of who you are as your plumage. Parrots care. As with us, the long-term parental nurturing and constant preening and feeding exchanges foster a sense of community. That's who parrots are, and who *Conuropsis carolinensis* was—an evolutionarily complex, stunningly beautiful creation whose time was cut short, in part, by individuals not so deeply feeling or thinking.

Choose wildlife conservation as a profession and you're surrounded by loss—marooned on an island of dwindling hopes surrounded by past practices, current lack of care, and emerging policies that can drive the conservationist into psychosis. It can be an unhealthy undertaking that drains one's reserves of hope.

My office walls are covered with portraits of birds gone past existence. At a glance I can see ivory-billed woodpeckers, Bachman's warblers, passenger pigeons, heath hens, great auks, and Labrador ducks. It's an ornithological pantheon of loss. Some Gone Birds, as I call them, especially the ones that would've inhabited my southern homeplace, have cast spells that I can't shake. As a result, I've carved, collected, and commissioned facsimiles of these birds. I have wooden ivory-bills in abundance and at least a half-dozen passenger pigeons scattered around. There are even a few Bachman's warblers skulking about. It's a fantastical aviary that serves to sate a desire to un-doom the wondrous loveliness.

Mourning Gone Birds isn't just a dive into a worry hole, it's a dirty crawl into a deep and sandy pit. For each species that is somehow recovered from oblivion—a bald eagle, for instance—more seem to tumble back in. Whooping cranes, Kirtland's warblers, Gunnison sage grouse, California condors, and many more teeter on the crater's edge of Almost Gone. Beyond the birds, I mourn the loss of places, too, because landscapes degrade and fall into the pit along with the birds. Longleaf pine forests, tallgrass prairies, and salt marshes shrink daily to mere fragments of once expansive swaths. I mourn the Gone Birds and the landscapes they inhabited because the whole of all of us becomes compromised in the loss of some of us.

There are fewer Carolina parakeets in my aviary than any other Gone Bird, though. I have a print or two—and even one life-sized figure fashioned from an artfully contrived kaleidoscopic conglomeration of pipe cleaners, a commissioned request from a young friend. That I have fewer parakeets than the other Gone Birds is odd, because for all the birds I've seen alive or dead, mourned and marveled over, all fall behind *Conuropsis carolinensis* in reverence. Thoughts of the extinct bird hang as a gnawing remembering I can't shed, a haint of times past. The idea of a parakeet's flourishes decorating a bald cypress like some sort of feathered ornament grabs me by the heart in a way the others don't. There are no known recordings of the bird's voice and only a few black-and-white photographs of birds kept as pets. Ghosted from existence, it sits now only in memory and museum trays.

Sometimes I seek the validation of what was in natural history museums. Behind what's stuffed and posed for the public façade of museum displays and dioramas, there are the museums' back rooms and basement catacombs where rows and stacks of dead things lie side by side. Here, the empty-eye-socketed souls of creatures killed and collected for science are kept cool and clean to reduce the chances for decay or insect infestation, and are essential tools for the scientist and for conservation.

A few years back, I visited the University of Georgia Museum of Natural History when there were several Gone Birds on display. It just so happened that at the same time, painter Philip Juras had a number of his relict southern landscapes—portraits of southern river valleys before they were dammed to slowing and scenes of old-growth cypress swamps—hanging around the displays of dead birds. I was drawn into a wormhole that featured the extinct birds, which seemed ready to fly back into the landscapes where they had once lived. There was a feather-worn ivory-billed woodpecker frozen forever in pursuit of a nonexistent grub, and a passenger pigeon perched in loneliness, brainlessly wondering how billions became none. And then there was the Carolina parakeet, which pulled at me with a mesmerizing gravitas. Yes, it was just as dead as the others. There hadn't even been an attempt to pose it on a branch like its peers—it was just a study skin, a tube of feathers meant to be measured and compared to other parakeets.

There was something different about this skin, though—it demanded something more than pity for its plight gone past. And then it struck me. I was being watched. Unlike any study skin I'd ever seen of any bird, the cotton-stuffed sack of feathers was watching me. Most stuffed birds have little tufts of cotton protruding from the holes where their eyes used to be, giving them a zombielike appearance. But this particular Carolina parakeet had glossy orbits of yellow glass eyes instead. It lay there unblinking with unsettling eyes, eyes that gazed through the display case and through me. Spend time in the company of parrots and you'll realize quickly (and sometimes uncomfortably) that the birds are thinking on levels beyond asking for crackers. They'll look you over and size you up. Some behaviorists maintain that intelligence in the parrot family can approach that of preschool children — maybe beyond. And although this bird was long past thinking, it appeared thoughtful nonetheless. Maybe it was begging to be released from extinction's damnation, to fly free and play again in the fragments of remaining bald cypress swamps and fallow fields rank with cocklebur.

Studying the parakeet in the museum and surrounded by landscapes that used to be, I began to imagine it among a cohort of others flashing green and gold in small, tight flocks through the used-to-be landscape. In the rendering of an old-growth, south Georgia swamp forest, I could hear the sociable shrieks and jabbering of roosting flocks echoing from the hollow trunks of the buttressed bald cypress. I was expecting the stuffed skin to up and fly away to join a flock wheeling over old fields. Juras's swamps expanded beyond the bounds of the picture frames that held them. Colonnades of gargantuan trees guarded the riverbanks and lorded over expanses of black water wetland. The parakeets flocked in and out of wilderness that exists now only in ragged remnants of parks and preserves. On the edge of the great swamps we now know by names like Congaree, Great Dismal, Black, Okefenokee, Four Holes, and Kissimmee, and all along the great South Carolina swamps swollen to flooding by rivers like the Savannah, Edisto, Santee, Cumbahee, Black, Little and Great Pee Dee, Waccamaw, and Ashepoo, the birds screeched and wheeled in unison. Dodging centuries-old trees and diving in and out of shafts of morning sunlight, they squawked their way to where the deep forest ended and yielded to open lands and farms.

I found myself completely consumed in my imagining: suddenly, I can see the flock circling once, twice, and then on the third pass settling into an old field gone fallow. The unplanted plot is a weedy, unkempt affair choked with ragweed and cockleburs. The burry bane of many a farmer's existence, the weeds are beginning to throw their sticky seed to whatever furred thing might pass by and offer a ride to the next patch of soil. To the parakeets, though, the burrs aren't pests—they're a delicacy. With great screeching in a celebration of food-finding, the parakeets land and settle in to a squabbling feast. They hang and dangle like green and gold chickadees from waist-high weeds. Tender bits from the tough burrs are consumed and the rough, sterile husks dropped to the ground. But then suddenly the whole flock is up in the sky again in a panicked, shrieking flurry—a watchful companion's warning shrieks suggest a raptor is overhead. The swallow-tailed kite wheeling below the clouds says danger in the moment. And then, just as suddenly, a calm falls over them; a rapid understanding of the lack of threat from the graceful raptor whose eating interests focus on dragonflies. The flock settles again in garrulous gathering to resume the meal. They are mostly welcomed there as they digest the undesirable weed in a form of service that the farmers—and the enslaved people working in the fields—appreciate. The more burrs the parakeets destroy, the less there is to do to prep the field for growing crops again. Like my grandmother Mamatha used to say: many hands make light work. It is a scene likely witnessed by many across the range of the species.

John James Audubon captured the essential character of *Conuropsis carolinensis,* painting them gleefully entangled in a thicket of cocklebur. In one of his most popular works, the birds seem consumed with consuming but acutely aware, too, of the world around them. They're engaged with their food, engaged with one another, engaged with us almost two hundred years beyond the painting. Facing the portrait, you count a flock of seven. A female on the far left raises a foot. Maybe Audubon meant to show the bird in midscratch or stretching to reach for the next cocklebur. Since art is also about what the seer sees, I imagine her waving at whomever might be looking from beyond the frozen frame of an existence that was already waning in Audubon's time. To me, it has always seemed an invitation to come closer—one knowing being to another.

Although America was burgeoning at its seams when Carolina parakeets flew about in abundance, it was a nation still wildly rough around the edges. What remained in the hinterlands is what eco-restorationists sometimes refer to as baseline—a reference condition for return.

As an ecologist of color, the restorative thinking is a bittersweet exercise. I've been steeped in the training (or brainwashing) of the "bring-back-the-natives-undam-the-rivers-pull-up-the-privet-and-release-the-bison" paradigm. It's a wistful conjuring to make North America great again—in an ecologically good way, I suppose. But beyond the uncomfortable verbiage about casting out exotics and eliminating aliens, there is the question of who—beyond the largely homogeneous choir of restoration ecologists and wistful wishers for the good old days of yore—gets to say what wild nature is. There has been a slow admission of indigenous American contribution to the landscape, and the ways in which they managed the land that sustained their communities and culture. For ecologists, it means recognizing the role that red, brown, and black people—who preceded ecologists and their almost exclusively white conservation "movement"—played in shaping nature, and what those people knew about the North American landscape before they did.

Wishing for a contrived, humanless wildness forwards a practice of belittling—or ignoring altogether—"colored" land connection. My own dark-hued roots are mired in the soil of the American South. When I drive by, fly over, or walk through most places "down here," I can see and often feel the actions of my ancestors who changed the land. By connecting the pain of that past to what we see now, I pay homage and deepen my personal connection with place. Yes, it's an exorcism of past pain, but also a progression toward helping others see the land's real history, and perhaps to become reconnected with the land. My desire to inform and inspire, beyond mere ecology, grows daily. Along with the fate of the Gone Birds and their lost worlds, it possesses me.

I wonder about the enslaved watchers who worked in the shadows of endless passenger pigeon flocks that passed overhead, or heard the ivory-bills that called from the tall timber, or glanced at the Carolina parakeets that flashed across work-weary eyes. I think about salt marshes modified and maintained by enslaved Senegalese—the spring crop waving thick with Carolina gold rice and sea-island cotton that created some of the richest men in the world. Beyond the monotonous thud slice of a hoe in pluff mud, what would my ancestors have noticed? The day-to-day work of survival required more than brawn and will. From where would hope emerge? Humans have always looked skyward for inspiration, imagining themselves unbound by gravity or the weight of oppression. Flight means freedom. It is not beyond the oppressed to lean hard on natural beauty as an uplifting beam. Survival draws on inspiration. Sweet sounds and beauty are no less worthy of notice because one is in chains—perhaps they are worthier because of the chains.

For the enslaved, there was more they would have noticed about the parakeets than just their beauty. The parakeets lived in tight-knit social groups comprised of relatives. Along with crows and jays, the parakeets would have been the avian intellectuals in a landscape where they had to make do with not only what was, but with what was to come. And then they were servants, too, clearing fields of cocklebur and sandspur menace. But when the birds exercised a desire to have more—to eat the fruit from plantation and farm orchards—the parakeets became targets of persecution. Because of their social nature, birds not killed or wounded in the first round of extermination circled around their fallen family members that screamed in fear and injury. In that empathy, more birds fell.

I imagine the flock, assaulted and driven out of a ripening orchard of plums and pears. On the edge of day, as katydids call dusk in, the birds retreat to the forests to roost in cavernous hollows. A depleted flock reenters a shrinking swamp domain—remnants of wild southern places already disappearing along with the parakeets. They are home, finding comfort in the shadows of last light. But daily, it seems, in smaller and smaller numbers and in fewer and fewer acres.

The birds aren't alone in the refuge. There are humans in the shadows, too. Torches lit from knots of fatwood throw long shadows onto the hollow trunks where the parakeets roost. The dark forms are Maroons, self-liberated slaves who once worked the same plantations that the parakeets frequent. They were once chattel, bound to the land at the cruel behest of white planters, but who have escaped terror and freed themselves from the very fields over which the birds have flown and fed. As the Carolina parakeets find security in wooded wetlands, so too do the Maroons—slave chasers and the "law" hesitate to pursue them into the swamps. Free from the plight of overseers and forced labor, they have lived for decades in thriving communities within mere miles of the plantations they had fled.

The Maroons shared the Carolina parakeets' requisite for free-

dom. They found sustenance in the wilderness, but also made noc-
turnal forays back onto the plantations to secure food, tools, and
sometimes weapons. They traced the same paths as the parakeets,
but worked the night shift. It was a life on the edge with constant
threats of persecution, capture, and death. But it was a free life
and that matters most. The land was flush with grain and fruit that
only existed because of black hands. What Maroons took was just
reclamation for work done.

By the time the Carolina parakeet's decline was noted by Audubon in the 1830s, the enslavement economy, fueled by whip-
cracked backs, had pushed the country toward a sinful prosperity.
It wasn't just the South that benefited. North of the Mason-Dixon
Line, wealth flowed upstream to financial houses and investors.
The numbers of black people in bondage exploded, and as enslavement swelled, the numbers of *Conuropsis carolinensis* dwindled.
And within little more than a generation of Audubon's lamenta-
tion that "our Parakeets are very rapidly diminishing in number,"
a civil war was raging across much of the birds' range.

Persecution of any kind ultimately demands relief, whether
through escape or revolt. It's all an inalienable flight to self-determination. It's a risky thing to seek one's own destiny, though. The
decision to leave certain bad for uncertain good is the balance
that must be measured. Enslaved people knew the gamble, and
some decided that liberty had to be sought at any cost, whatever
consequences might come. And so when the Maroons fled to the
southern swamps and found something way better than being held
captive, they shared the refuge with other beings that ultimately
found refuge there, too. In the convergence of demands for human dignity and freedom, and nonhuman survival and existence,
there are islands of empathy that emerge between our braided-
river beings.

Human trade and trafficking; genocide; driving other creatures
to extinction—it is all built on a corrupt human belief that some
are worthier than others. Racism and white supremacy lie at the
heart of enslavement—you could be bought and sold, whipped,
raped, or killed on a whim. It was custom, practice, and policy, and
it is the basis of so much of the brutality and bias we experience
today. It begins with the belief that some are superior and some
are inferior—whether racism, or sending another species into the
oblivion of extinction, they both grow from the same rotten core.

*

The parakeets' big-timbered bottomland world shrank even more rapidly after the Civil War and disappeared altogether into the ramped-up hypergreed of early-twentieth-century land grabs, rampant timbering, and swamp-busting agriculture. The fast-dwindling populations of Carolina parakeets were assaulted on several sides, sending the species plummeting. Beyond habitat loss, other factors probably contributed to the decline, including competition with introduced European honeybees for tree cavities, demands for bright feathers for women's hats, and persecution as pests. Although the birds cleared fields of cockleburs, crop depredation was likely an incentive for killing *Conuropsis carolinensis*. A flock descending on a ripening orchard or cornfield undoubtedly cost the species dearly, and the strong social ties that caused individual birds to flock around the fallen was a fatal compounding factor. As agriculture spread across the landscape, so did new diseases. Some scientists postulate that the parakeet's exposure to poultry diseases may have been a final nail in the forever-gone coffin.

And then there was the irony of rarity. As the reports of declines spread among the ornithological community, both professionals and amateurs "needed" to add birds and eggs to their collections. Collectors—many of them obsessed hoarders—shot whole flocks for the sake of "science." The museum bird that wouldn't release me from its gaze likely fell in the name of "knowledge" and the need to possess a rare thing with no thought of its extinction.

Today, when I lead others out to bird-watch in the remaining fragments of wild places, I cannot help but bring the history of the enslaved, and the landscape we tread upon, into the same head-heart space. I cannot tell stories of birds and of the cypress swamps and old rice fields I frequent in Lowcountry South Carolina without telling the story of those who moved forests, soil, and water through force and greed. There are stories in the soil that have to be plowed up.

Hate, enslavement, persecution, and the dramatic changes to the land wrought by all of us are heavy burdens to bear. Maybe it's why I yet seek birds, here and gone on. The quest renders the remaining feathered things precious gifts, passed forward to survival through it all. Black ducks and black rails in "managed" rice impoundments are reminders of what was created by a cruel society on the backs of black people. We can't separate one from the other. Can efforts to steward and make conservation a more inclusive effort be bolstered now by informing others of the past connections, even when they are painful recollections? Telling the full story seems the best start. Signs and monuments must tell the whole story—including the human elements—painful as it may be, behind the present things we see. Black land ownership and connections to nature languish in many places where Carolina parakeets may have once brightened the skies. History's shadow can be a long one, especially when cast cruelly or when remedies to right wrongs are made without consideration for everyone and everything. Do we readily reveal these chapters in history? Does conservation bear a responsibility to illuminate the dark corners where not only birds and beasts have suffered, but humans have as well? If Aldo Leopold's admonition to keep every "cog and wheel" is the first step in tinkering with the ecology, then the cultural gears and switches certainly warrant our consideration.

For those birds gone on, I mourn. I mourn the Carolina parakeets persecuted as pests and shot down for simply being who they were. Their plumage and behavior became easy marks to profile and possess for selfish purposes. I think of Incas, imprisoned as his species was on the brink of extinction, no crime committed other than being what he was. I see parallels between the Gone Birds and who I am as a Black American man. The mistreatment of nature, the disrespect for all those things believed unworthy of enough respect to not drive them into the pit of never-ness, has common plight among people who've been slighted by practice, privilege, and policy. Extinction by human hands is a sin. Racism is no different. It is a callousness built on judgmental whim. We are all part and parcel of nature, parakeets and people alike. How we treat one another determines who we all are—or might become. The good of it, our attempts to do better by birds and other species as well as each other, spells hope on one side. The upwelling of ignorance and denial of what's been, what is, and what could be, and a blind march headlong into some unregulated regained greatness with the past as the meter to follow—spells certain doom. It is an evil directed at birds and humans, too. It is a callousness toward life that spells endangerment, extinction, and exclusion.

In my constant quest for birds, thinking of those gone and then reveling in the ones still with us, I also find a peace and momentary freedom from the bad that exists in the world. In my escapes to places where birdsong drowns out the news stream and a soaring swallow-tailed kite blinds me to all else except the innate desire to fly in self-determination and free will, the bad disappears for a while and I too am marooned. I become a Maroon—escaping certain bonds to find freedom in the deep recesses of wildness.

One hundred years since Incas died. In the years of wishful sightings since—a disputed sighting on the South Carolina Santee Delta, ghosts in the Georgia Okefenokee, shadows flying across the Florida Okeechobee prairie—other species have fallen silent. Most have faded with no epitaph to mark their place in the Gone Birds book. For all the reasons posited for their loss, it usually comes down to a lack of caring. And more than that—pushing a living being into the abyss of extinction is, in the end, a hate crime; a lack of compassion for another's implicit right to exist. I feel some kinship in that place, where my being is seen by some as worthless.

Those responsible for Incas's well-being had to know the species' rare status as they watched his last moments. What kind of relationship did he have with those keepers in the Cincinnati Zoo? Did Incas respond to their voices in parrot squawks and chortles, or maybe knowing parrot nods of his big-beaked head? What were those last moments like? Was there a rift in the cosmos, or a ripple somewhere "out there"? For a species whose disappearance lies in so many ill lots, many believed that those final days of the last Carolina parakeet ultimately came down to a broken heart. His mate, Lady Jane, had died a few months before, and Incas was reported to be lonely.

A century later and there's talk of "reversing" the crime. Parakeet fanciers discuss resequencing genes from dead birds in museum trays to reassemble a Frankenstein-esque *Conuropsis carolinensis*. For me, the de-extinction discussion is a hollow one. How does an organism adapt to the missing gaps in time when it didn't exist? How does a species absent for a century react to a landscape so dramatically altered as to present a different planet than the one it knew? Technology tells us it may not be an impossible task, but maybe such tasks should be ones that we let pass. The whole of

what a Carolina parakeet or passenger pigeon or Bachman's war-
bler was, will always be more than the engineered sum of its parts.
In the century since Incas's eyes dimmed, we should let what we've
done to make living things gone stand as monuments, so as to not
let that history repeat itself.

At the time of Incas's death, there was no policy demanding
notice or care for Carolina parakeets as an "endangered species"
—such policies wouldn't exist for another fifty-five years. Maybe it
wouldn't have mattered. And although policy and regulation are
part of what we need to prevent tragedies like what happened to
the parakeet, maybe something simpler is needed just as badly. If
we see ourselves bound together in all of it—humans and nonhu-
mans alike—then maybe care takes on a deeper meaning. We all
require the same clean air and water, safe places to land, roost,
and love whomever we choose. Treat others, regardless of plumage
or color of skin, the way you long to be treated.

Even still, as I sat in my office, surrounded by my facsimiles and
replicas of the Gone Birds, the parakeet left me longing for something I can't quite explain. I wanted, in my own way, to see the bird
live again, to feel its animated, flying, screeching, and squawking
for myself. There's a bit of a god complex in most ecologists. Most
of us aren't just watchers and data miners; we're also wannabe cre-
ators.

And so I created my own parakeet, tacked and fastened together with wood glue and wanting. I worked for weeks researching the bird, trying to get a handle on the sense of it, its emergent
being. After days of measuring, cutting, discarding, remeasuring,
and recutting, I spent more days fitting and refitting the pieces
together as if I could bring *Conuropsis carolinensis* back again. The
wings at first were too wide—not fast enough to carry the bird
quickly through the past. I narrowed them and posed them downward. How to pose the tail in profile? I first splayed it out, but then
decided I wanted it straight as an arrow, so there'd be no delays
in its travel. The bird's face needed to be parrot-esque accurate,
parrot precise. I scroll-cut an eternal scream in the hawk-hooked
beak mouth, could almost hear a muffled squawk. I layered on
thin coats of painted plumage, then wiped them away to add another. Finally, after a fortnight of fussing, a last coat of subtle shad-

ing, and a little wish-conjuring, I set two bulging, brown taxidermy eyes in place, and shuddered a bit inside as something gone forever stared back. A Gone Bird lay in my hand ready to fly—and it seemed to be asking me why. I placed him among the rafters of my writing shack, where he now spins in the slightest breeze, bound for someplace far beyond my seeing.

LILI LOOFBOUROW

# Men Are More Afraid Than Ever

FROM *Slate*

IT IS A remarkable fact of American life that hordes of men are now defending sexual assault. It's not immediately clear why. It seems like the very definition of an unforced error. But a substantial group, many of them in politics, has taken to the internet to argue that a seventeen-year-old football player should get to do as he likes to a fifteen-year-old girl—say, for example, trap her in a bedroom, violently attempt to remove her clothes, and cover her mouth to muffle her screams—without consequences to his life or reputation. The "locker room" once invoked to normalize Trump's language (*every man talks this way behind closed doors!*) has expanded into a locked American bedroom with a woman trapped inside. *It's all in good fun,* defenders declare. *Horseplay.*

Here's the most surprising part: they've launched this peculiar defense despite the fact that the accused party *denies it ever happened.*

To be clear, there are perfectly feasible defenses of Brett Kavanaugh that others have attempted. One could respond to Christine Blasey Ford's allegation that he assaulted her at a party while they were teenagers by saying (as some have) that we can't know the facts or that more evidence is needed. But no: This group has opted instead to defend male impunity for sexual assault and frame a woman's story of coping with years of trauma as a true crisis . . . for men. A White House lawyer was quoted saying, "If somebody can be brought down by accusations like this, then you, me, every man certainly should be worried." Similar things were voiced by Ari Fleischer and Joe Walsh. Per this dark vision of the future, *any* consequence for committing assault—even being unable to move from one lifetime appointment to another lifetime appointment—is the beginning of the end of a just society.

There is a corollary, and it is that teenage girls should not expect justice for coming forward—which Ford had been rightly reluctant to do: "Even if true, teenagers!" tweeted Minnesota state senator Scott Newman, summoning a vision of American adolescence where being trapped and attacked is a boisterous fact of life. (He added, however, that he did not believe Ford.) Writing for the *Wall Street Journal,* Lance Morrow minimized the victim's side of things further by declaring that the incident wasn't serious enough to matter. "The thing happened—if it happened—an awfully long time ago, back in Ronald Reagan's time . . . No clothes were removed, and no sexual penetration occurred." What's a little assault—or fearing for your life and having to fight free and hide —if no penises made insertions and the Gipper was in charge?

This trend isn't really that mysterious, of course. The reason for this panicked defense of assault—even as Kavanaugh continues to firmly deny it—is fear. Not fear that the system will punish men wrongly but that it will punish them rightly. Sure, they will legalistically argue that the rules have changed on them, and it's true to a point that things were different in 1982: "Date rape" wasn't yet an available concept, meaning that women had no way of describing the peculiar horror of being sexually assaulted by someone they knew. But the times weren't quite as different as these guys like to pretend they were. Just because there was no socially validated vocabulary for a man forcing an acquaintance to have sex against her will did not, in any way, mean that *the man thought what he was doing was just fine.* Men are not idiots. As Caitlin Flanagan recounts in an essay, a high school boy who tried to rape her and then stopped, later sought her out to apologize. Why? Because he understood perfectly well that what he'd tried to do was monstrous. Sure, high-schoolers can have misunderstandings, but holding a high school girl down and muffling her screams is not a case of mixed signals. People understood that. Yes, even under Reagan.

But they sure got to pretend they didn't. "Boys will be boys" is a nostrum with the designated purpose of chalking male malfeasance up to innocent high spirits. It's a saying that meant to exonerate, but here's the funny thing: It only works on the agreed-upon assumption that boys *do shitty things,* the gravity of which we're supposed to ignore or dismiss. The message isn't that the boys don't know that the things they do are bad; it's rather that the rest of us should forgive, understand, and love them anyway, without their needing to ask for it.

Is it any surprise that an incentive structure like this one breeds entitled indifference to girls and women in the coddled party, and in the system that coddles them? Is it any surprise that men would panic at the realization that the system that they could depend on to look the other way is fast eroding?

We knew this moment would arrive when the #MeToo movement began. It was clear that men and women were universally comfortable with the movement as long as its targets were unregenerate monsters like Harvey Weinstein, and it was just as clear that the tides would shift once attention expanded to the scope of what women routinely put up with. Eventually, as I wrote then, there would be an attempt to "*naturalize* sexual harassment. If there are this many men doing these things, then surely this is just how men are!"

But I never imagined it would get this explicit. I never thought I would see a group that has spent years laughing at the very idea of anything like "rape culture" suddenly not just admitting that it exists but *arguing that it should*—nothing should be done about it; male malfeasance is an unstoppable cocktail of culture and biology. The subtext—stripped of all chivalric pretense thanks to the recent panic—is that victims don't matter. They're invisible because they're unimportant, and women's pain is irrelevant.

In contrast, during these past few weeks, nothing has been presented as more crucially central than men's pain. Almost as if they'd planned it, a clutch of disgraced men who were finally exposed for years of ongoing alleged abuse has been creeping back toward their long-lamented spotlight. There are quite a few. These reputationally injured parties range from Jian Ghomeshi and John Hockenberry to Louis C.K. to Bryan Singer. What they share— besides a history of inflicting their sexual attentions on the less powerful because they felt like it—is an itch to be famous once again. They want their time-outs to be over. They have *suffered,* they believe, and they wish us to know it. This should be laughable: Anyone who assaulted or harassed someone and escaped without a record should be thanking their lucky stars. Their minimal privation mostly consists of being economically comfortable and doing without attention for ten or eleven months. But it's not laughable! They mean it. They grew up in a world that taught them they "get to" do the things they did. They feel, accordingly, that they have been unjustly penalized. They believe they're suffering greatly.

And many of us (I include myself) are almost—*almost*—persuaded. Many of us have been trained from birth to believe that men (unlike women) are long-suffering and stoic. That means that their pain, when they *do* express it, strikes us as almost holy. It took me decades to realize that something like the opposite is true: It's not that men's pain isn't real; it's that our culture vastly overestimates it. A certain kind of man not getting *exactly* what he wants, precisely when he wants it, will truly believe he's suffering more than a woman in pain who has never been told that what *she* wants might matter. While this doesn't make him a liar, it does limit him and blind him to those limits.

It's as if men and women have different pain scales, emotionally as well as physically. Of *course* men believe they suffer more, and many women—having spent their lives accustomed to men's feelings mattering more than everyone else's—will agree with them. Most of us have been socialized to sympathize with men, the troubled geniuses, the heroes and antiheroes. They're the protagonists. And this meritocratic American dream stuff (which, let's face it, is 100 percent pitched as male) has a poetry that encourages pity. If men on that journey experience a setback, their plight scans as injustice. (The American dream does not reverse!) Their suffering must, therefore, be more acute.

The point of all this is that "he said, she said" accounts aren't the empty contradictions we often dismiss them as; they can tell us quite a bit about the different realities in which men and women get to live. We think of these testimonies as being equally valid, even if they're at odds. (Kidding: We usually assume that the woman has somehow exaggerated or misremembered or misread the context or lied: "I think she's mistaking something, but I don't know, I mean, I don't know her," said Senator Orrin Hatch of Ford.) We don't question the particulars of someone's account of their mugging, but rape inspires people to start panning the story for possible "misunderstandings." But given all of the above, there is, actually, a decent explanation for this: The painful experiences claimed by women make no impression at all on a certain kind of man's sense of reality. Her perspective is as unreal as it is inconsequential to him. Result: His and her story can be, in a limited and horrifying sense, equally true. It's believable, in other words, that Ford says she was scarred by the attack and dealt with it in therapy decades later. It's also believable that Kavanaugh pal Mark Judge "has no recollection" of being in the room while Kavanaugh allegedly attacked her—not because he was drunk (though he has a history), but because this incident with a struggling, screaming teen girl might be, to him, too unremarkable to remember.

It would be great if this appalling imbalance had been "fixed" by #MeToo in eleven short months. But if anything, the hysterical hypercorrection among men has combined our habitual sympathy for them with a plea to extend their exceptionalism. They're finally just willing to say what was once held in common: Women aren't full citizens whose bodily autonomy and personal liberty matter. The harm to a woman isn't worth punishing anyone over as long as you get yours. Convicted rapist Brock Turner was defended by his father on precisely these grounds: He should get probation, because jail time would be "a steep price to pay for 20 minutes of action out of his 20 plus years of life." (Note that the human person Turner attacked literally *does not factor* into this perspective.) Fox News columnist Stephen Miller reclassified the Kavanaugh accusation as "drunk teenagers playing seven minutes of heaven"—a game where the girl typically both consents and voluntarily participates, but is all that really necessary anyway?

It's useful to have naked misogyny out in the open. It is now clear, and no exaggeration at all, that a significant percentage of men—most of them Republicans—believe that a guy's right to a few minutes of "action" justifies causing people who happen to be women physical pain, lifelong trauma, or any combination of the two. They've decided—at a moment when they could easily have accepted Kavanaugh's denial—that something larger was at stake: namely, the right to do as they please, freely, regardless of who gets hurt. Rather than deny male malfeasance, they'll defend it. Their logic could not be more naked or more self-serving: Men should get to escape consequences for youthful "indiscretions" like assault, but women should not—especially if the consequence is a pregnancy. And this perspective extends 100 percent to the way they wish the legal system to work: Harms suffered by women do not rate consideration, much less punishment. (I recommend Googling the mortality rate for women when abortion was illegal.)

As if that weren't bad enough, this recent spate of attempted rehabilitations casts into sharp relief how little men socialized to think this way care—still—about the women (and men) they've harmed. The men exposed by #MeToo are testing the waters for their planned return, with a surprise performance here, a profile there, perhaps a giant self-regarding essay in a high-profile magazine. Some have offered to shade-in their experience of disgrace as if they were tragic heroes rather than prurient narcissists. Read those and search for any sign, however slight, that they've given their alleged victims' pain one-tenth of the consideration that they've given their own. Perhaps they erred, but what more do we want from them? Haven't they endured enough?

The answer is no.

TERESE MARIE MAILHOT

# Silence Breaking Woman

FROM *Pacific Standard*

I USED TO will chaos into my life. It was a gift of sorts. Mother said I was born to Thunder—which is an element of chaos and liberation in my culture. I have always believed that an electric chaos ran through my blood.

"It's a gift to be born this way," my mother said the first time I told her that I had a terrible dream of a large wheel spinning before me. It would not stop. "That is Thunder. This is a gift."

She saw the world differently, and I by proxy. Her willful nature to name the world as she saw it, not how *they* wanted us to see it, made me believe in the power of being an indigenous woman.

On one of our drives along the Fraser River, I asked her, "Is Sasquatch real?"

"His name is Sásq'ets. That is your brother," she said.

Mother's chiding brought to mind stories she gave me as a child. "Bigfoot" was a complicated man as I knew him—a thief, but part of an animal world. When he stole food from the fish camps along the river, my people recognized that was just the Sásq'ets tax. Like when a baby black bear climbed the tree in our front lawn on the rez. He was eye-level to my mother and me from the living room window. He watched us as we waited for his mother to come and get him. When his mother showed, she sat around. My mother took out her drum and started banging it, and then the pots and pans. Still nothing. We just had to wait for them to leave, and then my mother said, "I guess this was their home first." The bears left us alone and did not come back that way again.

She believed the natural world was familial. She saw our stories and myths as realities, and regarded every thing as a property worth protecting. I no longer know the beauty in that mindset; I only felt the power of it when I was in range of her. She felt a sense of belonging in the mountains, and would go alone to fast for several days at a time. No cavern or dark bothered her. She built her own fires, cultivated her own spaces, and never took from the land without making an offering first. It was a practice of power—as I know power to be: knowledge and understanding, with certainty and without shame.

I stopped believing in our power, in our Creator, and in our ancestors' looming spirits when my mother passed because I could no longer feel them—not the beating heart of the earth, nor the surging of the river, nor my ancestors. My mother was my medicine bundle and the blood of my holy life—and I felt the slip of the earth, watching her pass.

And then, at a dinner for authors, where I was asked to present my first book, a memoir, and sign 150 copies, I met a man describing his research on "bigfoot."

"Is this about the mythology behind bigfoot?" a children's book author asked him. "I love myths."

"In some ways," he said.

He was an elderly man who was generous and sweet to me, but as he started talking about his book, he kept prefacing with, "The Native Americans believe . . . ," over and over, as if we were one homogeneous group. It struck me as mildly offensive, because I was uncertain if he knew at least one Native American was at the table sitting next to him, cutting her bread and buttering it. This man had done extensive work with indigenous communities and was, most likely, only trying to impart knowledge to non-Natives in *their* language: coding for a room that doesn't appreciate the distinction between different sovereign nations in North America, and how our stories and beliefs are sometimes similar, but never the same. Native people are often absent from or uninvited to events like these, so it might not have struck him as insensitive, but I wondered if he would ever say, "The whites believe . . ." I often have to couch statements in this framework before I speak, in order to choose my words correctly, or decide if the offense is even worth noting. Because Native people are so underrepresented, and so often forgotten, I must ask myself, "What if anyone spoke like this about white people?" Like how is it possible to have a racist caricature like the Redskins, so overt and publicly defended, and where is the outrage? Is it because we're so underrepresented nobody is concerned with offending us?

When someone said, "Terese is First Nations—isn't that right?" the white authors around the table all turned to me.

"Yes," I said. "'Bigfoot' is a pejorative in my culture. He has a name."

As I said it, I became angry. This "myth" was my brother, and a white man was using our stories without respecting our sovereignty. I was upset that discussing "the Native Americans" was so interesting, and such a novelty, as if we weren't living and breathing at that very table. We don't even call these stories myths, unless we are speaking to people from outside of our culture. The invention of myth is a white thing, and it's often used to diminish the dynamism and functions of our work as storytellers and artists.

But then it rung true: *I claimed my brother in this moment.* I claimed our people. I felt my mother's presence in the room, and then felt her fade away as the white people moved on to discussing their favorite myths: fairies, leprechauns, and the like. What entertains them is not entertaining for me, but my lifeblood.

In my creative writing program there were Native and non-Native faculty teaching us how to cultivate our stories. During our graduate residency, I heard a Hopi-Laguna man defending his thesis. He was talking about how to incorporate myth into our contemporary fiction, which is a delicate thing. Native writers must sometimes adhere to protocol when using a story from our nation, or we must get permission to use a story from the speaker we heard it from, and sometimes we come from nations like mine, which accepts that story is meant to be shared. As this man was imparting the very delicate nature of honoring a story, and how high the stakes are, and why he's chosen to use a certain myth, a white author who wrote speculative fiction raised her hand and said: "I love myths. Look at my screen saver!" It was a unicorn.

She looked to me like the epitome of an East Coast writer: impeccably dressed, sharp, and content with herself. Of course I resented this, stumbling as I am when I walk into a room or try to impart why her sharpness confounds me. Her being able to enjoy fanciful things somehow intrudes on my sensibilities, because I suspect that people like her have never had to walk into a food bank where everyone knows your whole family. It shames me to be this judgmental, but it's always there in my mind—scanning the room for people like myself, and people who won't understand. Some part of me resents how angry I am with white women who love unicorns, who don't see the true nature of our stories, or consider what we do as something more than ancient.

Native writers tend to avoid the word "sacred," as we have marked it "too familiar," because we don't want to write the expected, or border on cliché, but these stories are quite sacred to me, and they have been maltreated for some time.

There is power in the reclamation of story—in the remembrance that these stories are real and tangible things, like my mother.

What Native writers do is art, both practical and sacred, as I know sacred to be.

We have a story in my culture about a "Wild Woman" or "Mosquito Woman" or "Cannibal Woman." Her name is Th'owxeya, and she came down from the mountain with a basket on her back. She took children away, and, if they were rotten, she ate them in her cave.

The stories vary, but the one I grew up with, the one told to me numerous times by my elders and the women in my home, was that Th'owxeya would take me away if I was out when the mosquitoes came.

They told me that little children were playing by the lake and then fell asleep on stones in the daylight. The eldest boy woke up to see Th'owxeya coming down her mountain. He could not wake up the little children, so he stayed behind to help them survive. The eldest take care of the younger ones, no matter what. This was a lesson I was taught early, from this story, and from babysitting my nieces and nephews—who were newborns when I was not yet a woman—protecting babies while their mother was out drinking. And I was happy to do it, for what felt like years. Soon after, I had my own babies, too young—and I say, with some pride, that I have taught myself, through story, how to do better by my children than those who came before me.

I remember one time the story of Th'owxeya was told to me in a circle, among other children—my cousins—and even though the story was about cannibalism and loneliness, the elder was soft-spoken and eager as she told us how Th'owxeya came down the mountain and put the children in her basket. Th'owxeya had a magical speed and strength, but a little boy in the bottom of the basket held a clamshell in his hand and began to carve a hole in the bottom to escape. He fell through, and one by one several little children followed. One boy, he could not fit. The children above him understood their fates if they did not devise a plan.

Th'owxeya took the remaining children to her cave, and had them line up so she could glue their eyes shut with pine pitch. The eldest was the smartest, and he whispered that they should not shut their eyes so tight. Some of them squinted, and therefore were not blinded by the glue. Th'owxeya danced around the fire and the eldest encouraged her, telling her how much he loved when she sang, when she danced. He whispered to all the children that when she came around close enough, they should push her in—and they did.

She cried and asked them to pull her out of the fire.

"We are," they said, but they did not.

Some people say she sang her song in the fire. When the flame took her, she became a cloud of mosquitoes.

Rule of thumb: When the mosquitoes come out, go inside. The buzzing is her song.

We know now, as a people, that though she is gone, there are many others who take our children away—the truckers and lecherous men who asked me if I needed a ride every time I walked along the highway to school or town, the social workers who still do not believe we are capable of raising our children.

When I was a child, I was intelligent enough to know a story does not breathe without engagement. Stagnant myths, or stories that exist without an active audience, they lose their power. When I was a child in the circle, I assumed Th'owxeya was not all bad. I assumed she had been raped, and that's why she lived up in the mountain in a cave like that. As a girl, from a reservation like mine, I assumed most women around me had been raped, and that most stories were burdened with that implicit truth.

In many ways, I am "Wild Woman," as the white men call her. In many ways, I am the eldest child, and the boy with the clamshell, and the fire itself. In many ways, these icons, deities, beasts, and holy beings are my only family now. Invoking them conjures my mother—admiring the beauty in my culture seems to conjure her too.

I've always been drawn to the story of "Wild Woman," because I feared it was my own. I often felt like an outcast as a child, and found solace in isolation. To escape the brutality of my home life, I often locked myself in our basement. In my mother's darkest moments, I could hear her outside my room, behind my door, shouting obscenities and telling me I wasn't anything at all. On the worst days, the only thing I could do was lodge butter knives in the doorway to keep her out—many children I knew did this.

Finding shelter in my dark room made me a more sinister character, I think, when I consider my origin and cannot remember any good stories to tell. Some people can't come to the light. I was the victim of sexual violence, and could not speak out against my father, not even to my mother. She was never ready to hear how she had failed to see the signs, or never thought what we endured was enough to leave him, until it was too much—and the police got involved. I understood, in my silenced time, how a woman could leave her home and dwell in a cave, and eventually learn to resent the beauty of children—to resent their innocence, even. There was a time I couldn't look at happy children because I couldn't bear it. I saw Th'owxeya's nature as one cultivated by the brutality of the world around her.

In many ways I am a broken woman who serves as a reminder that the world can be brutal to Indian children, and women. I often feel as if that is my role in my communities. My history feels brutal, unspeakable even, and sometimes carrying the weight of it makes me feel like a monster who refuses the cave.

My mother on her best days was constantly making an inventory of her children's gifts and traits, trying to discern how we would serve our community when we grew up. To prepare me to be powerful, she often took me to women's ceremonies. She taught me songs and asked me to sing them as we drove from valley to valley to pick medicine or visit elders. She raised all of us this way —traveling with us in our formative years to understand where we shined and what our interests were. When my father left, she became a better mother tenfold. I believe he stifled her with his presence, and she became liberated by his abandonment of us.

My father was incarcerated when he met my mother, who was doing outreach at the time. She encouraged imprisoned Native men to write and draw, or seek an education. It was always rumored he was in for assault. He was a monster, according to many.

I look at myself and see a lineage of monstrous desire and compulsion and beauty and power. When my mother said I was born to Thunder, she believed life would be hard for me, because Thunder is a liberator, and liberating is hard and thankless work. She believed I would disrupt things, but the world would be better for it. Thunder shakes and re-forms the composition of the space it occupies, and lightning is the product of its music. It is disruptive and wholly welcome.

It was a gift to have a mother who believed a disruptive woman is a gift to the world. Now that I am older, I've embraced my power in a room.

Some white people, after they find out I am Native, say things like, "I knew a Native American once." Or they impart to me some story about attending a powwow, or they ask probing questions I feel unprepared for about my culture or language. I tend to feel angry or resigned in these forced conversations. When I get angry, I become a type of brown battle-ax, and I resent it. I have learned to avoid these conversations at all costs.

In my creative writing program there was a teacher, a white woman, who had always been polite with me, but we rarely spoke. Perhaps I avoided her. After I graduated, she wrote a blurb for a white man's book, a friend of my husband's, saying the book was like "Wallace Stegner on peyote, Nathanael West in a sweat lodge, Larry McMurtry on a vision quest." I was raised to practice sweat lodge ceremonies, and my mother was a healer, a pipe carrier. She was a woman who built a sweat lodge for her community, and practiced the traditions. The woman who wrote that blurb, I believe, used those traditions as devices to inject something wild into the Stegner-like craft of the writer she was promoting. She was making an allusion, intentional or not, to the supposed savagery of Native cultures, and how they liberate ethnic enthusiasts in need of a "vision quest." We call people who do this cultural tourists. They appropriate our practices to serve their own liberations.

I confronted the issue of the book blurb in a public forum, and it spurred a discourse that eventually resulted in her stepping down from my school's faculty. There were other reasons for her departure, but my complaints were much more overt and public than those other complaints or rumors. The only thing I heard, constantly, was that I was being harsh or cruel, that I should not "fix" this, or I should speak out against her in a less public way. I felt like it was my fault she left. I felt monstrous. As if it had been my duty to bring her into the circle, like an ambassador, to help her understand, and speak to her like a sister, but instead I chose to be angry, to speak brutally, to be self-righteous. I felt savage.

Even Indians were upset with my callousness. Some told me that in the old days we'd have executed restorative justice and healing with her. But I knew Salish women did not operate this way, not where I'm from. I had watched my mother live through things like this—experiences with white people who deemed her too harsh or callous. Which she might have been, but racism is harsh to witness —it callouses us. My mother experienced a lot of racism as she was growing up, where we were relegated to a reservation and bused in to the white town for school. She used to tell me about the white children throwing rocks at her and her mother. I witnessed much of that racism myself. As a child, I remember my mother and I often weren't served quickly, if at all, in certain stores, and doctors rarely believed we were ill when we were, and my mother was often patronized by hairdressers, mechanics, or service people who seemed to resent having to serve a Native woman. My mother did not tolerate this treatment and lashed out every time. It was exhausting to watch. She swore at people, called them out, or she complained to managers, who could not acknowledge racism but sometimes apologized for the lack of service or outright disrespect.

It's difficult to acknowledge this, but I find myself experiencing this same exhaustion as a woman now, when my child and I are followed in certain stores, or when someone will serve my white husband before they acknowledge me.

Where I'm from, women received clubs and nets as a rite of passage, one item for protecting ourselves and the other for providing. We take care of our own, still, and are not so welcoming to those who betray us. When white men embezzle money from our nation, they are asked to leave, and when someone in our community hurts our children, and isn't registered to our band, that person is asked to never return. My father was forbidden from returning to my land after he was forced to leave my mother. We banish where I'm from, and, at worst, have been known to maim. There is a story that my grandmother had tried to pay for the murder of my father when he would not leave our house. I think of all of this when I consider how difficult it is for me to be fair, or calculated, or good to someone, like the writer of the culturally insensitive comment now gracing the cover of a white man's book.

The natural progression of my mother's beliefs is that this woman is part of this natural world. She is my sister. I've had to come to terms with this now—that while my anger was warranted and my voice valid, the way in which I treated my sister was not good for the world. It brought me pain, where it could have brought peace.

On the day I sold my book, my cousin Tyler, who had been adopted out, and, like me, wanted to know who our family was, wrote to say he found out why my father went to prison. Tyler said that my father's sister had turned him in because he, along with other men, were frequently—for a long period of time—sexually abusing children in the family home, where my paternal grandmother was often incoherently drunk. The duplicity I carry in myself, in having these two stories laid out so incongruently alongside each other—it is how I believe Thunder works. Disruptive and natural —part of me is chaotic, and I cannot escape it. I felt as though the myth of myself had been born on this day, when I could have the things I strived desperately for, but would always carry with them the weight of my history—and that, in order to liberate myself and women like me, I must acknowledge that my history is my gift. It disrupts the good in my world, but with purpose.

Sometimes the myths and stories get mixed up. Sometimes "Cannibal Woman" and "Mosquito Woman" are different myths, with separate stories, and sometimes white men take our stories and make them their own. I think about this when I think of my father, Ken—a name that still terrifies me when I see it or hear it —and Th'owxeya, these figures who serve many purposes, some brutal. All of these stories are maltreated, or used as moral tales: Don't go outside, or Th'owxeya will get you! Don't end up like your father, a drunk, an abuser of people. Don't die violently, like your father did. Don't love bad men, like your mother did. The stories serve their functions.

My work became my power. After finishing the book, I was offered the first Tecumseh Postdoctoral Fellowship at Purdue University, where I'm paid simply to write, to generate work. No more food banks, only abundance. I send money to my family, and we plan vacations—no more food banks for any of us.

I was also offered a faculty position at the institution I graduated from. "Your stories are your power," I say to my students. But
on my first day back on campus as a teacher, a white man pointed
his finger at me and indicted me for being cruel with the writer
of the book blurb, among other things. In front of our colleagues,
he shamed me for participating in call-out culture, but it felt as
though what he was really saying was "Shut your mouth." The man
had been my mentor once and wrote me letters of reference. He
was one of the first white men who ever really called me intelligent. Who asked to read my work. And now I was someone he
saw as a problem. I realized then that the work I had been doing
to make people who believed in me proud wasn't always going to
make them proud. I did not have the courage yet to own that I
wouldn't be everyone's success story. I had experienced this type
of shame before, but not as an established woman—not as the
woman who broke away from violence, poverty, and silence to become one of the first Native people to graduate from the program
and get a book deal.

I cried in the meeting. I was humiliated and scared. I was a
reckless, overly emotional brown person on her first day, already
a problem. After I cried, two white women expressed how they
needed safe spaces to make mistakes. None of the white people
openly empathized with me. They seemed put off by my emotion-
ality—they could not make eye contact, except for the man, who
still seemed angry. Later that week, in front of many indigenous
students, one of those white women dedicated a reading to the
woman who wrote the blurb. It didn't provoke me. It hurt to feel
that outcast in a space that exists to serve Native writers. It felt like
the cost of noting racism, and never doing things the right way, for
being Thunder, for being human too. I know that I am discordant,
but then, maybe all Indians existing after an attempted genocide
feel like a disruption or an anomaly.

The experience only hurled me toward my power. My outspo-
kenness was a hindrance, I knew, but why write, I thought, if I
would not be a disruption?

There was a moment at the river with my mother long ago when I
asked her why we pray. She told me that prayer was not begging or
asking for things, but an expression of gratitude for the way things
are. She looked at me, and behind her the river was not rushing.

There were so many spirals in the current of the river, and many undertows.

She saw what I was staring at. "That is your power too," she said. "The undertow can drown people." I knew she was pointing to the chaos of what we cannot see, and that the undercurrent—the chaos and conflict beneath every surface—is necessary.

Sometimes all I have is the power that she gave me—and the stories too. There might not be some mythological magic to me as a human being, but there is a reason I am drawn to spirals, to spinning things, to the disruptive nature of story, and to speaking out.

I am Thunder Woman, born to brutalities against me. I am Silence Breaking Woman. When I am told not to speak, by my father or anyone, there is a wielding thing turning inside of me that cannot be contained. It is a calling to be gifted with voice.

As an Indian woman, I feel a responsibility to be hard on the world, but love it as familial. I feel a responsibility to be hard on myself as well. I am both fallible and a gift. Even our perceived heroes are monstrous and imperfect sometimes. How easily Th'owxeya's story could have been different, had she made her cave a sanctuary of safety for children who needed a home. How different would the world be without mosquitoes or men like my father. In every person there is a myth, waiting. There are many reasons to survive.

DAWN LUNDY MARTIN

# When a Person Goes Missing

FROM *n+1*

WHEN MY BROTHER was a teenager and I was in grade school, he let some bullying kids from his high school persuade him to skip the day and invite them over to our house. He asked them to leave, but the boys refused. So my brother grabbed our father's shotgun and corralled them into the bathroom, the barrel pointed in their direction. The bathroom door now locked from the inside, my brother held the gun, luckily, up toward the ceiling, so that when his finger slipped and the mechanism went off, the bullet with its massive force went through the second-floor ceiling, the attic, and then out the roof of the house into the sky. How the rest of the family received the details of the incident, I can't recall. But to travel home now is to walk beneath the hole in the ceiling stuffed with newspaper from 1978. To return is also to encounter the past lurking behind me, contorting its face so I can really feel it—its truncated force, whispering a ghost voice into my ear.

If I believed in omens, I'd say the shotgun incident was the worst of omens, literary in its foreshadowing. We can smell a hint of devastation, can't we, a scent we can't quite recognize on first whiff but turn our noses away from knowingly. Where will our characters end up? Our armed protagonist? The girl who tells the story? When I began writing this essay I wanted it to be about fate—how two black kids raised by the same working-class parents could have radically different life outcomes because, as fate would have it, divergent occurrences compel divergent paths. Bruce never went back to the high school with the bullying boys. He dropped out. It's around this time that my parents got a call in the middle of the night that Bruce was in custody at the local precinct for being caught in a stolen car. It was the 1970s and no charges were pressed, boys being boys. That night, my father beat my brother mercilessly with a washing machine hose in the dank basement of our house. The chaos of a violence like that is astonishing. The cacophonous screaming. The inability of anyone to stop it. The cold pallor that hangs in the air afterward. A chasm emerged between us—me, floating off like some wandering balloon; my brother tethered tightly to a familiar story of trouble and poverty, like most of the kids in our neighborhood.

But the question of fate is a fake question. It's a refusal to see how the good daughter is a part of the problem. As a kid, I was the exception, the one who would "make it out of the ghetto," the one bused out of town for school. I liked being the exception. I loved the ways people's eyes would glimmer when I told them any little thing about my life, or when I simply said anything aloud. "So well spoken," the middle-class blacks would say. I basked, annoyingly, in their glow. I didn't mind either when my brother failed, because his failure meant my light shone even brighter.

When Bruce is seventeen, already dropped out of high school, and I am eleven, I'm allowed to go on ski vacations with the white families whose children I go to school with. I can't ski, but they are patient. I don't notice that I'm the only black face on the Vermont slopes. On the first trip, I've brought with me my beloved copy of Thoreau's *Walden; or, Life in the Woods,* not that I could understand much of it. I loved it anyway for its mysteriousness, and for how its *I* stands so solidly in the wilderness.

> Public opinion is a weak tyrant compared with our own private opinion. What a man thinks of himself, that it is which determines, or rather indicates, his fate.

When I return home, I look up each word that confuses in the hardcover *Webster's Dictionary.* I discover whole worlds of rebelliousness in Thoreau's words, fascinated by the prospect of being "born in the open pasture and suckled by a wolf."

I was drawn to orphan stories of all sorts, especially ones about wolves raising children. To stoke that fantasy, I also read the novel *Julie of the Wolves,* about an orphan Inuit girl, several times. After being sexually assaulted by Daniel, whom she stupidly marries even though he clearly has some kind of severe mental disability, Julie runs off to live in the Alaskan tundra with a wolf pack. I had some idea from *Walden* and *Julie of the Wolves* of a totalizing and enduring freedom of the wild—one that can only be obtained outside human society, particularly human family structures. By middle school, I already had this idea of myself as a person akin to Thoreau's first person, who would thrive by dropping out of the known social world.

Though literature is thick with this kind of adventure of the individual, the protagonists of these narratives are rarely, if ever, black. Toni Morrison's Baby Suggs makes the point: "Not a house in the country ain't packed to its rafters with some dead Negro's grief." In literature, being black is mostly about containment, or about the body as an obstacle to the wild freedom of roaming adventure. But it's a tricky containment, because the black body is contained in "blackness," and that blackness enables further containments. The containment of the body in its skin is the means by which we, as black people, are identifiable. This ability for us to be ID'd also facilitates our disappearance in plain sight. To disappear is opposite to the self-discovery made possible by encountering, with any measure of purity, a vast nature, no matter how badly we want it.

The night of Bruce's washing-machine-hose beating, the images would not leave me, and have not left me still. I sat with him upstairs in his room, watching his body swell up into big, bulbous bruises. He had not fought back. Instead, he hunkered and cried like a small boy, when in fact he was nudging up on manhood. This reduction was one result of his training by our tyrannical father. It was a private opinion made manifest in Bruce's body, a transference of thought into matter, a tyranny all supreme. Before this night, my brother was swallowed already—a person trapped within a person. He had ambitions that were entirely unrealistic: architect, golf course designer, business owner. He had begun to accumulate masses of random objects until his bedroom was so cluttered with things collected from yard sales and traded from friends that he was forced to sleep on a twin mattress on the floor. Though there were others less severe, this beating in particular seemed to cement him inside a very small world he'd likely never leave. One would think that the smaller your world, the safer you are.

What happens when a person goes missing?

My brother goes missing for almost two days in February 2017.

I find out on the Megabus en route from Pittsburgh, where I teach, to New York State, where I mostly live. It's a regular Megabus night, the cab darkened and quiet and most of us staring into the glow of our phones or watching something on our larger screens. I don't want to talk too loudly, so my voice is low, but since my mother is going deaf, it's difficult for her to hear me. Mostly, I listen.

My mother tells me the story of him being gone all night and her worrying. She says she thought maybe his car broke down on the side of the highway, and since he can't afford a cell phone he couldn't call. She also speculates that my brother's sudden disappearance is in some way connected to his owing past-due child support from a time when he was not working. There was a hearing, but where? She does not know. He could be dead by some sleight of hand, aggression, or accident. He could be in the hospital. Last year he became disoriented and dizzy at the wheel of his car, his hand tingling, which I revealed to him was likely a mini-stroke. My mother does not call the police. What would the police do? And anyway, as most black people understand, it is our work to stay clear of the police, as far from their notice as possible. My mother calls *me*. Absorbed by my busyness, I didn't, as is my habit, bother to answer or check my messages. I didn't answer until the next day, when the calls became more frequent, blowing up my phone.

To account for my brother's missingness is to put ideas together that in our United States don't ordinarily belong together. If we follow conventional knowledge, we follow a path that suggests that the *missing* black body is its very condition: the overt presence of the black body is an imposition. Any indication of "difference," particularly that which marks the black body as black, is an offense punishable by a range of containments, from regulation and imprisonment to death and genocide. The racist alt-right writer Colin Liddell put it very plainly when he wrote, "We should be asking questions like 'Does human civilization actually need the Black race?' 'Is Black genocide right?' and, if it is, 'What would be the best and easiest way to dispose of them?'" He wants to make a connection between genocide and order, the subtext being: allowing these niggers to exist causes chaos. Look how they run around stealing, selling drugs, raping, and killing. To "dispose" of something is to arrange it, to put it in place, to regulate it by containing it. Death, of course, is the ultimate containment; other, less final containments are conversely strategies toward genocide. Perfect chiasmus. Liddell's words are not simply rhetorical bluster. He wants to place the ideas in the room, uncloaked for the white readers who are looking for some language on which to hang their hatred.

When we were kids, our parents would drive from Connecticut down south to Florida once a year for a vacation to see our extended family. Our mother spent the entire day before travel cooking and preparing what seems to me now an extravagant cooler of potato salad, fried chicken, ham-and-cheese sandwiches, homemade pies, and grape and orange sodas. Our parents shared driving responsibilities, cursing at each other under their breath, while my brother and I lay in the wayback of the station wagon, sometimes with our feet dangling out the giant rear window. The middle bench seat between Bruce and me and the driving section gave us a feeling of being in our own world. We played games dividing up the junkyards filled with smashed cars, so that the first of us to spy a yard filled with metal junk could claim it was theirs. Bruce's and my aspirations of owning the virtually worthless filled our heads as we slept sweaty dreams in Carolina parking lots, pretending not to exist in case the cops or the Klan came tapping on the window. We were lucky. No one ever came tapping.

"Where is he exactly?" I ask, but at eighty-four years old my mother can't fathom a way of finding out. I spend over an hour frantically searching Google for information using my phone. Eventually, after searching the Connecticut Department of Correction Inmate Information database, I find Bruce's inmate name, number, and "Controlling Offense: purge civil commitment." His ex-wife confirms with my mother that my brother was arrested at the courthouse for some reason related to the unpaid child support.

How can he be put in jail for owing child support, I wonder, when he's been unemployed and unable to find a job? How can he look for a job to pay the child support he owes if he's in jail? What are the chances of getting a job to pay child support if you've been incarcerated? These are the times, says the President, when work for what we used to call blue-collar workers has been replaced by automation and the shipping away of jobs overseas—to Mexico and China. So where is the compassion for the American worker who, for a year, has no income? When Bruce was working, almost all of his paycheck went toward child support. His take-home pay was less than $100 a week. But this last point is not the point at all.

According to the Separated Parenting Access and Resource Center, once the court has determined that there is a valid support order (a valid claim that child support is owed), it's up to you to prove that you can't pay the amount owed and that you have no access to the money. If you fail to prove this, or if the judge believes you do have the money but don't want to cough it up, he or she can decide to slap you with criminal contempt and throw you in jail. On the other hand, "if the court agrees that your conduct is not willful and you don't have the ability to pay, you won't be found in contempt." That's the way it's supposed to work, anyway. A "purge" is the amount the court orders you to pay to "purge" you of contempt. In my brother's case, my mother had given him $10 for parking that morning. The judge finds my brother in contempt when he asks Bruce if he has any money. Bruce says no, thinking that the judge meant any amount of measure against the $13,000 he owes his ex-wife. The judge asks what Bruce used to pay for parking this morning and if he has any change in his pocket. He has $6 in change. "Then you have money, don't you?" the judge says. Bond is set at $1,500 and off he goes in handcuffs, easy as pie.

In the movies and once upon a time, the newly incarcerated were granted a single phone call. This call would be used to reach a loved one or a lawyer, presumably a person who needed to know about the jailing or could help. But I'm here to tell you there is no right to a single phone call, just as there is no black man hiding in the bushes in your front yard. When the phone rings, my mother tells me, a computer voice says that Bruce is trying to reach her from jail, but that in order for her to receive that call, she is required to add money to a prepaid account using her credit card. Something about the recorded voice signals "scam" to me, too, so I do a quick search to make sure the company is legit.

The "inmate phone service" they use at the Hartford Correctional Center, which, incidentally, has the same abbreviation as Hartford Community College, is called Securus—pronounced "secure us"—Technologies. It's like two cruel jokes at once. To load an account for my mother, I first must listen to a long, complicated recording detailing a rate system that befuddles me. Finally, I proceed through the steps and add $25, thinking that should be enough for a single quick phone call from my brother to my mother, so that he knows that she knows what's happened. That's the bone of it. Bruce became missing because, though there is an online record of where he is, for a while he is unreachable. He has no means to contact anyone to alert them to his whereabouts. My mother, whom the current technological moment has left in some other age, hasn't the ability to locate my brother beyond imagining him inside this vague concept, "jail." For her, it's like he's fallen inside a deep hole in the earth. As she likes to point out, if I had been out of the country, as I sometimes am, or hadn't just been paid from writing gigs, he might still be inside that hole.

*Miss,* the verb, has several definitions. To fail to hit, reach, or contact. To pass by without touching. To be too late to catch. To fail to attend, participate in, or watch as one is expected to or habitually does. To fail to see. To be unable to experience. To omit. When the word emerged in the late twelfth century its association was with regret, occasioned by loss or absence. But the adjectival version of *miss,* as in *missing,* was not recorded in English until the sixteenth century, and by 1845 became a way to describe military personnel not known to be present after battle. Whether missing soldiers were killed or captured is inaccessible data. In some parts of the world, we have transformed this state of indeterminacy into *disappeared.* Let me use this modified part of speech in an American sentence: "If recent trends continue, one in three black men in the United States will be disappeared into jail or prison in his lifetime." It strikes me that to miss or be missing, in my brother's case, requires a part-of-speech modification, too—one that could perhaps help me, at least, understand his particular condition, meaning the Condition of Bruce as it intersects with the subjugated identities we know are related, race and gender. To be *missing,* as a noun, would be the designation itself, like *a black,* the racial category without the noun *person.* A failed sight. A passed by without touching. A failed inclusion. An unattended. A missing.

Thoreau argues that "the mass of men lead lives of quiet desperation." It's an easy case to make when you can count on the centrality of your own unquestioned *I.* My brother, who is now fifty-five, in jail for the first time, is not singular in his missingness. Many of my first cousins have been incarcerated at some point in their lives, some serving long sentences for drug-related charges, others for more serious crimes. I myself once went missing for twenty-four hours—years ago, returning from the Washington, DC, party for my first book, swept up by the airport police for having (I didn't know) the tiniest bit of marijuana in my carry-on bag. My girlfriend at the time awaited me at Bradley airport, but of course I never emerged from the gate. One cousin, Dwayne, died from a heart attack after having chest pains for several days. He didn't have health insurance and was leery of going to the emergency room and racking up a bunch of unpayable bills, as he had once before. He might be called *an untouched*. In 2014, the Black and Missing Foundation reported that 64,000 black girls and women were missing in the United States. Passed by without noticing.

My brother and I grew up in Hartford, Connecticut, a small, poor and working-class city in one of the richest states in the country. The racial segregation, after my parents purchased their house in what was then a neighborhood equal parts black and white, began to anchor itself, thereby dividing us from all the thems. The Puerto Ricans in one neighborhood, the US-born black folks in another, the recent West Indian immigrants gaining a foothold around Albany Avenue, the artery connecting Hartford to the small, wealthy corner bordering West Hartford, where the white families from another time resided in their multiroom mansions with circular driveways. The whole of Hartford for me, though, was always a place I was set on leaving. By middle school I was desperate to roam, and by high school I was sneaking off to Manhattan, two and a half hours away, in order to experience what I understood as "the world." It occurs to me now that I don't think my brother has ever been to New York City. He has been locked in place while I have been profoundly out of place. Places uncomfortable and foreign felt more like appropriate contexts than the place where I was raised.

And here is the hard truth of the matter. If I am missing in any sense, it is a missingness I created for myself in order to be free, to reach toward Thoreau's solid *I*, roaming the world in wild adventure. I removed myself from the messy missingness that engulfs my own family—my brother, of course; my heart-attack-dead cousin; my ten-year-old niece already tracked by police, whom her school principal sent to her house in search of a stolen cell phone. Whenever I return home, I do so in a casual manner, just passing quickly through, so that I might avoid any contagion that might corrupt my good life. I am a welcomed ghost, but a ghost nonetheless, one called to a place forever fraught, the wallpapered walls peeling, the basement damp with wet clothes. It makes me feel bad to drive through the city where I lived for eighteen years. I get a sinking feeling. I often forget that the woman suing my brother for child support now is his second wife. I missed his marriage to his first wife entirely while I was living in the Bay Area after college. When I said before that the trick of the system is that it relies on the black exception, the thing is that I play right into it. I want to be your exception, because that means I get to escape, at least in part. I can be your shining example, and if I am, you can ignore the mass incarcerations, other disappearances, murders in plain internet view, what have you.

Via telephone I reach the officer on duty, who confirms, finally, that my brother is at the Hartford Correctional Center. While we're here, I'll pause and note the benign associations of the word *correction,* as if this place of punishment were a positive adjustment where humans are brought for the setting right of something previously misaligned. The logic is that the criminal element will be contained, rehabilitated, and released anew into society after the sentence is served. Jail, though, is mostly a holding tank for people too poor to post bail while they await their trial or hearing. Sixty-three percent of people in jail have not been convicted of any crime; they have been arrested and are trying to post bail. Under the law, they are presumed innocent. Bail, when it comes to minor crimes and civil infringements, is basically the freedom tax on the poor for being poor. The word *correction* is simply one of the many mindfucks of the way things work. If your jail has a population of 73 percent pretrial, in this case men, then why do you call it a correctional center, when there is nothing clearly determined that needs to be corrected?

All I have to do to get my brother "corrected" is to bring $1,500 cash the next day for his release, pending a new hearing in a month. My mother's voice sounds small and tired when she hears the news. "Did you talk to him? Is he OK?"

I think of a photo of Bruce I found recently when scrounging through my mother's old photo albums. He is about twenty years old and standing in the driveway of my parents' house, wearing a crisp white T-shirt, jeans, and a silver watch. His face is soft, thoughtful. He does not appear to know his picture is being taken.

He seems, in the photo, relatively "free." Not lost. I guess sometimes you can't tell. I am writing this story because it is impossible for me not to write it. It's my story too. And I keep trying to pull myself authentically into it. The photo albums themselves tell a story of an intense desire to capture our lives, the lives of my mother and her four sisters, my grandparents, my father, my brother, me. A record of existence like everyone's, but also a kind of testimony to black life, even and especially when we become uniquely aware of the multiple means by which black life is confined, made irrelevant, and eradicated.

What happens when a black person goes missing? I know that *I* am not missing in the same sense as my brother, but I also know that I am not entirely free. When I lived in western Massachusetts in graduate school, I was pulled over by police regularly. One night after a late-night fight with my then girlfriend, I went for a drive and was pulled over by police, who asked me simply, "What are you doing out at this hour?" What should we say in these moments of encounter? I am human. I breathe and eat and shit. I have ambitions. It is as ordinary and extraordinary as the first words of any nineteenth-century slave narrative: "I was born." I contribute something to society. I am not a vagrant. I sweat and ache and love and mourn. There will be many who will mourn for me if I die.

The literal opposite of *missing* would probably be *present*, but in my mind it's *free*, the radical opportunity to be present. This brings me back to *Walden*, which, honestly, I despise now for its naïve arguments about what is necessary for life. Thoreau never asks a basic question: What is a livable life? What does a human need to enact one's not-lostness, one's freedom? Though Bruce was incarcerated for only two days, it was for a civil offense, not a criminal one. What's recognized in the moment of random, unexpected jailing is the fragility of one's freedom.

The night before I found out about Bruce's being in jail, I hosted the writer Maggie Nelson in one of the university's big reading series. As it turned out, she read from a work in progress on freedom. Freedom, she asks: What is it?

I, too, have been attempting to think through the possibility that freedom—real freedom—might not be possible within society. We hardly even know ourselves in our ongoing encounter with the other, producing on the one hand what Du Bois calls double-

consciousness, and on the other, for black people in 2017, a radically distorted version of black selfhood. What else is possible given
the prolific, penetrating, and ongoing looking at oneself through
the eyes of an other?

To answer the question "What is freedom?" Nelson turns to lots
of thinkers, including Hannah Arendt. Arendt notes a difference
between political freedom and "inner freedom," the "inward space
into which men [*sic*] may escape from external coercion and *feel*
free." In my own work I have referred to this idea as a "freedom
feeling," a sensation of freedom even when actual freedom might
not exist. What I love about Arendt's distinction is that, for her,
in order to experience inner freedom you must first know outer,
political freedom. We like to think about this inner, "nonpoliti-
cal" freedom, she basically says, but we wouldn't know anything
about it had we "not first experienced a condition of being free as
a worldly tangible reality."

Neither I nor my brother is free in the way that Arendt describes. As a teenager, I often sat in front of my bedroom mirror in
an attempt to recognize myself. Many distortions from other people's perceptions needed to be smoothed out. Something about
an attempt to see my face as it was without mediation became, I believe, important for my growing sense of self, and thereby a sense
of my own power, real or imagined. Feeling free is a relationship
to *being* as much as it is to movement, travel, a sense of one's own
body in unfamiliar places. When Bruce moved away from home,
he moved in with a woman he'd just married. After he and his wife
divorced, he moved back into our mother's house, our father long
dead, and settled sadly into his old bedroom—the most familiar,
perhaps, of places.

The next night, instead of heading to East Hampton for a weekend away from the university, I end up staying the night in Brooklyn and waking up at 5 a.m. to catch a 7 a.m. Amtrak train to Hartford. My mother and I do some maneuvering around the ATM
withdrawal limits and pull together $1,500, in twenties and fifties,
which I stuff into a zippered compartment of my computer bag. In
the waiting room at the jail, the windows one approaches to talk to
an officer on duty are blackened so that you cannot see whom you
are talking to. Through a muted talk hole, the cop tells me that
it's going to take two to three hours to process my brother's re-

lease and that once I start the paperwork I cannot leave the premises. There's no vending machine, so I run across the street and grab fries at Burger King, then put my elderly mother in an Uber home. I have magazines and set up my iPad connection via my personal hot spot. At one point, I go into the bathroom and guzzle the Patrón nip I have in my pocket. Time passes quickly. The gate opens dramatically when anyone leaves or enters the door where I believe the release will occur. People—women only, actually—come to visit relatives. The guard comes out. The women go through the metal detector. The gate closes. I feel a tickle on my neck and realize that the rosary beads I bought in Mexico, even though I have no religion, have snapped, and the Jesus has fallen down into my bra.

After only an hour and a half, the officer on duty takes my cash and gives me a receipt. He instructs me to drive around the building and wait on the side of the road for Bruce to exit. I wait at Gate 5. You'd think there would be an official pickup area, but it's just a dead-end street, nondescript save the random fact that my father and I would often pass by that jail before the street was blocked. We'd drive over the railroad tracks on our way back from the bowling alley where we went on the off Sundays I wasn't forced by my mother to attend church, noticing but not really noticing the stone building with the barbed-wire fencing. Whenever I thought about who might be locked inside, I imagined rapists and murderers, or psychopaths like Charles Manson after I'd snuck and read my mother's copy of *Helter Skelter*.

Bruce comes out carrying a small, transparent plastic bag and a calendar. He hugs me long and hard. I can feel his body shaking as he towers over me and says, "Thank you, thank you, thank you." He tells me that his cell contained more than thirty men, all in situations similar to his, unable to pay bail. "Did you talk to each other?" I ask. "Not really," he says. "Mostly we just slept. There were no windows or clock so you never knew what time it was." The stench of bodies was overwhelming, he tells me, very stuffy, the air stale and hot, the smell of shit and piss from the open toilets. We drive down streets familiar and drenched in the memory of the life I lived before I left home. On Tower Avenue, the long street that leads to my mother's house, we pass the old house of Mrs. Alberta, a friend of my mother's so frightening to me as a child that I never addressed her in any way. She'd whack her children right in front of us, demanding their respect and discipline. The house looks so much smaller than it did when we were children. We pass a once-grand house on a hill, boarded up now, that belonged to a preacher and his typing-teacher wife. He was scandalized after being caught stealing money from his own church. When we finally pull into my mother's driveway, I'm staring at the shabby decay of her house, the three shutters that remain demanding paint. My brother says, "Seriously. I don't know what I would have done."

The bail system for nonviolent, misdemeanor offenses is currently under intense scrutiny in this country. More and more media outlets are reporting on jurisdictions that have increased their jailed population exponentially over the past two decades by locking up people who can't afford to post bail. Some, like Kalief Browder and Sandra Bland, suffer the direst consequences. At the less fatal end of the spectrum, pretrial detention keeps the poor poor. They get a choice: We'll release you if you plead guilty. It's a systematic and some say *illegal* practice that keeps commercial bail bond corporations making profit off poor people and coercing guilty pleas from those who may or may not have done the crime. As it happens, during day two of my brother's jailing, he received a voice message on our mother's landline for a job interview that day. It was a good job, paying well over the $10 minimum wage he'd been making at his last position. During his eventual quick Securus phone call with my mother, she alerted him to this fact. He thought about that, he said from his stuffed jail cell—the missed opportunity.

At my mother's house, things are surreally normal. She's propped up on the couch watching Martha Stewart on TV. "She's making something with 'ramps,'" my mother says. "What's a ramp?" I tell her it's a wild leek, like a kind of onion. Suddenly we're all in a discussion about Martha Stewart's recipes and her friendship with Snoop Dogg. "Are you spending the night?" she asks. "No," I say, "I have to get on the road in an hour or so, need to catch the last ferry. Deadlines tomorrow. Need to work." I am, in fact, desperate to disappear. But I need my brother's help in order to do so. I don't have my car, and my mother can no longer drive the hour and a half to New London and back.

To reach the freedom feeling, I must first reach the dock in New London, where the ferry departs to travel across Long Island

Sound to Orient Point. But in order to do that, I need to ask Bruce to come with us so that he can drive the car back home. I ask this of the very recently incarcerated brother whose wallet and other personal effects are still in custody at the Hartford Correctional Center. To retrieve these objects, he must return to the jail during an appointed time window on a weekday, and since he was released on a weekend, he is not in possession of his driver's license. My mother and brother and I reason it out, ignoring certain facts. We say, "Well, he *does* have a license and he's accompanied by two people with licenses. That should be enough." We say, "What are the odds that he's pulled over?" The risk we all take together is great. It's a risk I facilitate to some degree, unwilling as I am to stay one night in Hartford. I drive the fifty minutes to New London in my mother's aging Dodge Neon with a rebuilt engine so loud we can barely hear each other speak.

Above the engine's grumbling roar, I lecture my family on the school-to-prison pipeline and the systematic, institutional effort to disappear as many black people as possible. As the volume of my voice increases to drown out any protestations by my mother, who's always been more a bootstrap-theory gal, despite the evidence supplied by Exhibit A, Bruce, I feel an old impulse taking over: the impulse to dominate the situation, to control it. It's all swirling out of control, so I do what I do best, which is to try to analyze things to death. I gain my footing at the expense of my mother, who still has optimism for some long-annihilated black American future, and my brother, who is nodding heartily at everything I say. Repression occurs on the infinitesimal level. It becomes so much a part of you that you hardly feel it. Your heart rate increases when you see the police drive by, but you feel relief the second the car turns the corner. You've been spared, however temporarily, and that gives you peace.

KAI MINOSH PYLE

# Autobiography of an Iceheart

FROM *Prism*

## *1. Hunger as a Way of Life*

THE FIRST TIME I heard a windigo story, I was still a small child
living through yet another harsh Wisconsin winter. The storyteller,
an Anishinaabe elder brought in by the school to help young Native children connect with our cultures, had a knack for imitating
the sound of creaking trees and howling gusts and for dropping
long, dramatic silences at just the right moments. I wish I could
tell you his name, because Anishinaabe stories always, always come
with lineage, and windigo stories especially, but all I can remember from that day is the way he described the creature.

"It was as tall as the tips of the pine trees that surrounded it," he
told us in a hushed voice. "No meat on its bones, just skin wrapped
around its skeleton. When it opened its mouth, a terrible windy
sound rushed through the forest. It was human once, you know.
All windigos were once people, just like you and me. But this windigo, one cold winter all the food ran out. One by one the villagers
started to die. And the last one left, that one had no choice but to
eat that ripe human flesh."

We were gripping the edges of our seats, eyes glued to the storyteller, who needed no picture books to paint an image for us. He
let out a long sigh, and continued: "From that moment on, what
once was a man became a windigo. It was seized by an incredible
hunger—a hunger for more human flesh. With each person it ate,
it grew, until it was the size of the trees. But with each one it ate,
its hunger grew just as much. It could never be satisfied. And so it
kept hunting."

The elder bared his teeth with a small growl. Some of us jumped.

"Maybe . . . it's still out there hunting now."

I remember feeling like my skin had gone cold all over. My eyes were wide, and when I looked around my peers had the same look on their faces. It was nearly time for lunch, and the feeling of hunger in my stomach suddenly felt ominous. I've kept that story with me for some fifteen years, carrying it in the back of my mind. Haunted by the sound of that windigo, by the sight of pine trees, by the feeling of hunger itself.

## 2. *Culture-Bound*

When I tried to look up Anishinaabe culture and mental illness for the first time in my university library's catalogue, desperate for some kind of cultural guidance, I found almost nothing—except the windigo psychosis. Academics are obsessed with the windigo psychosis. Ever since it was first noticed by white observers (noted in *The Jesuit Relations* as early as 1661), the rare but occasional habit of individual Anishinaabe and other northern Algonquian people to become disturbed by a deep desire to consume human flesh has fascinated outsiders.

There are records of individuals taken by this disorder, people who engaged in cannibalism even in circumstances other than dire need. In some cases, the person-turned-windigo was only suffused with an incredibly pressing urge to become a cannibal, but never actually committed the deed.

Anthropologists have called this a "culture-bound syndrome," a mental disorder found only in certain, specific cultures across the world. Other illnesses deemed culture-bound syndromes include the sickness of those who fall under the evil eye, and *susto,* a Latin American phenomenon characterized by a sense of fright due to trauma. Some have debated if modern eating disorders, like anorexia and bulimia, may in fact be culture-bound syndromes found only in modern industrial societies.

I am not sure if the concept of culture-bound syndromes supports or disrupts the idea promoted by some Indigenous activists, that all mental illness among our people is caused by capitalism and colonization.

### 3. On Roots and Rootedness

I have combed my Anishinaabemowin dictionary for words that mean "crazy." Instead of a single word, there are several. In fact, there are four separate roots, maybe more that I don't yet know, that translate to one word in English. The first root is giiwashkwe, which by itself means "she is dizzy, feels unsteady." If you add the suffix that refers to a person's nature or character, you get giiwash-kweyaadizi: she is crazy, insane.

The next root is gagiibaad, which means something like "fool-ish" when attached to various endings. Gagiibaadizi means "she is foolish, silly, naughty." Gagiibaadaanagidoone means "she talks crazy, nonsense." And gagiibaazinam—"she visualizes crazy things, hallucinates."

The third root, giiwan, is difficult to translate. The dictionary lists its meaning as "disordered," but the words that it creates are more varied: giiwaningwaam, "she has a bad dream, a nightmare"; giiwanimo, "she lies, deceives"; giiwanaadizi, "she is crazy, insane."

The final root is mamiidaawendam. I've seen this word trans-lated in several ways: "she is struggling with her thoughts," "she is disturbed in her mind," "she is crazy." When I asked a speaker about it, they said it could mean anything from having a certain thought that you can't get out of your head, to being conflicted over a decision, to being mentally ill.

I whisper these words to myself as I read them, turning their meanings over in my mind. Am I giiwashkweyaadizi, dizzy-crazy? Am I gagiibaadizi, foolish-crazy? I return to mamiidaawendam over and over again, a self-fulfilling prophecy. The struggle with my thoughts continues even now.

### 4. Closets

I knew none of these Anishinaabemowin words when I first went crazy at age sixteen. Instead, what I had was a shut closet door I could hide behind, and a list of various mental illnesses printed out on several tear-stained sheets of paper. The rest of my family was out of town, leaving me to break down in utter desolation. After lying on the floor in silence for what may have been hours,

I finally sat up and pulled out the phone. I stared at the numbers for another minute, then pressed them.

My mother's voice was nonchalant, cheery. Mine was ragged, raw.

"I need you to come home," I said, throat scratchy and nose plugged from the hours of crying.

"Why? What's wrong?"

"I just need you to come home," I said again, and hung up.

## 5. *Tell Me (You Can Help)*

Despite my early flirtations with a rainbow of diagnoses—major depressive disorder, generalized anxiety, panic disorder, attention deficit hyperactivity disorder, autism, post-traumatic stress disorder, gender identity disorder—I managed to survive the next five years armed with a basketful of pills and a revolving door of psychotherapists.

The first therapist who assessed me listened to me talk for a while, then informed me, "You're going to need someone with a PhD."

The first psychiatrist who assessed me called me a bitch to my face in front of my parents, who said nothing in response.

My first long-term therapist once had me pick "my spirit animal" out of a book based on my horoscope, and refused to back down when I complained that it was offensive to my ancestral spiritual traditions. I stopped seeing her after we fought over my insistence that I shouldn't have to put up with being ostracized at school for being transgender and Indigenous.

"You can't change the way the world works," she said to me— shouted, really.

"That's exactly what I'm gonna do," I shouted back, and left her office for the last time.

I gave up on therapy entirely after my final therapist went on an extended rant about how dangerous the streets were with people of color walking around, apparently having forgotten my ethnicity in the face of my light skin tone.

The stories go on. There was the university therapist who believed I was faking my mental illnesses because I seemed "just so charming and put-together" in her office. The one who told me my diagnoses were wrong after a two-hour session together. The one who threatened me with institutionalization.

## 6. The Care and Keeping of Indians

Opened in 1903, the Canton Indian Insane Asylum served for just over thirty years as the single mental institution designated specifically for the care of insane American Indians. It was finally closed in 1934 after investigations revealed pervasive inhumane treatment of its Indigenous patients. The time period during which the asylum, known popularly as Hiawatha, was functional corresponds almost perfectly with the height of the Indian boarding-school era in the United States.

In 2016, Carla Joinson published *Vanished in Hiawatha,* a near-comprehensive account of the asylum's story from its origins to its downfall. The appendices list the names of every person who was ever institutionalized there. When I first found a copy in the local bookstore, I flipped to them immediately, following the names with my finger, hesitating for just a second whenever I reached one with the designation "(Chippewa)" next to it. The list includes the ages and diagnoses of each patient, and I was shocked by how many of the diagnoses were familiar to me—chronic depression, melancholia, manic-depressive, feeble-minded, imbecile—whether from my medical paperwork or from whispered insults throughout my life. I was shocked, too, by how many were the same age as I was when they were admitted—or when they died.

I would like to tell you about the conditions revealed in the book, of how the patients, known as "inmates," were treated. I would tell you the stories of Isabella Porter and Gaagigeyaashiik Martha Smith, Anishinaabe women whose lives were cut unthinkably short. I would tell you how over half the patients were under the age of thirty, some as young as sixteen. But I cannot bear to recount their pain, can barely stand to look at it myself.

What I will tell you is that in 2012, the first Honoring and Remembering Ceremony was held for the 121 people who had died while in the "care" of the Canton Indian Insane Asylum. It was held on the golf course that today encompasses the graveyard where they are buried.

## 7. On Recovery and Revelation

Though threatened with it on more than one occasion, I was never actually put in a mental institution. Instead I was placed in what is known as "intensive outpatient therapy," a process in which you attend group therapy every day for approximately eight weeks, plus individual sessions with both a psychologist and a psychiatrist.

The psychologist was, unlike most psychologists I had encountered, a relatively young Latina woman who kept an impressive rapport with the constantly shifting array of patients. Early on she pinned my motivation, or lack thereof, to the wall and forced me to recognize it hanging there.

"What did you accomplish yesterday?" she asked me. This was a reference to the worksheets we filled out every day, detailing our intended activities and how they would help our recovery.

"Nothing," I said without emotion. I rarely felt emotion in those days. Being crazy, for me, was not about sadness, or anger, or paranoia, but an overwhelming sense of disconnection from reality. Sometimes—often—that meant days lying in darkness, moving only to use the bathroom. Sometimes it meant lost time, when I would wake suddenly with no recollection of the past hours. Sometimes it meant scratching my skin until I bled, either out of complete lack of care for my body or out of genuine disparagement for my sheer existence. "Nothing" was my life.

My psychologist gave me a shrewd look. "Why nothing?"

"I don't know," I said, peeved. "I just didn't feel like doing any of it."

"The thing is," she said, eyeing my evasive apathy, "the only way you are going to recover is if you want to recover. Do you want to recover?"

I thought about it, really deeply, for the first time. And I said, "I don't think I do."

She leaned back with a satisfied smile. "There. See? You have to be honest with yourself. When you want to recover, you'll start making progress."

Great, I thought. How do I make myself want to recover? But she had a point. I felt lighter already, even if I was still shrouded in dark clouds. I don't want to recover. Not yet. It was liberating.

## 8. On Depression and Birchbark

There's a sacred story, what we call in Anishinaabemowin an aa-dizookaan, that I read for the first time in a book called *Centering Anishinaabeg Studies*. This time, I can trace the lineage of the story: Anishinaabe elder Ignatia Broker told it to Kathleen Dolores West-cott, who then recorded it in an essay coauthored with Eva Marie Garroutte. In the story, a woman loses her husband and falls into grief so deep that not even the year-long ceremonial practices of her people are able to touch it. She leaves her village and spends two years sitting at the foot of a birch tree, Wiigwaasaatig, day and night, numb to the world.

Her community is confused and concerned, so they do what Anishinaabe people do in such circumstances: they ask the elders. Garroutte and Westcott recall the elders' words: "She's thinking. She's thinking on our behalf. She is working on this carefully within her heart. This wouldn't be happening if there weren't something coming our way that we need to be prepared for. She's been called to go out and learn about it . . . We have to support her as though she's in a prolonged search for guidance, for com-munion. We may not even be alive when whatever it is she's seek-ing to prepare us for occurs." And it is said that the community was excited to continue to support her however they could, even though they did not yet understand.

And sure enough, one day in the summer of the second year of her vigil, the woman felt something stir in the tree behind her. Wiigwaasaatig spoke to her, calling her granddaughter and ac-knowledging her pain. Then Wiigwaasaatig taught her how to peel off its skin and to use the gifts of the other plant peoples to cre-ate baskets—beautiful things so tightly sewn that they could even carry water. Finally Wiigwaasaatig instructed her to return to her community and to pass on the knowledge she had been gifted. So she did, and her people loved her for it, and she began to heal.

## 9. Complex

The first time I talked with the outpatient therapy psychologist, she asked me about my diagnoses. Looking down at my chart, where my list of symptoms had been laid out, my body and history gutted open for anyone to see, she asked, "Have you ever experienced any trauma?"

I thought about it. I thought about the sudden death of my grandfather in the line of duty as a fireman when I was thirteen. I thought about the suicide of my good friend, a queer kid like me, my senior year of high school. I thought about the day I was sexually assaulted, and about the two terrifying years afterward, when I had to attend classes with the perpetrator. But mostly I thought about little things: the girl who had hit me with basketballs while calling me a sissy, the whispered taunts of "faggot" and "dyke" and "dirty squaw," the kids who cheered "Retard! Retard!" while pelting me with sticks on the playground.

"I got picked on a lot as a kid," I said simply.

The psychologist looked at me carefully for a long moment. "You know," she said gently, "a lot of new research shows that bullying can have the same kind of effects on a person that a single, major traumatic event has. It's called C-PTSD, complex post-traumatic stress disorder. The little things compound on each other and build up over time."

I didn't know it then, but research suggests that the rates of PTSD among Native children are about the same as the rates among combat veterans. I didn't know it then, but my bones did.


## 10. Brutality

In 2014, police killings of American Indians briefly got media attention. Though it was unfortunately often framed as being "the police killings no one is talking about" (as though African Americans were needlessly taking up all the space available, as though there is a limited space and time to discuss police violence), it spurred a bout of research that revealed that Native people, especially young Native men, are killed by the police at one of the highest rates in the United States.

It was the names and the stories I was obsessed with. Jeanetta Riley, Suquamish, "pregnant, homeless, and threatening suicide." Mah-hi-vist Goodblanket, Cheyenne and Arapaho, "diagnosed with oppositional defiant disorder." Christine Tahhahwah, Comanche, bipolar and off her medications. Paul Castaway, Rosebud Sioux, shot while holding a knife to his own neck. Karen Day-Jackson, Eastern Shawnee, a bipolar woman who allegedly shouted "shoot me" as the cops did just that. Philip Quinn, Anishinaabe like me, schizophrenic and suicidal, killed in the city where I now live.

Researchers at Claremont Graduate University estimate that fully half of all Native people killed by police had some form of mental illness. The news reports brim with stories of Indigenous people, young and old, of all genders, killed after their families or even they themselves called for help. The streets fill with Native activists crying their names. My loved ones and I wonder if we will be next.

## 11. Scratches

I was sitting in the office of the school's emergency therapist. She tugged on my arm until it was extended, forearm upward, to reveal the marks that showed just how crazy my illness had made me. The room was silent except for the scratches of her pen on paper as she assessed the damage.

"Do you know why you're here?" she asked me. Her voice was low and tired, like she'd done this a million times before.

"Uh," I said, and shook my arm a little. "Yeah. I guess." The night before I'd made a blog post about wanting to kill myself. Then, frightened by my own desires, I sent it to a friend who forced me to go see the emergency therapist.

"Look," she told me, "I'm not going to mince words. If you post anything else like that again, I've told your friend to call 911. The police will come and take you to the hospital. You'll have to stay there until they clear you to leave."

I said nothing. I was wallowing in the unfairness of it all, the fact that I couldn't even have an outburst of honest emotion without being threatened with law enforcement. But I accepted the anti-infection cream and bandages she offered, and I didn't post anything like it ever again.

## *12. Statistics*

The attempted suicide rate for Indigenous people is double that of non-Indigenous people.

Of transgender Indigenous people, over half have attempted suicide.

## *13. The Day My Life Turned Over*

The day my life turned over went like this:

I lay in the darkness all night. All day, too; my room was adjacent to the bathroom, and I had a not-insubstantial stash of nonperishable food that could be eaten without the use of kitchen appliances, so I could pretty well avoid leaving the dark imposed by my heavy blinds. I knew it was night mainly because when I refreshed my online news feeds, no new information appeared. I couldn't sleep, though. Mental illness traditionally fucks up one's sleep schedule, but on top of that I had a diagnosed case of delayed sleep phase disorder to deal with. So I tossed and turned for hours and hours.

Sometime before the birds began to do their damnedest to wake up the neighborhood, I got out of bed. My bones seemed weighted, but there was this anxious feeling throughout my limbs that made lying down for even one more minute seem impossible. Without turning on a light, I groped my way down the hallway into the kitchen.

Instead of a cupboard, we had a rickety plywood shelf that some previous inhabitant had installed. This was where we kept spices, sugar, flour, soup cans, and most importantly, tea. I wandered over to the shelf and squinted at its contents until their labels became clear; I had forgotten my glasses. The tea declared itself to be something called Lapsang souchong, a new addition my roommate had recently brought home to try. Figuring it probably couldn't make anything worse than it already was, I set the kettle to boil and brewed the tea. Thankfully, none of my roommates stirred.

As I sipped that smoky tea, light started to come into the kitchen. I followed its source to the living room, where sunlight had just begun to crawl over the tips of the Chicago rooftops and through the large, east-facing windows.

I had been up for over twenty-four hours. Feeling more awake than I had in days, I curled up on the couch and gazed out the windows with interest. The birds were chirping clear as day now. Once in a while, unusually early risers walked down the street past our front door. I cupped the mug of tea in my hands and began to hum a sunrise song.

### 14. On Assholes and Icehearts

My favorite aadizookaan is one not very easily told in polite company. It, too, is a windigo story. The most well-known version was told by a Bois Forte Anishinaabe man, Midaasoganzh, to the Meskwaki anthropologist William Jones, but I have heard it slightly differently: So it goes that a windigo was once again terrorizing the Anishinaabe people. They had done everything they could to destroy it, but still it continued to devastate their villages. Finally, our culture hero Nanaboozhoo reached the land where it was rampaging. He called on his friend Zhingos, the weasel, to help him hatch a plan. At the time, Zhingos was pure white and tiny. The perfect size for Nanaboozhoo's bright idea.

"Listen, my friend," Nanaboozhoo said. "I know how to kill the windigo. Its power is controlled by its heart, which is made of ice. If only we can destroy its heart, its power, too, will be vanquished."

Zhingos frowned. "But how do we get to its heart without being eaten?"

And Nanaboozhoo grinned and grinned, and told Zhingos the rest of his plan.

They waited until the windigo was nearby. Just as they expected, it came barreling into the village, looking for humans to devour. It barely noticed the tiny white weasel that scurried up behind it.

Zhingos looked at Nanaboozhoo as if to ask, Are you sure about this? Nanaboozhoo nodded and gave a thumbs-up. And without hesitation, that Zhingos leapt up, grabbed the windigo with its little claws, and crawled his way right up that windigo's asshole! Yes, up through its intestines he crawled, chewing his way through until finally he reached its icy heart. When he did, he chewed with all his might until the windigo faltered and then—fell.

Zhingos came creeping out the dead windigo's mouth at last to find Nanaboozhoo standing there. Around him the villagers were slowly coming closer to see who had defeated the dreaded windigo.

"How about that!" Zhingos exclaimed, proud of his deed. He went to preen, but realized at that moment that his beautiful white fur was now . . . well, less than pristine. Nanaboozhoo noticed too. With a chuckle, he picked the weasel up by the tip of his tail and, without hesitation, dipped him in a nearby stream of cold water. When he came out, Zhingos was shining and white again. All but the tip of his tail.

## 15. History

In 1907, the North-West Mounted Police of Canada arrested an Anishinaabe man for the murder of a windigo. Zhaawano-giizhigo-gaabaw, or Jack Fiddler as he was known in English, was famed throughout northern Ontario for his spiritual power and, in particular, his skill at detecting and killing windigos.

The Mounties were the first whites most of the community had ever seen. Looking for an excuse to impose Canadian law on the Indigenous north, they arrested Zhaawano-giizhigo-gaabaw and his brother for the murder of the latter's daughter-in-law, Wahsakapeequay. During a brief trip outside of their jail, Zhaawano-giizhigo-gaabaw escaped—and hung himself.

Fourteen windigos, he claimed to have slain. A hero of the community. Three years after his death, the Anishinaabe people of northwestern Ontario agreed to sign a treaty with the government and accept Canadian law. Today, Indigenous people look back on it as a moment when sovereignty was lost. But those fourteen windigos stalk me. I see Wahsakapeequay, who never succumbed to cannibalism, who was only delirious with illness before her father-in-law killed her. The laws of my people sanctioned this. I cannot judge the decision of a hundred years ago.

But I can mourn.

## *16. On Stories and Dreams*

I have heard many windigo stories, and many stories of windigo slayers.

Only once, I heard a story about a windigo who was cured. Like the story and its teller's name, the instructions for the cure are lost to me.

Only once, I dreamt of windigos. There was no cure for them there, either. But there were windigos who no longer wanted to be windigos. There were windigos who learned to fight their own natures, and there were windigos who learned to love again.

## *17. Sunrise*

Some days, I am deeply bothered by not knowing exactly how my ancestors would have treated me, a crazy transgender Métis-Anishinaabe. Would they have scorned me? Cared for me? Told me stories about others like me? Would they have had a name for me? Would it have been a good name, an affirming name, or an insulting one? Would they have had ceremonies for me? Would the ceremonies have worked?

I joke with my friends that I have gone through crazy and come out the other side. This does not mean I am no longer crazy. Maybe recovery works like that for some people, but I am not one of them. I will be crazy, in some form or another, for the rest of my life.

As I learn my language and my culture, these things weigh heavily on my mind. When I am mindful, however, they are not just questions of the past. They are also urgent questions for the future. If we revitalize our language, how will we talk about mental illness? How do we want to treat people with mental illnesses within our culture? There are things we bring with us from the past, things we come from in the present, and things we imagine for the future. We are creating the next world, one thought, one action, one movement at a time.

I have never woven a basket out of birchbark, but I can learn. I have always spoken English, not Anishinaabemowin, but I can pronounce giiwanaadizi one syllable at a time. I have gone through crazy and come out the other side, but I have come bearing gifts. Come, let's sing a sunrise song and melt the heart of a windigo.

GARY TAYLOR

# Death of an English Major

FROM *Tampa Bay Times*

I DID NOT anticipate this death. No one warned me that being chair of an English department meant that I would have to "manage" the grief, despair and rage caused by the political murder of one of our students.

The longer you teach, the more inevitable it becomes that you will have to deal, at some point, with the death of a student—especially if you teach, as I do, in a university with almost 1,200 English majors. Young people drink too much, and drive too fast; they experiment, sometimes dangerously. In Florida, they can be killed by a hurricane. Everywhere in America, they are exceptionally prone to depression, anxiety and suicide (and becoming more so all the time).

But Maura Binkley, who died early this month in a Tallahassee yoga studio, was the target of premeditated political violence. The white, straight American male who is accused of killing her went to that yoga studio intending to kill women.

Maura was not the only woman he is alleged to have killed, or the only woman who was shot. But Maura, unlike the others, was an English major. She was many other things, too; she was a treasury of particulars and potentials. But her death intersected with my life because she majored in English. I majored in English, too, many years ago, and now I chair the English department at Florida State, where she was, until last Friday, taking classes in the history of the English language, American literature and rhetoric.

I suspect that Maura Binkley was asked, at some point, as almost every English major is asked nowadays, "What can you do with a major like that? What good does it do?" Perhaps that's why the

*New York Times* misreported that she was a journalism major: journalism is practical and useful; English, not so obviously. And in the whirlpool of grief and rage after Maura's death, I have asked myself the same question: What good can I do? And it is not just a personal question. After all, Maura chose this, too. Maura's classmates chose this.

Other Shakespeare scholars might be able to stand in front of a room full of traumatized students and quote Horatio's response to the death of a young student named Hamlet: "Good night, sweet prince, and flights of angels sing thee to thy rest." Other Shakespeare scholars might point out that, four hundred years ago, the word "prince" was gender-neutral, and would therefore be perfectly appropriate for Maura Binkley. Other Shakespeare scholars might explain the traditional literary metaphor that equates death and sleep.

But although Shakespeare probably believed in angels, I do not. The Shakespeare quotation that first came to me, when I learned of Maura's death, was something much more brutal: "Why should a dog, a horse, a rat have life / And thou no breath at all? Thou'lt come no more, / Never, never, never, never, never." King Lear speaks these words to his young murdered daughter, half pretending to himself that she can still hear him. These are not words that any parent wants to speak, or to hear at a moment like this.

Father Lear also says, to his dead daughter Cordelia, "I killed the slave that was a-hanging thee." Shakespeare does not name the murderer, and unlike the press I will not dignify or memorialize the man who murdered Maura by repeating his name, or rehearsing his pathetic biography.

But Shakespeare does tell us something useful about the kind of man capable of murdering Cordelia, or Maura. In Shakespeare the unnamed "captain" explains, in an earlier scene, "I cannot draw a cart, nor eat dried oats; if it be man's work, I'll do 't." Killing an innocent and defenseless young woman is, for that nameless captain, what distinguishes him from a mere domesticated animal. It is what defines his manhood.

Unfortunately, anybody who is paying attention knows men like this, men whose identity and self-importance depends on their capacity for violence. The man who is accused of killing Maura was one of them. The man accused of killing eleven people in a Pittsburgh synagogue was one of them. The man accused of killing a random black man and a random black woman in a Kentucky supermarket, the week before, was one of them. The man who killed forty-nine people in a gay nightclub in Orlando was one of them. These men were all trying to kill generalities. The man who stands accused of murdering Maura was not seeing a luminous living individual; he was seeing a specimen of the category "woman," a category he hated. From his perspective, the category "woman" owed him something, something he as a "man" was entitled to have. The category "woman" had no right to choose to refuse him. Before the gun killed Maura, the generalization did.

What we do, in English, and in the humanities more broadly, what we teach, what we celebrate and investigate, is human particularity. That is why we become obsessed with individual authors, why we savor specificities of phrasing, why we pounce upon and explore a single word. It's why we value, above all, writers capable of telling many different stories, populated by many varieties of being, articulated in a kaleidoscope of styles. It's why I, personally, have always been most fascinated by playwrights, from Aeschylus to August Wilson: dialogue releases us from the monologues of one mind, clan, tradition.

We grieve, now, the loss of all the "brave, bold and kind" particularities of Maura Binkley: the sound of her voice, explaining the relationship between Old English and modern German; her cute cat backpack; her idealistic ambition to get accepted into the Teach for America program; her protesting gun violence earlier this year at the Florida capitol. "There was a daily beauty in her life," we can say, quoting Shakespeare but changing the pronouns, "that made his ugly."

What we can do, as English majors, is write about the particulars of her beautiful promise. What we can do, as Americans, is dedicate ourselves to erasing the ugliness that erased her.

JIA TOLENTINO

# The Rage of the Incels

FROM *The New Yorker*

LATELY I HAVE been thinking about one of the first things that
I ever wrote for the internet: a series of interviews with adult virgins, published by the *Hairpin*. I knew my first subject personally,
and, after I interviewed her, I put out an open call. To my surprise,
messages came rolling in. Some of the people I talked to were
virgins by choice. Some were not, sometimes for complicated,
overlapping reasons: disability, trauma, issues related to appearance, temperament, chance. "Embarrassed doesn't even cover it,"
a thirty-two-year-old woman who chose the pseudonym Bette told
me. "Not having erotic capital, not being part of the sexual marketplace . . . that's a serious thing in our world! I mean, practically
everyone has sex, so what's wrong with me?" A twenty-six-year-old
man who was on the autism spectrum and had been molested as a
child wondered, "If I get naked with someone, am I going to take
to it like a duck to water, or am I going to start crying and lock
myself in the bathroom?" He hoped to meet someone who saw
life clearly, who was gentle and independent. "Sometimes I think,
Why would a woman like that ever want me?" he said. But he had
worked hard, he told me, to start thinking of himself as a person
who was capable of a relationship—a person who was worthy of,
and could accept, love.

It is a horrible thing to feel unwanted—invisible, inadequate,
ineligible for the things that any person might hope for. It is also
entirely possible to process a difficult social position with generosity and grace. None of the people I interviewed believed that
they were owed the sex that they wished to have. In America, to
be poor, or black, or fat, or trans, or Native, or old, or disabled,

or undocumented, among other things, is usually to have become acquainted with unwantedness. Structural power is the best protection against it: a rich, straight white man, no matter how unpleasant, will always receive enthusiastic handshakes and good treatment at banking institutions; he will find ways to get laid.

These days, in this country, sex has become a hyperefficient and deregulated marketplace, and, like any hyperefficient and deregulated marketplace, it often makes people feel very bad. Our newest sex technologies, such as Tinder and Grindr, are built to carefully match people by looks above all else. Sexual value continues to accrue to abled over disabled, cis over trans, thin over fat, tall over short, white over nonwhite, rich over poor. There is an absurd mismatch in the way that straight men and women are taught to respond to these circumstances. Women are socialized from childhood to blame themselves if they feel undesirable, to believe that they will be unacceptable unless they spend time and money and mental effort being pretty and amenable and appealing to men. Conventional femininity teaches women to be good partners to men as a basic moral requirement: a woman should provide her man a support system, and be an ideal accessory for him, and it is her job to convince him, and the world, that she is good.

Men, like women, blame women if they feel undesirable. And, as women gain the economic and cultural power that allows them to be choosy about their partners, men have generated ideas about self-improvement that are sometimes inextricable from violent rage.

Several distinct cultural changes have created a situation in which many men who hate women do not have the access to women's bodies that they would have had in an earlier era. The sexual revolution urged women to seek liberation. The self-esteem movement taught women that they were valuable beyond what convention might dictate. The rise of mainstream feminism gave women certainty and company in these convictions. And the internet-enabled efficiency of today's sexual marketplace allowed people to find potential sexual partners with a minimum of barriers and restraints. Most American women now grow up understanding that they can and should choose whom they want to have sex with.

In the past few years, a subset of straight men calling themselves "incels" have constructed a violent political ideology around the injustice of young, beautiful women refusing to have sex with them. These men often subscribe to notions of white supremacy. They are, by their own judgment, mostly unattractive and socially inept. (They frequently call themselves "subhuman.") They're also diabolically misogynistic. "Society has become a place for worship of females and it's so fucking wrong, they're not Gods they are just a fucking cum-dumpster," a typical rant on an incel message board reads. The idea that this misogyny is the real root of their failures with women does not appear to have occurred to them.

The incel ideology has already inspired the murders of at least sixteen people. Elliot Rodger, in 2014, in Isla Vista, California, killed six and injured fourteen in an attempt to instigate a "War on Women" for "depriving me of sex." (He then killed himself.) Alek Minassian killed ten people and injured sixteen, in Toronto, last month; prior to doing so, he wrote, on Facebook, "The Incel Rebellion has already begun!" You might also include Christopher Harper-Mercer, who killed nine people, in 2015, and left behind a manifesto that praised Rodger and lamented his own virginity.

The label that Minassian and others have adopted has entered the mainstream, and it is now being widely misinterpreted. Incel stands for "involuntarily celibate," but there are many people who would like to have sex and do not. (The term was coined by a queer Canadian woman in the 1990s.) Incels aren't really looking for sex; they're looking for absolute male supremacy. Sex, defined by them as dominion over female bodies, is just their preferred sort of proof.

If what incels wanted was sex, they might, for instance, value sex workers and wish to legalize sex work. But incels, being violent misogynists, often express extreme disgust at the idea of "whores." Incels tend to direct hatred at things they think they desire; they are obsessed with female beauty but despise makeup as a form of fraud. Incel culture advises men to "looksmaxx" or "statusmaxx" —to improve their appearance, to make more money—in a way that presumes that women are not potential partners or worthy objects of possible affection but inconveniently sentient bodies that must be claimed through cold strategy. (They assume that men who treat women more respectfully are "white-knighting," putting on a mockable façade of chivalry.) When these tactics fail, as they are bound to do, the rage intensifies. Incels dream of beheading the sluts who wear short shorts but don't want to be groped by strangers; they draw up elaborate scenarios in which women are auctioned off at age eighteen to the highest bidder; they call El- liot Rodger their Lord and Savior and feminists the female KKK. "Women are the ultimate cause of our suffering," one poster on incels.me wrote recently. "They are the ones who have UNJUSTLY made our lives a living hell . . . We need to focus more on our ha- tred of women. Hatred is power."

On a recent 90-degree day in New York City, I went for a walk and thought about how my life would look through incel eyes. I'm twenty-nine, so I'm a little old and used up: incels fetishize teenagers and virgins (they use the abbreviation "JBs," for jailbait), and they describe women who have sought pleasure in their sex lives as "whores" riding a "cock carousel." I'm a feminist, which is disgusting to them. ("It is obvious that women are inferior, that is why men have always been in control of women.") I was wearing a crop top and shorts, the sort of outfit that they believe causes men to rape women. ("Now watch as the level of rapes mysteriously rise up.") In the elaborate incel taxonomy of participants in the sexual marketplace, I am a Becky, devoting my attentions to a Chad. I'm probably a "roastie," too—another term they use for women with sexual experience, denoting labia that have turned into roast beef from overuse.

Earlier this month, Ross Douthat, in a column for the *New York Times,* wrote that society would soon enough "address the unhap- piness of incels, be they angry and dangerous or simply depressed or despairing." The column was ostensibly about the idea of sex- ual redistribution: if power is distributed unequally in society, and sex tends to follow those lines of power, how and what could we change to create a more equal world? Douthat noted a recent blog post by the economist Robin Hanson, who suggested, after Minassian's mass murder, that the incel plight was legitimate, and that redistributing sex could be as worthy a cause as redistributing wealth. (The quality of Hanson's thought here may be suggested by his need to clarify, in an addendum, "Rape and slavery are *far* from the only possible levers!") Douthat drew a straight line be- tween Hanson's piece and one by Amia Srinivasan, in the *London Review of Books.* Srinivasan began with Elliot Rodger, then explored the tension between a sexual ideology built on free choice and personal preference and the forms of oppression that manifest in these preferences. The question, she wrote, "is how to dwell in the ambivalent place where we acknowledge that no one is obligated to desire anyone else, that no one has a right to be desired, but also that who is desired and who isn't is a political question."

Srinivasan's rigorous essay and Hanson's flippantly dehumanizing thought experiment had little in common. And incels, in any case, are not actually interested in sexual redistribution; they don't want sex to be distributed to anyone other than themselves. They don't care about the sexual marginalization of trans people, or women who fall outside the boundaries of conventional attractiveness. ("Nothing with a pussy can be incel, ever. Someone will be desperate enough to fuck it . . . Men are lining up to fuck pigs, hippos, and ogres.") What incels want is extremely limited and specific: they want unattractive, uncouth, and unpleasant misogynists to be able to have sex on demand with young, beautiful women. They believe that this is a natural right.

It is men, not women, who have shaped the contours of the incel predicament. It is male power, not female power, that has chained all of human society to the idea that women are decorative sexual objects, and that male worth is measured by how good-looking a woman they acquire. Women—and, specifically, feminists—are the architects of the body-positivity movement, the ones who have pushed for an expansive redefinition of what we consider attractive. "Feminism, far from being Rodger's enemy," Srinivasan wrote, "may well be the primary force resisting the very system that made him feel—as a short, clumsy, effeminate, interracial boy—inadequate." Women, and LGBTQ people, are the activists trying to make sex work legal and safe, to establish alternative arrangements of power and exchange in the sexual market.

We can't redistribute women's bodies as if they are a natural resource; they are the bodies we live in. We can redistribute the value we apportion to one another—something that the incels demand from others but refuse to do themselves. I still think about Bette telling me, in 2013, how being lonely can make your brain feel like it's under attack. Over the past week, I have read the incel boards looking for, and occasionally finding, proof of humanity, amid detailed fantasies of rape and murder and musings about what it would be like to assault one's sister out of desperation. In spite of everything, women are still more willing to look for humanity in the incels than they are in us.

DAYNA TORTORICI

# *In the Maze*

FROM *n+1*

ONE OF THE purposes of this section is to provide a testimony
of a moment—to recognize and record, as C.L.R. James said, the
questions and debates that preoccupy us. But sometimes life fur-
nishes situations that cannot be approached intellectually. None
of the usual keys fits the lock. An intellectual situation grades into
an emotional situation and becomes untouchable. How do you
write a history of the present, then? Sublimate, sublimate—until
that stops getting you anywhere.

Two years ago, in January 2016, I wrote to my coeditors with
a proposal for an Intellectual Situation about what I felt was an
impending male backlash. One colleague asked, "What backlash?"
Another worried it was too close to the bone. In the end I abandoned the essay because I couldn't find a way in. I couldn't figure
it out.

What was happening was that the men I knew were beginning
to feel persecuted as a class. They remarked on it obliquely, with
jokes that didn't quite sound like jokes, in emails or in offhand
remarks at parties. Irritation and annoyance were souring into
something worse. Men said they felt like they were living in Soviet
Russia. The culture was being hijacked by college students, humor-
less young people who knew nothing of real life, its paradoxes and
disappointments. Soon intellectuals would not be able to sneeze
without being sent to the gulag.

Women, too, felt the pressure. "Your generation is so *moral*,"
a celebrated novelist said to an editor my age. Another friend, a
journalist in her fifties, described the heat she got from online
feminists for expressing skepticism toward safe spaces. "*I'm* con-

servative now," she said, meaning to the kids. But the most persistent and least logical complaint came from men—men I knew and men in the media. They could not *speak*. And yet they were speaking. Near the end of 2014, I remember, the right to free speech under the First Amendment had been recast in popular discourse as the right to free speech without consequence, without reaction.

The examples in the press could be innocent and sinister. A Princeton undergraduate, the grandchild of Holocaust survivors, could not argue he was not privileged in *Time* magazine without facing ridicule on Twitter. A tech executive could hardly make a joke without being fired, a young tech executive told me. "Take Mahbod Moghadam," he said. Moghadam was one of the founders of Genius, and had been dismissed for his annotations of the shooter Elliot Rodger's manifesto. ("This is an artful sentence, beautifully written," he wrote. Of Rodger's sister, he added, "Maddy will go on to attend USC and turn into a spoiled hottie.") Once, on my way to work, I heard a story on NPR about a Pennsylvania man named Anthony Elonis who was taking a First Amendment case to the Supreme Court. He was defending his right to make jokes about murdering his ex-wife on Facebook, in the form of nonrhyming, rhythmless rap lyrics. "I'm not going to rest until your body is a mess, / soaked in blood and dying from all the little cuts," he posted. When she filed a restraining order, Elonis posted again. "I've got enough explosives / to take care of the state police and the sheriff's department." Posts about shooting up an elementary school and slitting the throat of a female FBI agent followed. When he was convicted for transmitting intent to injure another person across state lines, via the internet, he argued he was just doing what Eminem did on his albums: joking. Venting, creatively. Under the First Amendment, the government had to prove he had "subjective intent." His initial forty-four-month prison sentence was overturned by the Supreme Court but was ultimately reinstated by an appeals court. I learned later that he had been fired from his job for multiple sexual harassment complaints, just after his wife left him.

How did I feel about all this? Too many ways to say. The aggregate effect of white male resentment across culture disturbed me, as did the confusion of freedom of speech with freedom to ridicule, threaten, harass, and abuse. When it came to the more benign expressions of resentment, in the academy and in the fiefdoms of high culture, I was less sure. On the one hand, I was a person of my generation and generally thought the students to be right. Show me a teenager who isn't a fundamentalist, I thought; what matters is they're pushing for progress. The theorist Sara Ahmed's diagnosis of teachers' reactions to sensitive students as "a moral panic about moral panics" struck me as right. (Her defense of trigger warnings and safe spaces in "Against Students" remains one of the best I know: trigger warnings are "a partial and necessarily inadequate measure to enable some people to stay in the room so that 'difficult issues' can be discussed," and safe spaces, a "technique for dealing with the consequences of histories that are not over . . . We have safe spaces *so* we can talk about racism not so we can avoid talking about racism!") I also agreed with my colleague Elizabeth Gumport when she observed, speaking to a man in mind but also to me, "It's not that you can't *speak*. It's that other people can *hear* you. And they're telling you what you're saying is crazy."

Still, I had sympathy for what I recognized in some peers as professional anxiety and fear. The way they had learned to live in the world — to write novels, to make art, to teach, to argue about ideas, to conduct themselves in sexual and romantic relationships — no longer fit the time in which they were living. Especially the men. Their novels, art, teaching methods, ideas, and relationship paradigms were all being condemned as unenlightened or violent. Many of these condemnations issued from social media, where they multiplied and took on the character of a mounting threat: a mob at the gate. But repudiations of the old ways were also turning up in outlets that mattered to them: in reviews, on teaching evaluations, on hiring committees. Authors and artists whose work was celebrated as "thoughtful" or "political" not eight years ago were now being singled out as chauvinists and bigots. One might expect this in old age, but to be cast out as a political dinosaur by fifty-two, by forty, by thirty-six? They hadn't even peaked! And with the political right — the actual right — getting away with murder, theft, and exploitation worldwide . . . ? That, at least, was how I gathered they felt. Sometimes I thought they were right. Sometimes I thought they needed to grow up.

The outlet of choice for this cultural moment within my extended circle was Facebook. More and more adults were gathering there, particularly academics, and reactions to campus scandals ruled my feed. A mild vertigo attends my memory of this time, which I think of, now, as The Long 2016. It began at least two years prior. There were reactions to Emma Sulkowicz's *Mattress Performance*, to Laura Kipnis's essay in the *Chronicle Review*, to Kenneth Goldsmith's Michael Brown poem, to Joe Scanlan's Donelle Woolford character in the Whitney Biennial, to Caitlyn Jenner's coming out as trans, to Rachel Dolezal's getting outed as white, to the Yale Halloween letter, to Michael Derrick Hudson writing under the name Yi-Fen Chou to get into a *Best American Poetry* anthology, to the phenomenon of Hollywood whitewashing, to sexual abuse allegations against Bill Cosby and Roger Ailes. Meanwhile, in the background, headline after headline about police murders of black people and the upcoming presidential election. Many of these Facebook reactions were "bad"—meaning, in my personal shorthand, in bad faith (willful misunderstanding of the issue at hand), a bad look (unflattering to he or she who thought it brave to defend a dominant, conservative belief), or bad politics (reactionary). Yet even the bad takes augured something good. A shift was taking place in the elite institutions. The good that came of it didn't have to trickle down further for me to find value in it. This was my corner of the world. I thought it ought to be better.

The question was at whose expense. It was easy enough to say "white men," harder to say which ones and how. Class—often the most important dimension—tended to be absent from the calculus. It may once have been a mark of a first-rate intelligence to hold two opposing ideas in mind, but it was now a political necessity to hold three, at least. And what of the difference between the cultural elite and the power elite, the Harold Blooms and the Koch brothers of the world? While we debated who should be the first to move over, pipe down, or give back, we seemed to understand that the most obvious candidates were beyond our reach. What good would it do, for us, to say that Donald Trump had a bigger "problem" with black voters than Bernie Sanders did, or that Donald Trump would be kinder to Wall Street than Hillary Clinton would? To do so would be to allow a lesser man to set the standard for acceptable behavior. We would tend to our own precincts, hold our own to account.

This may have been bad strategy, in retrospect. Perhaps we lost track of the real enemy. Still, I understand why we pursued it. It's easy to forget how few people anticipated what was coming, and had we not attempted to achieve some kind of equality within our ranks, the finger of blame would have pointed infinitely outward, cueing infinite paralysis. Shouldn't *that* domino, further down the line, be the first to fall? Yes, but we'd played this game before. Women of color couldn't be asked to wait for the white male capitalist class to fall before addressing the blight of racism or sexism on their lives—nor, for that matter, could men of color or white women. It was not solidarity to sweep internal issues under the rug until the real enemy's defeat. Nor was achieving a state of purity before doing politics. But a middle ground was possible. Feminism and antiracism shouldn't have to wait.

Only they would have to wait. By summer 2016, Trump, the echt white-male-resentment and "free-speech" candidate, had proven all kinds of discriminatory speech acceptable by voicing it and nevertheless winning the Republican nomination. A low bar, to be sure, but even his party was horrified when the *Access Hollywood* tape leaked a month before voting day. Trump's remarks crossed a boundary his apologists didn't expect: the GOP's standing benevolent-patriarch attitude toward white women and sex. How depressing it would be, I remember thinking, to muster a win on so pathetic a norm as the purity of white femininity. But I was desperate. I'd take just about anything.

And then, despite the outrage, we didn't win. Although it matters that Trump won the election unfairly, it shouldn't have even been close. Perhaps I'd forgotten what country we lived in, what world. Sexual harassment was by and large accepted as an unfortunate consequence of male biology, and joking or bragging about sexual harassment was a comparably minor offense. Months later, I walked down the street in Manhattan and saw a row of the artist Marilyn Minter's posters wheat-pasted to a wooden construction fence. Gold letters on black read DONALD J. TRUMP above a two-tone image of his smiling face, and across the bottom, THE PRESIDENT OF THE UNITED STATES OF AMERICA. In between was a prose poem of Trump's words captured on the hot mic, iterated across the span of wall:

I did try and fuck her. She was married.
I moved on her like a bitch,
But I couldn't get there.
And she was married.
You know I'm automatically attracted to beautiful.

I just start kissing them. It's like a magnet. Just kiss.
I don't even wait.
And when you're a star they let you do it.
You can do anything . . .
Grab them by the pussy.
You can do anything.

*You can do anything* was the refrain of my childhood. I was a daughter of the Title IX generation, a lucky girl in a decade when lucky
girls of lucky parents were encouraged to play sports, be leaders,
wear pants, believe themselves good at math, and aspire to become the first female president of the United States. The culture
validated this norm. Politicians and advertisers loved girls. Girls,
before they became women, could do anything. (Women were too
old to save, an unspoken rule behind all kinds of policy. Need an
abortion? Better to keep the kid, who has not yet been ground
down by life.) But if girls were taught to be winners, boys were not
taught to be losers. On the contrary, to lose was a man's worst fate
—especially if he was straight—because winning meant access to
sex (a belief held most firmly by the involuntarily celibate). Even
then I understood that someone's gain was bound to be perceived
as someone else's loss, and over time, I learned not to be too brazen. I maintained a prudent fear of the falling class. Even when
men weren't dangerous, they weren't defenseless. Some still had
the resources to bring you down, should you be unlucky enough
to be crossed by one.

Combine male fragility with white fragility and the perennial
fear of falling and you end up with something lethal, potentially.
Plenty of men make it through life just fine, but a wealthy white
man with a stockpile of arms and a persecution complex is a truly
terrifying figure. Elliot Rodger, Stephen Paddock: both these men
had money. This is not to say that men punishing women for their
pain is a rich thing or a white thing or even a gun thing. It occurs across cultures, eras, and classes, and the experience of being
on the receiving end of it varies accordingly. As Houria Bouteldja
writes in "We, Indigenous Women":

> In Europe, prisons are brimming with black people and Arabs. Racial
> profiling almost only concerns men, who are the police's main target.
> It is in our eyes that they are diminished. And yet they try desperately to
> reconquer us, often through violence. In a society that is castrating, pa-

triarchal, and racist (or subjected to imperialism), *to live is to live with virility.* "The cops are killing the men and the men are killing the women. I'm talking about rape. I'm talking about murder," says Audre Lorde. A decolonial feminism must take into account this masculine, indigenous "gender trouble" because the oppression of men reflects directly on us. Yes, we are subjected with full force to the humiliation that is done to them. Male castration, a consequence of racism, is a humiliation for which men make us pay a steep price.

Women pay the price for other humiliations as well. The indignity of downward mobility, real or perceived, is a painful one to suffer, and a man takes it out where he can (Silvia Federici: "The more the man serves and is bossed around, the more he bosses around"). Whatever else it may be, sexual harassment in the "workplace context" is a check on a person's autonomy, a threat to one's means of self-support. It can feel like being put in place, chastised, challenged, or dared. *Sure, you can do anything,* it says. *But don't forget that I can still do this.* The dare comes from winners and losers alike. Either you accept it and pay one price or you don't and pay another. All of it always feels bad.

I imagine that some people feel good about bringing perpetrators to justice, such as it is under the system we have. But I imagine just as many do not want to be responsible for their offender's punishment. They might say: Please don't make it my decision whether you lose your job, are shunned by your peers, or get sent to prison. Prison, unemployment, and social exile are not what I want for men. I'm not here to be the police. I don't want to be responsible for you.

There are many obstacles to honesty in conversations about sexual assault. Loyalty and pity, fear of judgment or retaliation, feelings of complicity or ambivalence—all are good enough reasons not to talk. Alleging sexual misconduct also tends to involve turning one's life upside down and shaking out the contents for public scrutiny. It's rarely done for fun.

When victims do want to talk, however, the litigiousness of men proves an obstacle to honesty. It is not unusual for women who speak too liberally about men to be threatened with legal action. Of all the striking things in Ronan Farrow's *New Yorker* articles about Harvey Weinstein's sex crimes, what struck me most were the allusions to Weinstein's lawyers. "He drags your name through the mud, and he'll come after you hard with his legal team," said one woman who asked not to be named. Another chose to pull her allegation from the record. "I'm so sorry," she told Farrow. "The legal angle is coming at me and I have no recourse."

In the weeks after Jodi Kantor and Megan Twohey first reported the story in the *New York Times,* as colleagues and strangers on the internet moved to identify the Weinsteins within their own industries, I felt uneasy. Behind every brave outing I saw a legal liability. I suppose that's what happens when you know enough men with money. Such men are minor kings among us, men with lawyer-soldiers at their employ who can curtail certain kinds of talk. While I do believe in false allegations, and I do believe that women can be bullies, it's hard, sometimes, not to be cynical about the defense. Some men love free speech almost as much as they love libel lawyers.

"Smart or reckless or both??" I texted my friends when I first saw the Google spreadsheet, titled "Shitty Media Men," that compiled the names, affiliations, and alleged misconduct of men in my field: writers and editors of books, magazines, newspapers, and websites. The document had been started anonymously, and though intended for circulation among women only, it was visible to, and editable by, anyone with the link. I saw the names of men I knew and men I didn't, stories I'd heard before and a few I hadn't. "The List," as it came to be called, didn't upset me, but neither did it give me comfort. Mostly I worried about retaliation: the contributors getting sued or worse. "Reckless," a friend texted back. "Not sure how but definitely reckless."

By then I was once again preoccupied by backlash. The day the Weinstein story broke in the *Times* and five days before Farrow's first article, an investigative piece on *BuzzFeed* had described the range of people who'd sustained an email correspondence with Milo Yiannopoulos, the former *Breitbart* editor who'd once been the face of the company. In addition to the usual alt-right characters, there were "accomplished people in predominantly liberal industries—entertainment, tech, academia, fashion, and media —who resented what they felt was a censorious coastal cultural orthodoxy." Named among them were two writers I knew, both men, who according to the article had tipped off Milo for stories. One of them was a Facebook friend. He vehemently denied the allegations and said he hadn't written the emails provided by *BuzzFeed* as proof. The other, as far as I know, said nothing. He was the managing editor of *Vice*'s feminist vertical (he once profiled Ann Coulter) who emailed Yiannopoulos with the request, "Please mock this fat feminist," linking to a story by Lindy West.

The article had made me feel naïve. These were the people I'd given the benefit of the doubt, the professional acquaintances who adopted such strong anti-identitarian poses that I often couldn't discern their true sympathies. I figured that like the liberal professionals in the throes of a moral panic about moral panics, they shared the goal of collective liberation but disagreed about how to reach it, and in their disagreement came off as more resistant to change than they were. But what if some of them were not just acting like reactionaries? What if they didn't share the goal?

In the case of Milo's pen pals, their connection to the right was far from abstract: they talked, griped, shared notes. The lesson was that if someone sounds like an enemy and acts like an enemy, he may in fact be an enemy. I wasn't sure what this meant for the men on the List. These were men I'd known to say "woke" in a funny voice, to make intellectual arguments against the redistributive efforts within their control—whom they published or how they assigned. They lamented the intrusion of politics on quality art and warned of the perils of hysteria, witch-hunts, and sex panics. To prove myself worthy of their confidence I tried not to leap to conclusions. But the allegations against men like this were damning: rape, attempted rape, sexual assault, choking, punching, physical intimidation, and stalking; "verbal intimidation of female colleagues"; "sexual harassment, inappropriate comments and pranks (especially to young women)." Even if half of it was false, I knew at least some of it to be true. At some point it's irresponsible not to connect what a man says with what he does. In the days following the *BuzzFeed* article, "Who Goes Nazi?," Dorothy Thompson's famous *Harper's Magazine* piece from 1941, sprang to the collective mind:

> It is an interesting and somewhat macabre parlor game to play at a large gathering of one's acquaintances: to speculate who in a showdown would go Nazi. By now, I think I know. I have gone through the experience many times—in Germany, in Austria, and in France. I have come to know the types: the born Nazis, the Nazis whom democracy itself has created, the certain-to-be fellow-travelers. And I also know those who never, under any circumstances, would become Nazis.

None of the men I had in mind were Nazis. None resembled the men who'd marched through Charlottesville with tiki torches, shouting, "You will not replace us!" But there was another spin on the game, and this was the one that worried me: Who in a show-down would accept the subjugation of women as a necessary political concession? Who would make peace with patriarchy if it meant a nominal win, or defend the accused for the sake of stability? The answer was more men than I'd been prepared to believe. I'd have to work harder not to alienate them, if only to make it harder for them to sell me out.

And so I talked to men. Men on the List, men not on the List, men secretly half disappointed that they'd been left off the List, mistaking it for some kind of virility ranking. In the past I'd argued that it shouldn't be women's job to educate men about sexism, and I sympathized with the women who said so now. But reality isn't always how it should be.

Perhaps it was just time for my shift. People take turns in the effort to explain collective pain, and I'd tapped out plenty of times before, pleading exhaustion, depression, and rage. The fact that I had the emotional reserves to discuss harassment at all implied that it was my responsibility to do so. ("It is the responsibility of the oppressed to teach the oppressors their mistakes," Audre Lorde wrote in 1980—"a constant drain of energy.") This is not to say I was good at it: I overestimated the length of my fuse, listening, talking, reasoning, feeling more or less level-headed—then abruptly shutting down or crying. It was nevertheless more than some friends could muster. From each according to her ability, et cetera.

If my approach was too much about men, my defense is that the situation was about men from the beginning. The shared experience of sexism is not the same thing as feminism, even if the recognition of shared experience is where some people's feminism begins. It was to be expected that the discussion turned to men's fates and feelings. How could guilty men be rehabilitated or justly punished? Under what circumstances could we continue to appreciate their art? As think pieces pondered these questions, other men leapt at the opportunity to make their political enemies' sexual crimes an argument for the superiority of their side. It might have been funny if it weren't so expected, so dark. When a friend and former colleague mentioned the "male-feminist" journalist who had choked her at the foot of his stairs, right-wing outlets rushed to "amplify" her voice. The pro-Trump website *Gateway Pundit* quoted her without permission; the men's rights activist and alt-right personality Mike Cernovich retweeted the blog post to his 379,000 followers; *Breitbart* followed up with its own story. "My therapist said that I should sign every tweet with 'also the alt right sucks' so they can't use my tweets in any more articles," she joked.

Leftist men celebrated the fall of liberal male hypocrites, liberals the fall of conservative ones, conservatives and alt-rightists the fall of the liberals and leftists. Happiest were the anti-Semites, who applauded the feminist takedown of powerful Jewish men. It seemed not to occur to them—or maybe just not to matter?—that any person, any woman, had suffered. Outrage for the victims was just another weapon in an eternal battle between men. I remembered the emergency panel Trump assembled in response to the *Access Hollywood* tape with Juanita Broaddrick, Kathleen Willey, and Paula Jones—women who had accused Bill Clinton of harassment or rape. A fourth woman, Kathy Shelton, had been raped by a man Hillary Clinton defended in court as a young lawyer. As the adage goes: in the game of patriarchy, women aren't the other team, they're the ball.

All this posturing made optimism difficult and clarity imperative. Patiently, my peers and I explained to men that we understood the difference between a touch and a grope, a bad time and rape, and mass online feminist retribution and a right-wing conspiracy (how credulous did they think we were?). Meanwhile, we wrung as much change as we could from this news peg. We called meetings, revised workplace policies, resumed difficult conversations we'd have preferred not to. As we learned during the Long 2016, the self-evident harm of sexual assault is not self-evident at all: no automatic mechanism delivers justice the moment "awareness" is "raised." Donald Trump remains the president. Social media, the staging ground for much of this reckoning, remains easy to manipulate. Our enemies pose as allies, and our allies act like enemies, suspicious that our gain will be their loss.

Must history have losers? The record suggests yes. Redistribution is a tricky business. Even simple metaphors for making the world more equitable—leveling a playing field, shifting the balance —can correspond to complex or labor-intensive processes. What freedoms might one have to surrender in order for others to be free? And how to figure it when those freedoms are not symmetrical? A little more power for you might mean a lot less power for me in practice, an exchange that will not feel fair in the short term even if it is in the long term. There is a reason, presumably, that we call it an ethical calculus and not an ethical algebra.

Some things are zero-sum—perhaps more things than one cares to admit. To say that feminism is good for boys, that diversity makes a stronger team, or that collective liberation promises a greater, deeper freedom than the individual freedoms we know is comforting and true enough. But just as true, and significantly less consoling, is the guarantee that some will find the world less comfortable in the process of making it habitable for others. It would be easier to give up some privileges if it weren't so traumatic to lose, as it is in our ruthlessly competitive and frequently undemocratic country. Changing the rules of the game might begin with revising what it means to win. I once heard a story about a friend who'd said, offhand at a book group, that he'd throw women under the bus if it meant achieving social democracy in the United States. The story was meant to be chilling—this from a friend? —but it made me laugh. *As if you could do it without us,* I thought, *we who do all the work on the group project.* I wondered what his idea of social democracy was.

As for how men might think about their role in a habitable future—or how anyone might, from a position of having something to lose—a visual metaphor may be useful. Imagine walking through a maze, for years and years, to find that your path has dead-ended near the exit. There's an illusion of proximity, of closeness to the goal: you can see the light through the brush, hear the traffic just outside. It's difficult, in that moment, to accept that you're not in fact close—that you can't jump the hedge, and that to turn around would not be to regress but to proceed. You turn around not because it is morally superior or because it will get you into heaven, but because it is your best and only option. Perhaps redistribution is like that. To attempt it is not to guarantee that the future will be better than the past, only to admit that it can be.

# Contributors' Notes

RABIH ALAMEDDINE is the author of *I, the Divine, The Hakawati, Koolaids, The Perv, An Unnecessary Woman,* and *The Angel of History. An Unnecessary Woman* was a finalist for the National Book Award 2014 and the winner of the prestigious Prix Femina Étranger. His most recent novel, *The Angel of History,* won the Lambda Literary Award.

MICHELLE ALEXANDER is a legal scholar, human rights advocate, and the author of *The New Jim Crow: Mass Incarceration in the Age of Colorblindness,* a *New York Times* bestseller. She is currently a visiting professor at Union Theological Seminary and an opinion writer for the *New York Times.*

HEATHER ALTFELD's poetry collection *The Disappearing Theatre* won the 2016 Poets at Work Prize, selected by Stephen Dunn. Her poems and essays appear or are forthcoming in *Conjunctions, Orion, Aeon, Narrative Magazine,* and the *Georgia Review,* among others. She lives in northern California, where she teaches humanities and honors courses at California State University, Chico.

MARIO ALEJANDRO ARIZA is a Dominican immigrant to the United States. He is the author of the forthcoming *Disposable City: Miami's Future on the Shores of Climate Change.* He holds an MFA in poetry from the University of Miami and a master's degree in Hispanic cultural studies from Columbia University. His poetry, journalism, and nonfiction writing can be found in places like *BOAAT,* the *Atlantic,* and the *Believer.*

JABARI ASIM is the author of several books. His most recent, *We Can't Breathe: On Black Lives, White Lies, and the Art of Survival*, was a finalist for the PEN/Diamonstein-Spielvogel Award for the Art of the Essay. He lives near Boston, where he directs the MFA program in creative writing at Emerson College.

ALEXANDER CHEE is the author of the novels *Edinburgh* and *The Queen of the Night*, and *How to Write an Autobiographical Novel*, a collection of essays. He is a recipient of a 2003 Whiting Award, a 2004 NEA fellowship in prose, and residency fellowships from the MacDowell Colony, the VCCA, Civitella Ranieri, and Amtrak. His essays and stories have appeared in *The New Yorker*, the *Yale Review*, the *Sewanee Review*, and *The Best American Essays 2016*, among others. He is currently at work on a short story collection and teaches at Dartmouth College.

CAMILLE T. DUNGY is the author of the essay collection *Guidebook to Relative Strangers: Journeys into Race, Motherhood, and History*, a finalist for the National Book Critics Circle Award, as well as four collections of poetry, most recently *Trophic Cascade*. Dungy has also edited anthologies, including *Black Nature: Four Centuries of African American Nature Poetry* and *From the Fishhouse*. Her essays have appeared in *The Best American Travel Writing*, the *Georgia Review*, *New England Review*, *Virginia Quarterly Review*, and elsewhere. She is a professor at Colorado State University.

MASHA GESSEN is a journalist and the author of ten books of nonfiction, most recently *The Future Is History: How Totalitarianism Reclaimed Russia*, which won the 2017 National Book Award for nonfiction. Gessen is also the author of the national bestseller *The Man Without a Face: The Unlikely Rise of Vladimir Putin*. Gessen is a staff writer at *The New Yorker* and a national fellow with New America Foundation.

JEAN GUERRERO is the author of *Crux: A Cross-Border Memoir* and is a recipient of the PEN/FUSION Emerging Writers Prize. She is an Emmy-winning investigative journalist covering the US-Mexico border for KPBS, NPR, the *PBS NewsHour*, and other public media. Her writing has also appeared in the *Wall Street Journal*, the *Seattle Times*, *Literary Hub*, and more. She lives in San Diego.

LACY M. JOHNSON is a Houston-based professor, curator, and activist, and is the author of the essay collection *The Reckonings*, the memoir *The Other Side*—both National Book Critics Circle Award finalists—and the memoir *Trespasses.* Her writing has appeared in *The New Yorker,* the *New York Times,* the *Los Angeles Times, Virginia Quarterly Review, Tin House, Guernica,* and elsewhere. She teaches creative nonfiction at Rice University and is the founding director of the Houston Flood Museum.

WALTER JOHNSON—a founding member of the Commonwealth Project, which brings together the efforts of academics, artists, and activists in support of arts-based social action in St. Louis—teaches history and directs the Charles Warren Center for Studies in American History at Harvard University. He has written for the *Boston Review,* where he is a contributing editor, *Dissent,* the *Times Literary Supplement, Raritan,* and the *New York Times,* and is the author of two books, *Soul by Soul: Life Inside the Antebellum Slave Market* and *River of Dark Dreams: Slavery and Empire in the Mississippi Valley's Cotton Kingdom. By the Rivers of Babylon: St. Louis and the Broken Heart of American History* will be published in the spring of 2020.

ELIZABETH KOLBERT is a staff writer for *The New Yorker.* She is the author of *The Sixth Extinction,* which received the Pulitzer Prize for general nonfiction in 2015, and *Field Notes from a Catastrophe: Man, Nature, and Climate Change.*

J. DREW LANHAM'S work probes the intersections between nature, race, and identity. His book, *The Home Place: Memoirs of a Colored Man's Love Affair with Nature,* was named a John Burroughs Association Book of Uncommon Merit in 2017, and won the Southern Environmental Law Center's Reed Writing Award in 2018 and the Southern Book Prize. His work appears in *Orion, Places Journal, Oxford American,* and numerous anthologies. He is the poet laureate of Edgefield, South Carolina, and the author of *Sparrow Envy: Poems.* He is the Alumni Distinguished Professor of Wildlife Ecology and Master Teacher at Clemson University in South Carolina.

LILI LOOFBOUROW received her MFA from the University of Alabama. Her work has appeared in the *New York Times Magazine, Virginia Quarterly Review,* the *New Republic,* the *Guardian, PMLA, Post 45, The Week, The Cut,* the *Los Angeles Review of Books,* and the *New Inquiry.* She has twice won the Staige D. Blackford Prize for nonfiction. She is a staff writer at *Slate.*

TERESE MARIE MAILHOT is from Seabird Island Indian Band. She is the *New York Times* best-selling author of *Heart Berries: A Memoir* and the winner of a 2019 Whiting Award. Her essays have appeared in *Guernica, Granta, Pacific Standard,* and elsewhere. She teaches writing at Purdue University.

DAWN LUNDY MARTIN is the author of four books of poems, including, most recently, *Good Stock Strange Blood,* which won the 2019 Kingsley Tufts Poetry Award. Her essays can be found in *The New Yorker, Harper's Magazine, n+1,* and the *Believer.* Martin is a professor of English in the writing program at the University of Pittsburgh and director of the Center for African American Poetry and Poetics. She is also the recipient of a 2018 NEA grant in creative writing.

KAI MINOSH PYLE is a Michif and Sault Ste. Marie Nishnaabe writer and Indigenous-language advocate. Their work has been published in *PRISM International, Nat. Brut, Transgender Studies Quarterly,* and *Red Rising Magazine.* Currently they are a PhD student in American studies at the University of Minnesota, Twin Cities.

GARY TAYLOR is the general editor of *The New Oxford Shakespeare: Complete Works* and of Thomas Middleton's *Collected Works.* He has written for the *Washington Post* and the *Guardian,* and has re-created Shakespeare's partially lost play *The History of Cardenio* (based on *Don Quixote*).

JIA TOLENTINO is a staff writer at *The New Yorker* and the author of the essay collection *Trick Mirror.* She formerly worked as the deputy editor at *Jezebel* and contributing editor at the *Hairpin.* She received her MFA in fiction from the University of Michigan and lives in Brooklyn, New York.

DAYNA TORTORICI has served as coeditor in chief of *n+1* with Nikil Saval since 2014. Her writing has appeared in the *Atlantic,* the *Guardian, Harper's Magazine, n+1,* the *New York Times Book Review,* the *Village Voice,* and elsewhere. She has edited three small books with *n+1,* most recently *No Regrets.* She lives in Brooklyn, New York.

# Notable Essays and Literary Nonfiction of 2018

SELECTED BY ROBERT ATWAN

DAISY HERNÁNDEZ
Grammatical Disquisitions, *The Iowa Review,* Fall

JAMES TATE HILL
Do Audio Books Count as Reading?, *Literary Hub,* January 11

JEN HIRT
Going to See the Body, *The Turnip Truck(s),* Spring/Summer

JACK HITT
In Search of the Perfect *Ulysses, New York Times Magazine,* June 17

J. D. HO
We Will Return After These Messages, *Michigan Quarterly Review,* Fall

TONY HOAGLAND
The Cure for Racism Is Cancer, *The Sun,* September

BRANDON HOBSON
How Tsala Entered the Spirit World and Became a Hawk, *Conjunctions,* #71

RICHARD HOFFMAN
Wheels, *Tahoma Literary Review,* Fall/Winter

HUA HSU
Varieties of Ether, *Lapham's Quarterly,* Fall

SONYA HUBER
Between One and Ten Thousand, *Another Chicago Magazine,* December 5

NICOLE IM
On Sharks and Suicide, *Freeman's,* October

KRISTEN IVERSEN
A Good Ghost Story, *Hotel Amerika,* Spring

MITCHELL S. JACKSON
Exodus, *The Paris Review,* Fall

ROWAN JACOBSEN
Deleting a Species, *Pacific Standard,* September/October

JOANNE JACOBSON
Thoreau's Body, *Bellevue Literary Review,* #35

RUSSELL JACOBY
Diversity for What?, *The Baffler,* #41

CATHERINE JAGOE
The Ambassador and the Assassin, *Under the Sun,* #6

LESLIE JAMISON
The Breakup Museum, *Virginia Quarterly Review,* Spring

TERESA H. JANSSEN
My Fifth Sense, *Gold Man Review,* #7

BROOKE JARVIS
Paper Tiger, *The New Yorker,* July 2

CLAIRE JARVIS
Object Relations, *n+1,* Winter

HA JIN
In the Margin, *Bellevue Literary Review,* #35

FENTON JOHNSON
The Future of Queer: A Manifesto, *Harper's Magazine,* January

GEORGE JOHNSON
When Racism Anchors Your Health, *Vice,* December

HEATHER JOHNSON
Nowhere Place, *Prairie Schooner,* Spring

TROY JOLLIMORE
Dressed in the Absurd Clothes of Time: Thoughts on Translation, *Conjunctions,* #70

JONATHAN WINSTON JONES
Bison Clouds, *Ruminate,* Summer

ROSEMARY JONES
The Beach at Trouville, *Cherry Tree,* #4

DAVID JOY
At the Crossroads, *The New York Times Magazine,* April 8

JENNIFER KABAT
The Digital Blues, *McSweeney's,* #54

*Artforum,* What Is Enlightenment?, ed. David Velasco, Summer

*The Baffler,* Mind Cures, ed. Chris Lehmann, #41

*Booth,* Women Writers, ed. Robert Stapleton, #11

*Boston Review,* Fifty Years Since MLK, eds. Deborah Chasman and Joshua Cohen, 43/1

*The Briar Cliff Review,* Thirtieth Anniversary, ed. Tricia Currans-Sheehan, #30

*Broad Street,* Small Things, Partial Cures, ed. Susann Cokal, 2018

*The Chattahoochee Review,* Lost & Found, ed. Anna Schachner, Fall/Winter

*Conjunctions,* Sanctuary: The Preservation Issue, ed. Brad Morrow, #70

*Creative Nonfiction,* Embracing Uncertainty, ed. Lee Gutkind, Fall

*Daedalus,* Unfolding Futures: Indigenous Ways of Knowing for the Twenty-First Century, guest eds. Philip J. Deloria et al., Spring

*The Florida Review,* Latinx Feature, eds. Lisa Roney and Nicole Oquendo, Fall

*Foreign Affairs,* Is Democracy Dying?: A Global Report, ed. Gideon Rose, April/May

*Freeman's,* Power, ed. John Freeman, October

*The Georgia Review,* I Am What Is Around Me: Opening Up the Environmental Dialogue, eds. Stephen Corey and Douglas Carlson, Fall

*Granta,* Generic Love Story, ed. Sigrid Rausing, #144

*The Hudson Review,* Seventieth Anniversary, ed. Paula Deitz, Autumn

*Hunger Mountain,* Everyday Chimeras, guest ed. Melissa Febos, Spring

*Iron Horse Literary Review,* Best of *IHLR* Prose, ed. Leslie Jill Patterson, #20

*Lapham's Quarterly,* States of Mind, ed. Lewis H. Lapham, Winter

*Manoa,* Becoming Brazil, eds. Frank Stewart, Eric M. B. Becker, and Noah Perales-Estoesta, 30/2

*The Massachusetts Review,* Asian American Literature: Rethinking the Canon, eds. Cathy J. Schlund-Vials and Lawrence-Minh Bui Davis, Winter

*McSweeney's,* The End of Trust, ed. Kristina Kearns, #54

*The New Atlantis,* The Space Renaissance, ed. Ari N. Schulman, Summer/Fall

*The New York Times Magazine,* Losing Earth, ed. Nathaniel Rich, August 5

*North Carolina Literary Review,* North Carolina on the Map and in the News, ed. Margaret D. Bauer, #27

*North Dakota Quarterly,* The Humanities in the Age of Austerity, ed. William Caraher, #85

*Notre Dame Magazine,* What Could Go Wrong?, ed. Kerry Temple, Spring

*Oregon Humanities,* Owe, ed. Kathleen Holt, Spring

*Oxford American,* Southern Music Issue, ed. Eliza Borné, Winter

*The Point,* What Are Intellectuals For?, eds. Jon Baskin et al., Spring

*Provincetown Arts,* Helen Frankenthaler, ed. Susanna Ralli, #33

*Room,* Queer, ed. Leah Golob, 41/3
*Salmagundi,* This Age of Conformity: Politics, Groupthink, and the Academy, eds. Robert Boyers and Peg Boyers, Winter/Spring
*Slice,* Flight, ed. Elizabeth Blachman, Fall/Winter
*The Threepenny Review,* A Symposium on Shame, ed. Wendy Lesser, Spring

*Tin House,* Candy, ed. Rob Spillman, #75
*The Turnip Truck(s),* Bodies, ed. Tina Mitchell, Spring/Summer
*Vice,* Privacy and Perception, ed. Ellis Jones, June

Note:

The following essays should have appeared in "Notable Essays and Literary Nonfiction of 2017":

MICHEL BOGAN, On Fighting, *Southwest Review,* 102/3&4
KRISTA CHRISTENSEN, World, Heaving, *Booth,* #11
B. G. GAYLORD, The Beast in His Belly, *Sycamore Review,* Summer/Fall
JEFF STAUTZ, Third Shift, *Event,* 46/3
AMY YEE, In Kenya, a Transformation in Shades of REDD, *Undark,* July 28

# THE BEST AMERICAN SERIES®

*FIRST, BEST, AND BEST-SELLING*

*The Best American Comics*

*The Best American Essays*

*The Best American Food Writing*

*The Best American Mystery Stories*

*The Best American Nonrequired Reading*

*The Best American Science and Nature Writing*

*The Best American Science Fiction and Fantasy*

*The Best American Short Stories*

*The Best American Sports Writing*

*The Best American Travel Writing*

Available in print and e-book wherever books are sold.

Visit our website: hmhbooks.com/series/best-american